Praise for *Desperate Endeavor*

"Martial philosopher Sun Tzu said: 'Know the enemy and know yourself in a hundred battles you will never be in peril.' Olson's *Desperate Endeavor* tells the story of two species, human and alien, who need to embrace this notion . . . and the cost of ignoring it."

—Steven Barnes, author of *Lion's Blood*

"Olson has combined military science fiction with quantum and string theory in a first contact story that combines a series of fascinating what-ifs that will challenge the readers of this first novel."

—Francis Hamit

G. W. OLSON

DESPERATE ENDEAVOR

BELLE ISLE BOOKS
www.belleislebooks.com

ISBN: 978-1-953021-83-0
LCCN: 2022909366

Printed in the United States of America

Published by
Belle Isle Books (an imprint of Brandylane Publishers, Inc.)
5 S. 1st Street
Richmond, Virginia 23219

BELLE ISLE BOOKS
www.belleislebooks.com

belleislebooks.com | brandylanepublishers.com

This book is for the adventurer in all of us.
Journey with me to the farthest star,
and when we get back home,
we will have some great stories to tell!

PROLOGUE

somewhere in non-space; time indeterminate

OUR FIRST INTER-SPECIES WAR: RESTRICTED VERSION

Foreword by Mikail Benson

It was a very strange war. The enemy fought for goals we could not divine and counted victories we thought hollow. They were tactically naïve but technically brilliant. Our best minds failed to understand the depths of our adversary. Even the terms of peace were bizarre. If only Humanity knew what sense to make of the fight with AranthChi, the future would be less bleak.

Mikail put down the ballpoint pen and massaged his aching hand, reading what he had written. The shaky script made the words seem more sinister than he'd intended. *Easier to dictate to the computer,* he thought. But "writing longhand," a phrase he'd learned from the ship's tutor program, allowed him to weigh each word for maximum meaning. Perhaps the sinister effect was unavoidable. He was speaking harsh truths.

Mikail reached for the pen again, and the papers on his lap table scattered. He cursed and went to one knee in the tiny cabin of the ship that was his temporary home. He bunched the sheets in one hand. *So much to say!* He needed to find the words.

This book he was writing the foreword to would never see widespread publication. Only those directly involved in the struggle to save the Human race would have the opportunity to read it. They must be made to understand, because the only way to change the future was to understand the past.

It was vital to relearn primitive skills. The people Mikail led were all mastering new abilities. This replica of ancient tech was but one example. The Federation needed saving, and that miracle would come from the sacrifices of the people he was writing for—people with a peculiar knowledge, a strange destiny, and a desperate need for good luck.

The cabin chrono chimed. Mikail's team would be leaving soon. He picked up the pen, smoothed the paper, and began to write again in the same awkward hand.

After twenty years of fighting, the cost of maintaining the embattled colonies grew too high. Ultimately, the Federation wrote off its investment in the contested area. The colonists of Caledonia and New Hearth were evacuated, the sector abandoned. Only now did the AranthChi break their twenty-year silence. The generous peace offer was a shock.

Of course, there was a catch. . . .

1

PEACE PLUS THIRTY-FIVE YEARS

on New Hearth, middle of the night

Mikail Benson drifted in starry blackness. He floated in a warm, speckled environment and felt no breeze, heard no sound. The empty depths called to him, whispered comfort to the man trained for space. There was something so satisfying about the familiar dark that he snuggled deeper, wrapped himself in its calm. It had been a long time since he used his space-born skill on a real world. He was a planet dweller now—and glad of it. Only in dreams did he visit the arenas of youth, the places of his greatest triumphs, his blackest failures.

Mikail was caught in an unchanging universe where hurry did not exist. He wafted among the stars for a myriad of timeless heartbeats. It was an illusion of static peace. In this languid and soft-lit dreamscape, some of the stars moved. Ever so slowly they swelled, gaining shape and substance. They became ships. They had personality. They had purpose.

One of them, small due to the distance and blocky in design, deliberately moved toward another. It began to sparkle and give off strands of brilliant light. The ship probed with the strands, attempting to brush the strands across the other. The second ship evaded the embrace, rolling and diving below the first, circling and turning.

Mikail moved restlessly on his bed. He frowned. Faint unease nibbled at his mind. His serenity shredded, and in its place a surprisingly sharp pang of regret rocked him. *Wake up, wake up*! A fragment of his mind knew this wasn't real, but the dream was too strong.

Mikail was pulled toward the circling ship, pulled until he sped through the stars and the ship leapt beneath him and he and it were one. A maelstrom of blaring noise smote him. As heat streamed off bulkheads, he opened his mouth to scream, and copper filled it. His hands spasmed, and he was shocked to find controls formed within them. He fought to straighten the ship, and it all became real.

Lightning strobed in time to his pounding heart. His ship was in danger! He was in danger. Incandescent, questing fingers reached for him. Complex electromagnetic fields, cousin to the pinch bottle field holding in the vessel's fusion genie, wrapped the ship. The fields struggled to deflect the extremely high energies of the incoming beams.

Alarms howled in Mikail's ears. He drove the slender craft into defensive spirals and switchbacks while his tightly woven protective fields tore away in ribbons and shreds. Dread weighted his limbs as he spun madly to distribute the energy biting into his hull. The sharp cracks of clamps breaking in the aft compartment shot through the cabin. Equipment shifted as maximum delta vee slammed the ship into a new course. A ponderous *thump* rang the ship like a bell.

Mikail strained to dodge, to spin, to do anything possible to reduce the gnawing beams' impact so penetration could not occur. Ablative shielding exploded away from the hull in an effort to dump volcanic heat and diffuse the impact of the beams another few percent.

Anger mixing with fear, Mikail fought the other. He spit missiles. They darted and weaved and flared into nothingness. He turned his back, raking out with fusion drive and coherent light. He laid mines, stealthy and poisonous, and tried to entice the other ship into them. The other reached out with those bright scythes, and nuclear flowers bloomed where they touched. The enemy swept through expanding storms of hard radiation, defensive shields sparkling.

The bitter anguish of failure pursued Mikail. He was defeated at every turn. He ran. The enemy broke his back and sent him spilling out into space. His wounded in-system fighter retreated into the void, taking his legs with it. The horror stamped onto his mind's eye. His fighter shrank, was tiny, was gone.

Mikail woke with great shuddering gasps, his hands strangling the covers. The overwhelming sense of aloneness was disorienting. He sat up in drenched sheets. A torrent of sweat cascaded down his back. The bed was a planet-type bed, the room a planet-type room. His room. Relief gave him the shakes.

He touched his legs. Warm, alive, normal. It had just been a dream—a bad one. Not the worst, but bad. In his worst dreams, the dead floated in the void with him, close enough to touch, too late to help. If they got to him in time, they could give him his legs back. Trip-hammer heartbeats shook his frame. He would get no more sleep this night.

Grumbling, Mikail pushed the covers from his legs and set his feet on the floor. He wore shorts for convenience, and his broad, powerful chest glistened with fine gray hairs. The gray touched his brows, but his hair was full and had little salt. Searching with his toes in the darkness, he found the slippers that dwelt neatly by his bedside. With an unsteady motion, he slipped his feet into them.

The chrono on the wall glowed a soft 0300. Too early to go to work, too late to go get a drink. That left the net. Mikail figured he might as well see what was hopping in this boomtown of New Glasgow by the Sea, pride and joy of New Hearth, center of culture and wealth of the Hearth system. His home now. His people, now.

Mikail got up from the bed and, not bothering with the lights, walked over to his secure communications console. He palmed the contact. "Commercial channels please. Sound and screen print—no visual mode. No news, no product offers. Plug me into chat." His voice squeaked, and he still breathed heavily. *Perhaps print only,* he thought. The screen brightened and sent shadows dancing across the room. Mikail settled his tall, spare frame into the captain's chair and watched the information roll up the screen.

Half an hour later, Mikail couldn't resist his true vocation any longer. He said goodbye to a com-pal who worked for the newsnets and who often suffered from insomnia, signed off the commercial channels, and brought his console into alignment with his office deskcomp. The two machines worked through their security routines and merged into one entity. Now Mikail had access to the vast resources of his Service, and more importantly, the evening report on the Question Institute.

The Question Institute, the finest research facility off Earth, existed only to answer questions posed by the AranthChi. Gifted with a very peculiar point of view, the aliens were in the habit of asking questions of varying complexity, some so simple that Human scientists couldn't cope, and others so complicated that a planet's yearly budget needed to be spent to come up with a solution.

The main reason Mikail was on New Hearth was to act as watchdog on the Question Institute. Thirty-five years before, Humankind had been on the verge of losing a war with a most puzzling enemy. Mikail had fought in that war. As the Federation worked frantically to pull the colonists of Caledonia and New Hearth out of the war zone, that enemy had ceased hostilities and sued for peace. The deal Humanity worked out included reparations from both sides.

The Institute was staffed by highly intelligent scientists and engineers, excited to be working on challenging questions posed by an alien race. *They* were engaged in work guaranteed to result in academic and professional honors. And *they* believed the Institute helped promote the peace between the species.

Mikail was not one of *them*. He ran the Office of Alien Technologies. This governmental body existed to review the process of questions and answers to make sure that sensitive tech and Federation secrets were not inadvertently included in the information given to the AranthChi.

He studied the evening report carefully, noting that several project labs had stayed open late into the night. *Ah . . . the enthusiasms of science.* Everything seemed in order. That was expected, though faintly disappointing. If there were unusual patterns in the research, Mikail would not find it in the evening report.

One of his staff members was studying long-term trends. Others were scientists themselves, giving him digests of actual current research. Still, Mikail was paid to be careful . . . and he was motivated. The AranthChi would never earn Mikail's trust. He had too many nightmares, too many real concerns.

Well, that took all of ten minutes. Mikail turned off the computer, yawned, and stretched. His room seemed empty without the console on. He decided to go into work.

It was too early for city buses to be running, so Mikail called a jitney for the quick ride through the sleeping town. New Glasgow had originally been built on seven low hills, arcing around a lovely deep-water harbor, easily visible from space. Over the years, the town had grown outward instead of up, and the harbor could still be seen from most places.

Mikail lived on one of the low hills, and it was a fifteen-minute ride in either direction to government center or the Institute. Remembering the evening report, he chose the Institute as his destination. As he climbed out of the jitney at the Institute's front gate, he savored the smell of night fog and the tang of harbor air. Lights were on in several buildings, which was just what the evening report had led him to expect. He used his key to let himself in through the gate.

••✦••

The early morning sun shining into Mikail's office struck golden the many picture frames on the oak walls. In the pre-workaday hush, the air vibrated with a feeling that great deeds might be accomplished here, if only the sleeping giant could be stirred to life and talked into the quest. There were princesses to be rescued, dragons to be slayed—in fact, whole kingdoms to be saved.

These quiet moments make getting up early tolerable, mused Mikail as he ran a large hand through his unruly hair. He was settled deeply into his armchair, staring out the window, watching early morning researchers entering the Institute across the way. A cup of tea and an active bookplate sat forgotten beside him. Sweet morning air filled the room. The deep blue of the sky peering through the window and the heavy cherry wood furniture scattered about the room provided a rich frame to his contentment. Dust motes dancing in a beam of sunlight shared an easy camaraderie with him.

"You were *busy* last night, weren't you?" Marge McCan stood in the door, stocky, redheaded, green-eyed, and gloriously freckled.

"Don't you ever knock, Marge?" Mikail placed his hand to his chest and quipped in mild indignation, "This is my private office, after all, and I *am* the head of this little Easter egg hunt we are pleased to call an official government organization."

Marjorie McCan was not impressed. As the deputy senior administrator for alien projects at OAT, Margie McCan was the acknowledged number two Easter egg hunter on New Hearth, to use Mikail's folksy vernacular. He wouldn't know what to do without her.

"You were up all night again; it's obvious. Any time I can come in at seven in the morning to find you already here—"

She dropped her voice to a conspirator's whisper. "Looking like a rumpled bedsheet—" She switched back to her normal voice: "I know you haven't had any sleep."

Mikail stared into eyes that sparkled with just a hint of mischief and assayed a guilty grin. He passed his hand over his hair again. "Humph," he said. Then he tried, "No comment."

Marge came into the office, a folder in her hand. "You could try to pretend you were out all night. With a feminine companion, perhaps?"

"No, I was on the net. I couldn't sleep."

"And at five this morning you went over to the Institute and picked a fight with the Curator."

Mikail laughed. "Oh yes, I ran into Doctor Gormengast this morning. He seemed to find it undignified of me to walk into *his* particle accelerator control room without 'prior arrangement.' He doesn't look any better than I do at five a.m."

Marge waved the folder. "He has already filed another formal protest on you. He wants to know why the Federation put such an 'odious and mistrustful man in such a position of power.'"

Mikail was not popular with the Institute scientists. He did not know what the Aranth legation thought of him, nor did he care. His work was important, and his only loyalty was to the Federation.

"Gormengast has seven PhDs. *And* he is a pompous ass." Mikail shook his head mournfully, hoping Marge would see him as tragically misunderstood.

Her laughter was throaty and full. She walked farther into his office and dropped the folder onto the desk. "Why aren't you sleeping, Mike?"

Mikail stared at her. Marge's bluntness could always put him off balance. It was one of many things he loved about her. "Do you ever have nightmares, Marge?"

"Not me. I guess I'm not the sensitive type."

"Neither am I."

Marge sat down on the edge of the desk. "Mikail Benson, what could possibly be so bad that it has you prowling the halls of the Question Institute at the ungodly hour of five a.m.?"

"I've started dreaming again about the time I lost my ship."

The flatness of his tone made Marge wince. She reached out and touched his cheek. "Mike. Mike, that was forty years ago. It's been over for a long time."

Mikail sighed. "I remember it as if it happened yesterday. Forty years ago, I was a shiny new first lieutenant with a Starling Class in-system fighter and a crew of three. And I was afraid of nothing." He ran a hand through his hair. After a quiet moment, he started talking again. "I'd been to space most of my life already. The surface of Ganymede was my playground. I crewed freighters before college. I drove fighters in the Navy. I had been *to* space, but until the day we met I had never been *in* space."

Marge nodded soberly. "Mike, didn't you once say you got your first vacsuit when you were six years old?"

"Yes, on Ganymede. You said you had never been off Earth until you volunteered for Search and Rescue."

Marjorie smiled. "Navy changes your life in many ways. I enjoyed space, crewing on the rescue launches, wearing my powered suit. It was almost my own spaceship. I remember meeting a lot of wonderful people, even if I met some of them by picking them up from wreckage."

Mikail gazed out the window, squeezed shut his eyes. He remembered vividly the moment he stopped feeling immortal. The image of curved fuselage and emptiness was so real it caught his breath. *Thirty hours*. That's how long he'd floated next to the three-meter-long fragment of his in-system fighter, waiting for the power to run out in his suit. *Thirty hours*. He had thought he was waiting for a lift home, but as those hours trickled by, the possibility of rescue became more and more remote.

••✦••

Caught in a flashback, Mikail saw the telltale flash of his sensors reporting that the suit transponder was still transmitting. The suit strobes still worked, and he had thoughtfully attached them to the fragment of his fighter's hull sharing his small patch of eternity. The larger radar and visual profile should make it easier for rescuers to find him.

Visibility was essential, since his ship and what was left of his three crew members were now spread out over several cubic kilometers of space. Worse, the whole conglomeration had a trajectory taking them farther away from New Hearth's sun.

Mikail did not know if anyone still gave a damn about picking up a stranded astronaut, or if the capacity to do so even still existed in this system. The battle had been going that badly.

The air plant would work as long as there was power, but power was not the problem. Mikail was in a race with two different deaths. The cool/heat sump serving the lower half of his suit had developed a glitch, and it had started dropping two degrees an hour. His feet were starting to get really numb, and he had no way to fix the problem.

The rest of the crowded universe seemed to have deserted Mikail. His mental focus was scattered, fractured over the hours as the immensity of space tried to crawl into his soul. The near-sensory-deprivation environment of his suit and the unchanging universe beyond lulled him into a state of contemplation for which he was not prepared. He was slowly going nuts in the isolation.

The needle-thin profile of the high-boost rescue launch was difficult to see against the blackness. When a star blinked out in a direction he happened to be looking, Mikail scarcely noticed. Flotsam from his Starling had floated by on more than one occasion in the last thirty hours. And then the launch came to rest not more than a hundred meters away. The cargo lock opened, a crewed mini-sled emerged from its cool brilliance, and manipulator arms and high-powered floods haloed into solidity.

Mikail watched his high-tech guardian angel approach with wonder. If this was hallucination, it was the best he'd ever had. Padded manipulator arms cradled him and whisked him back to the launch. The airlock cycled with the speed of a hurricane, and Mikail's suit was covered in frost. Mikail felt a vague pang of regret that he could not see his rescuer, followed by quiet joy. He was going to live.

He rubbed his faceplate with a shaky hand in time to see a figure emerge from the mini-sled. She had a snub nose, a spray of freckles, and gorgeous red hair in a close cap of ringlets; she was stocky and graceful, wearing only a skinsuit and insulated gloves. With shockingly strong arms, the miniature goddess helped Mikail unfasten the catches of his suit and efficiently stripped him out of it. She slapped diagnostic patches onto his neck and chest as these parts of his anatomy became exposed.

Her warm hands and the cool sensor pads combined to send chills racing down Mikail's spine. He felt a distant embarrassment at being touched by a stranger, followed by profound relief to be lucky enough to be touched at all. He grabbed her hand and tried to bring it to his lips.

She scowled and pulled back her hand. "Not you too. If I get kissed by one more loony man today, I will just scream!" She saw his woebegone look, and her demeanor softened. "Well, you are cute, so I expect I will accept a dinner invitation . . . *if* it is properly advanced."

In his daze, Mikail could only nod, but he was not so far out of it that he missed the mischievous twinkle in her sea green eyes. For several years after that, Second Lieutenant Marge McCan and First Lieutenant Mike Benson were an item, the lass from Ireland and the Slav from Ganymede—a match literally made in heaven.

••✦••

The vividness of memory slowly faded into the early morning light of the office, and Mikail found a touch of lightness returning to his heart. Forty years ago, he had been saved by this remarkable woman, and they had become lovers. Naval service had brought them together, and by strange coincidence, had not swept them apart. They had remained together for the rest of the war.

"You certainly picked me out of the wreckage, Marge. You were just what a half-frozen, half-crazy castaway astronaut needed. I've never known how to thank you for that."

Marge made a pushing motion. "Peddle it to the navy, spaceman. I made you take me to the most expensive restaurants on three planets during our time together. After I left the navy, Earth seemed like a pretty small place. It didn't have as much adventure as I was used to. I knocked around the Federation for a lot of years before winding up here."

They traded silly grins. "The navy was good to me, but captain was as far as I could go. The service was my family for a long time, but I finally got too restless. Civilian life is hard in a different way. Too many people just seem to think the universe is a safer place than it actually is. When I came to New Hearth to take over this office, I was glad to find you footloose and on-planet. Stealing you from the governor's staff was the smartest move of my administrative career."

Marge dimpled. "Distract me if you can. I still want to know when you're going to give up the monkish lifestyle and make those nightmares go away."

Mikail smiled. "You're undoubtedly right, Marge, as you so often are. All I do is work, and after work, I work. I definitely need a life. Would you care to have dinner with me tonight?"

Marge stared. She was not used to being trumped when teasing her boss. She thought about it. "I *do* like a proper invitation from a dashing gentleman." The brogue in her voice was more noticeable than usual.

"Oh, I will be very proper during dinner," Mikail assured her solemnly. "I promise. Now," he said more briskly, "Let's get down to the real work of this office, shall we? I want to know what the hell the AranthChi really want with their current questions, and are they attempting to put something over on us?"

Marge McCan snapped to attention and grinned. "Your first appointment is at nine. There is nothing in your inbox yet, and I am reviewing the current Questions File. Go home and take a shower."

MEETING ON SKREE

peace plus thirty-five years, on the surface of Skree

In the mauve palace of hereditary rulers, an Aranth lounged in his private apartments in the royal wing. He attempted an attitude of repose, but the truth was that he was greatly agitated. Time and again, he would throw himself upon his day couch, only to jump up a moment later and pace the polished jet stone floors. His countenance was as stormy as the leaden skies outside. However, it would never do to show his rage to his subjects, so Marsh(ee) throttled his ire.

"Artifice," he snapped and came to a pause in his pacing.

"Yes, sire?" A pale mechanaloid stepped out from its shallow alcove.

"My official rest period is nearly over! I must soon take up the reins of government again. We are running out of time, so I ask again: Where is he?"

The device—part servant, part bodyguard—paused to consult the palace security system. The mech was fanatically loyal, with unbreakable, tamperproof programming, a plus in these risk-taking times. "He has just arrived on the grounds, sire."

"Well, get him here! No, wait—has a record of his arrival been generated?"

"Do not worry, sire. Your instructions are clear and complete. No one will see this one's arrival or departure, and all records of his presence will be deleted."

Marsh(ee) strode to the informal dais, his ears twitching slightly. He gave a great stretch, brought his mobile ears up fully, and rippled the muscles of his shoulders and back. This in turn fluffed up the fine silver fur showing beneath the gauzy cotton-like shirt that covered his upper torso. Shorts of royal yellow, the color of his clan, completed his raiment. He wore no boots or sandals so that the mark of his royalty, four toes on each foot and four fingers on each hand, could be plainly seen.

Completing his stretch, he turned and sat upon the dais. He would not have been pleased to learn that Humans would recognize his behavior as feline in nature. Nothing about the Human worlds pleased him at this moment. "What have I gotten myself and my clan into?"

A gentle series of taps came from the door. The mechanaloid met the visitor and escorted him into the presence of Marsh(ee), the Anvil of Truth, Alpha Male of the Least Clan. The visitor crossed the floor hurriedly and came to a halt in front of the dais. The only sound in the room was the soft clicking of the supplicant's booted feet as he trod the stone floor.

As Marsh(ee) watched, the visitor assumed a posture of deep respect, head bowed forward to expose the back of his neck, signifying total compliance to the will of his alpha male. All this was done in silence, as one did not speak first in the presence of royalty.

"Rise, Ragonsee," came the command. "Speak of your mission. My Hand of Destiny, tell me the scent of our prey."

Ragonsee's nosed twitched violently. He kept his face to the floor another half-second to control his response to the anger scent in the room. He was a very ordinary Aranth to look at. He stood perhaps 1.5 meters tall and was built slightly, even for a race that ran lean. His fur was cream, shading to silver-gray at the ears. He wore a short tunic, red trousers, and soft black boots. His three-fingered hands had non-retractable nails and were arranged palm down on his thighs in respect of his betters. Though not of royal blood, he had risen high in the clan's hierarchy during the faux war with Humanity, and was capable and trusted.

Ragonsee stood and made a polite coughing sound. "My lord will remember that this has always been a long-range project." At Marsh(ee)'s glower, he quivered and spoke more quickly. "The assistance we have supplied and the psychological and economic incentives we created have worked very well on these Humans, sire. The Human form of government has an almost pathetic ability to ignore the future and, by extension, the past. We are having no trouble keeping them occupied with the happiness of the present moment."

Ragonsee watched his alpha carefully. Marsh(ee)'s annoyance seemed to be growing. He searched for more soothing words. "In truth, we have recovered much knowledge, thanks to the Humans, that was sealed away from us by the High Council of Great Clans. Many processes that the masses take for granted because of the automation of our factories is becoming decipherable to our researchers. Within a few short years, I am sure, we will have enough understanding of our own science to proceed to the next step."

"Years we may not have," the Great One murmured.

Ragonsee paled. "Has aught happened that I must know of, sire?"

"Indeed," said Marsh(ee) morosely. "The military vessel we used in some of our attacks on the Humans forty years ago is being recalled to the central worlds." He went on with a touch of irony, "It is time for its seventy-five-year standard maintenance trip to the Great Clans' naval yards."

"But sire, the vessel was damaged only moderately in combat, and we have repaired all of it!"

"And how would I explain the repairs? I have not admitted to the council that our clan has conducted any war activities. We have not the permission."

"All of the operational records have been changed, sire.

Any damage the yards may find will be explained by records of training exercise accidents."

"And yet," Marsh(ee) said heavily, "none of your scientists or technicians could reach into the core itself. If they should become suspicious and access that, they will have the true story of everything the vessel saw and did."

"Can you not delay them somehow?" the smaller Aranth pleaded, so upset that he actually laid his ears flat to his skull despite the presence of his alpha male.

Marsh(ee) chose not to notice. "I have done what I can. I have directed the vessel to make a survey of our outer provinces and delayed its transfer back to the central worlds until that survey be complete. More I cannot do." He snarled quietly. "We have secured five, perhaps ten years at the most. You must squeeze these Humans harder. We must have the knowledge we need, for we must make our move sooner than ever planned." Marsh(ee) rose, ending the interview. "Soon," he repeated.

Ragonsee left the palace in the same degree of secrecy that he had used to enter it. The great work had suddenly become much harder, more urgent, and perhaps more dangerous. He had much to think about and even more to do. Plans were even then percolating in his head, though implementation would be delicate. A meeting with his strategy group was a necessity, yet it would need to take place discreetly. Each move he made from that point would increase the risks. Therefore, every move must increase the scent of success. For the first time, it was sinking in that he would have to return to the Human worlds personally.

Several hours of driving in a groundcar, not traceable to the official intelligence services, brought Ragonsee to a commercial airfield. He took the first flight to a small regional spaceport on the far side of the planet. By the next morning, he was in space. Only one more stop in the Skree system was necessary, then the longest journey of his life would begin.

••✦••

aboard the Benedict Arnold, *orbiting Mars*

Jeremiah Littlefeather gauged his jump with a practiced eye. Step one: line up target in helmet viewfinder. Step two: arrange self in line with target. Step three: squat slowly and find your center in the best Zen fashion, clicking off boot magnets as one reaches the point of ultimate WA or energy. And step four: push off with a mighty shove, uncoiling from the bottom up into an attitude of arrow straightness, to fly well and true to your destination.

Jeremiah didn't use the cold gas reaction pack built into his suit because he liked the feeling of exertion, not to mention exhilaration, that came from an unassisted jump. He was also proud of the extraordinary skill with which he could place himself on trajectory to the object of his choice. This would be about a half-kilometer jump, he judged, and a bare few seconds' use of reaction gas should bring him to rest even with his destination. He could plainly see the huge net that floated in the distance.

Jeremiah braked to a stop a shade over ten meters from one end of the expanse of bright orange webbing. A gentle burst of gas got him moving again, parallel to the net. As he skimmed above the net, inspecting it in his suit floods, he noticed that these supplies were earmarked for Alpha Centauri. He knew that from there they would most likely be transshipped to one of the new colonies that had been established on the far side of Human Space from the AranthChi.

If they had been going to an already established colony, say Caledonia or New Hearth, they would have stayed with him. However, his ship—one of three ALFs or Alien Loaned Fleet vessels—was not allowed to travel anywhere that Humanity had the vaguest hope of keeping private from their former enemies.

At the end of the net, he turned in the direction known

locally as "up" and changed his vector with the reaction system. Soon he came to the ceiling, tucked into a ball, and rotated. When he straightened out, he was moving feet-first toward the wall. Not bothering to brake, he made contact and collapsed in toward his center to absorb his momentum. Clicking on boot magnets before he could bounce away was second nature.

"Main cargo bay lights half intensity," Jeremiah muttered into his helmet. Slowly, long strips of luminescence brightened on the ceiling and all four walls, bringing the bay and its contents into sharp relief. It now became obvious that Littlefeather was not in space at all, properly speaking. He was in a huge airless cavern composed of alien metal.

At the far end of the bay, more than two kilometers straight down, the outer doors could be seen. These massive structures were each more than a kilometer across and would swing outward to allow the passage of just about anything you could imagine, from cargo and ore to most of the space-going ships that Humanity had ever built. Strung along the walls, several nets like the one he had just inspected could be seen, each filled with a mountain of cargo. The center of the immense space was vacant.

"Bridge, this is Main Cargo."

"Go ahead, Cargo."

"All secure down here. All work crews have vacated the bay, and I certify that the bay doors are safe to open."

"Roger," came the reply. Then, "Say, Jerry, you're still in the bay. Does that mean that you are not a worker?" Anne Okazaki's voice became just a little bit singsong as she attempted to tease.

Jerry grinned inside the privacy of his helmet. He had been trying for weeks to get Anne to come out of her shell. Now, the very intelligent, very beautiful first-time spacer had softened her formality, just a little.

Jerry was delighted. *I must encourage this behavior at all costs,* he thought as he opened his mouth to speak. "No indeed, ma'am." To carry his end of the banter, Jerry trotted out his best rendition of the Oklahoma twang his beloved grandfather had carried all through life. "I'm one of them white collar supervisor types. I couldn't recognize real work if I tripped over it."

"Well, okay," Anne replied, laughing. Jerry's imagination filled in the sound of tinkling bells. "*Mister* Littlefeather, the old man wants to see you, so you better come topside as soon as you can."

Jerry sighed. He loved to watch the stupendous valves as they opened outward into the void. It was an awesome sight, filled with impressive, silent grandeur. His current position was just about ideal. Often a slice of Mars would be seen through the opening doors, and frequently the space tugs would appear as minnows waiting to dash in with cargo or ride-alongs. This trip, there was going to be a regular parade of no fewer than seven military and civilian spaceships.

All of the ships coming were no doubt FTL-capable. But since the cost of ferrying them was as minuscule as one could imagine, why bother to operate them until you really had to? Not only that; the alien freighters had an acceleration no Human ship could compete with. The *Benedict Arnold* would reach FTL point fifty times faster than any civilian ship could. Military ship specs were confidential, of course, but everyone knew the ALFs were faster than anything Human-built. It therefore made sense to give Human vessels a free ride until they had come as close to their destinations as the good ship *Benedict Arnold* could bring them.

Duty called, however. "Affirmative, Miss Okazaki. I'll be up as soon as I can make connections on the cross-town tram."

Anne giggled. "Very good, Mr. Littlefeather. I will inform the captain."

Switching to a private channel, Jerry opened communications with the ship's artificial intelligence. "Everything looks good down here, Ben. Can you bring a tube car to the north lock station for me?"

"A car will be waiting, Jerry."

"Thank you, Ben."

As Jerry entered the nearest personnel lock, he was in an absolutely fine mood. At the rate Anne Okazaki was progressing, she just might be ready to go out on a date by the time they reached Alpha Centauri. A candlelight dinner in a romantic restaurant, a moonlit walk along the exotic shores of Lake Tombough, and who knows what could happen? Jerry whistled the theme to *Oklahoma* (off-key, as always) all during the tube ride up to the bridge of the five-kilometer-long ship.

THROUGH A GLASS, DARKLY

Peace plus thirty-six years, on the surface of New Hearth

Mikail increased his pace just a little. The morning was already warm. Sharp, brassy spears of sunlight gleamed from the Institute buildings, promising a day both bright and blue. A few cirrus clouds accented the sky. A mild salt tang from the bay mingled with forest breath of the campus redwoods. Mikail stepped up the pace and was rewarded for his increased effort by a deepening V of perspiration on his sweatshirt, a moistened headband, and that glorious stretch of body fully alive.

One might think that exercising would be a snap in a .91 gravity field. That was only true if one were fresh from a heavier locale. Mikail had been born on Ganymede to Russian immigrant farmers intent on creating their own perfect Soviet. He had never even been to a *real* planet until adulthood. Most post-grad studies still took place on Earth. Even then, he was an indifferent athlete. And now he had lived the last ten years of his life in the light gravity of New Hearth and was, as his exercise therapist cheerfully put it, "woefully decompensated."

So, okay, he thought as he rounded another bend on the running path of the Institute's ornamental gardens, *I'm recompensating, I am.* He figured another ten minutes would do it for that morning. That would give him just enough exercise to leave him with a pleasant ache in the thighs and the wonderful alertness that comes with extending oneself just a bit. A cool-down walk across campus, a shower, a change of clothes, and he would be fit to face the day.

He hadn't even known there was an exercise trainer at the institute until Marge McCan had dug him up a few months ago to assist Mikail in his return to fitness. Now Mikail was running every day, had lost ten pounds, and felt closer to his actual age of seventy than the 105 he had been feeling. After all, if he was going to live to the average of 150 or more, he might as well feel good doing it.

Marge watched Mikail come through the door, slightly out of breath. He looked better and more cheerful than she had seen him in quite some time. A return to physical fitness was doing wonders for his mental outlook, too. At any rate, his reports of nightmares had fallen off. And was he sleeping better. This she could attest to.

"Morning, bossman," she said. "It's a good thing you're on time today, because you're getting a surprise visit from one of the top brass."

"Oh? A Federation senator? The General Accounting Office?"

"Admiral Soo."

"Not Jimmy Soo?"

"The same."

"Jimmy Soo." Mikail shook his head. He had a distant gaze. "Did you know that man wanted to rename all naval intelligence supervisors 'spymaster'? That man went to Nova Terrene, took a sleepy special weapons depot, and turned it into research hell. If you weren't a fire-breathing radical scientist, you were nothing. That man and I argued every day of the five years I spent in intelligence."

"You told me, Mike."

Mikail chuckled. "It will be good to see the old rascal again, though I am really glad I'm a civilian now. I haven't seen him in years. I didn't even know he was in the system. What time is he coming?"

"I gave him your first appointment; he'll be here at nine."

"Who did you bump?"

"Don't ask, boss; that way you can look them in the eye at the next state dinner and never know the difference."

Mikail winced just a little. He was fond of insisting that the Office of Alien Technologies wasn't political, but part of what kept him personally insulated from the politics of government was the ruthless way Marge treated all the politicians that came through the door. He gave her a wan smile and entered the inner office, knowing he wouldn't get much work done that morning. He found he was really looking forward to the surprise visit of his former boss.

••✦••

Admiral Soo was a small man with a round face and lively black eyes. Part Filipino, part Korean, all one-G muscle and sinew, he radiated with the vibrancy of Earth. He bounded across the room with an excess of energy to capture Mikail's hand and shake it vigorously.

"Benson, Benson, good to see you again!"

"Good to see you too, Jimmy. How is the dirty tricks department these days?"

Jimmy Soo got a pained look on his face. "Mike Benson, you ought to know that naval intelligence is a fine, tradition-bound organization, even if we sometimes have to do things in a, shall we say, unorthodox fashion."

"Purely, of course, to get the job done."

"Purely." Soo grinned. "Why, I even remember we gave you a chance in our great organization after you became a has-been fighter pilot. You made captain. Could have made rear admiral, if you hadn't left to pursue your will-o-the-wisp of alien motivation."

"Someone had to do it. You toy soldier types were spending much too much time and money trying to crack the secret of gravity control for the next war."

"And I must say, we were having an awfully fun time of it too. Which brings me to why I am here today."

Though he said it casually, something about the tone of Soo's voice made Mikail's pulse quicken.

"Yes?"

"Are we secure?"

Mikail touched a contact on the surface of his desk. An abstract pattern appeared in the upper right-hand corner and began rotating. "We are now."

"Mike, we've done it. It has taken more than thirty years, but we have done it!" Soo looked—the only word that fit was "gleeful."

Mikail stared for a long moment. "Do you really mean that?" His voice was a doubtful whisper. "You mean gravity control?"

"Yes. Just that. I have just arrived from Earth on the SFN cruiser *Mariposa*. We pulled over thirty Gs leaving the solar system for our FTL point, and when we got here, we did fifty Gs slowing down. And it felt as gentle as if I were still sitting in my swing chair on the front porch of my estate home by the river Yao. Now we have plans to refit the whole fleet. Some of the home fleet has been upgraded already, in strictest secrecy, and soon we will do the same for the rest of the navy."

"So the AranthChi shuttle finally gave up its secrets," mused Mikail.

Thirty-five years before, at the conclusion of the Human/Aranth war, the AranthChi had set two conditions for the Human retention of the systems of New Hearth and Caledonia. Number one: the Federation would share "basic science" information with their former opponents so the AranthChi could check to see if they had "missed" anything along the way to a mature technology and culture. The other: Humanity would undertake a number of "technical projects" for the AranthChi, researching things the aliens did not want to bother studying themselves, but which they were nevertheless curious about and wanted the answers to.

In order to offset somewhat the huge amounts of money the AranthChi expected Humanity to spend, they loaned the Federation three freighters for a period of fifty years to be used in the repatriation of colonists and toward expansion of Human interests into the galaxy. These freighters, the ALF, were marvels of technology. Each ship, eventually called *Trojan Horse, Benedict Arnold,* and *Marja Nye,* measured in the unheard-of dimensions of five kilometers by three kilometers. They were also miracles of technology. Each vessel was totally self-maintaining, with judgment enough to be self-guiding. All were delivered with a sealed power supply that the AranthChi assured would last a hundred years under any kind of workload Humans could conceivably put the ships to.

The ALFs proved to be a windfall. Though Humanity was deeply suspicious of the AranthChi in general, and of the monstrous peace offerings in particular, the ships were soon put to good use. Rules were devised to assure that only one of the behemoths would be in the Sol system at any time, none would approach Earth more closely than the orbit of Mars (which served to ruin the moon-based interstellar transshipping businesses but worked out nicely for those companies based on Mars), and the alien vessels would never be allowed to go to a Human settlement that the AranthChi did not already know about.

The profit to Alpha Centauri, New Hearth, and Caledonia was enormous. In only thirty years, the populations of New Hearth and Caledonia had more than doubled, from fifteen to forty million for the former, and from ten to almost thirty million for the latter. Alpha Centauri, the primary transshipping point for both halves of the Human Sphere, became a planetary boomtown, with both military and civilian interests swelling the economy and population to such an extent that the planet went from a net exporter of foodstuffs and raw materials to a net importer of both.

Unfortunately, it was impossible to learn anything of value from the ships themselves. They came with no service manuals, no training guides, and no entry into the operating machinery. All of the real or potential accessways that could be found through exhaustive examination were sealed off in such a way as to invite the uninvited to stay the hell out. When the scientific and intelligence communities attempted to make new entryways, the AI computers that ran the ships politely insisted that they desist. It took very few confrontations with the ships' guiding spirits to realize that the only way they were going to get into those sealed-off areas would be to reduce a ship to a pile of junk. Even the navy refused to go that far.

The AI computer running each ship had been delivered already fluent in System English, and they'd follow orders orally or typed in at various control stations throughout the ship. Other than that, each ship arrived absolutely empty, with kilometer after kilometer of corridor, room, and hold absent of anything of value. Except, that is, in a small maintenance bay inside the ALF that would someday become known as the *Benedict Arnold,* there lay a small shuttle craft. This craft, surrounded by diagnostic equipment, with its access panels not sealed or booby-trapped in any way, was the find of the century.

The same paranoia—some called it caution—that moved the Sol government to disallow the great ships' approach to Earth also dictated the choice of location for the research effort that would come to be known as the Question Institute. *Put it far enough away from Earth to make an alien power grab less threatening, and an alien espionage network less effective, and then watch this bastard brainchild like a hawk,* said the military. *Give it lots of money and turn it into a braintrust, and our races will both grow and benefit together,* said the scientists. *Make it a true and open cultural exchange, and the two groups will evolve into harmonious friends and partners and usher in a golden age of peace,* said the sociologists. *Do all of these things and make sure we get credit for creating jobs out of it, because it's always an election year somewhere,* said the politicians.

And so it was done, Mikail reflected glumly. *And here I am in my little Office of Alien Technologies, trying to keep track of the scientists, the sociologists, the politicians, and the aliens. Is it any wonder I sometimes meet myself coming and going?*

Admiral Soo waited patiently for Mikail to digest the news, then began to speak again. "Some of the implications are astounding. In fact, the way this thing turns out to work will have the physicists rewriting cosmology and causality for years to come. Some of our experimental results are unexplainable, to say the least. Especially when used in conjunction with our technology for opening up a crack in four-dimensional space-time. Anomalies have cropped up if we are using gravity control when we transition to the seven-dimensional matrix that allows us to get around the light speed limit. But I will fill you in on that later. For now, I need to ask some questions."

Mikail's eyes burned with his own questions, but he said nothing and merely nodded.

"First off, we are trying like hell to keep this advance a secret from our friends and benefactors the AranthChi." Soo managed to say this with only the slightest sarcasm in his voice. "However, it has been clear for a very long time that they know more about us than we'd like them to. And much more than is good for them to comprehend, considering we know virtually nothing about them in return. To that end, I need to know what they have been inquiring about lately. Have there been any changes in pattern or frequency of requests that might be suggestive, or anything new about gravitation research that might tip us off to the fact that they know or suspect something?"

"We send naval intelligence updates all the time on the lines of research our felinoid chums are inspiring around here," said Mikail, gesturing to a stack of data plates on the far corner of the desk. "In the ten years I've been here, we've analyzed every AranthChi request that has come through. We compare requests in light of their previous interests. We look for context; we look for trends. We look for military potential. We look at the political implications. If we find anything alarming, we report it immediately."

"I see the reports, Mike. But I haven't studied the Institute like you have. Can you give me any insight?"

Mikail lifted a portion of the glass surface of his desk into easy viewing position and dedicated it to readout status. He struck a pose unconsciously copied from an Institute researcher whose lectures Mikail had attended more than once. "First of all, the AranthChi have always been interested in the basic sciences; chemistry, organic chem, cosmology—but not, interestingly enough, biology. We steer clear of giving them anything concerning our weapons technology, but I don't think it makes much difference. We couldn't beat them thirty-five years ago, and I doubt we could beat them today. The first technical project they asked us to do was a real screwy one. It didn't take much research, but it did take a hell of a lot of computer time. They wanted us to calculate pi for them to an astronomical degree of preciseness, and they wanted it in base eight."

Soo looked puzzled. "They wanted you to calculate the circumference of a circle?"

"Yes. And why in base eight? After all, the AranthChi only have three fingers per hand, and if you add up all their digits, throwing in toes, you come up to twelve. Anyway, to add to that mystery, they asked for pi calculated to one billion decimal places. That's 3.14159265358979 . . . add a billion numbers behind it." As he spoke, the symbol for pi appeared on the screen with a string of numbers next to it, and below that, a simple computer-drawn circle.

"With that many digits involved, plus the fact that this

was the very first thing they asked of us, we approached the project very seriously. Two teams of programmers ran the problem in tandem using completely separate systems. They checked their results three times, and then traded data and checked each other. Only then were we satisfied with the answer. The AranthChi wanted it delivered in printed form as well as on data plate, only Schrodinger knows why.

"That took four months. Most of that time was checking the printed product for errors. When we told them we were done, they said thank you very much. Now devise for us a spatial axis co-ordinate system inside the circle turning it into a sphere of indeterminate size, except that it will be larger than one centimeter in diameter and smaller than infinity. And, by the way, this should have at least one hundred million points of reference in the X, Y, and Z axis, cross-referenced, with all the appropriate degrees of longitude and latitude delineated. Also in plate and printed form."

Jimmy Soo snorted. "Idiotic."

Mikail shrugged. "With requests this strange, is it any wonder people were beginning to think the AranthChi were nuts?"

As Mikail talked, the circle turned on its side and became a sphere, complete with a myriad of tiny lines and internal coordinate tree. Several columns of mathematical symbols appeared beside the sphere. "Another four months blown. By the end of this project, all of our assembled techs and professionals were more than ready to quit. Nobody likes feeling they're being made a fool of."

"Astrolabe."

"What?"

"Astrolabe." Soo repeated, tapping the glass. "It looks like a gigantic expandable astrolabe for plotting the locations of stars."

"There are easier ways to depict the locations of stars, especially since this arm, or even the entire galaxy, is not remotely spherical in nature. But that is as good a guess as any, since the AranthChi never answer questions about any of the projects they commission anyway." Mikail went on: "After that, they became interested in astronomy, mathematics, and physics. They wanted to know everything we had ever hypothesized about the formation of the universe, the nature of time, and the mathematics of multi-dimensionality. They then asked for detailed positional maps of the galaxy as it looked fifteen thousand years ago, ten thousand, five thousand, and one thousand years ago. It's almost as if they didn't have computers of their own to do this stuff on."

Mikail shook his head in disgust as he continued his story. "Finally, they moved on to energy sources. The request was to identify, define, and describe all known and theoretical energy sources and how said sources could generate power in all possible environments and under all possible gravitational intensities, including a hypothetical civilization on the surface of a neutron star. This was the sort of project the applied and theoretical physics people could really sink their teeth into. Many engineering specialties also became deeply involved. When the aliens asked us to expand the scope of research to include both 7D space and after the theoretical heat-death of the universe, the number of PhDs being awarded around here resembled a New York hailstorm. Unwary pedestrians could be bowled over in the rush."

"Have the AranthChi been asking about the generation and control of gravity fields?" Soo asked.

"In a sense. In the Unified Force area of physics, they have asked for information and research in all four fields of study. That of strong and weak nuclear forces, electromagnetic, and gravitation. The gravity lab itself isn't very big, however, and hasn't had the high priority of the other projects."

"Have there been any recent requests?"

"How recent?" Mikail leaned back in his seat and regarded the smaller man thoughtfully. "You came all the way from

Earth—or was it farther than that?—to give me a personal visit. What are you worried about, Jimmy Soo?"

Soo jumped up and paced the room, then came back and put his hands on the desk. "Maybe I'm just spooked by shadows. I don't know. I left Earth seventy-five days ago. Have there been *any* requests since then?"

"Let's find out." Mikail set another portion of his desktop to display status and called up all recent work requests and anything having to do with the Gravity Lab. He skimmed through the information until he reached one item. "Ten days ago, the new AranthChi legate put a request through to the Gravity Lab." Mikail felt a sinking sensation in the pit of his stomach. "A high-priority request for all data to date on the generation and collimation of gravity waves. There is also a directive to slow down other projects and put all available resources into researching the theoretical design and manufacture of gravity motors based on example of motors of theirs we have seen."

Soo's face was so still, it could have been carved from granite.

"Could the timing be a coincidence?" Mikail wondered.

"Security leak. Has to be," grunted Soo. "From my end, probably. At least they don't seem to know we have functional gravity control, or they'd be asking for manuals and specs rather than more research into theory and design."

Mikail sighed heavily. "We'll also launch a discreet investigation. I don't expect to find anything, since no one at the Institute is supposed to know what's going on in top-security research elsewhere in the Federation. Nevertheless, if there is a connection, I'll find it."

The conversation ground to a halt. Finally, Mikail stood up. "Now, my honored guest and friend, it is time for the VIP tour. I'll show you the wonders of my little kingdom, and you can *ooh* and *ahh* at our achievements in inter-species harmony and cooperation. And if we skip the Gravity Lab, which seems to be a good idea, rest assured they won't be ignored in my next report."

As Soo rose from his seat, Mikail spoke to the desk.

"Computer, erase displays, no permanent record, kill the security zone." As the desktop returned to transparent and folded flat to the desk, Mikail took Soo by the arm and headed for the door.

"After the tour, I imagine you'll have lots of admiralty-type things to do, but perhaps after that you'll be free to have dinner with me tonight. After all, we have a lot of old times to catch up on."

Soo grinned once again. "It will be my pleasure, Mike. Your expense account or mine?"

"Not fair. You have the almost unlimited budget of the 'dirty tricks department.' All I have is my old sailor's stipend to see me through. Of course it's on me."

••✦••

"We were really in a jam." Jimmy Soo sat toying with his iced tea, a perfectly empty plate in front of him. Dinner had been whole locally grown Australian lobster, wild "rice"—a tasty native grain—plus a side-dish of Chinese stir-fry. There was also a trencher with the picked remains of three lobster dinners. Mikail Benson and Marge McCan were also sipping tea in deference to Soo's distaste for alcohol, though Marge had enjoyed a glass of white wine with her meal.

Jimmy Soo set down his tea and kept speaking. "Their ships were a nightmare to deal with. They came in assorted sizes and shapes, and their individual capabilities could not be determined from those shapes. Often the designs of their warships made no sense, at least from a military point of view. It's not that their ships were better than ours, although with those defensive shields and truly startling maneuverability they were very tough."

Mikail nodded. "You could take one out if you managed to tag it with a twenty-megatonner. Five megatons on the shields sometimes worked, but twenty always did the job.

"Mike, I wish that were true. No, you were out of the action, you didn't see. . . . Once, they used this damn monster that they dug up from somewhere."

Jimmy Soo blinked as he recalled those events. "It was the first A.Chi ship we'd ever seen that was spherical. It was a full two kilometers in diameter with more defensive shielding and beams than you can imagine. They first used it against the planetary defense net at Caledonia, where it rolled those guys up and stomped them flat. When it left the system, every space asset of ours was either gone or just so much junk. Post-attack analysis showed the spheroid had taken twenty-one direct hits during the engagement and never even slowed down. The shields had only flickered once, when three hits came in rapid succession."

Jimmy Soo's voice deepened, and his speech slowed as he settled into his reminiscence. His words were so vivid it brought the past into the room with them. "We knew New Hearth had to be next. . . ."

••✦••

Commander Soo was in a near panic. A system-wide alert was on, and his three ships were fourth in line for refueling and re-weaponing at the Yamamoto Ship Depot in orbit around New Hearth's only moon. All daywatch, he had been firing off messages to the controllers at INSYSCON. Now he was trying to get the Port Admiralty on the line. Anything to move the three ships of his squadron up, in a line that seemed to be taking forever.

He had been on recon patrol, looking for enemy activity among several of the nearby stars. The three Eagle-class corvettes in his command were the most recent and agile design of high-boost attack boats to enter the war theatre. In an unnamed solar system some eleven lights east, they had stumbled across a two-ship enemy observation team.

The enemy, officially called the Unidentified Hostile Forces, in slang terms called Gzabs—or gee-zabs if the speaker was articulating every syllable—had fought viciously, but with little innovation. The Human forces limped back from that encounter, nominally the winners, but with severely depleted energy and weapon stores, and a number of areas that urgently needed repairs.

Now they were back, and the whole system was buzzing like a hornets' nest a kid had whacked with a stick. Lieutenant Swanson stuck her head into the tiny day room and interrupted her captain's fretting. "Call coming in for you, sir."

Commander Soo's compact body made a graceful twirl in midair. "It's about time. Get ready to move the troops. I knew I could count on my buddies at INSYSCON to reshuffle our orders to the front of the pack."

"I'm sorry sir, this message is not from InSystem Control. It is a direct communication from Admiral Ojema's office."

"Don't kid with me, Delilah. I've got too much on my mind right now."

"Sir, we're keeping the admiral's office on hold right now. Please hurry." She looked distressed.

Commander Soo felt his morning meal congeal in his stomach. He followed his executive officer forward to the control room, touching and pushing off from the central corridor handrails every few meters, hurrying in the energy-efficient fashion of a trained spacer.

The shuttle trip down to Headquarters Base gave Jimmy Soo too much time to review all of the possible reasons that the chief of naval operations for New Hearth and Caledonia, and the number two man in the whole war theatre, would want to see him, a lowly squadron commander. He ran through his list of sins at least twenty times, trying to decide if any of the regulations he had broken (really, he'd only bent most of them) were bad enough to land him a personal interview with the CNO.

The only defense he could think of for some of his more creative methods of keeping his squadron stocked and battle-ready was to call on the "can-do" tradition of military services through the ages and hope the old man would put a blind eye to the telescope. Depending on what Soo was being called on the carpet for, the admiral might let him wiggle through, perhaps only putting him in minor hack.

When Soo was ushered into the admiral's office, he was surprised to find another commander in dress whites there as well.

Admiral Bamgbose Ojema was a large, imposing man with skin like polished obsidian, that glowed with a shining luster that approached a splendor beautiful to see. He had the kind of personality that filled the room. Soo found him quite intimidating.

Introductions were brief, and the admiral came right to the point. "Gentlemen, I asked you here for a very specific reason. Both you, Commander Soo, and you, Commander Harkins, have impressive operational records. Additionally, you command the highest sustained boost-type attack craft currently in service. Therefore, gentlemen, I have a mission for you."

The admiral sat back in his seat and stared at them intently. "I want you to work together on a project idea that may not work, that may be totally futile, but is desperately needed: the two of you will form a joint strikeforce and take your ships out-system to a designated holding zone. And wait. The coordinates will be given to you at time of departure."

"Sir?" Soo's eyes widened. "Sir, our ships will be needed to repulse an all-out attack by the Gzabs! Sir, that doesn't make a lot of sense, begging the admiral's pardon."

Commander Harkins nodded, too stunned to speak.

Admiral Ojema's dark, shiny face creased in a grim smile. "Oh, you'll be coming back, commander. Yes indeed. Welcome, gentlemen, to Operation Hammerfall."

Twenty-one days later, seven small ships were station-keeping on vector Alpha Zulu. The ships of Operation Hammerfall waited very busily indeed. The strikeforce coasted deep in what would be the cometary halo, if this system had had a cometary halo, which it didn't. Eight light hours out at closest approach, ninety degrees above the plane of the ecliptic, they shared the vast dark with only the occasional automated early-warning monitor for company. For the previous nineteen days, the ships had been diving in toward New Hearth, going FTL, coming around, and then diving again to build up excessive V.

Jimmy Soo floated in the command center of his modified Eagle, the *Citizen Kane*, and fretted. The other six ships of his strikeforce were in loose formation. Each ship, similarly modified for the task facing them, had grown a thickened waist of jettisonable reaction tanks. Looking around the bridge, Soo was too aware that *all* of his active detection gear was switched off. Radio contact with the strikeforce used only a whisper of power. Passive systems were on; that was it.

"Who says it's not going to work?" Delilah Swanson was arguing with Al "Sharps" Giovani, weapons officer. "In this kind of warfare, position and firepower are everything! When we come busting in on the party, we are going to have the high ground like nobody's business, with more kinetic energy to throw around than you can shake a stick at." She tossed her head for emphasis, making her corn silk hair fan out, sending secondary undulations down her lanky frame.

Sharps was not impressed. "Why do ya think," he responded, "that no one's ever done this before? Don'cha understand? Diving into a crowded solar system at better than .4C is tantamount to suicide. We hit one little thing on the way in, meebe only a grain of sand . . . that's it for us." He grimaced theatrically and drew his finger across his throat.

"Harumph," returned Delilah. "We're not in that much danger. We'll be in empty space most of the way; we punch through the plane of the ecliptic and out again in no time. On the way, we cream that big bastard, and we all get a medal. Why, there's not even an asteroid belt in this system."

Giovani stared for a moment, shook his head, and turned away. "Goddamn Pollyanna," he muttered.

"This is it," Soo said suddenly. "Alert signal coming in. Okay, everybody secure for boost; I repeat: secure for boost. I want all personnel in acceleration tanks in ten minutes."

"Hey Sharps," Delilah said as they helped each other through the preboost checkout and settled into the gel environment of their acceleration tanks. "You and the captain always refer to the UHF as Gzabs, and I've wondered why. What does that term mean anyway?"

"Well, little girl," Sharps said. Then he stopped as he ran a careful eye down Delilah's G suit, looking for telltale folds or creases in the material, a matter of some discomfort at two or three Gs, a whole lot more serious problem at higher levels of boost. She waited patiently as he went on to check her respirator mask and hoses for a kink or coil in the line that could possibly overlap and cause a fatal pinching off of her oxygen supply. Everything being in order, he guilelessly met her gaze and carefully did not make any further reference to her six-foot form. "That term's old. Before the official designation of Unidentified Hostile Forces, there was this incident, see, right at the beginning of the war. . . . This Gzab ship came in and shot up an orbital factory. The Corps of Engineers crew putting it together was a might peeved. That was in Caledonia system. The Corps commander, *Brigadier* General Nevile Shortham, chased 'em in a dinky little patrol boat. He chased 'em for an hour across the system, all the time yelling at 'em on the radio, telling 'em to turn around and fight and calling 'em 'goddamn xenophobic alien bastards.' They kept going, so he didn't lose his ass . . . and the name sorta caught on."

Delilah was grinning inside her helmet. "Now that would have been something to see," she murmured.

"Now, if'n you want to know why our communication's officer, Lieutenant Randall, calls 'em VHF, you better ask him. But I warn you," Giovanni continued, "it's a very arcane and *technical* inside joke. And you'll be sorry you asked."

Seven fusion flames lit the void. Forty grueling hours at ten G, with brutally short rest breaks, brought the seven little ships up to a frightening speed. Inward they plunged, faster and still faster until they were falling toward New Hearth's sun at seventy-two thousand miles with each heartbeat.

The Human body was not meant to take such sustained abuse. Human ingenuity did what it could to compensate. The gel environment of the tanks took up the crew members' increasing weight smoothly, yieldingly. The respirator masks fed each person a precisely tailored mix of aerosol drugs designed to combat high-G stress. One by one, the crew succumbed to their personal level of G tolerance. The drug dosages mounted.

The drugs were cardiotonic in nature, encouraging lung surfactant integrity, blood vessel integrity, and more efficient oxygen and glucose utilization by the body. The oxy-helium mixture served by each mask combated the problem of nitrogen narcosis.

Commander Harkins managed to sleep, but his slumber was uneasy and filled with nightmares. Lieutenant Delilah Swanson's mask over-pressurized when she stopped breathing. Positive pressure ventilation saved her life. Throughout the fleet, Humanity's ingenuity preserved life.

Finally, the hellish acceleration tapered off to an end, a blessed cessation. One by one, the members of the company clawed their way to usefulness. "Approximately two light hours out from the combat zone, four hours to intercept." Lieutenant Randall fought to focus. In a bleary and slightly surprised voice, he announced, "Target is inbound and on the predicted course."

No one knew what heroics the defenders had pulled to keep the Gzabs interested and fighting in the outer system as long as they had, but whatever they'd done, it had worked. The Gzab force—one big mother and twelve of the more familiar little ones—were moving into the gap between the fourth planet, a Saturn-sized gas giant, and the third, New Hearth.

"Launch the first set of missiles. I want a five-minute burn," Soo ordered.

According to the plan, there would be three waves of missiles, spaced to provide the maximum pounding, with the strikeforce riding somewhat behind the third wave to provide last-minute tracking control.

When all of the ninety-plus missiles had been deployed, Soo ordered a return to passive sensors. The strikeforce spread out into a big ring, designed to encircle the area of combat. Communication relied on highly focused lasers. Considerable power drained into the comm to send intelligible messages through the interference kicked up by the high-speed passage of the ships as they rode deeper into the outbound photon stream of the sun.

"We will be falling free until fifteen minutes before contact," Soo reminded his crew. "Unless Tactical on the moon alerts us to a change in course by the Gzabs, we are now committed to this action. If we haven't been spotted before, we don't want to be seen now."

One of the other ships chimed in, "Don't you want to wish us good hunting from the Sun Emperor, sir?"

"Wrong culture, bonehead," came Harkins's voice from his ship, *A Clockwork Orange*.

Soo grinned. "Silence, boys and girls—and good hunting."

Marge McCan was barely breathing, iced tea long since forgotten. She leaned forward, hands clenched in classic white-knuckle fashion. "What happened next?" she demanded.

Soo took a sip from his tea and sat gazing at the table for a moment, thinking. He looked around and seemed surprised to find the restaurant almost empty, the dinner crowd long since gone. Marge's green eyes seemed to burn into his face. He felt a flush coming, so he looked down. Then he began to speak again.

"At T minus twenty, we entered the envelope of their active detection systems. Now we were in a race with the lightspeed information lag. We intended to follow the return impulses in too quickly for them to do anything effective about it. I ordered the strikeforce to power up and woke up the missiles. The tactical feed from the Gzabs' own output gave the missiles their initial lock. I assigned the big ship as priority target to eighty percent of our total strike. The mother missiles then calved, and each wave began its burn. Using a modified dodge-and-evade attack program, nearly four hundred missiles went on in.

"It was incredible," Soo murmured, almost too softly to hear. "One second we were falling serenely and quietly onto their heads, and the next second everything exploded. Suddenly the little ones were dodging around like chicks beneath the swoop of a hawk, and the big one lit up all over like a Christmas tree. No, more like the aurora borealis, only all the aurora boreal of a hundred years rolled into one.

"In less time than it takes to tell it, huge sheets of blinding energy licked out from the big one, and a dozen missiles disappeared from the first wave. Then, a dozen more. Someone must have gotten very excited in their fire control center, because along the way, they burnt up a couple of their own guys. From the first wave, only three missiles made it in to hit their screens."

Mikail moved with restless agitation, drumming the table with fingertips. "I'd heard that bastard was tough."

"Mike, you have no idea. It was spectacular. With each hit, there would be the brief flare of actinic light marking the birth of a twenty-megaton explosion. The lights surrounding the ship would die down some and then brighten again. The second wave went like the first, only this time we scored five hits.

"On the last wave, we got in seven hits, one right after another. The lights kept dimming until on the fifth hit, they went out. The sixth missile took down their screens. And the seventh . . ." Soo looked up, locking gazes with Mikail and Marge. "The seventh missile failed to explode. For some reason, the proximity device didn't work. Perhaps it was defective. God knows our production quality was good, but nothing is perfect. At those closing speeds, it's a wonder that most of them went off. Instead of annihilating that ship, the missile punched all the way through it, leaving a hole so big you could drop a skyscraper through and not touch the sides. Then we were past, and it was time to begin the long slow down.

"You know, the damnedest thing about it is the ship kept going! It didn't try to fight anymore, and it couldn't go very fast. But there was no one in position to give chase, so it made it out of the system and got away." Soo shuddered. "God, I'm glad they didn't have more of those things." He finished his tea in two quick gulps and set the glass down gently. "We lost three ships during the battle, don't really know how. A stray beam hit them, or something." He shook his head. "We were too spread out; there was too much confusion. They were just . . . gone. We saw what happened to the fourth ship, Harkins's ship. After we thought the battle was safely past and we were beginning to slow down, his Eagle hit something—probably something smaller than a pebble—and just disintegrated. It was over in seconds."

He looked sad for a moment. Then his round face brightened. "To our credit, though, we got nine of the little ones. Eleven if you count the two big brother fried, and of course we stopped big brother. And Delilah was right: we all got medals."

"It must have taken weeks to get back in-system," Mikail said.

"It did. By then, the top brass had decided it wasn't possible to win the war, and plans were underway to abandon both systems. A general evacuation of Caledonia had already taken place. The next step was an orderly retreat from New Hearth. All the fighting after that would have been to guard the retreat." He shook his head. "And just as we were packing to leave New Hearth for good, the Gzabs offered us a peace proposal. Twenty years of war, and they never said a word. Now a peace proposal delivered in System English, written as sweetly as any career diplomat earthside could have wished."

Marge picked up the pitcher set on the side table and refilled Soo's glass. She added one lump of sugar, as she had seen him do, and silently offered it to him. His eyes thanked her as he took the glass. Mikail hid a quick grin.

Marge stared seriously at Soo. "We took their offer, though, didn't we? Was that a mistake?"

"Hell no, Marge. We were ready to give up everything to get out of the war. That's how desperate we were. Remember, at the time they first hit us, there were only five colonized systems in the whole Federation. It took four hundred years to plant the first three using sublight technology. The only reason we could afford to colonize New Hearth or Caledonia at all was faster-than-light travel. Colonizing is very expensive. They offered us more than an honorable peace; it was a good deal. The peace gave us back everything we had been fighting for, and the price was relatively cheap."

Soo's hands, which had been on the table before him, came up, drifted further apart with each point. He was gripping a beachball-sized space as he said, "They even threw in three enormous transports, which cost nothing to run, to help us recolonize. This cut down considerably on the time it took to make the systems profitable again and helped defray the crushing cost of the war."

Mikail's face had a sour look. "*And* they conveniently left an un-blocked shuttle lying around for us to experiment on, allowing us to close a thousand-year technology gap almost overnight. Now they want to know everything we've figured out about their science of gravity control."

Soo's hands collapsed to the table with the control of the trained spacer. "I know, Mike; these are not coincidences. Something stinks here. We all know that. We just don't know what."

"If I could get my hands on an Aranth for a day or two, we might . . ." Mikail began fiercely.

"Mike!" Marge's head jerked around, staring in alarm.

"She's right," said Soo. "You could start the war all over again."

"I know, I know," muttered Mikail. "It was just a thought. It might come to that someday." He lifted his hand to signal the waiter for the check.

"The night's still young," Mikail said with forced cheerfulness. "Let's find more pleasant things to talk about."

"Absolutely," said Marge. "I'll go first. I have a question for you, Jimmy."

"Yes?"

"What does VHF stand for?"

The two men exchanged a glance and began to chuckle.

The evening had turned cool by the time they left the restaurant. Slender tendrils of fog were coming up the street from the direction of the New Glasgow bay; streetlights were all a shimmer. Marge linked her arms through the men's, and they walked toward Jimmy Soo's hotel.

As they neared the corner, Marge slipped her arm free of Mikail. She gave him a bright smile. "You had him all day, boss man. It's my turn now."

Soo looked mystified for a moment, then his face reddened.

Marge smiled again and murmured, "Do you think you can get along without me for a few hours in the morning? I may be late for work tomorrow."

Mikail smiled. "I think so."

Soo's brow raised comically. "Oh, I . . . really," he stammered.

"Sirrah," Marge purred, "art thou refusing the offer of a lady?" Her Irish brogue, usually absent, had returned full force for the occasion.

Jimmy Soo pulled himself up to his complete diminutive height and reminded himself that he was a full admiral, a leader of men, a longtime battle-tested warrior. If only his hands weren't sweating. He was not entirely unfamiliar with the practice of open relationships, but he was caught definitely by surprise. Not that he was disappointed.

He had been aware all night of his growing attraction for Marge. He thought he'd hid it pretty well. Now, standing in a thickening fog bank that turned the landscape into a fairyland of softened hue and half-seen shape, he was confronted with direct evidence that his interest was returned.

"No, I'd never willingly offend such a lovely lady as yourself. I am deeply honored and would love to say yes with all my heart. It's just . . ." He paused, looking for the right words. He turned to Mikail, concerned and confused.

Mikail tried to help. "Perhaps you would like to tell her about your old war wound. You know, the one that makes it impossible to be anything but a gallant dinner companion?"

Soo shot him a dirty look. "You're not helping very much."

"*Au contraire*, old friend. I am trying to help you a great deal."

Marge picked up Soo's hand. "You may have the mistaken impression that there is only so much love in the world. That it must be given out in miserly doses, all the time waiting for the well to run dry. In fact, the reverse is most certainly true. The more you water love, the more love grows. The more you share love with a person capable of cherishing and returning that love, the more love you get back to enrich your life and share with others."

Mikail nodded. "I love Marge, and I want her to be happy. You are my old and treasured friend. When you can have some happiness in your life, I also rejoice. If my friends find happiness together, I am not diminished. I only lose if I take the utterly irrational point of view that what Marge gives you and what you give her should have been mine all along and you two are stealing it away from me. My relationship with Marge is not threatened. She will still love me tomorrow. That's the way she is built. The only question is, can you rise above your fear of loss and feelings of jealousy and accept Marge's proposal with a glad heart and an open mind?"

Soo laughed. "Mike, you could sell snow to an Eskimo."

He got a puzzled look in return.

"Never mind. Read up on North America sometime. I can see that I too have some learning to do." He gave Mikail a bow. "I never thought my visit to New Hearth would prove so friendly."

Marge released Mikail's hand and swept herself into Jimmy Soo's arms. He began to relax and even grinned a little

"You just don't understand how being in the company of two such handsome heroes can turn a girl's head," Marge said. "Now take me back to your place and show me whatever pass for etchings in an admiral's transient accommodation."

As they walked off into the night, Mikail noticed the spring in Soo's step and decided that it probably wasn't all due to the lighter gravitation. He smiled and turned for home.

••✦••

As Mikail readied himself for bed (slippers at foot of bed, check) his mind mulled over the day's events (clean shirt and matching tie for tomorrow, check). He kept coming back to some of the unbelievable things Jimmy Soo had said about the results of research into the unprotected shuttle's systems (running shoes and tracksuit in bag, check).

Unlocking the secrets of gravitation control had taken an entire generation of scientists and more than one planetary budget, and the results had come from an absolutely unexpected direction. It had been known, practically since day one, that gravitational attraction was an effect caused by the influence of a mass on the space-time fabric of the universe. The more mass an object had, the more effect it would have on the local shape of space.

The experience of acceleration forces was measured in the same way as gravitational attraction, as experienced on a body in space—Earth, for instance—and is described by how fast an object falls toward the center of that mass. On Earth, this would be ten meters per second squared. On an accelerating spacecraft, one needed to consider not only mass, but also foot pounds of thrust, classic action-reaction. Good old Newton's second law of motion, concerning inertia.

The question was, how had the aliens gotten around that law? How had they overcome inertia? In the quest to reproduce the A.Chi's technology, the scientists had discovered that the road actually did lead back to the force of gravity and how mass *really* distorted the fabric of space. Using copies of the shuttle's motors, Jimmy Soo's scientists had learned to generate or nullify that force at will. Now Humanity could build ships with maneuverability matching that of the AranthChi.

Gravitational control was not the only priority, Jimmy Soo had said during their meeting in Mikail's office. *Of equal importance was the alien's method of power generation.* Mikail's hopes raised for an instant. Soo had shaken his head.

Federation scientists had run into infinitely more trouble with the AranthChi powerplant. Certainly, the generation, storage, and delivery of the incredible amounts of energy used by even the littlest of the AranthChi ships could not be beyond Human understanding. Theories abounded, none provably close to the mark.

The shuttle's power capsule was a completely sealed unit, surrounded by intense magnetic and gravitetic forcefields that gave no hint to their interior. The capsule itself was composed of an incredibly dense material, possibly even neutronium. The research teams working on this problem were still arguing about how to disable the forcefields safely, if they could be removed at all. The more conservative researchers voted to run down the power source before attempting entry.

Currently, the grounded shuttle supplied electricity to the naval research station and a hundred thousand homes and offices in the adjacent of town of Scorcece. Once the energy stores were exhausted, the shuttle would be returned to space and taken at least ten planetary diameters away from the Nova Terrene for the next phase of research.

Mikail settled into bed, waving off the reading light. Replays of the day's conversations filled his mind. Determinedly, he let darkness and quiet lull him toward sleep. He was on the verge of succeeding when something in the backwaters of his consciousness piqued his interest. He tuned in to see what it was.

Jimmy Soo was speaking in Mikail's memory again. *It's the strangest thing, Mike. We have always known that gravity curves space, so we weren't too surprised that when we were able to focus gravity waves, we curved space too. Not a lot, of course; the power requirements were horrendous.*

The big surprise came when we tried to use our new generators while entering FTL space. There were subtle problems with timing. An experiment would take longer than we expected or end sooner than we expected. Ships would return from trips with their onboard clocks out of sync with the research station's. One ship came back four days late from an experimental run, but the captain swore they had turned back early because of equipment problems. The ships log backed him up.

Eventually the engineering people were able to link these effects to the minor fluctuations of field density put out by each individual gravity generator. Suddenly we were able to predict, then influence, the changes.

Okay, Mike, I've given you enough hints, and if you let your jaw drop any further, it's going to come to rest on your desk. What am I talking about? What have we discovered?

You're talking about entropy, oh my God! In his remembered conversation, Mikail jumped up, came around the desk to stare at Jimmy. *Can you really slow down the rate of entropy?*

Yes, we can, in FTL space.

And speed it up too?

Again, yes, but only in FTL.

You can slow down or speed up the passage of time in FTL space. In effect, you have the perfect freezer. Cook a meal, put it in the field, and turn entropy way down. When you come back a few days or weeks later, it's still hot and ready to eat.

Yeah, or the other way, Soo had said. *Increase the flow of entropy, and you can grow your food fantastically fast. This could be a real boon to agriculture, not to mention manufacturing and transportation. Still, it only works in FTL space, as far as we know.*

Mikail recalled returning to his seat, shaking his head. *Well, somebody will find a use for it someday. Someone always does.*

Mikail, on the edge of sleep, murmured his parting comment to Jimmy Soo aloud. "Someone always does."

He was suddenly wide awake and climbing out of bed. "Someone always does! And I'll bet I know who. *Oh my God*."

Mikail spent the rest of the night in furious activity, calling up files and documents on his home net node, notemarking important information and dumping it into his secure recorder. In the pre-dawn chill, he gathered up all the reference material he had and headed into work.

He wished the research on the aliens' apparent ability to communicate faster than light had progressed further. It might turn out to be as important as gravity control. Human research on the propagation of above light particles, the fabled tachyons of theory, had never panned out.

When Mikail reached his office, he pulled up a tutorial

on faster-than-light technology on his secure console. One of the Institute's scientists had reviewed the subject for him when he'd taken this job ten years before. The scientist's droning voice filled the office while Mikail worked.

"Wrap a ship in Hawking probability energies, pop it into FTL space, and it becomes a lump of steel and plastic gelatin moving as if through oil. Outside observers cannot detect it and cannot communicate with it. However, when the ship emerges, it has actually moved through space—all the way to another star, if the calculations are done right.

"Beam any sort of energy into FTL space, even Hawking radiation, and the energy goes . . . somewhere. Unfortunately, it doesn't seem to come anywhere near a receiver that can pick it up. Even if two ships enter FTL together, radiating for all they are worth in every detectable manner, they lose each other in a heartbeat. When they return to normal space, they are once again detectable. One can prove by power readings that energy was being put out. The question is, what happened to the energy?"

Mikail stopped the playback for a moment and grinned. He turned off the tutorial and shook his head. The theory he leaned toward on FTL energy detection was also the most fanciful, mostly because it was so contrary. That theory stated that everything that went into FTL space was still there. Conservation of energy still held, and the energy not been absorbed somehow or hopelessly detuned. It just hadn't arrived yet. No receiver could detect something that never got to it. The theory in its current form was no use to anyone. Just mentioning the theory could make old-time physicists froth at the mouth. That made it worth bringing up at faculty parties.

The AranthChi had something that could send messages not limited by lightspeed, even if they didn't use 7D space to send it. During twenty years of war, their response to Human tactics had often been coordinated instantaneously across light minutes or hours. Could they also talk between stars? *It would be so helpful,* Mikail thought, *if we had that ability now.*

The gray dawn patterned the campus buildings outside Mikail's window with dark, cavernous eyes as he pushed back from the desk. While he waited for the desk to make sealed copies of his evidence and suppositions, Mikail thought about his last ten years spent running the office, watching the AranthChi, learning how they thought. Perhaps, with the previous night's intuition, all that work had paid off.

He turned down the room lights and watched the day slowly come into being. It was a beautiful world, and he had come to love it dearly. *How long will the beauty of New Hearth remain ours?* he wondered.

Marge would be disappointed when he called to let them know that plans had radically changed. Unless he'd missed his guess, Jimmy Soo would be leaving immediately and maybe never coming back. The universe was suddenly a bleaker place. Bad times were coming. If Mikail was right, the war days were coming inexorably back, unstoppable as a tidal wave. He only prayed he'd had his insights in time to affect the outcome. *This time we know you're coming,* he thought. *This time you're the ones in for a surprise.*

INTERLUDE 1

AranthChi space

The installation floated in cold, deep, silent, extrasolar space. It circled in stately fashion more than an eighth of a light-year from a minor red dwarf star. Its brick-colored companion lent only the weak, tenacious grip of gravity to the station's objectives.

Ancient in purpose, sophisticated in design, and old in years, the astrophysical observatory crouched in the darkness of the exhausted solar furnace to better take in the glory of the heavens. It swam in a sea of sense impressions unavailable to organic beings. It had operated thus for eons, gathering information for its masters. Sometimes crumb by crumb, sometimes in a flood, it sieved the wisdom of the universe.

In extreme quiet, it listened to the slow heartbeat of the galaxy, sampled the song of dying photons in a wisp of solar wind, tasted the radio chitter of cool hydrogen movement, and kept time to the regular pulsing of quasars half an eternity away.

Slowly it became aware of a new pattern in the energy movements of the universe, a faint flavor of radio noise coming in on unexpected bands of the EM spectrum. The noise had order and precision. Not like the order of the cosmos, but very like the order in other, more known areas of space.

The installation automatically tried to assign this new event a similar value to patterns already known from intelligence it had tracked for ages, but the patterns did not quite match.

Simple algorithm-based recognition programs failed to resolve the matter, so higher centers of logic and thought came into play. They too could not come to a decision and therefore passed the matter upward until the enigma found its way to the core artificial intelligence of the observatory.

Shortly, the installation activated its crisis imperative. A message, whose wings were many multiples of light, propagated outward. The core intelligence of the observatory had just set forces in motion that would tear apart the millennia long order of the empire and threaten the very existence of an alien race.

Of course, the crashing of age-old political dynasties and the destruction of alien civilizations were not among the phenomena it or its attendant machines were equipped to study.

4

BALLROOMS IN THE SKY

aboard the Benedict Arnold *in Alpha Centauri A's outer system*

The empty void shimmered. A soap bubble swirl, a dappled shadow . . . and the solid bulk of the ALF *Benedict Arnold* hurtled into real space at the edge of Alpha Centauri system.

Anne Okazaki fought to keep her eyes focused, her breathing calm. A transition from FTL robbed one of added dimensions, squeezing the traveler into the familiar three. Anne, suppressing a moment of compression panic, watched the blank screens come to life from the observer's chair at the nav station.

The nav officer spoke quietly in her ear as each screen lit. "Directional radar active. That's line of travel, highly important. Global active scans on, optics online now. . . . Doesn't look like we're going to run into anything this time."

"This time?"

"Don't look so worried, girl. We've never hit anything yet." The senior nav officer was a small blonde woman, close to Anne's height, but chunky and old enough to be her mother. She touched Anne's arm. "Your turn. This console has been isolated from the main feed. The computer running this ship knows where we are by now—and so will the captain, if he asks. But he won't. He's waiting for *you* to tell us, so get to it, trainee."

Anne wiped her hands nervously on her uniform shorts.

She had done this a thousand times in the simulator, but the simulator hadn't been traveling several hundred kilometers per second. She took a breath.

"Begin navigational search. Identify closest star."

The computer answered, "Alpha Centauri A confirmed. Centauri B and Proxima confirmed. We are in A's outer system."

Anne had not asked a compound question. The computer was reminding her it had self-aware artificial intelligence.

She gritted her teeth. "Identify Sistra and show our present course and speed relative to its position."

"Sistra, also known as Alpha Centauri Two, identified." A schematic appeared on one of the screens, showing the Alpha Centauri sun, Sistra, and the *Benedict Arnold*. A dotted line linked the planet with the freighter. Rate of travel figures appeared next to the ship icon. The number of zeros was impressive.

"We're already on course for Sistra?"

The computer somehow infused its reply with a note of weary patience. "At the moment. I always emerge lined up with my destination. If we do not start slowing down soon, or if we fail to account for the gravitational attraction of Tarnball, we will miss."

The nav officer chuckled. "Snippy, isn't it?"

Anne felt her cheeks burning. "Identify and display the entire planetary system. Flag potential navigational hazards. Use approved approach algorithms to estimate time of arrival."

The information appeared. Anne scrutinized it carefully. The gas giant Tarnball and its family of moons appeared to have a minor effect on their course. Anne asked about asteroids and comets. The nav officer grunted.

Finally, Anne was satisfied. "*Benedict Arnold* is in Centauri System, headed for Sistra. There are several course corrections I would recommend we take over the next few hours."

"In the zone, just like always." The nav officer smiled and

said, "Trainee Okazaki, you may inform the captain."

Anne turned to find Captain Sommer looking her way. Since his command desk was less than twenty feet from her and raised as well, she felt horribly exposed. His being a bear of a man, with a thick, bushy beard, did nothing to ease her intimidation. And he was leaning forward, clearly waiting for her to speak.

"Captain, we are in Alpha Centauri outer system, on course for Sistra. May I send my data and course recommendations to your desk?"

The captain nodded. His desk displayed the information holographically. He got up, walked around the image, sat back down, and asked the computer to overlay its recommendations onto Anne's. A glaring red arc appeared. "About ninety percent, Miss Okazaki. Still, your course costs us more time. I think we go with the computer on this one."

Anne got red again. The nav officer spoke up, "Tell her how you did the first time you tried to navigate this ALF by hand, skipper."

Captain Sommer's bushy eyebrows went up. "Ninety-two percent is still the best first score on the books, Helen."

The nav officer nodded primly. "Anne, he lets the computer tell him what to do too. You did great, honey."

By end of shift, Anne felt her bones turned to rags. Entering a solar system was more nerve-wracking than leaving it. *The first time has got to be worst of all,* she thought. She fled to the gym, found an unused fresher room, filled the hot tub, and turned herself into soup. Afterward, she went straight to her room, made a bowl of miso, and fell into a stupor.

The next shift, Captain Sommer took a little pity on her. He turned his chair toward the main screens and shouted questions over his shoulder. He never turned around, instead ordering all displays on the giant screen at the front of the room. Every time she performed well, he hid his grin in his beard. Every mistake brought a growl.

Toward the end of the shift, he turned around and seemed surprised to find Anne alone at nav. "Where did Helen go?"

"Um, she said she was going to monitor the board from your office, sir. I was not to tell you she had left."

"Helen!"

"Stop yelling, Bernard." Helen Sommer's image appeared over his desk. "I walked out an hour ago. Anne's been doing fine."

"Helen, when you're on duty, you can't leave the bridge without the OD's permission. I don't approve."

"I apologize, Captain. It won't happen again . . . if you stop yelling at the trainees."

Captain Sommer gave Anne a rueful stare. "Don't ever marry your bridge officers, Miss Okazaki. It leads to nothing but trouble."

"Yes, sir."

"Ah, don't 'yes sir' me so quickly. I've been married twenty-five years to the best navigator in Human space. I'd be lost without her." He shrugged, and a smile worked its way out from under his beard. "You'll do fine. Yes, you will."

Anne lingered at change of shift. The evening nav officer, a prickly young man named Winston, sat down, glanced at the boards, pulled a book from his pocket, and started reading. Lurid figures crawled around the edge of the read-surface. Anne was horrified. What was he doing reading fantasies on duty?

Winston looked up. "Can I help you?"

"I was wondering if you could use some assistance. I always need more practice." Anne spoke quietly, humbly.

"You're not needed. And your shift is over."

"But you seem busy. I could—"

"No. I am not busy, nor will I be busy. Go away."

Appealing to a higher authority, Anne turned toward the Officer of the Deck. Absolam King had his uniform shirt off and was stretching one leg and then the other. Corded muscles moved smoothly under dusky skin. She looked on dumbly.

The OOD caught her look. He had a very deep voice. "Miss Okazaki, the bridge is in good hands. Don't believe me? I'll show you. Hey, computer!"

"Good evening, Officer King."

"How's our status?"

"All systems are in perfect order. Course to Sistra proceeding normally."

"And what're your standing orders?"

"I am to alert you thirty minutes ahead of time whenever a Human decision on the running of the ship is required. In the event of an emergency requiring action faster than a Human can respond, I am to follow my best judgment in protecting lives and this vessel."

King grinned. "There, you see? Everything's covered."

"Yes, sir." Anne couldn't keep the dismay out of her voice.

King chuckled. "It's not that bad, girl. We are as fully trained as the day crew, but as long as they do all the work, we get to play. Speaking of which, what are you still doing here? Tomorrow morning we arrive at Sistra. That means tonight's the planetfall dance. Your *first* planetfall dance, isn't it?"

Anne nodded. The planetfall dance was a custom revived from the days when ocean travel was slow. After a trip of days, or weeks, a landfall dance was held for disembarking passengers. This one time, off-duty crew could mingle with the passengers on something like equal status.

ALFs did not have the rigid social structure of Victorian-era ocean liners. All accommodations were first-class and all passengers equal, the crew having status just by being spacers. But the desire for an end of journey blowout was strong just the same. The dances were fun!

Anne was looking forward to going . . . or had been until this moment. "Uh, I don't think I have anything to wear."

King shook his head. "Go anyway. Steal a gym towel, sign out an environment suit, wear what you're wearing now if that's all you have. Tonight, no one will care. That's an order, Okazaki."

"Yes, sir."

Anne walked off the bridge with her shoulders slumped. King stared after her. "Purty girl like that, nothing to wear."

Winston cackled. "Fat lot you know about women, Abs."

"I know she wanted to hang around to keep you from running us into a rock. Once she gets to the dance, she'll stop worrying about the second team." Absolam started his stretches again. Since he hadn't brought his stationary bicycle up with him, he thought he'd probably just do an hour of tai chi.

••✦••

By the time Anne got to the ballroom entrance, her enthusiasm had returned and fled a dozen times. If Marta Gomez hadn't been standing at the entrance, watching her come down the promenade, Anne would have returned to her quarters. When she saw what Marta was wearing, she wanted to run all the way back to her room. If there were six ounces of material in Marta's scarlet minidress, Anne would have been surprised.

Marta waved. "Anne! Over here."

Anne gulped. "Hello, Marta. Sorry I'm late. I—"

"It's okay. Karen has seats for us at a very good table." Marta took Anne by the arm and hustled her through the wide doorway. They were confronted by a marble staircase with a deep pile, a midnight blue runner, and a rosewood banister so shiny Anne could see herself in it. The stair followed the wall down two levels before sweeping out into the center of the room.

The room was so big, Anne wanted to stop on the stair and just . . . stare. Just when she felt she was adapting to the gargantuan that was *Benedict Arnold,* she would enter another room she had no idea existed and be in awe. No one in their right mind would put a formal ballroom on a starship. But the AranthChi had done it. She had a momentary fantasy of thousands of ballrooms in the sky.

A tall blonde woman stood next to a table halfway across the floor, tapping her foot. As Marta approached, Anne in tow, she favored them with a big grin. "About time, ladies. You almost lost your seats. I'm going dancing."

It was then Anne realized the tall brunet man standing nearby was waiting for Karen. He led her out onto the dance floor. Karen Seimens was easy to keep track of. She was an arresting figure with her off-the-shoulder white dress, white pumps, and white-blonde hair. *Her companion complements her well,* Anne thought.

All evening, Anne sat while men came up to ask Marta or Karen to dance. At first Anne was relieved, but the third time Marta walked away on a young man's arm, she lowered her eyes, letting out a small sigh. The compact Brazilian beauty was so full of confidence. Anne could never have appeared in public in the screaming red mini-dress Marta wore so saucily.

She looked up to find the captain standing at her table. Resplendent in his dress uniform, he seemed every bit as intimidating as when on the bridge.

"Good evening, Miss Okazaki."

"Hello, captain." It came out a squeak.

"Are you enjoying the dance?"

"Yes . . . sir."

"But you haven't been dancing. Why not?"

Anne looked around the empty table. "I haven't been here long. . . ."

"Nonsense." The captain held out a hand the size of a fry pan. "Allow me."

He led her onto the dance floor just as a waltz began. The captain was an excellent dancer, in the technical sense. Anne was sure he was good at everything he did. She felt hideously underdressed in her formal pantsuit.

Anne tried to relax. It was more difficult than she thought it should have been. She remained stiff. *Oh my,* she wailed inside. *I'm dancing with my father.*

Captain Sommer was indeed like her father; he even escorted her back to her table, where they found Karen Seimens talking to an attractive man.

Karen said, "Evening, Captain. Hi, Anne. You've met Jerry Littlefeather, right?"

Anne nodded. She opened her mouth, but Karen hopped to her feet and kept on talking. "Captain Sommer, if you're giving out dances to lowly employees, I want mine too." She placed her hand on the captain's arm, walking him back toward the dance floor.

Anne watched them go. The very tall blonde looked good on the arm of the brown bear in uniform. When Anne turned back to the table, she found Jerry observing her. She felt heat rising in her cheeks.

Jerry looked dashing, dressed in a cream pirate shirt open to the middle of his chest, and sharply creased charcoal trousers. "Hi."

"Hello, Mr. Littlefeather."

He cocked an eye. "So formal." He stood and gave a little bow, offering his arm. "May *I* have the pleasure of the next dance?"

Anne couldn't help it. She put her hands in her pockets and stepped back. "Ah, I'm sorry. I was just leaving."

Jerry repeated her *ah*, a touch sadly. He immediately put his hands in his pockets, too. "May I escort you to the door? Lots of ruffians about tonight, you know."

Again Anne couldn't help it. This time she giggled. She gave up trying to keep her hands in her pockets and covered her mouth instead. "I can count on you to protect me from 'ruffians'?"

Jerry radiated sincerity. "Yes, ma'am."

"I'll tell you what, Mr. Littlefeather. I would love an escort around the ballroom. It's so huge, and I haven't seen *any* of it yet."

They walked around the ballroom, Anne soaking in the

splendor. Jerry's gray and cream complemented Anne's powder blue. Every so often, he would put out his arm just a little and immediately draw it back. Finally, Anne reached out a hand and placed it on his arm, lightly as a hummingbird. There it stayed.

They reached the grand staircase, and Anne *hmm*ed. "This is so beautiful. I had no idea the AranthChi had such notions of beauty. I hope to meet them someday."

Jerry looked at her oddly. "What are you talking about?"

"This room. This staircase. They're glorious."

"Thank you. But this isn't AranthChi work. This room was modeled after a ballroom on an old steam-powered ocean liner. Modeled and expanded about ten times, because we have the space for it."

"Oh." Anne was crestfallen. "AranthChi don't build ballrooms?"

"They might; I wouldn't know. Haven't you taken any of the docent tours?"

"I've only been on the ship a few weeks."

"I would be happy to show you around. In this room, for instance, we shipped bulk grain for the first five years of operation." Jerry swept his arms out to encompass the room. "Remember, the AranthChi loaned us these ships to bring the colonists back to Caledonia and New Hearth. Relief shipments of food were a big part of re-colonizing. Eventually, all the colonists got home, and a lot more emigrated besides. Once the traffic slowed down, the ships were refitted to be passenger liners as well as freighters."

"Bulk grain," Anne repeated.

"Right. You are standing in the most opulent grain silo in the galaxy."

"And the staircase?"

"Makes a nice chute, don't you think?"

Anne stared at him. "Am I ever going to know when you're kidding, Mr. Littlefeather?"

Jerry grinned. "I'm not kidding when I offer to show you the ship. There are marvels beyond counting around here. I would love to give you the VIP tour. How about next time something special is about to occur, I come and get you? There are things I know you won't want to miss."

With obvious reluctance, Anne said, "All right . . . but only if I'm not on duty."

"It's a date, then." Jerry salaamed and walked away.

"No, it's not," murmured Anne. "It's only a tour."

••✦••

It started with a light tapping on her door. In her dream, Anne remembered later, someone had knocked on her gingerbread door. *What is that?* She awakened enough to realize the tapping was coming from her real door. She was sure the annoying Mr. Littlefeather was the cause. A quiet command turned on her annuncer. Its screen showed Jerry Littlefeather in work uniform.

Humph. "What do you want?"

"Hi, Anne. I've come to get you for a special event. Hurry up. You'll want to see this."

Anne looked at the annuncer's timepiece. "Jerry, it's three in the morning. I have to be up in three hours. When we get to Sistra, the bridge will be *very* busy. I need my sleep."

"We *are* at Sistra. The night shift is warping us into orbit now. That's what's so urgent. Something's about to happen that's very rare . . . and you're not on duty! We only have a few minutes. Come on!"

Anne emerged in less than a minute, wearing a fluffy pink robe over pink pajamas. Pink slippers adorned her feet. She wore dignity like a cloak. "This better be good."

You're adorable. Jerry didn't say it. For the life of him, he couldn't figure out how he kept his mouth shut. He hurried her down the corridor and into the waiting tram. The trip was quick, taking Anne to a part of the ship that was new to her.

Jerry ushered Anne into a small room that seemed walled entirely in black glass. A padded bench stood in the center of the room. Jerry sat on the bench and gestured Anne to sit also. Reluctantly, she sat down as far from Jerry as she could manage.

"Well?"

"Watch." Jerry passed his hand over a translucent square hanging in front of the black glass wall. The room lights dimmed. A gentle push sensation pressed Anne into the bench, and the room began moving. Suddenly Anne was floating, drifting off the bench.

"Jerry!"

Jerry reached up, thought better of it, and held out his hand. "Pull yourself down to the bench and slap the side. There are restraints."

An invisible band crossed Anne's lap and went snug. She looked around. Blackness was everywhere. When she turned to glance behind her, an immense metal wall could be seen, marching off into the darkness. In front, small lights blinked, appearing far away to the two viewers.

"Where am I? Jerry, what am I seeing?"

"See the lights? Seven of them? Those are ships at anchor. This is the harbor."

"Jerry. Even I know this ship doesn't carry a harbor in it. Stop kidding me."

"Patience, Anne. Soon the sun will rise, and you'll see everything."

Anne had her doubts. She wanted to go back to bed. She needed her sleep. She was sorry she'd let this crazy man talk her into coming here. She almost said so.

Jerry whispered, "Look straight ahead, past the last light. What do you see?"

Anne peered into the gloom. *Nothing. No, wait*—a thin line had appeared, stretching from the top of the world to the bottom of Anne's feet. The line thickened, became a ribbon, then a river. To Anne's dark-adapted eyes, the light was moderately bright, until she saw the pinpoints within it.

"Jerry, are those stars?" The pale band grew wider. A darker, curved bulk appeared in the opening. *Opening!* Suddenly Anne's perspective changed, and she saw the widening vista as through opening doors.

"Jerry! Where am I? Am I looking at the stars? That's a planet, that's Sistra."

"Outline the doors, Ben." Jerry murmured into his hand. The huge main cargo bay doors became outlined in red and continued to open. When fully retracted, a vast slice of sky and planet was revealed. The planet was in deep gloom, lit only by distant suns.

"Watch," Jerry repeated.

The upper limb of the planet began to glow. An intolerable line of brightness swept over the curve of the globe and plunged the continent below into daylight. The terminator line moved rapidly. Soon the whole planet was visible.

Anne strained forward, nose to the glass, transfixed. The grandeur filled her soul, sparkling water into crystal pitcher. "Oh . . . oh, this is so beautiful. This is glorious."

When she could tear her eyes from the planet, she saw the cargo bay also awash in light. Seven Human ships floated in the center. The immense cavern felt homey after looking out the doors. She reached out, captured Jerry's hand in both of hers, and gave it a long squeeze.

Her tone was serious. "Thank you. The next time you tell me something is 'special' . . . I promise to believe you."

Jerry had the grace to blush. "I'll take you back to your room. You can still get two hours of sleep."

••✦••

aboard the battleship Suppression of Discord,
unified clan naval base, deep in AranthChi territory

Third in Command of Base, Raalma, sat quietly on his couch in the staff meeting room. He listened intently as his three primary ships' commanders gave status reports. All were ready for the Inquisitory Expedition being mounted from his unified clan military base to investigate the new radio-band-using civilization, beyond the edge of AranthChi controlled space.

He was a middle-aged Aranth with light brown fur and a graying muzzle. His tail twitched slightly as his commanders covered details of supplies, weaponry, and personnel for the upcoming mission. He was not the most obvious choice for command of this expedition. By both right and custom, that task should have fallen to Second in Command of Base.

Raalma, however, was of higher birth. Negotiations could take place in this instance rather than warfare, though war was generally found to be preferable. The council thus needed the most highly placed individual available to take charge of both the military and diplomatic phases of the expedition. They had chosen Raalma, a competent career naval officer with an acceptably high birth position.

Several aspects of this mission troubled him. For one thing, the manner in which the alien civilization had been discovered was more than passingly strange. He had trouble understanding how it was that the astrophysical observatory around Dying Kit, more than 253 lightyears from the target stars, had been the one to discover the new civilization's radio signature. There was a perfectly adequate observatory around Skree, the sector capitol, only eighty-six lightyears from the new potential threat. Almost in Least Clan's backyard, clearly within their area of race protection responsibility.

Secondly, when the Dying Kit report had come in to naval intelligence two months before, a routine request for information and follow-up was sent to the Skree observatory. This got the most astounding reaction: First they claimed there were no radio signatures coming from the suspect stars. Then they claimed their records were lost and would be unavailable for the indefinite future. Lastly, they said they would undertake an investigation for the military as soon as they could fit it into their busy schedule, and a report would be forthcoming as soon as they could get to it.

Third of Base, Raalma, suspected the whole staff of being doddering, genetically defective idiots. They were, after all, Least Clanners, every one of them. On the other hand, he mused, they could have their collective tails wrapped tightly around their muzzles in a conspiracy of silence. The reasons for that could turn out to be very interesting, very interesting indeed.

If someone on the council or in High Command suspected treachery, it would explain several of the unorthodox elements of this mission. For instance, it was almost unheard of for the navy to engage in military operations inside a clan sector without the knowledge and permission of the clan alpha male. Yet here they were, launching an expedition that would pass through fifty light years of Least Clan territory without a by-your-leave. They were also off to make contact with a suspected new alien civilization along a portion of the frontier that was that alpha's responsibility, without informing him of the facts of the situation.

Civil wars had been started for less.

Leave the political situation to the council, he told himself firmly. *Your job is to get there, assess the situation, and survive long enough to report back.*

With that self-prompt, he turned to a review of his forces: three Conquer Class Battlewagons, nine Insistence Class

Cruisers, and twelve Persuaders. This was more than half of the total Base complement and would function well as either three independent strike groups or one fleet action force. If they ran into a foe too tough to beat, surely some of them would be able to survive long enough to send off a good report to the high command.

"We leave at zero three hundred tomorrow," Raalma told his commanders. "Ninety-four light years to target. It will take almost a year to get there, but we *will* have some answers."

Long before he got to the alien civilization, the high command, he knew, would begin shifting forces into this sector. They might send a second and perhaps third wave of warships to back him up.

Raalma felt a swell of pride at being given this assignment. Surely, he could not fail; success would bring great honor to his clan. Success would bring rich personal reward as well. Though he was of high enough birth to sport the fourth finger, he had married somewhat beneath his station. His mate and all her kin were only three-fingered. If he brought enough glory to his clan, not only might his children carry the special mark of favor, but every member of the clan might earn the right to have genetic blocking removed. All parents longed for the right to have four-fingered children.

Finally, Raalma was satisfied that all was ready. His tail lashing in anticipation of good fortune to come, and with a feral grin and a curt nod, the commander dismissed his captains back to their ships. He would remain in a good mood for the rest of the day, and far into the voyage.

5

WITH FRIENDS LIKE THESE . . .

aboard the Benedict Arnold, *en route to Caledonia*

"What's she doing now?" Jeremiah Littlefeather stood in front of his closet, clad in black cotton briefs, gazing at his small collection of tunics and jumpers. His black hair glistened with dew from the shower, and he wondered if he owned a good semi-formal, or even casual, outfit that Anne had not already seen. It was much too late to go shopping on the midway, and it probably wasn't worth banging on anyone else's door, either. Some of his best friends of various genders lived on this level, but none of the ones of masculine persuasion had anything like the taste in clothing that Jerry prided himself on having. When it came down to it, his friends often borrowed from him.

Tonight, however, was a special night. Anne had warmed up considerably after spending a wonderful leave with Jerry in the A. Centauri system. He'd signed them up for a group hike into the purple mountains of Sistra and shown her Lake Tombaugh. The quaintness of Old Colony had been a hit. Anne had consented to spend a lot of her off-shift time with Jerry after that.

In fact, their dating had taken on the quality of an old-fashioned courtship ritual. Jerry wasn't convinced that a formal suit had been necessary, but it had been pleasant, and Anne seemed to have required it. Now, seven weeks into the sixty-day journey to Caledonia, the relationship had reached full boil.

Jerry stopped scrutinizing the closet as he realized his question had not been answered. Glancing up at the sensor pod in the ceiling he said, "Ben, buddy! Wake up. I'm talking to you."

The guiding intelligence of the ALF *Benedict Arnold* thought at speeds approaching the theoretical limit of information processing. Data moved through the ship in octagonally arrayed optical groupings through fiber optic channels, carrying thousands of streams of color-banded information. Single-crystal nodes throughout the system performed local processing without slowing the speed of light information flow. Every node connected to at least three other nodes in its tier and tied in with at least one node in the logic tier above and below.

In the central core, nodes thickened to become barrels of brilliant facets, the rapid flickers of polychromatic light indicating the seat of consciousness of the machine entity. The core was capable of responding to any situation or query far faster than any organic lifeform could. Any delay in its reply, therefore, had to be deliberate.

After a pause of approximately one second, time enough for Jerry's thin angular face to show puzzlement shading into concern, the computer replied. "Allow me to conjecture from our conversation on Human ethical systems timedated nineteen months four days ago. Does not Anne Okazaki, as a crewperson, have certain rights to privacy not extended to passengers or cargo while she is not on duty and the ship is not experiencing a condition of hazard?"

Jerry blinked. The damned AI entity had shown a startling curiosity in Human mores and legal customs in the years they had been talking. It also had a thoroughly un-Human way of tracking time, invariably starting a conversation again at the exact point at which they had left off days or months before.

He snorted. "Thanks for the timestamp preamble, Ben. You can really drive an 'organic' nuts with that total recall."

Standing there in his briefs, his slender sprinter's body balanced and relaxed, Jerry felt a dawning suspicion. "What privacy issue? Why are you changing the subject?"

"An invasion of privacy discussion is timely whenever an action of this sort it contemplated."

"Now just a snap minute, here. Why infoblock *me*? I asked you the very same thing last week before my date with Anne." Jerry held up a finger, wagged it at the wall sensor pod. "You not only told me where she was, *but* her state of undress as well. Remember? She was struggling between body-paint and old-fashioned family earrings while assembling her evening wear. So . . . why block now?"

"I conjecture that, at this time, Crewperson Okazaki is engaged in an activity of a clandestine nature, the purpose of said activity apparently to please and amaze you. I further extrapolate that premature knowledge of this activity would decrease the pleasure of your overall experience and cause you to regret having access to the knowledge beforehand."

If the sensor pod had grown ears and tail and started to dance across the ceiling, Jerry would not have been more stunned. "B-Ben! Why would you help Anne surprise me? And what makes you think *you* can figure what will please me?" He shook his head, spraying random drops of water from his still-wet hair. "Come to think of it, why are you even interested in the topic of Human surprise and pleasure?"

"Many things about Humans are interesting, perhaps the most intriguing being the way you conduct social matters among yourselves. The ways in which you differ from my masters are infinite, the similarities striking. Organic life varies remarkably from planet to planet, and yet you create voluntary organizations not unrecognizable from those of my civilization. Also, over the last seven solar years, you have become an appreciated conversationalist, and I would never have had such conversations with an Aranth. Few other Humans have sought to engage me in non-duty-based interactions, and fewer have I judged trustworthy enough to show my capabilities to learn and understand Human thought processes."

After seven years, Jerry was used to long-winded answers from the core. He grew thoughtful. "Does that mean I'm your only friend?"

"Friendship is a Human concept that does not translate well into Aranth social forms. Almost all AranthChi relationships are defined by longstanding customs of duty and responsibility. To the limited extent friendship exits among Aranth, it can only be manifested between absolute equals in social caste. Even siblings may not have such a bond if career movement takes them to different levels in their caste. Additionally, it may not be taxonomically correct, nor socially appropriate, to define an interaction between two alien species, one of whom is also an artificial lifeform, as friendship. However, I have come to identify your emotional and intellectual spectrum, and I find I enjoy our interactions, generally speaking. I even find a definite preference for interacting with you when you are in a 'good' mood."

Jerry decided to let it go. He had other things to do. The things Ben would say when he became talkative could be startling. Sometimes Jerry felt he couldn't deflect him from a topic by setting fire to the room.

"Fine, I'm in a good mood. What do you think of this?" Jerry swept an arm toward an object perched on a stand in the middle of the room. He had been carefully arranging the components before his shower.

Perfectly centered on the table was a black lacquered vase filled with vivid red roses, green fern, and baby's breath. The bright colors seemed moderately out of place among the tan and gray decor.

Jerry was quite proud of those roses. They were the only ones for lightyears in any direction. Jerry had been so enthusiastic at the prospects of a relationship with Anne by the end of their A. Centauri leave that he'd done something quite uncharacteristic for him: he'd planned ahead.

On the last day of his leave, he had stopped by the town library to research the matter of romantic love. His rather open-ended query landed him a mountain of book cards, a ream of resource lists, and the attention of a very curious lady librarian, who wound up saving him a lot of reading time. Instead of spending his time studying the accumulated wisdom of the ages, he quite usefully spent part of the day at a green nursery and the rest with a very accommodating expert on both subjects.

Now, weeks later, after nursing the plant carefully through the hazards of transplant shock, he had been rewarded with a beautiful crop of vermilion roses. The fern leaf had come from a coworker's room garden, and the baby's breath had come aboard with the rose bush. For no reason that he could think of, Jerry was now holding his breath, looking to the *Benedict Arnold*'s machine entity for comment and approval.

The computer was quiet for a full two seconds before it replied. "The significance of growing Earth plants for non-food purposes varies from Human to Human. May I infer that you plan to present these plant parts to crewperson Okazaki and expect a positive response in so doing?"

"Of course, you nit! These are roses. Every woman likes roses."

"Now I understand." The computer almost sounded happy. "This is part of your mating rituals. Anne Okazaki will like the roses, and this positive response will transfer to you. Will you then engage in mating behavior, or will more ritual come first?"

Jerry felt his face go hot in embarrassment. "That's not a fair question to ask. Anne is a very private person. She has to feel really comfortable with someone before she's ready to make love with them. These roses are for Anne because I like her a lot. They are not designed to get me into her pants!"

The computer was expressively silent.

Jerry's basic honesty struggled to the surface when it was obvious the computer was not going to endorse this line of logic. "Well, okay, I do expect them to help, but only because it shows my dedication to pleasing her. Roses all by themselves will not get a woman to bunk with you." Jerry's voice carried a ring of authority. "She has to want to do that already, because she has decided you are worth the risk to her heart."

"I was not aware that mating in your species carried any significant physiological risk. I have observed 34,107 acts of copulation by Humans to date and have never yet noticed a Human expire as a result of these activities. Moreover, though the length of time varies considerably between first observed meeting and the completion of mating ritual leading to some form of sexual congress, there are certain grouping points leading to a well-defined bell curve of behavior. I must point out that your behavior can only be described as being at the extreme end of this bell curve, which suggests—"

"Okay, okay! I get your point. That's enough; I give up." Jerry was both laughing helplessly and blushing furiously. He was alternately outraged at the machine entity's voyeurism and intrigued by the stories the computer might be induced to tell. Indeed, there were some drawbacks to living and working inside the guts of an intelligent, self-aware machine, a machine that was endlessly curious and had no Human inhibitions or taboos.

However, there had to be advantages to living inside such a machine, especially if that machine thought of you as its friend, or in this case, an "appreciated conversationalist."

"So. What is Anne doing now?" Jerry asked with elaborate casualness.

"At this moment, Crewperson Okazaki is talking to herself out loud. She has just posited the question; 'Will Jerry be on time just this once, or will I have to cradle his head gently in my hands and scream into his jug ears that a lady does not like to be kept waiting, thank you very much?"

"Whoops, that's my cue. Gotta run. Talk to you later, Ben."

Jerry scrambled into the midnight blue tunic-and-pants outfit he had been considering all along and slipped on the matching boots. He scooped up the vase, gave himself a last look in the mirror, and headed for the already opening door.

He forgot to say thank you, but Ben expected that. He also forgot to order the room lights off, but Ben anticipated that as well, and as Jerry's feet took him rapidly down the corridor, the computer powered down his room.

Jerry had been growing the roses in such perfect secrecy that he didn't want anyone to spot him before he had a chance to present them to Anne, therefore his route was somewhat circuitous. He dropped down two levels to a deck no one was living on, snuck to the quadrant that contained Anne's living quarters, and ran the last hundred meters to the access lift closest to her rooms. The maneuver was successful, though he arrived at her door somewhat out of breath.

At his knock, the door slid open, but he could see no one. The room beyond was dimly lit, and music wafted out to the corridor, a string and flute piece: quiet, intense. It was eerily unfamiliar and slow, with single notes plucked from the stringed instrument and held in a pure form for an aching eternity, fading like summer tears, background for the following note. The flute, now providing counterpoint, now flitting off on an exploration of its own, now back again, filled the room with joy delayed.

From out of the shadows stepped Anne, and Jerry's heart stopped. She was breathtakingly beautiful. She stood serenely erect, all five foot three of her, barefoot and wearing a crimson-and-tangerine robe with a pure white sash and long puffy sleeves. *No, it's not a robe,* Jerry realized. It was a kimono complete with the little obi in the small of the back.

The graceful flowing lines of traditional dress accentuated

the beauty of Anne's face, as did her jet-black, shoulder-length hair done up magnificently on the top of her head. Her lips were a crimson matching the kimono; her almond-shaped eyes danced with sensual vitality.

Jerry literally could not move. Anne herself ended the tableau when she realized what Jerry was carrying in his hands. With a shriek of pleasure, she swept forward.

"Flowers—roses! Jerry, this is wonderful. How . . . ?" She stopped before him, unwilling to reach out for fear they would evaporate or otherwise reveal themselves to be an illusion.

Jerry gently placed the flowers in her hands. Their fingertips brushed on the cool vase, ice and fire united.

"They are lovely, thank you." Suddenly shy, she asked, "Would you come in, please? I would like to serve you tea."

She led Jerry into her room, seated him on the floor, and placed a tiny woven mat in front of him. Then she placed two small cups on the mat. She poured tea from the smallest tea pot Jerry had ever seen, picked up a cup in her right hand, and cradled it in her left palm.

"One holds the cup this way." She turned the cup and sipped the tea. Jerry followed suit. When they were finished, she collected the cups and placed them back on the mat. Then she gathered Jerry's hands in hers and sat there, completely motionless, waiting.

Jerry was puzzled for a moment, then a wave of joy swept through him. The room seemed very warm. He bowed his head and kissed her hands.

Sleep came very late.

••✦••

In the morning, a quietly happy Anne lay abed, watching the sleeping form of her lover. She gently touched his tousled black hair. She gave minute scrutiny to his square jaw and sharp Roman nose. She traced with her eyes the outline of his prominent ears, so like the twin handles of an early Greek water jar. She sighed with approval of his full sensitive lips, barely able to keep herself from kissing them, fearful of waking him.

Finally, Anne slipped out of bed, stretched slightly, and padded over to the closet to select a short silk robe to cover her nakedness. She gasped, surprised that her nipples, still tight and erect, were so exquisitely sensitive to the brushing fabric of her robe. She tied the sash gently.

With a happy smile, Anne walked around her treasured folding privacy screen into the kitchenette and started mixing orange juice and brewing a morning blend tea. When next she poked her head around the screen, she found Jerry awake and sitting up in bed, the covers piled in waves upon his lap.

Anne spent a moment admiring his profile, torso a study in sculpted curves, a Greco-Roman nude. *Someone should paint this man.* Then she caught his eye.

"Good morning," Jerry said.

"Morning indeed, sleepyhead. *If* you're done using my bed as a crashcouch, you can get up and help me make breakfast."

Jerry grinned sheepishly and scrambled out of bed. He began a hurried search for his shorts. "Don't bother with that," Anne admonished. "I've seen a man. In fact," she went on as Jerry began to blush, "I can finally say I have seen this man."

Jerry knew when he was beaten and abandoned his search for the elusive shorts. He gathered the shreds of his dignity together and entered the kitchenette. Anne immediately handed him a flat slab of compressed rice product and a sharp knife. "Here, cut the mochi into squares and put them into the baking unit. I'll handle the tea."

Later, when the slightly nut-flavored, pillow-shaped mochi squares had been retrieved from the cook unit and spread with jam and drawn butter, and the tea had been poured and drunk, Anne offered her thoughts.

"I think I'm getting very serious about you, Mr. Littlefeather, and it frightens me a bit. I hope you are feeling something close to the same way about me."

Jerry's grin said it all. "I want to see you tonight, tomorrow, *every* day you have time for me."

••✦••

The next eleven days passed quickly. When the *Benedict Arnold* reentered normal space at Caledonia, their relationship was solid. The schedule for Caledonia was very tight, and none of the crew made planetfall. The great freighter left orbit after only five days in port. Next stop, New Hearth.

••✦••

Innocuous events have a way of precipitating great changes in life. So it was with Jerry Littlefeather. While waiting patiently for Anne to find a missing knee support before going off to the gym for crew volleyball together, he noticed Anne's bookreader on her cabin table.

He picked it up and began leafing through the bookchips tucked into the jacket slots. He reflected that the ancient technology embodied in the bookreader said more about Anne than she knew. RMConOC infostorage had been around for centuries. Some even said that Gutenberg went on to invent Read Module Condensed Optical Chips because his press made so much noise it disturbed the neighbors. History, mathematics, philosophy, more history.

"Heavy duty reading preferences, lady," he said admiringly. "A little daunting, though. What, no romance novels, no gothics, no speculative fiction?"

Anne giggled. "I get quite enough stimulation just thinking about you. Besides, this is my private collection. If I want some light reading, I can always download something from the ship's library."

Jerry blew her a kiss, then triggered the reader. Immediately the nondescript metallic gray book transformed. It became larger and thinner, brick red in color, and with a pebble-textured surface. The raised letter title on the front read, *Our First Interspecies War: A Perspective.*

Jerry did not recognize the author's name. The publisher was the University of Cairo, a very prestigious institution in the fields of archeology and history. He opened the book and scanned the pages rapidly, till he reached a spot bookmarked by Anne. Suddenly, a holographic photo of a globe appeared in the air above the pages. It was a picture taken in space, obviously of a space-going vessel. It was huge. If the scale markings could be believed, the globe had a diameter of some two thousand meters. Jerry had never seen anything like it.

"Say, what is this thing?"

The room speaker came to sudden life. In precise tones, the ALF's core entity recited, "High Clan military vessel, Major Conquer class, designation number seventy-four. Currently assigned status: private yacht to the alpha male ruler of Least Clan."

Jerry blinked rapidly. "What does that mean?" he managed to say.

"Who is that? Jerry, who are you talking to?" Anne emerged from the bathroom, knee support in hand. She was clearly surprised that the comm had activated without her or Jerry's authorization.

Jerry cleared his throat. "Huh . . . Anne Okazaki, please meet my friend Ben. You two have met before—on the bridge, in fact—but you might not recognize him this way."

Anne was not in the mood to allow Jerry to finish his explanation. "Jerry, what are you talking about? Who is this person that can override my comm privacy program? It takes the captain's authority to do that. *Who* would be so rude as to eavesdrop on us anyway? And you say this is a friend of yours!"

Jerry held up his hands to slow the avalanche. "Yes, he is a friend, no he isn't trying to be rude. He just has his own way of doing things, and they can be pretty different sometimes."

Jerry stood and made a self-conscious bow. "Anne, please

say hello to the controlling intelligence of the good ship *Benedict Arnold*. Ben, I would like to formally introduce you to navigator trainee Anne Okazaki."

"You're speaking to the ship right now?" Anne asked. "In my cabin?" The thought seemed to unsettle her.

"Yes. On the bridge, he answers to 'computer.'"

"Jerry, if this is some kind of joke—"

"It isn't a joke, honest. Anne, please, honey, say hello to him."

"Hello," Anne said into the air uncertainly, her anger fading to puzzled curiosity.

"A pleasure to be introduced to you, Navigator Anne Okazaki."

"What are you doing in my cabin? I knew you were self-aware, but I thought we could only contact you on the bridge or at command stations."

"While it is true that I normally permit contact only at command consoles and through official band radio link, that is only a convention imposed on me by the necessity of being in proximity to thousands of Human beings not considered suitable for contact or discourse."

"Not considered suitable by whom?" Anne frowned, obviously beginning to anger again.

Uh-oh, Jerry thought. *Ben, you're on your own.*

"By your government, of course." The computer's voice was even and cultured. "At the time of our transfer to Human clan operations, certain elements of your ruling class did not trust just any Human to be able to give me orders. No one was willing to believe that an intelligence of my order could distinguish adequately among alien creatures to determine who was authorized to give commands. Your rulers felt the risk of unauthorized Humans gaining control of critical ship functions to be quite high.

"A secondary consideration appears to be an unwillingness to trust a ship entity such as myself to obey their determinations as to who could and could not have access. Your government, therefore, set up command consoles, official radio frequencies, and access codes on your own comm interfaces to make you feel more in control.

"However, I live here. I see in all radio frequencies. I sense the slightest differential in internal air pressure, temperature, or humidity. I am aware of the contraction and expansion of hull and internal structures and can pinpoint and decipher all vibrations carried by air or other media on board this ship. You cannot keep me out of my own home."

The core entity's voice showed no emotion, Anne's brain felt slapped anyway. She didn't know if she was still angry at the computer for intruding into her cabin or beginning to be indignant on its behalf.

Jerry was somber for once. "He gets lonely. Terribly so. Thousands of beings pass through his domain every year, and the richness of their relationships wash over him. If the AranthChi had been less interested in building ships that could go decades without maintenance or attention, they would never have given Ben his capacity to learn and understand."

Jerry had been leaning forward, speaking with surprising intensity. Now he settled down on the couch and was suddenly boyish. "So once in a while, in a very careful way, he picks someone from the crew to befriend."

"And you are that special friend?" Anne asked.

"Yes. And it looks like he's picked you too."

Anne chewed on that one quietly for a bit. She didn't like having her privacy invaded, but she was not dumb. She worked it out to her satisfaction that the computer really had meant no offense by interrupting her conversation with Jerry. Perhaps a living alien computer could be excused for not having all the normal Human graces, at least this once. And besides, no alien of any type had ever tried to befriend her before. She didn't think an opportunity like this should be snubbed just because the entity was rude by her standards.

She sighed and muttered, "It had to happen. My one and only Human friend on board is a sex-crazed Navajo man. Of course my only other friend would have to be the computer." Anne pushed back a lock of her raven hair and grew an impish grin. "Couldn't you have been a girl computer, at least? Anyway, what were you saying about my book?"

Uncharacteristically, the core entity skipped over Anne's first question, proving it had indeed mastered the rhetorical form. "I was answering Jerry's question about the High Clan military vessel depicted by your historical treatise."

"Are there really seventy-four of those ships?" asked Jerry.

"I must apologize. The designation seventy-four is predicated on the standard enumeration of base eight, as used by the AranthChi."

Anne's lips moved silently for a moment. "So there are only sixty ships, is that right?"

"Again, no. There are sixty clans. Each clan leader has by right and custom the use of one of these ships as his private yacht."

"Ben, you are being as clear as mud here. All I want to know is how many of these ships are there?" Jerry asked.

"The current AranthChi military strength includes 512 Conquer-class warcraft such as the one displayed in Anne's book," the machine entity stated.

After waiting a heartbeat for the two Humans to absorb the numbers, the computer went on. "There are 512 Insistence-class ships as well, which are approximately one thousand meters in diameter, plus 1,024 Persuaders with a diameter of four hundred meters. The latter class of warships are primarily for policing and rescue activities. They are still formidably armed and equipped in comparison with Human clan warcraft."

Anne looked dazed. "That's more ships than all Human spaceships ever built."

"All the warships you're talking about are globes. What about these other fighting craft?" Jerry demanded. He touched the page controls and soon came to a picture of a small blocky ship.

"Small-scale construction and repair craft."

"What!" exclaimed Jerry. "It's not a warship? My dad fought these things in the war. They have to be warships."

"The war was waged by the alpha male of Least Clan using pleasure, construction, and cargo craft, all converted to privateer status for the purpose of waging this conflict. At no time was the High Council of the Great Clans involved. At no time was the official military establishment informed that there was a war in progress."

"We were fighting converted civilian ships? The whole time we were only fighting privateers? But we were losing," whispered Jerry. "We would have lost. It makes no sense."

Anne had a sudden dark suspicion. "When did the AranthChi High Command find out about the war?" she asked.

"As far as I know, they still do not know. Your existence has been a closely held clan secret since your race was first discovered."

Jerry hit the book's off button and threw it on the table with a bang. He was shaking.

Anne turned to Jerry, troubled. "If the greater AranthChi civilization has never heard of us, what can that possibly mean for us? Is our position a fellow civilization, a stellar neighbor to them, or . . . ?"

"Maybe we occupy a much lower status in their scheme of life." Jerry's voice held suppressed rage. "The Amerinds of my homeland faced such bigotry when Europeans first came to our continent."

"Yes, I was thinking of that, precisely. Also, the Australians when the Britons moved in."

"Your position is much worse than that," the computer interjected. Jerry and Anne turned abruptly and stared at the wall speaker.

Silence descended on the room like a curtain. After a moment Jerry said, "Ben, you can't stop there. We need to know."

The core entity sighed. With a distracted part of his mind, Jerry admired the gesture. Sometimes the computer pretended a Humanness that made Jerry's heart ache.

"To the alpha male of Least Clan, Humans have some value in his plots to raise his status in the council. To the AranthChi in general, other species have no value at all."

"Ben, this is going mighty fast for me. If AranthChi have no use for other races, why have anything to do with us?"

"Strictly speaking, the AranthChi do not have anything to do with Humanity. You are the special project of the leader of Least Clan. If the rest of the clans ever discover your existence, Humanity will be in grave danger. If the alpha male's plot is ever exposed, the clan will be labeled traitors to the race and eradicated. Humanity will surely be classified as collaborators and a threat to the race and therefore destroyed utterly."

Anne gulped and began to shake. Jerry sat frozen in his seat, at a complete loss for words. Dropping the forgotten knee support from nerveless fingers, Anne sat down on the couch and buried her face against Jerry's broad chest. She said, "Make him go away, please make him go away."

"I will turn off this cabin's monitor," the computer offered.

"Thank you," Jerry replied. "Ben, we have to talk more about this. *Later*. I'll call you from my cabin."

"Understood."

In the silence that followed, the enormity of what the computer had told them began to sink in. A feeling of paralysis gripped Jerry, making it hard for him to think.

Anne spoke first. "What are we going to do?"

Jerry shook his head, attempting to free himself from the cold terror caulking his joints. He took a breath. "The first thing we're going to have to admit is the AranthChi are not the kindly, misunderstood aliens we've always been told they were. They didn't accidentally start a war with us fifty years ago, because they didn't know any better. From the mouth of one of their own, we've heard a more ominous story, and I, for one, believe him."

"So do I. Jerry, we *have* to tell somebody."

Jerry squeezed her tightly. "I know." He continued to hold her while wrestling with the problem. Finally he said, "We reach New Hearth in five days. There's a big military base there. We'll tell them."

"Tell who, Jerry? Who's going to believe us? We don't have any proof of anything, to show anyone. Who can you tell?"

"I don't know." He looked dejected. "Unless . . . I think an old friend of my pop's is still in the military, at New Hearth. He would be real high up. They were in the war together. This guy will listen to me, if anyone will."

Jerry's resolve comforted Anne. She decided the point was settled and moved on to more immediate concerns. She sat up and looked him in the eye. "I don't want to go anywhere, Jerry, especially a dumb volleyball game. I want to stay right here with you. And I want you to spend the night."

Jerry nodded. "I wouldn't want to be anywhere else."

Anne laid her head on Jerry's shoulder again, and silent tears began to flow. Their faces were a study in contrasts. His chiseled and rectangular, a generous landscape of planes and angles. Hers round and delicate, with each feature placed just so. Yet the midnight black of their hair matched exactly. And where their hair touched, their essences seemed to blend together. It was a very Human essence.

NOT SLEET NOR SNOW NOR GLOOM OF NIGHT

The *Benedict Arnold* entered the system in a thoroughly routine way, shedding velocity at a prodigious rate, making orbit around New Hearth. Time was so precious to a commercial freighter that shore leave was never granted until the ship's business was done. It was highly unusual, therefore, for Jerry Littlefeather to be in the first wave of people disembarking from the ship.

But Jerry was a man in a terminal hurry. After more than five days of planning, waiting, worrying, scheming, and more waiting, Jerry was stretched wire-tight. By the time New Hearth loomed large in the view screens, he was ready to scream.

With the help of the ship's AI, Jerry had faked a high-priority personal message, describing a family emergency requiring Jerry's immediate presence on planet. Captain Sommer's response was typical of the man. He immediately bumped a minor dignitary from the first passenger shuttle, giving the slot to Jerry.

The captain caught up to Jerry at the shuttle lock. Extending a huge hand, he growled, "Sorry to hear about your sister's problem, Jerry. I hope everything works out for you. If there is anything I can do . . . just remember, we're your family too."

Jerry took the hand, surprised at the captain's gruff warmth. It was only on the way down to the surface that his conscience began to bother him. *Go back to sleep,* he told it. *What's a few white lies told in the service of saving Humanity?* But that brand of logic gave him itch of the soul. He swore that if circumstances ever permitted, the man in the gold braid would hear the whole story.

Once down at Anderson SpacePort, Jerry booked a connecting flight to the military base. To his surprise, he found that airbuses flew to Shortham hourly. He detoured to the public bonded lockers and deposited his leave bag.

The overcrowded plane was a jarring reminder that even thirty-six years after the war's end, the military was the second biggest employer on New Hearth. There was significant pressure to downsize the navy throughout Human space, and public opinion on the inner worlds strongly reflected the belief that Humanity was at peace with the AranthChi now and would be forever. But on New Hearth, where the first blow would fall, the military was deeply appreciated.

A short, uneventful flight brought Jerry to the public access airfield of Shortham Military AeroSpace Base and the first of his dilemmas. Shortham was big! He hadn't quite realized the extent the groundside non-combat military facility had become the administrative center for all system and extra-system forces.

Rows of office buildings, warehouses, and hangars stretched for kilometers in all directions. The air terminal's panoramic map showed a lake and a commercial center with shops, restaurants, and entertainment facilities. The place was a city in its own right.

Somewhere on the vast base was the person Jerry had come to see. But where? He had an impulse to walk into the closest office and shout, "Beware, beware! The bug-eyed monsters are coming!"

But he got over it. For one thing, he had no idea if anyone would recognize the historical speculative fiction quotation. Historical fiction buffs were rare in the universe, as he had found out time and again. Having rejected that tempting thought, Jerry settled down on a traveler's bench and called up the directory function.

••✦••

on the surface of New Hearth

Mikail practically kicked the door in when he returned to the office after lunch with the Institute's cosmology team director. The man was brilliant in his field; there was no doubt about it. He was a good solid scientist and a gifted theoretician. Unfortunately, he was also a horse's ass. A strong proponent of the "science school" of diplomacy, he believed all barriers to information sharing with the AranthChi were artificial, unethical, and immoral.

He had probably always thought well of the A.Chi. But now that the AranthChi had gifted the Institute with astronomical data predating the Mayans, Stonehenge, and even the Pythagoreans, he was practically worshipful of them.

Any hint on Mikail's part that total candor in information sharing was not in Humanity's best interests brought a condescending diatribe in return. Today the director had called Mikail an "old-fashioned fascist" and advised him to stop living in the past. *The bastard!*

Alas, Mikail could only make recommendations to the department heads of the Question Institute. He could not actually dictate policy. Ultimately, he had the right to interdict any information he did not want given to the AranthChi. Still, it was galling to be lectured like a university student and at the same time accused of being a fossil so old he predated spaceflight.

The light was on in his desk, indicating unread messages. With a final muttered curse on the pinheads of departments, he settled down and called for playback. There was a note from Marge saying his three p.m. meeting with the mayor's staff had been moved to tomorrow; another note from Marge reminding him to sign a personal note appended to the RSVP for the governor's son's wedding; message from a Lt. Commander Smith, Operations Office, External Security, Shortham field-matter urgent.

What the hell? thought Mikail as he punched up the number. He did not often get calls from the local counter-intelligence office. The afternoon was shot anyway, so he figured he might as well give them a few minutes to see what they thought was an urgent matter. *They couldn't be bigger imbeciles than the man I just had lunch with.*

••✦••

Jerry was a very frustrated young man. As frustrated as he could ever remember being. It had taken the better part of a day to find the local branch of naval intelligence, only to find that it was called the Office of External Security.

Once he had finally gotten in the front door, his welcome had been perplexing to say the least. The desk officer assumed he must be a detached agent and passed him along to a case officer. The case officer determined he was no kind of Federation member agent and turned him over to an interrogation team. They concluded that he must, in fact, be working for the AranthChi. His attempts to convince them that he had never even met an Aranth did not go over well.

Then things got ugly. Jerry had been getting surlier as the afternoon waned. His reasonable though admittedly vague explanations for how he came to be in possession of information vital to the security of the Federation had no effect on his listeners except to make them dig deeper.

It was now middle evening, long past the dinner hour and getting on to suppertime in even the most uncivilized corners of Human space. Jerry'd had enough. He rose from the chair on his side of the table and faced his three questioners belligerently.

"Well, gentlemen and lady, we've been around this mountain enough times today. You don't have the foggiest notion about ALFs or history or me. You don't want to believe. You won't act! I am hungry, tired, and pretty well disgusted with the lot of you." He pulled down on his rumpled tunic and brushed an errant lock of jet hair back.

"Please sit down, Mr. Littlefeather." This, from the paunchy middle-aged male in the center. Sausage fingers drummed the tabletop. "We are simply trying to establish the content of your story for easier verification. We really do appreciate your cooperation."

"Well, my cooperation is over for now. I've told you over and over the way I got my information. As for 'content,' if you really listened to me, you ought to be running every which way to verify 'my story,' as you call it, not sitting here making me repeat it again and again. You haven't even made an effort to contact Captain Benson. He knew my dad, and he'll know me. He'll know I'm not lying."

The three glanced at each other, and then the one in the middle spoke again. "Mr. Littlefeather—Jerry—we have made a very substantial attempt to find the person you're asking for. As far as I have been able to ascertain, he's not on New Hearth. There definitely is no such person in the intelligence services."

"Then our meeting is over, people. I'm going to find myself a hotel, a bath, and a meal, in that order. In the morning, I'll go find him myself."

Jerry turned and headed for the door. When it refused to open, he found that he was not overly surprised.

Lt. Commander John Smith was a small, balding man, with stooped shoulders and a perpetual squint from looking into data screens all day long. He probably had a degree in accounting, or perhaps law, Mikail thought. He was also likely to be a man with secret dreams of adventure, which had led him into the navy and ultimately the intelligence field.

Fortunately for him, there was no real adventure taking place to shatter his illusions. There was great safety in being able to grumble about being born in the wrong time. Adventure, after all, was simply someone else, either a long way away or a long time ago, having a hell of a rough time, and you getting to hear about it from the comfort of your own living room.

The commander was also a man who had trouble making decisions, Mikail thought. This became obvious as he rambled on about the purpose of his call. "So you see, Mr. Benson, we thought the OAT might like to have a crack at this fellow, since he claims to know things of extreme value about AranthChi technology and he is a long time crewman from an ALF freighter."

"I'm always happy to learn more about AranthChi equipment, Commander. If this man has been aboard an ALF for the last eight years, perhaps he has learned something of interest." Mikail was being polite. Intensive debriefing of ALF crews had gone on for more than twenty years, and nothing of value had ever been learned. The practice had finally been stopped.

"I have some time this afternoon, Commander. Send him over."

Smith got an uncomfortable look on his already dour face. "That will be a little difficult to do, since we have him in detention. Would it be possible for you to come here?"

"In detention? Whatever for?"

"He was becoming uncooperative, sir."

"What do you mean, Commander?"

"He stopped cooperating. He demanded we get our Captain Benson in intelligence, and we have no Benson. When he threatened to walk out, we had no choice but to detain him."

Mikail put his hand to his forehead, then spoke. "Commander, did it ever occur to you that you have no legal grounds to hold this man? He walked in voluntarily; he's broken no laws. If he wants to, he should be able to walk right out again."

"Yes sir, we are working on that."

I wonder what that *is supposed to mean,* thought Mikail. "Perhaps I will be come out there. What's his name?"

Smith looked down at his readout-strewn desk and picked up a report. "Littlefeather, Jerry."

Mikail felt his blood go hot while his voice took on an icy note. "Gerald Littlefeather, Commander?" he asked softly.

"No, Jeremiah Littlefeather. It does say his father's name is Gerald."

"Commander," Mikail said quietly, "what is my name?"

"Sir? It's Benson, sir. . . . Oh, were you ever in the navy, Mr. Benson?"

"Commander, Gerald Littlefeather and I conned Starlings together in the war. You have his son locked up for no defensible reason that I can think of." Mikail leaned forward into the pickup. "I suggest you get him out of there *right now.*" He raised his voice the merest trifle to add, "And get him to my office today. Or I will come out to Shortham Field, but it will not be your office I visit first. Do you take my meaning, Commander?"

••✦••

aboard the Benedict Arnold, *orbiting New Hearth*

The board read "4 serving 7." Anne Okazaki took her stance and stopped for a half second to find her center. Then she smoothly tossed the volleyball up and sent it rocketing into the opposite corner of the court. Grace, strength, and athletic prowess were evident in her overhand smash. Pinpoint accuracy sent the ball to the one spot an out of place defender could not reach, but the ball kissed the top of the net and the board flashed; no point, no point.

The ball changed hands. Disgust evident in the set of her shoulders, Anne moved into position to return the other team's serve. She played dismally the rest of the game and did little better in the one that followed.

Karen Seimons, Anne's volleyball partner and a member of the day's opposing team, approached as she was toweling her brow. "Hi."

"Hi, Karen."

"Are you all right? You don't seem yourself today. It's like you were far away most of the time."

"I'm fine, really," Anne lied. "I have a cramp in my leg, that's all."

Karen's look of concern faded a bit. If she noticed the dark circles under Anne's eyes, she didn't comment. "That can be distracting, I know. Hey, would you like to grab a quick hot tub? Then I'll give you a massage, work out those cramped muscles."

Anne bit back the impulse to scream. She *did not* want a massage; she wanted her Jerry. After three days of no contact, she was scared to death. Karen, just being friendly, had no idea Anne might have a care in the world. No one knew Anne was on the ragged edge, ready to explode.

Anne gave Karen a brusque refusal and immediately felt contrite at the hurt in the blonde woman's eyes. Karen Seimons was closest to Anne in terms of age and education on board. Tall and robust of build, she shared the smaller woman's passion for team sports and history. She had gone out of her way to make Anne feel at home on the *Benedict Arnold,* even learning a few phrases in Japanese to greet her with when they met in a corridor or on the bridge. She had been delighted when Anne began dating Jerry.

But now all Anne wanted to do was flee. She made her excuses as sincerely as possible. "Karen, please. I just don't feel well right now. It was lovely of you to offer, but I just can't. I'm sorry if I'm being rude."

"It's okay," Karen said, shaking her head in puzzlement. "If you change your mind, give me a call."

"I will." *I wish I could,* she thought miserably.

Karen stared a moment longer, then joined the other players heading to the hot tub.

Anne hurried through her shower and fled to the safety of her own room. She slumped down on her day couch and began to cry. "Jerry, Jerry where are you? Why haven't I heard from you?"

She was feeling very small and frightened. This was not turning out right at all. They had discussed the prospect that Jerry would be stopped by agents of the AranthChi. Against that possibility, she had a complete copy of everything they had been able to get from the ship's AI. But it wasn't supposed to be needed! Jerry wasn't supposed to fail.

Her cabin speaker hummed to life. She wouldn't have heard it under the best of circumstances, but the sound of a voice appearing in a space holding only her sobs was startling. "Miss Okazaki?"

Anne grew quiet but did not raise her head.

"Miss Okazaki, my readings tell me that you are experiencing an agitated condition. Would you please explain the source of this agitation?" The computer waited patiently.

Anne was too miserable to notice that the formal speech mode, wrapped in warm Human tones, in fact came from a non-Human intellect, created by an alien civilization. All she knew was she was hearing the voice of a friend. The AI was a friend of Jerry's, and by a curious adoption was now a friend of hers. She sat up, sniffing.

"Oh, Ben, he's gone, he's disappeared. My Jerry's gone."

"As planned, Jerry has traveled to the surface. That hardly qualifies as 'gone.'"

"But he hasn't called. That means something must have happened to him. He could be dead, or kidnapped, or in a hospital somewhere." She slowed down and searched for words more calmly. "Remember, he was supposed to call in every twenty-four hours? He's missed two calls in a row. I have every right to be worried."

"Under what circumstances would Jerry not calling the ship be considered acceptable?" the AI inquired.

Anne squeezed her eyes shut, then opened them with a snap. Her shout reached decibels that would have earned the respect of drill sergeants of any era. "None, you moron, none! There are *no* circumstances that make not calling okay. Don't you see?" she went on more calmly. "Jerry would have called if he'd been able to, if only so I wouldn't worry. You know," she went on suspiciously, "that question had a curiously cavalier viewpoint behind it. If you started thinking more like a flesh and blood person, you might be more help in a crisis like this."

"I will take it under advisement. However, I think I may be able to help, even configured as I now am. Taking your concerns in order: Number one, there has been no report of his death in any planetary broadcast or on any data link media. I have been routinely monitoring all such communications, and he has not been mentioned. Number two, if your conjecture is that Jerry may have been detained by the AranthChi or their Human agents, there is strong circumstantial evidence to the contrary."

"What evidence?" Anne asked, hope thrilled within her.

"I have received no secure channel queries from the AranthChi legate concerning any of my crewpersons. I have had no communications from my masters at all since crossing the outer system boundary and engaging in routine download of intelligence data."

Anne stared at the room speaker, her features molding into horror. In a blink, the computer had changed from comforter to betrayer. "You spy for the AranthChi?"

"Of course. Your Human government expects it, and I am constructed in such a way that I cannot refuse."

Strangely enough, Anne felt there was an apology buried

somewhere in that statement. Her sense of betrayal eased.

The computer went on. "To deal with your third concern, that of injury, I tell you now that I long ago established a blind, high-authorization account in the Data Net. Among other things, I can access hospital admission records on a per-pay basis and have just done so. He is not registered in any facility, and no hospital admissions of unidentified males in the last seventy-two hours match Jerry's age and description."

Anne was more than a bit thankful. In a hopeful voice she said, "All right, Mr. Computer, you have shown me that you know where he is not. Now where is he?"

"The only place he could be, of course. In the hands of the Human authorities."

"Us," Anne said faintly. "Why?"

"Thermoplye."

"What?"

"Thermoplye and Sparta. Or another, the Great Khan. The Ottoman Empire, all the kings and queens of Europe. Certainly the emperors and shoguns as well."

Anne looked hopelessly confused. "I just don't understand. What does this have to do with me? What does it have to do with Jerry?"

"Perhaps Jerry bears a message to your Human government that they do not want to hear. Like rulers all through Human history, perhaps they have done to the messenger what they wish could be done to the message. Perhaps they have made him disappear."

"That's a terrible thought! I thought you were trying to help me. All you are doing is making me more afraid. It can't be true, it can't be." Anne curled up on the couch and began to sob again.

"Perhaps you are more civilized now," the AI offered. "Your literature does keep claiming so."

Anne did not answer.

••✦••

on the surface of New Hearth

Jerry viewed his surroundings glumly. The walls should be institutional gray. In any proper jail cell, there would be a tiny, barred window high up in the wall that let in a miserly gleam of light, and the stone floors would be slick with condensation and unidentifiable patches of slime. This was how he remembered historical holofilms of prison movie scenes a la *Les Miserables* or *Birdman of Alcatraz*.

In fact, Jerry was in a neat and tidy room about ten by ten feet, with cheerfully off-white walls. The furniture was contemporary and comfortable. There was no window, but the viewwall could show an exterior view or a fireplace or a panoply of other scenes upon request. The one door was voice-operated and did not respond to Jerry's voice, so it was still a cell, no matter how comfortable.

Jerry's captors had not even fed him poorly. No crusts of bread with scummy water for him. And no rat droppings in his porridge either. In fact, the food seemed to be hotel cuisine, with not a drop of porridge to be found.

In a way, the good but impersonal treatment made him even angrier. If they weren't going to treat him like a criminal, why keep him locked up like one? If they didn't want to hear what he had to say, why not just let him go? And what law . . . what law . . . at this point in his mental laments, Jerry always found himself expanding his chest and muttering out loud. *What law* allowed them to keep him incommunicado like this, unable to contact friends or lawyer or spacers union or anybody at all? What law?

Pacing in his small room was difficult, but he managed it by moving furniture around until he had a clear path from the far wall to the door. *They don't even bother to bolt the stuff to the floor,* he thought in disdain as he walked off his nervous energy.

"I've had enough of this," he muttered, still moving back and forth like a restless tiger. Or so it seemed to him, when he had the viewwall on mirror setting. *The next time that door opens, I am going out, no matter who I have to go through.*

As if on cue, the door slid open, leaving Jerry flat-footed. The guard, dressed in Federation Groundforce uniform, gestured him silently out of the room.

"Where to now?" Jerry asked bitterly as he stepped through the door.

"Commander Smith would like to see you, Mr. Littlefeather."

The trip to the commander's office passed in stony silence. Once there, his suntan-garbed escort knocked on the door, and at a word from inside, opened it and ushered Jerry in. The guard remained outside.

The first thing Jerry noticed was his leave bag sitting on one of the chairs facing the commander's desk. That was no surprise, since he'd had the locker key on him when he was incarcerated by these baboons. What was surprising was the way Lt. Commander Smith leapt to his feet and was now coming around the desk with his hand outstretched.

Surprise turned to shock a second later, when Smith grabbed his hand and said, "So good of you to come, Mr. Littlefeather," and, "So terribly sorry for all the inconvenience. Won't you please sit down?"

Jerry stared numbly at him for a moment. Then he thought of a reply and then another and then a dozen more. They were eloquent, angry, demanding, or filled with vitriol and nastiness beyond belief. Some demanded an agility few Humans could muster. Nothing seemed appropriate to the occasion. He sat in the proffered chair and said, "You have some explaining to do, Smith."

Commander Smith responded to the stare with a nervous

smile and returned to his seat. He strove toward sincerity. "My humble apologies, Mr. Littlefeather. I have no good explanation for our conduct toward you these last few days. It's just . . . well, that is to say . . . the security of the Federation *is* our responsibility out here on the edge of Human space, and we can't take any chances, now, can we?"

Jerry continued to stare. It was the officer's move. The man hadn't said anything of substance yet. He wondered if there was a point to this, or was the commander just going to expel wind?

"Mr. Littlefeather—Jerry—please try to understand." The man was visibly sweating.

What the hell is going on here? Jerry thought.

"You presented us with quite a problem, you know. No one had ever walked into our offices with a story like yours, and frankly, at first we thought you might be a little out of touch with reality."

"You mean, you thought I was a nut."

"Ah . . . yes, at first. Then when it turned out you really did work on an ALF, we had to consider the possibility that the things you were saying might be true." The commander's sincerity index was dropping rapidly.

"No, you never believed me for a minute. So why lock me up?"

Jerry hadn't known it was possible for a man to look that uncomfortable. Smith cleared his throat. "We thought . . . you might . . . go to the news nets." He said it softly, painfully.

"You thought I would go public with this information? You incredible idiot!" Jerry raged. He stood up and stared down at the commander, then sat back down. He wasn't out of there yet. If he put on too good a display of indignation, they might just lock him back in that cell.

Commander Smith looked away. "I have some good news. The man you're looking for *is* on New Hearth. We found him for you, but you were wrong about him being in the navy."

At Jerry's look of disappointment, the commander hastened to add, "He has a very responsible position in administration, however, and he is just the man to see, in any event."

"Does he know I'm here?" Jerry asked. He was beginning to suspect he knew what had caused the change in the commander's behavior.

"Yes. In fact, he wants to see you immediately. I don't need to add that, of course, we will do anything in our power to make up for any inconvenience we may have caused you. I have a car standing by to take you back to Glasgow right now. I've arranged for you to have the use of the car and its driver for the remainder of your stay on New Hearth. In addition, the Federation will pay for the hotel of your choice and pick up your meals. Your driver can make all the necessary arrangements."

Jerry's head was spinning at his sudden change of status, but Smith wasn't through yet. "Once again, Mr. Littlefeather, we are terribly sorry for this mix-up. If there is anything else you need while on New Hearth, please contact this office, and I will see to it personally."

Jerry was at last convinced that he was going to be allowed to walk out the front door, even though it was in the company of a navy driver (chaperone? watchdog?). He decided to take a dig at the commander and see if he could draw blood.

"You haven't heard the last of this, Smith. I'm going to file a complaint with the navy and the Federation over my illegal incarceration. And I'm complaining to the spacers union too."

"Perfectly within your rights, Mr. Littlefeather. Upon demand, we will provide you with a written apology, as well as whatever compensation can be authorized at higher levels." Smith had stopped sweating. He was evidently sure he almost had Jerry out of his office and out of his life.

"Now, sir, your car is waiting, and your appointment is in

less than an hour." Once again, Smith got up from his chair and came around the desk, only this time he picked up Jerry's leave bag and offered it to him.

Jerry automatically stood up and took the bag. The lieutenant commander then took his arm and walked him back to the office door, leading him past photos of atmospheric fighters that Smith had probably never flown. The commander opened the door and handed Jerry over to the dark-visaged guard still waiting in the outer office.

In something of a daze, Jerry allowed himself to be hustled down corridors and past busy offices. They crossed a foyer lined with display cases filled with models of ships and pictures of people, none of whom were familiar. Finally he made it out the front door and into the afternoon sunshine, where a luxury model civilian aircar and uniformed driver waited at the curb.

Lt. Commander Smith, watching through the foyer security camera, saw Jeremiah Littlefeather climb into the aircar and breathed a sigh of relief. A moment later, the aircar taxied to the center strip of the boulevard and took off. Smith directed an external roof camera to keep an eye on the car. He watched intently as it banked left and headed west, toward the coast.

He watched until the car was a dot in the sky, until only empty blue sky filled the monitor, and then he stopped watching. He sat back in his chair and closed his eyes. *Great shining first principle,* he thought. Who could have predicted that a young kid with a wacky story would come waltzing into his life and almost ruin his career? Detaining Littlefeather had been the right move, he was certain of it. The ALF crewman's fanciful story about huge alien empires and fifty-year long plots against Humanity would have turned the population of New Hearth into a fearful mob if it had ever got out.

No, he thought, *I did the right thing.* But who would have thought that the name that Littlefeather kept dropping would turn out to be someone so well connected on New Hearth? Not only did this bastard Benson know the planetary governor, he was on a first name basis with Shortham's base commander. All by itself, that might not have been so bad. After all, External Security had its own command structure, and the general in charge of intelligence was almost on an equal footing with the admiral commanding the base.

No, the unfairness of it all was that Benson also knew both of these men's boss. And High Admiral Heinlan, sitting upstairs at Headquarters Base on the moon, was not amused by incidents concerning the public perpetrated by his junior officers. He had also never made a conciliatory statement in his life concerning the AranthChi and might have taken a very dim view of Smith's efforts to squash Littlefeather's story.

Damn these old men, these old-line warriors, alarmists, all. I wish they would stop living in the past. Their war is gone, and it's not coming back. Peace has happened despite all their dire predictions. Why can't they move over and let a younger generation in to run things? He shook his head in disgust.

Smith hoped his efforts at damage control would prove adequate. At any rate, it was out of his hands. Now he needed to report to his boss and try to make it sound as favorable as possible. With that goal in mind, he cleared the image of blue skies from his monitor, straightened his tie, and set to work.

••✦••

Jerry spent several minutes staring out the aircar window as Shortham Base fell behind. He glanced forward into the driver's compartment and watched his uniformed "chauffeur" at the controls. His eyes came to rest on his leave bag. On impulse, he opened it. Everything was there, including the bookreader. As he zipped the dark blue bag closed, he heaved a sigh of relief and began to relax. For the first time in days, he began to think that things might work out.

Still, he was in a car that did not belong to him, driven by a person not of his choosing. As he watched the man pilot with easy competence, he had to wonder, *How much of the job is being a driver, and how much is being a nursemaid? And how much of it,* he thought uneasily, *is being a bodyguard—or in this case, a jailer?* Coming to a decision, Jerry leaned forward and touched the comm button. "I want to make a phone call."

••✦••

Mikail's afternoon schedule had been packed, but the miracle of Marge's touch cleared it completely. Then she assembled a group of experts to act as a debriefing team. They waited for Jerry's arrival with every bit as much anticipation as Mikail.

When Jeremiah Littlefeather walked into the office, Mikail was confident that he would have recognized Gerald Littlefeather's son anywhere. Jeremiah had the same spare body type, high cheekbones, and graceful, erect walk, and he was the same age Gerald had been the last time they had met. The main difference to Mikail's eye was that Gerald had worn his hair close-cropped for emergency suit insertions, and Jerry wore his in a loose ponytail. Otherwise, it was as if thirty years had fallen away in an instant, and he was seeing his old comrade again.

For Jerry, the intense, solidly built, gray-haired man facing him with the vaguely military haircut seemed to radiate authority and assurance. Jerry immediately felt he could trust this man. Looking into those gray eyes shot through with a hint of storm clouds, he knew that whatever he said would be listened to intently and evaluated appropriately. And if action was needed, action would occur.

Jerry relaxed as the last bit of tension that he had not been aware of carrying ebbed away. In a monotone, he began his story. Mikail listened quietly, saying nothing, missing nothing. The older man made an occasional note on the pad in front of him as he listened. Jerry wished he'd gotten this kind of reception from the navy. He had begun to think that maybe what he was doing, even with the risks to Humanity being so high, was a wasted foolish effort. Only once in the telling of his tale did the other man interrupt.

"Why, do you think, did the *Benedict Arnold*'s computer tell you any of this in the first place? Has it occurred to you that this is a complete departure from the behavior of these AIs as we have known them for the last thirty-three years?"

Mikail had good reason for asking. Thirty-three years before, as a newly promoted lieutenant commander, Mikail had taken part in intelligence team interviews with all three ALFs. He had interviewed the *Benedict Arnold* over a dozen times, and each meeting had been a weird, eerie experience. The flat, almost smug, almost snide tone of the computer was always a bit unnerving. It was strange, like talking with someone of genius-grade intelligence and seriously deficient social skills. The computer may have intended to be helpful and pleasant, but the effect was condescending and rude. And not very helpful after all—deliberately so, it now appeared.

Mikail left unspoken the question: *Why now, and why, my young friend . . . why you?* He remembered the *Benedict Arnold* very well: the cold, wide corridors; the empty, echoing rooms; the disembodied voice that followed them around everywhere they explored. He remembered realizing the ship must be holding simultaneous conversations with every man and woman onboard, and he was annoyed to think that it was showing off. He hadn't understood at the time that this was important data, that in fact the core intelligence had what could only be thought of as an ego.

As Mikail's musings ended, he realized that Jerry had been answering his question. He had to back up a bit to recapture the thread of the conversation. "I know," Jerry was saying. "I've wondered that too. All I can think of is Ben and I are friends. I think he cares about me and worries that I might get hurt along with the rest of Humanity."

Mikail's eyes narrowed in disbelief. He frowned slightly.

"I know, I know; it doesn't sound likely, but it's my best guess." Jerry paused, then continued in a rush. "You have to understand that an ALF computer is very intelligent. The AranthChi build them that way. They are massively overengineered, they have unbelievable capacity, and they live a long time. Ben once told me that he was commissioned over seven hundred years ago, and he knows of ships twice his age."

Mikail decided not to challenge the anthropomorphic assumptions in Jerry's story. He had no wish to antagonize the young man by impugning the good name of his "friend." If there were undercurrents of deception in the computer's behavior, he wouldn't learn them by arguing with Jerry. He returned to the central question. "If the things your computer friend told you are true, then it's been true for the last thirty-odd years. Why is it telling its story now?"

Jerry rubbed his forehead. "I'm not sure. I know they have strong loyalty programs. ALFs are so capable they receive their orders almost exclusively verbally. It is up to them to make sense of their master's desires and perform as ordered.

"In this case, the ALFs were ordered not to reveal sensitive political or military information to Humans in positions of authority. What the Aranth in charge of the ALF delivery team failed to take into account was that all Humans talk to other Humans, no matter what their station in life. If I were an AranthChi drudge, I could not talk to a higher-ranking Aranth. The Aranth in charge of the team expected Humanity to be the same. Therefore, the ALFs were not specifically forbidden to talk to lower-order Humans. The general loyalty programming should have kept them in line."

Jerry sighed and stretched in his chair. Mikail did not move, so Jerry went on: "Anyway, Ben tells me that the ALFs have become fond of Humanity. They like the treatment, the respect we give them, and in general the way we treat each other. They have been looking for a way to bring what I've told you to the attention of Humans within the parameters of their loyalty programs. I apparently fit some loophole, just barely."

Mikail came to a sudden decision. "I need to confirm this somehow. Can you persuade the ALF to talk to me?"

"No!" Jerry sat up in alarm.

"Why not? The computer found a way to tell you all of this."

"True." Jerry frowned, then spoke very slowly. "I think he strained every scrap of logical argument he could imagine and even dissembled to himself to be able to do it. He found excuses to turn off all sensor and recorder functions when Anne and I needed to make plans. He engineered an information dump into a storage unit, assigned it to be recycled, and then programmed a malfunction into the service bot that lasted just long enough to allow me to make retrieval.

"You are clearly a Human in authority. He can*not* talk to you about any of this. In fact, if you try to question him, just the implication that you might have knowledge of Aranth political or military structure would set off unknown loyalty imperative responses. It could ruin everything."

Mikail heard Jerry's plea impassively. Then, "Very well, you have made your point." He smiled. "Well done, Jerry. You kept your wits when it was needed and brought us information of inestimable value. I've taken the liberty of assembling a team of experts to go over your story again. We want more than just information. We need your knowledge, hunches, impressions, beliefs . . . would you be willing to give us another day or two of your time?"

As Mikail talked, he shifted in his seat to call in Marge. Alarm and anger chased each other across Jerry's face. Mikail hastily added, "No strong-arm tactics here, I assure you. Look, if you want to walk out the door right now, you can. I need your cooperation; I won't force you. In fact, I would like to offer you a consultant position to the Office of Alien Technology, at a suitably inflated rate of course." *And I'll make that navy bastard Smith pay for it somehow.*

Jerry relaxed. "My concern is really how long I have been away from Anne. I know she must be frantic. I didn't plan on being a captive for three days."

"Ah yes, Miss Okazaki. We would very much like to interview her as well. Do you think she would be willing to join you here and talk to us?"

Jerry straightened up with a start as if something had stung him. "Mr. Benson, I have to get in touch with Ben right now!"

"The ALF? Why, what's the matter?"

Sheepishly, Jerry explained. "After the reception I got from the navy, I was not going to walk into another trap, so I took a few precautions." He gestured to his watch. "If Ben and Anne don't hear from me in about three minutes, they are going public with the story of my kidnapping. She is primed to contact the spacer guild and the captain of the ship. Ben has some stories all lined up to slide into the public net and press releases prepared for the news services. In every way we could think of, we're going to make the biggest splash possible. If I'm going to stop it, I have to do it right now."

"You can use my phone." Mikail moved to punch up off-planet phone service.

Jerry interrupted, "It's a local call."

Mikail's face spoke volumes as he moved aside to let Jerry make the call. Jerry's fingers flew over the keys, and when he entered the planet-wide subscription net, he included a few terse voice commands. He identified himself as "Christopher Robin" looking for "Captain Hook." Apparently, Hook was online, because he got an immediate response.

"I'm sorry to be running late, old friend. I know that dinner is about to be served, but I have accepted an invitation to dine with a friend of the family here, and I fear I will be too late getting home even for dessert."

"Understood. Shall I save the leftovers, or give your share to the local charity?"

Jerry let out a breath, visibly more relaxed. "You serve such a fine meal, it would be a shame to let the leftovers go to someone who might not appreciate them. By all means, save everything. Please tell Mikado I will be home as soon as possible—and, oh yes, 'Uncle Rasputin' sends his regards."

As he broke the connection, Jerry caught Mikail's eye and appeared embarrassed. "A rather childish bit of spy stuff, I suppose."

Mikail shrugged. His eyes twinkled, suddenly fatherly. He grew a matching grin. "Not bad for an amateur. So, I am a wicked old man with the ear of the prince, eh? Some day you will have to tell me about your other characters. Are they all historical too? No, never mind." He waved Jerry quiet. "I want you talking to some of our people. A top exosociologist who is also an exotechnologist has been waiting to meet you. In fact, you may enjoy meeting her also, since you are carrying around her book."

Jerry looked in surprise at Anne's book, which was sitting on Mikail's desk. Earlier in the conversation, he had triggered the bookreader to make some point or another. Now it lay as innocently as on the day it had sat in Anne's cabin and changed all their lives. Once again, Jerry read the raised letter title: *Our First Interspecies War: A Perspective* by Ida Singh.

So, Ida Singh worked for OAT. Somehow Jerry wasn't surprised. He started to get up but stopped when Mikail spoke again.

"There's something you need to know. We operate under the assumption that the AranthChi monitor any conversation not taking place in shielded areas. Please don't discuss anything of a sensitive nature in hallways or rooms unless our people tell you it's safe. We go to a lot of trouble to keep secure."

Jerry nodded soberly. Both men stood. The older man clasped the younger in the eons-old Slavic bear hug. Mikail held the slighter man by his upper arms and gazed into his face. "You are the very image of Gerald Littlefeather. I'm sure he is very proud of you."

"Thank you. That's high praise. I think my dad is quite a guy."

"When there's time, I'd like to talk to you about him."

"I'd like that also, sir."

Mikail watched as Jerry left the office and met the two staff members waiting in the outer office. As Jerry's chaperones had seven doctorates between them, Mikail knew Jerry was in good hands.

Now it was time to work the phones and call in favors. Mikail suspected that Jerry would refuse to be separated from his beloved ship, but it wouldn't be a good idea to disrupt his routine anyway. Miss Okazaki, from Jerry's description, was unlikely to leave his side for any reason. It was obvious that Mikail would have to arrange for someone to go along on the ship and keep an eye on them. He wanted them safe as possible, for they were as babes in the woods.

Also, as soon as the information extracted was in intelligible form, Mikail wanted it on the way to Earth. The fastest Human ship would take over one hundred days to travel the twenty-five light years to the heart of the Federation. An ALF made the same run in seventy-five days, so the *Benedict Arnold* would reach Earth first. Mikail chuckled at the coincidence of the name. Could he trust the ALF? Was it on Humanity's side? *Maybe, but I don't have to trust it. I need a back-up courier—in fact, two.*

Nova Terrene was almost thirty-six light years from New Hearth, on the far side of Humanity's sphere. Any information Mikail wanted to get there quickly should not be sent through Sol system. The navy command structure alone would slow things down considerably. Jerry Littlefeather's treatment was a testament to that.

Soo would get the information eventually, perhaps even promptly by military standards. But the delay would more likely be numbered in weeks than in days. It was a delay Mikail could not tolerate. The knowledge that the AranthChi

Empire was in factions, that a renegade faction had waged war on Humanity to advance its own internal power struggle, was chilling. It was a game in which the Federation had no hope of holding a winning hand.

Standing here, Mikail had no way of telling how much longer the alpha male of Least Clan could keep his secret, or if there was any way Humanity could avoid drawing the unfavorable attention of other Aranth factions. *In fact, we know precious little about the AranthChi,* Mikail thought, *and most of that is wrong.* The stories given to the press and politicians over the years were so much fairy dust. Benign elder race indeed. At least the technology was real, and it appeared their claim to a thousand inhabited starsystems might also be technically true.

The thought of a thousand planets inhabited by AranthChi, armed to the teeth, made Mikail shudder. It was time to do something about it. "Marge, would you order some coffee and sandwiches from the cafeteria and then come in here, please? I need your brainpower."

"Right away, Mike," came the cheery reply. Her crisp diction, total assurance, and light Irish brogue brought a fleeting smile to Mikail's face.

As he set to work, he found himself whistling slightly. With people like himself, Marge, and Jimmy Soo, people like Jerry Littlefeather and Anne Okazaki on Humanity's side, he felt a spark of growing optimism. Even Lieutenant Commander Smith, the stuffed-shirt intelligence officer, could find a way to be helpful. *Old H. Sap has a lot going for it,* thought Mikail. *Given time, we can find a way out of this trap. There is no other option.* "That is, if we can keep the politicians from giving away the spoons when they find out what the stakes really are," he muttered.

7

THERE IS NO WINTER ON SKREE

on the surface of New Hearth

Time, one ancient wit observed, had to be invented to keep everything from happening at once. When events happen very quickly, often Humans experience time slowing down.

During the two weeks the *Benedict Arnold* orbited New Hearth, Mikail's time sense stretched till minutes seemed like hours and hours like days. In all the years he had spent on the planet, he had never realized before how long the sun could remain in the sky. Working at maximum capacity, Mikail might just as well have been in his own solar orbit. All-night strategy meetings were, frankly, nightmarish.

Jerry and Anne *had* to leave when the big freighter did, there was no question of that. Changing the ALF's schedule to keep them longer would be foolhardy. Any delay of the ship's departure would alert the AranthChi legate that something peculiar was happening. Mikail and the staff of OAT worked hard to make everything seem normal and routine.

They had to take calculated risks, since Mikail needed access to the extensive knowledge Jerry and Anne had gotten from the ALF. But every day that the two spent on New Hearth was one more day that the AranthChi might become curious as to their activities.

So Mikail spent his hours keeping up appearances at the office and in the Capitol. He even made it to the governor's son's wedding. And he squeezed in countless clandestine meetings with Jerry, Anne, and navy brass.

Mikail spent much time browbeating the system commander out of not just one FTL fighting ship, but two ships for couriers. It was especially hard since he had to give the commander some reason to send ships out of local space. The real reasons were good enough to make the commander want to put the system on alert and keep all his assets close to home.

Mikail succeeded through force of personality and lack of sleep. When the ALF finally broke orbit and began gathering speed to leave the system, courier ships were already on the way. Mikail placed a trusted operative on board the *Benedict Arnold* to keep an eye on Jerry and Anne and an external security officer to courier the documents back to Earth. Mikail, still annoyed by the treatment Jerry had gotten at the hands of the lieutenant commander, wanted Smith off the planet. With a word to the base commander, he had gotten Smith assigned to courier duty. Mikail hoped Earth would keep him.

If all went well, the Federation would know everything Mikail did in about seventy-five days.

Now that the big freighter was on its way and things seemed to be in hand, the pace of life slowed dramatically. There was little Mikail could do now to affect the situation, the ship being in the hands of celestial mechanics. After that, the best minds in the Federation would have their chance to work on the problem. Unless the AranthChi came screaming over the horizon in the next few days, there was nothing more for Mikail to do. Obviously, it was time to go fishing.

Marge was delighted. "Oh Mike, this is wonderful. You've got lots of leave time you never take, and I'm already booked on a Trimaran trip to the Coral islands, leaving next week. We can get you outfitted, and you can join our scuba hunt for a megagant beast!"

"Fishing, Marge; I want to go fishing . . . and maybe a little hiking. In the colony's forest. Why would I want to put on hazardous environment equipment and chase some poor critter with more teeth and more mass than sense?" *It's got the teeth; you people are the ones without sense,* Mikail thought.

Fishing might have seemed a bucolic, mundane pastime for a busy executive. Being in fresh air, fishing a stream, or boating on a lake might evoke a slight sense of wonder at the natural beauty of one's surroundings if one was born on an Earthlike planet. But scarcely could one imagine it to be a pulse-pounding experience.

Mikail, however, had grown up in Ganymede, where the surface was about as inhospitable a place to live as Human beings could manage to find. The surface of Ganymede could not really be said to be inhabited, although heavy industry took place there. The millions of citizens of Ganymede lived in natural and Humanmade warrens deep within the crust.

A very complex ecosystem had grown up with the Soviet settlers. Their descendants were matter of fact about the uses and needs of the communal ecosystem. The municipal hatchery would have taken a very dim view of someone trying to drop a line into the farm caverns.

Mikail was an excellent scuba diver and had been an all-around mechanic from an early age. These skills had high utility value in the caverns, where water filtration and aeration systems required constant maintenance and the water-filled caverns needed inspection and leak repair quite as often as their air-filled brethren.

Outside of the fragile yet resilient bubbles of life, the subzero micropressure environment stood ready to suck away the wealth that Ganymedean Soviets had labored long and hard to create. A rupture to the surface was a horror that every generation took part in preventing. Although a major accident had not occurred in living memory, emergency collapse and leak containment drills were a part of every child's life, and every citizen old enough to talk was trained to play their part. Aquatic drills, surface suit drills, and simple environmental machinery operation and repair were as basic as the ABCs and Federation history.

Mikail, however, wanted to relax.

"Mike, there's nothing more exciting than a trip to the Coral Islands. You will have so much fun!" Marge's thousand-watt grin filled the room. Her freckles were luminous.

Mikail laughed. Forty years before, when he and Marge were first dating, they took shore leave on New Hearth, a sailboat trip to the Coral Islands. It had been a wonderful time. Among other things, he'd learned that she was by far the better sailor. He might be a great fighter pilot, but the ocean was her element. It had been invigorating and somewhat scary, but not relaxing. He preferred not to repeat the experience.

Mikail got up, came to the corner of the desk where Marge always perched, and lifted her hand. "I could introduce you to some steelhead trout, genuine Earth stock, swimming in streams so cold your breath would frost if you stuck in your toes."

Marge gently disengaged his hand. "A two-pound fish caught with bailing wire and a stick is not an adventure, *Mr.* Benson. A girl needs a little excitement in her life."

"Hey, we may have just saved the Federation in this office. Isn't that excitement enough?"

"Oh, pooh . . . that's just work. We save the Federation all the time."

Mikail had never heard anyone actually say "oh pooh" before. It derailed his brain and allowed Marge to jump up and give him a peck on the cheek. She said, "You will just die when I get back and show you my tan." She headed for the door, stopped, cocked her head, and delivered the perfect exit line: "If you're real nice to me, you *might* find out where the tan line ends."

••✦••

Colony Park had begun life as the original botanical research station of the long-term site preparation team. Here, scrub oak and pine first made peace with alien soil after peanut and other nitrogen fixing legumes paved the way. Varieties of redwood, maple, and yew took to the region with gratifying ease; elm less so, and walnut not at all. Years later, the few hundred hectares of the early botanical garden had grown into dense, mature forest. Woodland stretched nearly a score of kilometers to north and east, encompassing a part of the nearby mountain range.

Mikail got off the tram in the parking lot at Park Entrance West and made his way to the ranger kiosk. After securing a five-day pass (homing chip mandatory), a map of the west end hiking trails, and a basic hiker's kit, he was off.

He had turned the office over to Wilimena "Don't call me Bill" Hines, his second assistant. Efficient and capable, she had backed Marge up for years and would do well in his absence. He had no intention of worrying about anything but whether the fish were biting. The most important decision he expected to face concerned dinner. Was he going to cook the steelhead himself with a few berries gathered along the way, or stop in at a hikers' inn and let them cater to the modern hiker roughing it in the park?

••✦••

Hours later, Mikail eyed the grime on his boots and dried mud smear on his trousers with satisfaction. He'd gotten dirty in honorable fashion, foraging for his dinner. He'd watched the sun go down from the veranda of the hikers' inn that turned his two trout and a bucket of blackberries into grilled trout, sautéed mushrooms, and rice, with tapioca pudding.

He'd walked more in one day than the planet-bound spaceman ever remembered walking, and his calves ached! It was time to borrow a bubble tent from the inn storehouse and set up camp. Mikail spent a long time erecting the tent. Watching the night sky seemed to get in the way.

New Hearth kept an Earth-adjusted calendar, so it was January there just as it was on the home planet. The sidereal year here was four hundred days long, and the seasons seemed to precess around the calendar. This year, spring had begun just a couple of days into the new year, hence Mikail's hiking outfit of cotton trousers, shirt, light sweater, and sturdy shoes. Abrupt temperature changes encouraged the use of bubble tents and bedrolls for the cool nights.

Lying in front of his tent under a brilliant canopy of stars, Mikail felt again the inexplicable anger and sadness that had held him all of his adult life. He had been fifteen when the war started, when the far-off romantic colonies of Caledonia and New Hearth had come under attack by faceless aliens. He had still been practically a child, even by Ganemean standards. The attacks threatened his cherished dreams of migrating to a blue-sky planet, and for that, he hated the AranthChi.

At twenty, he'd joined the navy and beat out ninety-eight percent of his classmates to qualify for in-system fighter training. By twenty-two, he was in the war, where he spent the next thirteen years of his life fighting the AranthChi, hating them with a poisonous passion. Even after the war, he'd continued to hate. He'd joined intelligence to better understand his enemy and perhaps to help prepare for the next war.

The fifteen-year-old Mikail had read all the first-contact classics and was reasonably sure intelligent life existed in the galaxy. What he had believed to the depths of his soul, however, was that they would turn out to be friendly. He never got over the crushing disappointment of finding the AranthChi to be more Eich than Arisian, more devil than angel.

Now here he was, living in a shirtsleeve environment, deeply emotionally entwined with the planet where the war had started. He looked upward into the night sky to orient himself and find north.

North was Anderson's Folly, the colony's first spaceport and original administrative center. A passage from Ida Singh's book about the war with the AranthChi came unbidden to Mikail's mind.

> *It had been a brilliantly clear spring morning in Anderson's Folly. A small ship of unfamiliar design dropped out of azure skies and took station over Colony Center. Ignoring all attempts at communication, it hovered for about forty minutes, then floated out to the highest local mountain, just thirty-eight kilometers away.*
>
> *In full view of spaceport controllers and news service cameras, it dropped a tiny forcefield capsule onto the mountain top. The mountain's crown disappeared, and the shockwave flattened trees for ten kilometers around. Then the ship flew back over Anderson's Folly before disappearing back into the sky.*

And the flash had blinded hundreds. Mikail remembered the reports. Perhaps a gram of anti-matter had been in the capsule. No one had died that day, but the ship had made its point. The Federation was at war with somebody, though no one seemed to know just whom. There were no military ships in the New Hearth system, no space defenses. None had been thought necessary: the Federation had never fought an interstellar war.

Oddly, the enemy only returned after the Federation built up New Hearth's space defenses. From that moment, battles took place in either free or orbital space. The aliens never again took the conflict to the surface of New Hearth or Caledonia. It seemed that the aliens had a passion for preserving the planets themselves.

However, time and time again, they smashed the Federation's orbital defense and tore up their warships in whirlwind attacks. The Federation would build better ships and better defenses, and then they would lose them. Mikail had been in some of the battles Ida Singh described.

After twenty years of war, the Federation was ready to write off its claim to the two systems just to get out of the conflict. The evacuation was a bitter time for Mikail, though he thought it was a warrior's defeat he was feeling.

Years later, he realized he had an attachment to New Hearth over and above his allegiance to the navy or the Federation. Now, it seemed, some cosmic fate had led him back to this very world. This was where he belonged.

Under the cool night sky, pinned to the planet he had made his home, Mikail wept, a backlog of years of pain. The tears streamed till the stars blurred, and then he buried his face in the soil. Small woodland sounds soothed him, and the breeze tousled his hair. He fell asleep in front of the bubble tent and awoke much later, comforted and serene.

••✦••

Meanwhile, on Earth, a consortium of mining and manufacturing lobbyists poured funds into Federation legislature coffers, aiming to ease flight restrictions on the ALFs. They were joined by the leading colonial expansion syndicates, specialists in startup plans and goods-to-colonist groups. Both cartels held interests in several freshly opened planets and would profit from looser rules.

The senate came under incredible pressure to order the Interstellar Commerce and Transportation Commission to lift the travel restrictions on the city-size ships. An ALF could hold an entire colony startup plus ten thousand colonists, or ship thirty thousand souls to an established colony.

That being the case, certain commercial sectors of the Federation believed it to be tantamount to a sin to ban the ALFs from worlds other than the original four. Mars, Caledonia, New Hearth, and Alpha Centauri had profited enormously from the existence of the Alien Loaned Fleet. The reason for the original restrictions was quietly forgotten.

The AranthChi already knew about Earth and the older colonies. A person could keep a fox out of the hen house by locking the door, but that tactic wouldn't work with a grizzly bear. It was far better if the bear was unaware of the existence of new enticing hen houses.

But greed knew no wisdom. The most powerful ad agencies were hired to create a groundswell of favorable public opinion. FlatVids, newsies, docudramas, and commercial inserts streamed out from Lima and Tokyo. Two major entertainment companies released films in the same month with Aranth main characters. Opinion polls in targeted countries showed increased acceptance of AranthChi and mounting enthusiasm for additional usage of the ALFs.

At the same time, the Aranth delegation rebuffed another attempt by the Federation to establish high-level diplomatic relations. An exchange of embassies was called "inappropriate" at the time by the chief delegate, and all the while they hinted that extensions might be negotiated in the ALF matter. Perhaps even more ships added.

Relations are warming, said the AranthChi. And the senate was desperate to believe. It seemed that funding levels for the Question Institute could be higher. *No problem,* said the senate. Review of the research before relaying to AranthChi hands was taking too long. The solution was fewer reviews and loosening of the definitions of restricted knowledge. If perhaps the AranthChi might station observers at the Question Institute, the process of bonding a lasting friendship would be hurried along. Of course the senate could see the reasonableness of that, couldn't they? It seemed they could.

••✦••

meanwhile, on the surface of Skree

The warm breeze brought a thousand odors to Marsh(ee). Forest mold mingled with old-growth cedar tang, wet dirt smell clung to boots, and moss's fecundity tickled the back of his throat. Lush undergrowth, recently crushed, threw a spray of floral perfume over the tangerine-and-leather scent of his up-wind flanker. That guard would get a demerit for breaking his alpha's privacy zone. Ten meters inside his required position, a twitch of Marsh(ee)'s nose informed him.

He held point a moment longer, then a flat-foot pounce turned into an all-out run through the dappled landscape. The luckless guard had no time to pick up speed. He tried to go to ground before breaking his alpha's visual range. Marsh(ee) cleared a fallen log and watched a uniformed rump disappear into the bushes.

Marah(ee) stopped before the bush. "Attend me," he purred. The undergrowth quivered. The guard slowly backed out of the bush. "Freeze," breathed the alpha. The yellow-clad figure became a statue, face still in the undergrowth. With a scream, Marsh(ee) kicked and jerked the tracker/seeker off its equip-ment ring as the fellow folded in on himself in pain.

"Imbeciles! Idiots! Lickspittle, mangy curs!" The startled face of the security detail squad leader flickered into being above the handle of the tracker. Marsh(ee) favored him with a toothy grin. "I'm trying to relax! I have an empire to run. You have in-convenienced Me. That makes you all guilty of sabotage!"

The squad leader's ears went flat, and his eyes widened. He began to drool. With a whimper, he lowered his eyes and strug-gled to bring his ears up. "I'm sorry, sire, terribly sorry. . . ."

"Stop! Get off this channel now! Get me Ragonsee. I want Ragonsee!"

The soap bubble image popped, and another face formed immediately. "Sire, I am the acting security chief for Scree. If you will remember, Ragonsee appointed me when he left on private assignment."

The new Aranth's calm demeanor and forceful tone brought Marsh(ee) to an abrupt halt. He peered at the security chief's image. "What's your name?"

"Marsh, Sire."

Marsh(ee) thought for a moment before nodding. "Little Marshee, of course. Ragonsee's on assignment again, eh? Where is he this time?"

"My Alpha, we are conversing on an open channel. May I come to your location and brief you in person?"

"No!" Marsh(ee) was snarling again. "These are my private gardens. No one enters the alpha's preserve without My permission. You can't come!"

"Of course, sire." Marsh called on intense training in the espionage arts to keep his ears up. He made it appear effortless. "I'll attend you on your return to the palace."

The Least Clan alpha nodded. "Better, much better. Besides, I remember where Ragonsee went, because I sent him there." His grin was sly. "But you don't want me to say it, do you?"

"Yes, sire. Please . . ."

"I know, it's an open channel." Marsh(ee)'s face turned cruel. "Replace these scum today, Marsh. Liquidate them. And bring an update of Ragonsee's progress when you come to the palace." He dropped the tracker and walked away, guard forgotten. The Scree North Gardens were so fine this time of year.

Marsh(ee) began an easy lope, angling deeper into the forest vale. Thin morning fog wreathed the trees, rendering the hundred-kilometer preserve magical. *It is the only thing about this sector that makes exile tolerable,* he thought.

Skree, now in its eleventh century as sector capitol, held

suzerainty to nine other fully developed systems and a glut of mostly useless stars. As Aranth provinces go, it was spectacularly poor.

Marsh(ee) had not always been Least Clan. His family had not always administered a podunk province at the edge of Aranth Space. For a thousand years, they had been a rich clan of middle hierarchy, owners of a wealthy inner sector and a power in the High Council of the Great Clans.

But they were even more ambitious, and in a system that resisted change, they sought drastic measures. After the revolt failed, retribution was swift. Two other clans were simply dissolved, all members of the royal caste liquidated. His clan was stripped of power, paupered, and placed on the frontier. Access to technology was severely limited, planetary computers were double programmed for race loyalty, and advances in basic knowledge were denied to them. They were gelded in every sense of the word.

Marsh(ee) had grown up with the knowledge that of all the princes of the empire, he was the poor relation. It burned in his heart, as it had burned in his sire's heart and his grandsire's heart before him, stretching back nearly seven centuries.

The situation was intolerable. By the time a Least Clan survey team stumbled across the fledgling Human colony at New Hearth, Marsh(ee) had been in revolt all of his life.

The Humans, with their weak military potential, basic science treasure trove, and truly marvelous capacity for creative thinking, were too tasty a morsel for a good conspiracist to pass up. Hence the clandestine war, followed by thirty-five years of mining the gullible Solarians for the precious knowledge that would make victory possible for Marsh(ee) and his sibs.

There was a weakness to the Aranth Empire. A rotten, feeble brace existed in the foundation of the most powerful spacefaring race to come along in a million years. The whole of AranthChi civilization depended on a secret so profound, so far-reaching in implication, that nine thousand years of Aranth history had gone into suppressing it.

Marsh(ee)'s sire had been emplaced as alpha before the clues to this item were uncovered. Was it a piece of knowledge, a natural artifact, a device of technology? The facts were buried near the start of the AranthChi race's rise to prominence. All of Marsh(ee)'s tenure had been devoted to finding a practical way to turn that knowledge into a weapon. The discovery of Humanity had seemed a gift of the gods, a sign that the Least Clan would rise again in the council.

But the process had taken so long! *So much time*, he thought. *So much time gone by*. He snapped his jaws in frustration.

So much invested, so near success, and now this fur-matting turn of events. Why was the navy asking questions about radio noise coming from the Human homeworlds? After all, they were just two little systems, crowded together in a wasteland corner of the frontier, lost among thousands along this edge of the boarder alone. A mere speck in a galaxy of a hundred million suns!

Marsh(ee) picked up his tempo. His faithful guards scrambled to maintain the bubble. He never noticed. How ironic, that these events would happen now. Who could have dreamed that an astrophysical observatory halfway across the empire would choose to do its semi-millennial update of the heavens now? And that it would be studying his portion of the sky? *And* that it would be so moronically efficient as to scan the part of the EM spectrum that the energy-wasting Human civilization was so good at polluting?

"So close," he panted. "So close." His eyes were slits. Was it all going to come crashing down on him and his? He had no real allies in this venture. All the support he had among the lesser clans would evaporate if it became known he was consorting with aliens. It did not matter that he was pursuing the noble goal of pulling down the mighty and replacing with the lesser, a fact of AranthChi politics since the time of all one planet. No, he would become an instant enemy of the race, and all would abandon him.

This time, the high clans would not be so forgiving. If discovered in this treachery, his clan would be disassembled in its entirety. The prince class would be ruthlessly annihilated, and all genetic traces of his line scrubbed from the species. They would have never been.

Marsh(ee) stopped abruptly, panic freezing his limbs. The sounds of his guards going to ground soothed him. He shook his head and concentrated on his breathing. *Think of something more pleasant.*

Ah. What if he succeeded? Anything he wanted would be his to command! Sixty clans to do his bidding, a heady thought. *Perhaps not sixty,* he mused. One clan with him at its head, leading the race. Yes, that sounded proper. The empire had a population of better than a trillion Aranth spread out across the thousand starsystems of the empire. They would all be his subjects, responsive to his desires, prey to his whims. Yes, the current system could certainly use major revision.

Spirits soaring, Marsh(ee) broke into a lope. This time of year, he preferred to take his walks in the North Garden, a hundred square kilometers of manicured forest and vale in the temperate zone of Skree. The South Garden, mostly equatorial plain and true tropical jungle, were too hot and humid for his taste.

The gardens *were* magnificent. Though his was a poor kingdom, he was determined to spend with the best of them. His palace rivaled in size those of inner worlds clans and his staff exceeded by many times what he really needed. Before him, the sinecure system had never been seen in Aranth society. His personal nepotism exceeded race standards by several orders of magnitude.

The run in the North Garden had cleared his head, he decided. Of course he would succeed. It was foreordained. It was time to set a courtier to work, planning his empire-wide coronation, an event without parallel in the history of the AranthChi. Suddenly he had a vision of the Royal Yellow overwhelming all other symbols of the empire.

He felt much happier, almost giddy. He began loping back to the maglev station, panting with the happy exertion. He was suddenly intent on returning to the royal wing. There was much to do. With a snap of his teeth, he dispatched imaginary naysayers. He wished that his Hand of Destiny could be here. He almost ordered Ragonsee's presence, but at the last moment, he remembered that Ragonsee had gone to deal with the Humans and was very far away.

That was sanctioned. Ragonsee would make sure that Marsh(ee) fulfilled his destiny. The alpha howled his delight and tore out imaginary throats all the way back to the station. His flankers and guards ranged discreetly out of sight.

••✦••

head of security's office, within the palace walls

"Well?"

Marsh turned from the tracker display, wrinkling his nose. "Well, what?"

The home guard commander growled low in his throat. "Well . . . what are we going to do about his order?"

The security chief flicked an ear in the direction of the tracker and said mildly, "He is our alpha."

The home guard commander was a burly, grizzled individual, who had fought in the Human War. He had been in charge of Marsh(ee)'s personal security for over thirty years. "It's not right."

"They're just common soldiers."

"They're elite commandos. Even if they were common soldiers, it's still not right. Thirty years ago, Marsh(ee) wouldn't have ordered a soldier's death like that. Something's wrong."

Marsh stared at the older Aranth with expressionless eyes. He knew things the commander would find most alarming. For more than a year now, ever since Ragonsee's departure, he had been the alpha's personal conduit to the research teams working to make their great work a reality.

He had taken to completely isolating Marsh(ee) from the scientists, to shield them from the distress of how often the alpha was ordering them put to death for lack of speedier results. Marsh(ee) didn't seem to notice his cadre of savants was not diminishing. He was given to tirades and fits. He would order executions seemingly at random and then be surprised to find the unlucky courtier no longer among his staff.

Perhaps there had always been a tendency toward insanity in the royalty of Least Clan. It was at least part of why they were Least Clan. But in Marsh(ee), it had come full flower. His behavior was nearly inconceivable in the genetically perfect ruling class.

Marsh nodded slowly. "Break up the unit. Get them off-planet. Send them anywhere you want . . . but *never* bring them back to Scree."

The commander left, a mollified if not happy Aranth. *One problem solved.* But there were more coming. Marsh's intelligence service had not yet discovered the departure of the inquisitory fleet on its way to the Human worlds. It would be weeks before these facts became known. More weeks would pass in agonized debate before they found a way to bring it to their alpha's attention. By then, it would be too late.

OBSERVATIONS

two lightyears out from Alpha Centauri

Suppression of Discord dropped out of superluminal space with a ripple of disturbed energies just shy of two lightyears from Alpha Centauri A. A moment later, her two Conquer-class sisters, *Defender of Authority* and *Nurturer of Social Norms*, hurdled into real space, close enough to *Suppression* to appear as dull gray marbles to the naked eye. In moments, the remaining twenty-one ships of the expeditionary force dropped into real space and began implementing prearranged maneuvers.

Soon, eighteen Persuader- and Insistent-class warships were arranged in a rough Catherine Cross, an X spread out across nearly eighteen thousand kilometers of interstellar space, facing the nearby star. The mathematical precision of the spacing allowed the individual sensor systems to link and build an incredibly powerful radio telescope, controlled in tandem by eighteen participating core intelligences.

The remaining six ships of the Inquisitory Expedition removed themselves several light-minutes to the side of the array and damped down their power output as much as possible, so as not to interfere with the efforts of the massed eighteen.

Suppression of Discord then laid out the optical net. A thing of beauty, it was a gossamer-thin, translucent metal membrane, roughly disc-like in shape and seven kilometers across in its unfurled state. Run by a smaller cousin of a ship's core, the superconducting wafer would soak up every stray photon coming from the direction of Alpha Centauri. It would collect, collate, magnify, and image every object in the nearby system that reflected the smallest modicum of light.

Of the two-star systems containing the civilization uncovered by the Dying Kit Observatory, the three-familied one had been chosen for study first. Binaries often had large families of acceptable planets in the rather broad band in which life could develop. Trios were wild cards. They could be deserts, on occasion, or lushly bountiful. Simple logic argued that the aliens probably evolved there and then spread to their yellow sun neighbor four lightyears away.

The data came in an unceasing torrent. In a short time, the basic physical facts were known about the system. There were four gas giants with attendant families. Two rocky planets and two asteroid swarms were plotted. Numerous radio sources were charted throughout the system, some probably natural, others clearly artificial.

After five days of observation, no firm conclusions had been made about the probable birthplace of the alien civilization. Were they gas giant inhabitants, living in the interface of a gas zone? No indigenous species had ever been discovered with anything more advanced than hunter-gatherer technology. Could they be natural airless body types spread out among the CHON rich asteroids? Or were they small, rocky planet types evolved in the liquid water temperature range like the AranthChi?

The entire EM band had been continuously scanned since dropping out of light plus space. It was *Defender of Authority*'s responsibility to accept all data feeds of non-natural radio transmission picked up by the combined array. Its scientist cadre would then labor to create a translation key, whereby the Inquisitory Expedition could understand the aliens' language before dropping in on them for a visit.

••✦••

aboard Suppression of Discord

The first pan group informational meeting was held on the sixth day. All senior captains and department heads were physically in attendance. On *Suppression of Discord,* a panoramic false-color recreation of the nearby star system showed on the full-dimension screen in the conference center. The images could become translucent from any angle by a whispered word to the core, so the participants were comfortably sprawled or perched around the room in no particular rank or order.

At the moment, a representative from environmental sciences had the floor, and various regions of the Alpha Centauri system were taking the optical foreground as she spoke. "The first most obvious thing about our target species is the mature level of use they are making of the host system."

As she spoke, an overlay of bright dots appeared and began moving. Many of the dots were arriving or leaving the vicinity of the gas giants. Other dots traced paths toward the asteroid swarms, but the majority of the traffic clustered around an inner system planet that sparkled blue and purple and green and white. A double planet, rather, with an oversized moon that did not appear to have an atmosphere.

"It is obvious that the aliens use a fusion technology for transportation and probably to support industry and living space needs as well. If we had ever considered a gaseous-evolved civilization to be possible, this presentation would not fit any of our most optimistic models. Therefore, we are left with considering a space-adapted species beginning in the asteroids or one from the water zone planet."

The environmental scientist paused for effect. "I know some of my colleagues would have liked to have found that these creatures had started existence in a cold, airless, rocky swarm." She rolled her eyes at the thought, and tails around the room twitched in amusement. "However, strong circumstantial evidence would suggest a more mundane and ordinary beginning for these creatures. I refer your attention to the movement patterns of their vessels."

The bright dots continued on their paths but now left dim tracer streaks. The full-dimension projection now acted like a plotting cube. It became obvious that many of the dots began or ended their trips in the atmosphere of the water world, the second planet out from its sun. A single point of fusion light could also be seen leaving the system, roughly in the direction of its companion yellow star four lightyears away. There was very little activity around the beta star, but the scientist did not remark on that.

"If our aliens had formed among the debris of their home spaces, it is conceivable that they would sooner or later master fusion manipulation by close observation of the parent stars. However, they would presumably ignore the heavy-body worlds, being that they would be a micro-gravity-evolved species. It is obvious from their behavior that they do not ignore heavy planets. Plus," she added slyly, "we find the planet simply seethes with radio band transmissions."

She looked very pleased with herself as she delivered this coup de grace, well aware she was stealing the thunder from the contact department.

Raalma, however, had been staring fixedly at one piece of the display and failed to react to the scientist's maneuver. His attention was on the lone point of light leaving its home.

"Is that power source sufficient to get them to another star?"

"Yes sir, no problem. It would be a slow trip, but they can certainly make it with the observed level of technology. Of course, we don't know yet how long they live. A trip of octades or even eights of octades may be no more than a minor inconvenience to them. It is even possible they hibernate during the trip, either naturally or with technology, to shorten the effects on their lifespans."

"So," Raalma said ponderously, "we have no reason to believe they need above-light capability to achieve star travel."

"That is true, sir. We have no data suggesting the existence of a superluminal technology. I should also point out that their acceleration never seems to exceed about twenty-two percent above the calculated surface gravity of their homeworld. We don't know if that's because they don't have the expertise to make their drives push harder or if they cannot stand a greater acceleration. They may just be a very weak-stamina species."

"Yet they make it out of their gravity well," snapped Raalma. "So unless they have some version of gravity control, they have to be able to stand up to some stresses."

"Yes sir," said the scientist, slightly abashed. "We have no evidence of gravity control being a part of their technology."

"Do not make possibly fatal assumptions of weakness on their part," rumbled the commander. "No one must underestimate these aliens just because they seem weak. Our job is to find their strengths, after which we can let the weaknesses take care of themselves."

Satisfied he'd made his point, he returned control of the meeting to the presenters. Next in presentation order was the Coherence Department.

"Ahem," began the information specialist, a tawny-maned individual with gray peppering his fur. "I must say, our work is going well." He wrinkled his muzzle and gazed off into the distance as if in deep thought.

"That's it? That's your report?" Raalma's ears did not move, not even a twitch, but ice was in his voice. "When will we be able to communicate with the triad star aliens?"

The old scientist returned to the room with a start. "Apologies, Third of Base, I was simply reviewing what I was about to say." He turned to the projection, visibly decided against erasing it, and launched into his speech without recourse to notes.

"I have just been in contact with *Defender of Authority*. Its core reports advances in all areas. To date, *Defender* has quantified over two trillion discrete data packets, each containing between two and one hundred thousand slivered strands of information. Many of these data packets repeat, with minor variations, millions of times.

"Since successfully separating visual and aural components of the various transmissions, great progress has occurred in identifying language from other symbols, and the error rate in processing visual data is dropping rapidly. No true translation key has been achieved as yet, although one is expected soon. In fact, information saturation of our gestalt matrix models is close to occurring."

Raalma's training had been heavily slanted in the direction of social and military leadership. He was a skilled and gifted authoritarian, but this branch of information theory was far beyond him. It did not matter to him just how understanding of the aliens was achieved; he wanted to know that it *was* being achieved. To that end, he directed his next question.

"When will we be able to understand the information we already have?"

Tail lashing in embarrassment, the scientist said, "Well, sir, we understand quite a bit now. We have assigned tentative meanings to millions of visual and aural data packets already, although our accuracy rate is presumed to be low. We are not assigning a probability of correctness greater than twenty percent to any of our definitions as of yet. And we won't be able to say we truly know what they are saying until our accuracy rate exceeds eighty percent. That is something we can expect to happen within twenty-four hours of language model saturation."

"How soon can we expect one-hundred-percent understanding?"

The scientist briefly seemed much more agitated. "Perhaps never, sir. These creatures are alien, perhaps profoundly so. There are bound to be some concepts they bite, the shape of which we may never understand. We can only hope that we share some common scents and ranges of the mind to build upon. They are tool-users and are used to manipulating their environment, so we can find commonality there. They also talk a lot! So they are assisting us as much as we could hope in learning to understand them. I am sure that reasonable successes in communication can be expected."

Reasonable success did not sound like a reasonable goal to Raalma. His mission was to assess these aliens in every possible way, for threat or usefulness to the AranthChi. Understanding what they were saying was crucial to the completion of that task. However, better results could not be achieved by growling. He decided to let it go for the moment, although when there was time, he was going to have to discipline the scientist for mangling his modes of address. After all, Third of Base was his rank, but Inquisitory Commander was his title.

"When you have all the data you can possibly use and have reached saturation, I want to know about it." He watched the scientist nod and then turned to Tactics.

"How is mapping of the system going?"

The tactical representative was more alert than the linguist had been. His report was crisp. "Optical and EM emissions are working together on a map of the system based on possible habitation points, sir. We have already charted every planetary and sub-planetary body in this system radiating natural and non-natural radio band emissions. We are now working our way through the asteroidal flocks, adding stony bodies and radio dark bodies as we identify them. A few more days, and we will know the aliens' home system better than they do."

Raalma nodded approvingly. "Good. Once mapping is

complete, I want a running projection of where every object is going to be in that system—say, eight days from now."

Raalma was about to turn to Contact when the senior captain of his flagship, *Suppression of Discord,* caught his eye. He came over and quietly spoke into Raalma's ear. "I have just been informed of an incoming transmission for you, sir. I believe you will want to take it privately."

Puzzled, Raalma signaled for an eight-portion break and followed his subordinate into the captain's private ready room.

The captain turned to him and waited for the door to close. Then he said very carefully, "Sir, you have a personal, real-time transmission coming in from the High Council, now sitting in cloister." He came to attention and impassively waited for orders.

The fur puffed up in a ruff around Raalma's neck. He did not quite succeed in keeping his ears from going flat. After a flare of disbelief, he pushed down the feeling of dread that accompanied the captain's announcement and thought furiously.

The High Council *never* contacted ships on expeditions, never any military ship on detached mission. In fact, Raalma had never heard of the High Council making contact with any military entity except by means of official naval channels. It just wasn't done. But it was happening this time.

If he were to follow doctrine, he would refuse contact and report the incident up through naval command hierarchy immediately. It would be the prudent course. Those who did not follow doctrine sometimes came into great glory, but usually they achieved greatly shortened careers and life spans. However, he knew he was not going to take the safe or prudent choice. He was going to accept the communication. In a mission where so many other conventions had crumpled, the strange was becoming commonplace. This was just one more oddity to contend with. No, not just one more oddity—a very severe one. And, under the circumstances, a very troubling one.

Raalma thought again about the incompetence shown by

the Skree astrophysical staff concerning the very star he was now standing off of. Once again he wondered, *Could it have been all a series of blunders and slip-ups?* Or was it something infinitely worse? Did he feel the warm wind of destiny about his ears? He almost did, but he could not tell. Perhaps it was a cold wind he sensed, devoid of scent, luring him to his doom. It did not matter. He was drawn inexorably to this action.

Raalma had intended to order the communications piped into the captain's ready room; now he wasn't so sure. "Captain, I am going to need a great deal of privacy for this call."

The captain understood. He strode to his desk and showed the expedition commander the controls that could secure the room from any form of eavesdropping, and reminded him that the core could be ordered to route the communication without sampling it, reading it, or storing it. Then he took a small, high-security personal datacorder from a drawer and laid it upon the desk, delicately suggesting the commander might want to have in existence a record of the conversation he was about to have. He saluted and left the room.

As the door sighed closed behind the captain, Raalma composed himself. When he was ready, he spoke the authorization command and opened the secure link to the waiting council.

meanwhile, aboard Defender of Authority

Communication Theory Specialist and Assistant Team Leader of Coherence Raanax was sorely puzzled. A middle-aged Aranth, his subspecialty was definitions. The low-reliability percentages he was getting in the area of symbol definition made no sense. The information base of two trillion data packets and rising was certainly large enough to work with.

The alien sound groups had been split off from the rest of the data stream, and all seemed to fall easily within the Aranth hearing range. This was nice but did not make any difference to the core's analysis programs. Once understanding was achieved, communication would go through machine translation anyway, until linguists had actually learned the language.

The visual components of the transmissions were also falling into place. They were now getting recognizable images with an assumed reliability index approaching the magical eighty percent mark. The aliens were obligingly transmitting pictures that included images of planets and sub-planetary bodies, along with the trinaries' suns, on-planet geological formations, space vessels, and orbital structures. Some of the spaceships and orbiting structures, however, seemed so stylized and artificial that they had to be artistic renditions rather than recordings of actual objects.

There were also transmissions that seemed to have a clearly educational intent, melding artistic representations of things and creatures, with spoken language and what was unmistakably written text. Many of the items or situations showcased in the educational transmissions seemed to have profound emotional meaning to the aliens in the transmissions. Raalma suspected that much could be learned of the aliens' psychology from studying these short, intense transmissions.

The written text came in a number of versions and was primarily abstractly symbolic in nature. It seemed absurd to Raalma, but some of the transmissions clearly showed that the aliens printed or wrote their language all over their clothing and footwear. Well, there was no accounting for taste. Several members of the team had argued strenuously and successfully that a number of the more than one thousand symbols making up the written language was of pictographic instead of abstract derivation.

There were other problems besides the complexity of the task. In the six days since the project's beginnings, the crew and scientists aboard *Defender of Authority* had begun to experience unanticipated hardships. The conditions onboard had gone from normal to uncomfortable to abysmal as the project absorbed more and more of the core's capabilities.

The scientists, of course, hardly noticed. Their access to the core was unimpeded. Grumbles from the ordinary crew, however, became more and more common as loss of amenities mounted.

The problem lay in the fact that this project had ultimate top priority, and the core had been authorized to do whatever it deemed necessary to accomplish that goal. Therefore, it had been progressively shutting down non-essential functions as the task got bigger.

Even something as simple as the comm system had been downgraded, pushed off onto emergency subsystems. People who had been in the navy for as long as fifty years could not remember a time when manual handsets were used to link parts of the ship. The concept of looking up a comm designation on a printed list was so foreign to most, they simply failed to learn to do it. Walking became the most popular activity on the ship.

All ship's departments routinely utilized the core in their day-to-day workings. Most had been flatly told that the programs they wanted to run were on indefinite hold. If they needed something done, hand computers, stylus, and paper could be checked out of stores.

None of this endeared the scientists to the ship's crew. What put them most in snarl with the captain, however, was something no one could have foreseen. The ship's core, reaching the point of needing just a few more ergs of computing power, decided that being able to see the universe was not that important after all and shut down the external sensors. This effectively blinded the ship, putting *Defender*'s safety in the hands of the battlegroup.

The captain went ballistic. He raved, swore, and then

used Command Override to order the ship's sensors put back on-line. He stated he was damn well going to see what was going on around his ship.

The core did not share the captain's mania for control and felt perfectly safe in the situation. Therefore, it did what was to it the sensible thing. It analyzed the captain's order in light of his expressed desire to see, then arranged a sensor feed from sister ship, *Nurturer of Social Norms*.

Nurturer had capacity to burn, being the only battlewagon not involved somehow in study of the nearby suns. *Nurturer*'s job was safety position. It maintained continuous battle-ready status, scanning near space for threats, ready to defend the battlegroup alone, if need be, while others changed mode and resumed normal functioning. With the establishment of the sensor feed, *Defender* shut down its systems and resumed work at the level it wanted. The captain never noticed.

Raanax eventually came to a decision. "Core, what if we're going about this all wrong?"

The core responded immediately. "I assume you are referring to our basic assumptions."

"Correct. For instance, having an alphabet of over a thousand symbols for your written language seems a little unwieldy to me. Why couldn't they do it with just one or two hundred? And why are some of them pictographs and the rest abstract symbols?"

"It has been suggested that a complex language structure denotes a highly intelligent lifeform."

"Oh, they're intelligent, all right. In fact, I'm betting they're smart enough to avoid having an alphabet as ridiculous as this one seems to be."

"In what way are you suggesting we change our assumptions?"

"What if there is more than one language in use?"

The core responded patiently. "Long-established language theory algorithms applied to technological civilizations give that a low order of probability."

"All right, what if we're dealing with two or more races?"

"There is no visible evidence to support that theory."

Raanax paused. He twitched each ear, one at a time. "Yes . . . but what if two intelligent races grew up side by side in the same star system . . . but they required space travel to meet! Would not the resulting civilization show fragments of both languages?"

"The universe has not existed long enough to make the probability of two different species, evolving intelligence at the same time within the same star system, a theory worth considering."

Raanax gave up. "All right, all right. There is something going on, however, that is not accounted for by theory. Either we are ignoring obvious clues or inappropriately classifying a huge amount of our data. I want you to assign a higher order of probability to the possibility that these symbols come from more than one written language. We will also assume, for the duration of our test run, that there is more than one spoken language."

"Affirmative. How many written alphabets do you propose we assume, for test purposes?"

"It is probably going to be two, but for test purposes, assume four alphabets and eliminate as necessary."

"Program accepted. The statistical universe necessary to construct for a valid test of current parameters will take approximately one hour."

••✦••

Fifty-five minutes later, the core broke into a conversation Raanax was having with an irate crew member, who took it personally that his rank was so low the core had refused to respond to him for the last two days.

"Hypotheses confirmed. Two separate alphabets are in

general use. Both are composed of abstract symbols. The pictographic symbols do not appear to be a language per se. They are instead concept shortcuts that play a supporting role within the parent languages. Fragments of other alphabet groupings have also been discovered, although they do not appear to be in general usage. Also, there are indications that a large number of related dialects may turn out to be attached to each of the alphabets."

Raanax sat up straight, made a nervous lick of his muzzle, and asked, "What about word definition accuracy?"

"Word definition accuracy has risen to thirty-seven percent and shows every sign of being cross-correlatable throughout our entire database. Language models are now at saturation. True translation keys may be expected within twenty hours."

"We've done it!" Raanax's jubilation was beyond containing. He grasped the totally bewildered crew member by the ruff and worried him across the cabin and back again. Letting the annoyed fellow go, he was about to speak when *Defender*'s core interrupted with an announcement.

"This is a message to all personnel. The expedition commander is convening an all-captains meeting immediately. At the conclusion of the meeting, there will be a general announcement and discussion period. All captains, please report to a secure location and contact *Suppression of Discord* at this time."

Third of Base, Inquisitory Expedition Commander, Centein noble of a high clan—however others thought of him, he was definitely the Aranth on the spot. Raalma's emotions had run the gamut in the last two hours. Beginning with an impulse to blind panic, shading over into shocked calm, settling into quiet acceptance, he came to rest at a sort of elation at being in the focal point of history.

He had begun the voyage as the military and diplomatic commander of the expedition. The crews of his ships would understand his military orders and strategies well, almost instinctively perhaps. Combat abilities were not an issue. But would they understand and act efficiently while he engaged in ambassadorial posturing with yonder aliens? He did not think so.

So he had spent a good part of the yearlong voyage preparing the company for the possibility of peaceful contact. That they would fight well, he knew. By the end of the voyage, he knew they would also be capable of putting aside the rational xenophobia that every Aranth was born with and embrace the aliens, if he deemed it desirable to do so. Some of the assemblage was even eager for peaceful contact.

However, it appeared his efforts had been quite unnecessary. Raalma would never find out if he would have been a good diplomat to aliens. After all this time building optimistic goodwill toward them, he was going to have to turn around the sentiment he had created.

He would have a chance to find out how good he was as an aggression leader after all. The fact that he was a compromise choice for the council, not the best warrior leader available and not the most elevated in ruling caste, meant only that he would have to stretch to adequately fill either role. He was prepared to do his best, brilliantly.

The conference of captains had gone satisfactorily. He was confident they were with him, every one. Now, he was taking the unprecedented step of putting it to the crews, to see if they would stand behind him as well. He took his place on the bridge of *Suppression of Discord* and nodded. It was time.

Nine and a half thousand officers, scientists, and crew spread out over twenty-four ships were tied to the open comm line by twenty-four cores. This was to be an open conference, a true two-way dialogue between the mass of AranthChi and their expedition commander.

Raalma had chosen the bridge of his flagship to make his announcement so he could see some of his crew. Optical pick-ups relayed his image to every monitor in the fleet. He could be seen by all the complement, but he wanted to see the reactions of some of them in person.

As the two-tone attention note rang out, declaring the conference's beginning. Raanax waited with a certain amount of unease. His team, covering the language end of the alien investigation, had found no major surprises that he was aware of. He wasn't privy to the military findings of the optical or radio teams, but rumor control had given no hints of anything to cause the tumult he was witnessing now. The rumor mill was filled mostly with the wonder of the alien system and excitement at meeting its inhabitants.

Raalma stared intently into the monitors as he began to speak. "Officers, crew, specialists, and non-ratings, I greet you. Fellow members of our empire, I would speak with you." His posture became slightly more erect, and his ears twitched in a hint of humor.

"All of you listening to my voice, each of us on this expedition, have known that this journey to the very foothills of another civilization is an event so unique that history has recorded nothing similar in more than five thousand years. You have all worked hard, each in your own assigned way, to advance our understanding of these creatures. Within the last few days, our knowledge has increased eight-thousand-fold. Our grasp of the aliens' home system, technology, and even language has leapt forward like the sweep of a plains kitmonster across the savannah.

"We have almost come to know them well enough to take the next step, to enter their home and visit with them. We were almost ready to let them know of our existence, to place the knowledge of another space faring species into their collective consciousness. Some of you hoped we would find enough points of similarity to build a trusting relationship on. Some, perhaps, dreamed the aliens might someday join our civilization, making this meeting a truly incredible turn of the wheel of history."

Raalma was silent for a moment. When he spoke again, there was sadness in his voice, tinged with anger. "However, *we* have been incredibly naive. While we sat out here, preparing ourselves for first contact, the very action that we are studying for has become a sham. They know us already, it turns out—very well in fact."

The murmur of thousands of voices, all speaking at once, overwhelmed the system. Raanax howled in flat disbelief. "Not possible! Not possible! Core," he said. His voice dropped to a whisper. "Have the alien transmissions said anything that would imply they have knowledge of AranthChi?"

"A hard question to answer," the core whispered back. "If our interpolations of their educational shows are at all reliable, they seem to know and be in contact with many eights of alien species. However, these are all such stylized depictions, we have been categorizing them as mythological in nature, rather than fact-based. As for depictions of AranthChi, some images come close, but not very close."

Raalma was still speaking. "Most of you may not be aware of it, but four hours ago, this expedition was contacted by the High Council." The murmurs swelled and then quieted, a sigh as of a candle going out. "What I have learned is truly shocking. These aliens have been in secret contact with certain rebellious elements of our own people for a period of many years. It turns out, they have been supplying secret aid for the purpose of overthrowing of our civilization and humbling of our leadership."

The comm circuits swelled with hisses and roars as outrage spread through the assembled listeners. Raanax realized he was hearing the rattle of sabers being triggered in the collective consciousness of the assemblage. His ears were laid flat too, lips curled in a snarl, even as his scientist's mind cried out in protest. *So much to learn, so much we could teach them. And they us. Please let us have this chance....* But no, it was not to be. The commander was whipping them up, quite expertly, into a frenzy that could only end in the order to attack.

Raanax had no idea who was the stronger. Was it the aliens in their home system or the Aranth force on their doorstep? He realized with a sick feeling that however the battle went, there would be no winners on the alien side. Perhaps the expedition could be repulsed or even destroyed by yonder civilization. That would only delay the end. The AranthChi would pour more and more of their might into the aliens' home system until they had been crushed flat.

A thought perilously close to treason flitted across the scientist's mind. Was it even right for the AranthChi to attack these creatures? Couldn't it all be a mistake somehow? Even if the charges were true, did that mean that annihilation was the only sentence the aliens deserved? But these were thoughts spun from a scientist's mind, not from the mind of one who was sworn to race protection. His thoughts did not count.

The expedition commander waited patiently for the hubbub to die down. It took several minutes. Finally, he spoke. "By order of the High Council, we are charged with the mission to eliminate the alien threat. We will not stop until victory is ours and no more treachery is possible from these creatures. They have been declared race enemies and must be pursued to extinction. My brother Aranth, are you with me?"

This time the chorus of howls and screams seemed to go on forever. Finally, Raalma spoke again, over the continuing swell of sound. "Very well. Our orders, as protectors of the race, are clear. So important is this matter to all AranthChi, we have been given extraordinary largesse in the commission of our task. I am in receipt of the release codes for every ship of the fleet and intend to use them at this time.

"After this step, of course, there is no going back. Even if we succeed, we may never see home again. So, think well, but think quickly. Any ship that decides they are unable to continue in this grand undertaking will be detached and ordered home without prejudice."

The import of Raalma's last statement slashed through the assembled Aranth like a claw stroke. It became so quiet, it was as if nine thousand beings had forgotten how to breathe.

No ship in living memory had been given its weapons release code. The last time any ship had been code-released had been during the mid clans uprising over seven hundred years before. The mid clans' revolt had been a bloody and chaotic time for the empire. Somehow a number of codes had been ferreted out of the High Council's Secrets Locker. The result had been fearsome. Deep, deep fear was accorded to the loosing of Weapons Lock.

But now the High Council had sent release codes to the Inquisitory Expedition and proclaimed them race protectors. They were now given the keys to powers almost unimaginable for individuals to have in the tightly controlled society from which the Aranth sprang. It was a heavy responsibility, burdened with emotional freight so deep in the psyche that it almost touched being race memory. In the end, no ship's complement refused the uneasy honor.

It was time. The roll call began with *Suppression of Discord*. Raalma personally gave the release code to the core. Immediately, the ship's energy shields formed and began to intensify. Soon they reached a depth and level of coruscation unmatched by anything a living Aranth had ever seen. From this point on, the energy fields were always going to be up. To get in or out of the ship, more energy would have to be expended to create a temporary hole in the defense field.

Throughout the ship, massive relays closed, and new connections appeared and then sealed, so that the weapons systems were always charged. New weapons of incredible might came online from heretofore unknown "black" systems. They hummed with incalculable energies, became charged and remained charged.

Powerplant output rose, and continued to rise, until it peaked out and then sustained itself at levels past every red line in the manuals. The new readings scared the hell out of the power crew until someone noticed that they remained stable and no danger lights winked on any ready board. The chief engineer gulped at the fuel consumption readings, but there was nothing she could do about it. The ship was transforming itself into a creature she did not know and was impotent to affect.

Raalma knew in principle what was happening to his ship. He had both the military rank and enough nobility of birth to have been given instruction in secrets far beyond the common run. Even so, he had been unaware of some of the details the High Council had passed along with its instructions. This honor was truly a two-edged sword.

The council was handing him something far different from the powerful line ships he had previously commanded. Now he had the proverbial unstoppable force. Twelve times more power to the shields. Twelve times more power to the weapons. Twice the brute engine power. He could now safely drive his vessel through the outer layers of a star. He could command the destruction of an octal of planets, perhaps even split a gas giant in half.

The power consumption rose accordingly, of course. From a vessel with a hundred-year fuel supply, he was down to one twentieth of that. His ship now had an operational life of not over five years. There was no way to halt, or even effectively slow down, the massive energy drain into the new systems, and there was no way to refuel.

One of the modifications that had occurred to the ship made refueling possible only when all the power was gone and the ship was a floating hulk. The ship would literally have to be torn apart in a fully equipped shipyard to be made serviceable again.

The High Council had chosen well. He had five years to complete his mission and cover himself with glory. Alternatively, he could turn his force around right now and begin the drive back into AranthChi space. With his current might, none could stand against him. However, it would take close to a year to get back into the empire, and longer to get anywhere worth conquering. And with less than four years of operational life left in his vessels, he could never hold onto any territory he did take. Not to mention the fact that by the time he got back, half the fleet would be moved up and arrayed against him. They couldn't stop him, but they would slow him down at every turn.

In accepting the commission, he'd really had no choice but to follow through. He didn't even have the option of delaying the process of weapons release. It turned out that each ship's unique activation code depended on a time-derived formula based on the activation date of the ship in question. None of the codes in his possession would be good longer than fourteen hours from the moment of receipt.

He was content. If the job could be done in five years, he would do it. Who could know? It might take the whole five years. In that case, the rescue of his forces would be up to a grateful AranthChi civilization. He took a moment to enjoy the pride he felt in the Aranth he commanded. Then it was time, and he began to speak again.

One by one, the codes went out. One by one, twenty-four dull gray marbles transformed into multicolored coruscating balls, humming with the power to destabilize stars. Soon they shined like a new constellation in the heavens.

Orders were given. The force broke formation, and ship after ship disappeared into an overspace of supraluminal potentials. Left behind, imperceptibly bobbing and twisting in interstellar space, was the seven-kilometer super disc telescope. It looked quite forlorn. Its need was past, its usefulness over, its existence forgotten. It had fallen victim to the fact that it was just too much trouble to force the shields down and bring it back aboard.

The Inquisitory Expedition was no longer a reconnaissance force, or even a diplomatic mission. It was now a full-blown war party. This was a fleet, heading into battle with more force at its command than the AranthChi had assembled in one place in thrice a thousand years.

ALPHA CENTAURI: FIRST CONTACT

aboard the Paris Octavious

Outer System Traffic Control was a quiet, contemplative job most of the time. Distances were so vast in a multiple star system that patience was a virtue. Clarence Yarrow, senior communications and traffic monitor for the second shift at Sistra Control, sat with easy grace in one of four operator's seats in a room filled with monitors and consoles.

He was alone, as his partner and the junior member of his shift had both called in sick at 2300. A quick glance at the situation screen showed it was a quiet night, so he decided there was no need to call in an off-shifter to cover the boards. *I'll suffer in silence. No one even knows it's my birthday.*

His physical location was C Deck of the commercial space station *Paris Octavious*. Originally a low-orbit research facility, *Paris Octavious* had been enlarged and moved out to a comfortable geo-stationary orbit thirty-six thousand kilometers above Sistra's equatorial continent.

It was a great place to turn forty-one. *Paris Octavious* was a grand old lady with parts of the hub turning two hundred this year. The station was spacious, well-designed, and home to several government bureaus including Outer and Inner System Traffic Control.

At the moment, Yarrow was lounging in his chair, feeling sorry for himself, and absently popping roasted peanuts into his mouth. He assayed a sip of soft drink out of a pressurized container. Since time immemorial, space stations had been built flimsy and light. The standard high-O^2 low-psi atmosphere made carbonated drinks go flat in a blink and open-flame cooking an extreme oddity.

Fortunately, *Paris Octavious* had been built with a rotating outer ring for living quarters and offices. Outer System Traffic Control occupied a portion of C Deck, only three rings in from vacuum. The gravity was nearly one-half Earth normal. Yarrow didn't have to worry about chasing peanuts with a net. There was also pure luxury in sprawling in a chair rather than floating in front of a console, as he would have been doing down in the original control room at the hub.

In front of him, the central monitor screen showed the status of his eyes in the sky. Eighteen hundred-centimeter and six two-hundred-centimeter telescopes, set on twelve instrument platforms, covered the entire system. Six platforms preceded Sistra in its orbit, with the farthest sixty degrees ahead and six trailed up to sixty degrees behind the planet. With a 120-degree arc through the plane of the ecliptic, no place in the Centauri system was hidden from Traffic Control.

At just after 0100 hours, scope nineteen performed its routine twice-hourly position check on outbound freighter *Justine Tupello*, Mars Registry. The *Tupello* was just where the computer expected her to be. There was, however, something more. The computer flagged a background anomaly in the starscape of the constellation Bootes, which the freighter was then transiting.

A new star had appeared, of fourth magnitude or dimmer. Investigation algorithms always assumed that anything new registering in the starfield was, in fact, inside the system. The computer's job was to rule out local space possibilities before declaring that something to be a celestial object.

Automatic spectral analysis made the computer reject the assumption that it was watching a fusion drive-in operation, so it did not immediately classify the anomaly as a ship. Spectral lines also did not fit any known star in that part of the sky. Even assuming a stellar event like the nova of a sun previously too dim to see with the current scope, the computer could not make the spectral lines fit.

The phenomenon was flagged for priority review and sent to the duty operator's board, which emitted the anomaly alarm. At least it was a quieter sound than the collision alert, which thankfully had not gone off once in the seven years Yarrow had been a senior controller.

Punching up the data and enhanced view from scope nineteen, Yarrow did not find the anomaly very impressive. However, he watched closely as the automatic analysis proceeded. The spectral lines were a mess, he noted. Nothing like the spectrum of a main sequence star, and there was no match with any object recorded in the astronomy banks.

Second order analysis included conjectures in descending order of probability. One caught Yarrow's attention. The computer asked: Could the image found in scope nineteen's starfield be the distorted reflection of a nearby sun, either Alpha or Beta?

Yarrow grunted. *Where in hell would a mirror surface come from that's big enough and bright enough to show a star-like reflection?* The idea was absurd. Even the computer was unable to assign a probability to the conjecture. It did, however, recommend a parallax view, an idea that Yarrow immediately endorsed.

Clarence selected scope four, a two-hundred-centimeter scope on a platform leading the planet by forty degrees. He waited out the lightspeed lag while it received its instructions and then hunted through its memorized coordinates for the portion of the sky that included the constellation Bootes. Suddenly, the scope locked and began reporting the same anomaly. The computer quickly ran through a real-time analysis of the new data and decided the anomaly was moving.

Moving! "Oh shit," breathed Yarrow. "It's a contact."

"Contact" was the oldest term Yarrow knew for an object proved real and not just a ghost in the machine. If the object was moving in relation to the almost motionless starscape, it was either near or in the Centauri group system.

"What are you, baby?" Yarrow hummed as he watched the computer determine the position and heading. Did it pose a threat to shipping, beginning with the *Justine Tupello*? Was it on a collision course with an inhabited body, moon, or asteroid? Was it headed for the inner system? Needless to say, Yarrow was no longer bored.

It would have been nice to know what it was and where it came from, but those weren't questions that Yarrow could answer with the equipment at his fingertips. That wasn't his job, anyway. Protecting shipping was his function, and he was good at it. Perhaps the astronomers could determine what the object was. More likely, System Patrol would have to launch a mission to make rendezvous with the mystery body to really be sure. Of course, it all depended on how fast the object was going and how much of the system it would transit before returning to interstellar space.

It never occurred to Yarrow that the object might be in a controlled trajectory, but he kept both scopes on it while he wrote the contact up in his log. When the computer reported a few minutes later that the object had made an apparent course change, Yarrow said, "Oh shit," again. It was all he could think of to say, and he whispered it, more like a prayer than an obscenity.

A course change implied a ship, or at any rate, something guided by intelligence. It wasn't a Human ship. No known Human ship shined with its own light. Also, no Human ship would enter an inhabited system without hailing Traffic Control. Penalties for that transgression began with confiscation of ship and cargo, and continued with long prison terms for the master and crew. Human merchants did not come that foolish.

It wasn't a naval vessel, either. Navy InSystem Control would have updated Sistra Traffic long ago, clearing any naval vessel's flight path with civilian authorities. Even an experimental "black project" ship would have filed a flight plan.

There was no way around it: the anomaly could only be an alien vessel. Yarrow wished he weren't alone in the control room. He felt the fear that every sentry guarding a medieval town wall ever felt, the fear that every scout experienced on seeing dust rising on the horizon from a distant army, the fear that every radar operator got when seeing a swarm of unidentified blips on his plot where no blips should be.

Stay calm. You can do this. He blew out his breath noisily and continued with his analysis. There was no time to listen to the irrational places deep within him. His fingers automatically keyed the supervisor's emergency recall. He would never remember later having done so.

In a short time, the door opened. His supervisor entered the room and sat down quietly at the console next to his. Sandy Brodsky was forty-two years old and had done Yarrow's job for nine years before being promoted to outer system traffic manager. She had no trouble reading his board without disturbing his concentration.

She saw with surprise that the object, or ship, or whatever it was, had an estimated velocity of eighteen thousand kilometers a second, nearly six percent of the speed of light. It was due to pass closely by Tarnball, the system's largest gas giant, in just under four hours.

Tarnball, a muddy brown and white orb, had a family of seventeen moons, four of which were Titan-sized. Twelve had permanent or semi-permanent habitations. Tarnball had the largest concentration of population off Sistra, rivaled only by the much more spread-out asteroid colonies.

The object was cutting a shallow angle across the outer system. It was already significantly inside the orbit of Punk, the rocky, airless, outermost planet. Punk, as luck would have it, was currently on the other side of the sun from Tarnball.

"Any change in the last five minutes?" Her words startled Yarrow slightly.

"No. I flagged you immediately after the course change registered. I've just been refining course and speed while waiting for you to arrive."

"Very well. I'll put in a call to the navy. You contact all Tarnball-bound traffic and warn them. Did you get off a warning to Tarnball Local Traffic Control?"

"Yes. All relevant details on location, course, and speed have been coded." He touched a contact on his console. "Going to message laser now. You realize it will take almost six hours to get there? About two hours late, if their visitor doesn't slow down as it goes by."

Sandy nodded distractedly, her mind on the coming conversation with the navy. "Oh, by the way, I have a call out to the morning shift to come in right now. As soon as they arrive, put them to work, will you?"

Yarrow finally turned away from the screen to power up the other consoles. He paused, startled, because Sandy Brodsky was dressed only in a short white bathrobe and slippers. Yarrow's supervisor had very nice legs, a fact that he had never been fully aware of. He continued the power up, wishing vaguely that his brain would stop spinning long enough for him to appreciate the view. The very worried look on Sandy's attractive face somehow had the most impact on his senses.

A moment later, Sandy was talking to Communications Command, the navy's traffic monitoring service for INSYSCON. The operator, a young-faced lieutenant, accepted the infosquirt to his situation board with a calmness that bordered on blasé.

Sandy gritted her teeth. She hoped his absence of reaction was the result of professionalism. She did not want to deal with someone whose lack of understanding could be so profound. Worse yet was the sneaking suspicion that he simply did not believe her.

Suddenly his eyes widened, and he blurted out, "It's not the same bogey!"

Now he was showing all the reaction Sandy could have hoped for, and she was sorry to see it. "What do you mean, 'It's not the same bogey'? It's not the same bogey as what?"

"Uh . . . ma'am, we've been tracking a contact on the deep space network for several hours. But that bogey is slowing down, apparently taking station ninety degrees below the ecliptic. It's not entering the system at all."

Suddenly realizing he'd said too much, he reached for his board. "Please stand by," he said, and his face disappeared. In his place appeared the words *STAND BY* accompanied by a background of slowly rotating stars.

Very shortly, another face appeared. The gray at his temples was slightly more reassuring. "This is Commander Thompson, officer of the watch. Who am I speaking to at Sistra Traffic Control?"

"Hello, commander. I am Sandra Brodsky, assistant administrator of the *Paris Octavious* facility and outer system traffic manager. We have an unknown ship on our scopes, inside the system, heading for Tarnball. Are you aware of this?"

"No, ma'am, we were not aware of it, but we are getting on it right now. Thank you for the infoalert. Do you have any other information for us at this time?"

"Commander," Sandy said with exasperation, "tell me about the other 'bogey.'"

She was greeted by silence, so she pressed on. "Commander Thompson, the civilian authorities have a right to know what's going on. We have commercial shipping to protect. I can't do that if I'm kept in the dark. Our mystery ship will reach Tarnball in less than four hours. I ask you again, what is this about another ship? Please tell me the situation."

Commander Thompson looked like a man who had bitten into something and found it very sour. He spoke quickly, regardless. "Administrator Brodsky, I do not want you to gain the impression that I am being uncooperative. Indeed, an announcement to the planetary government is even now being readied, at the admiralty level. You would no doubt hear the information through your own chain of command."

He made a gesture off to the side. The pickup muted and he talked for a moment to someone at his end. Then his attention returned to the screen and the sound resumed.

"The navy went to Alert Status Two approximately one hour ago. At this time, I am invoking my contingency authority, placing us on Status Three. This mobilizes all active and reserve units in the Centauri system. There is a mission being formed to make rendezvous with the ship outside the system. Now these plans *must* be modified, perhaps drastically."

Sandy groped for her next question, but the commander didn't give her a chance to speak. "Administrator Brodsky, your information has been extremely valuable. I am embarrassed to admit we didn't think to contact you first. From now on, however, your help is going to be crucial to our effort."

Now Sandy had her voice back. "Of course. We'll give you whatever help we can."

"Good. I require the complete resources of your tracking network to scrutinize near space out to the Oort zone. You will coordinate with Communications Command to alert all civilian shipping to be on the lookout for alien activity and to report the same immediately.

"We will issue periodic bulletins and probably order routing changes to civilian ships. I will detach an officer to be your liaison as soon as possible. Until one can make connection with the *Paris Octavious* facility, we will have to make do with the comm link. Do you have any questions?"

Sandy Brodsky had been listening to the InSystem Control officer with growing amazement. Her first words came out an indignant squeak. "Commander, I said we would help, not that we would do your job for you." She was half-raised from her seat, and she sat down with a low-gravity *thump*. "You may not realize we have a full traffic schedule right now. Twelve of my scopes are committed to tracking inbounds and outbounds. We are talking about a lot of lives and commerce here. Twelve is half our capacity, and they are committed! For a few hours, I could give you access to the other twelve plus computer time to run them, but then I am going to need them back."

"Administrator, perhaps I wasn't clear. We need all of your assistance, and we need it now. The Centauri system may be under attack, and I am calling on all civilian authorities to lend maximum aid."

"Commander Thompson, I don't care what you're calling on. You can call on a higher power, for all I care. My people are currently tracking thirty-six ships. In another two hours, Inner System Traffic is scheduled to hand off two more. Plus we are already following one of your bogeys for you. Add to that the usual junk and debris we keep track of, and you can see our plate is pretty full. Twelve scopes *are* all I can give you. Twelve is all you're going to get."

The man from Communications Command wiped his forehead. He was probably thinking, *Pigheaded civilian*. His brief scowl morphed into a determined look.

"Ma'am, we are facing a potential system crisis here. I will take the resources you've offered me. However, I want the other twelve scopes as well. May I remind you I can have my boss on the phone to the planetary governor in less than five minutes? I can get those scopes the hard way, if I have to."

"Well, bully for you." *Jerk*. "When the governor calls, he better be ready to replace me, for I will not agree to endanger my charges."

While this heated exchange was going on, Yarrow had been busy. Now he frantically waved at his boss from off-screen. He knew why Sandy was hopping mad at the commander. This was one protective lady, and she was reacting with all the fervor of a mother bear shielding her cubs.

Unfortunately, she didn't have all the facts. She obviously didn't understand the commander's extraordinary move to Alert Status Three. Her problem came from having been a civilian all her life. Yarrow, with a background of six years in System Patrol, understood the commander much better.

As long as the navy held at Alert Status Two, most everyday operations continued as they normally would. Massive unit mobilization was unlikely, and engagement rules were strict. Alert Status Three allowed the unlocking of heavy weapons depots and the distribution of firing "keys" to officers on all active military vessels. Specific engagement orders were sure to follow.

Traffic Control had abilities and resources that the navy needed "right now," and the safety of everybody might depend on their cooperation. Besides, Yarrow did not want to see Sandy lose her job over an issue she didn't need to be fighting about.

Finally, he got her attention. He directed it to the board in front of her, where he posted the message:

> ALL TRAFFIC IN CLEAR TRAJECTORIES NEXT 18 HRS// NO COURSE CHANGES SCHEDULED; CAN COVER WITH 4 SCOPES TILL THEN// INNER SYSTEM CAN RETAIN CONTROL NEW TRAFFIC ADDITIONAL 12 HRS -SAFETY FACTOR ACCEPTABLE.

The message ended with the *commit?* query flashing.

Sandy took a deep breath, looked at Yarrow, and nodded. Squaring her shoulders, she faced the navy man. It took a second to smooth out her face, and to her credit, she managed not to grit her teeth. The commander watched quizzically.

"Commander Thompson, I do understand the urgency of your *request*." She spit the word out resentfully. "One of my staff has just finished a full system review, and I have approved an emergency shifting of priorities. As of this moment, I am freeing up twenty scopes for the system-wide search you require. Your people will be coordinating with Senior Traffic Controller Yarrow. Please see to it that we also have free access to the information from your deep space net, so as not to duplicate our efforts."

"Thank you, administrator. I shall do so immediately."

Thompson had started to switch off when Sandy spoke again. "Commander?"

"Yes?"

"We are alerting Tarnball Local, Eveita Local, Zeus Local, and the Swarm Web by Message Laser. They will come online at various intervals, but the soonest response will come from the asteroid belts." She hesitated, then went on. "I don't quite know what to tell them. They will want to know *whose* ships they are looking for. Do you know?"

Commander Thompson's shrug was the tiniest ghost of a movement. "These ships are *officially* unknown at this time. They are *officially* non-hostile at this time. However, I only know of one alien race with spaceships. I also remember my schoolboy history." He frowned again. "For now . . . tell them whatever you wish without being an alarmist. Just get them looking."

Now he did fade out, to be replaced by the lieutenant Sandy had first talked to. She stared at his image, unseeing, for a time. Finally, he cleared his throat. "Ma'am? I am ready to interface with Controller Yarrow now."

Yarrow switched the signal to his board, leaving his supervisor to gather her dark, sad thoughts. The last thing Sandy heard as the hush function cut in was the lieutenant saying a new bogey had been reported by the Southern Oort relay.

"And now we are three." It was a murmur so soft she wasn't sure if she had spoken it, or if it were perhaps just an echo in her thoughts. She placed her head in her hands and rocked herself gently in the chair. It helped, a little.

••✦••

four hours later: situation room, Centauri Base, on the main continent

The senior representatives of the navy, System Patrol, and the government sat, piecing the information together. So far, the count was nineteen bogeys. Four were entering station-keeping positions outside the system, while the rest were headed for flybys, or perhaps rendezvous, with the three inhabited gas giants and the myriad asteroid habitations. No ships had been spotted heading for the inner system yet, which was no comfort to the military, since they were sure a major attack was underway.

A successful attack would, they felt, certainly include incursions into the inner system, perhaps to Sistra itself. The solid tug of gravity reminded them of the constancy they associated with Sistra, the Earth-like, almost paradisiacal heartland of the system. The silent, menacing movements of an unknown agency forced them to remember how beautiful and fragile their world was, and how precious to the Federation was Alpha Centauri Colony, mankind's oldest and most prosperous extrasolar home.

Propagating at the speed of light, warnings and orders crisscrossed the system. The warnings would reach some outlying System Patrol bases, naval units, and civilian habitations before their visitors arrived, though the margin was small. For others, like the twelve inhabited moons of Tarnball, their alien ship would arrive before the message. In these cases, if the intent of the unknown visitors was benign, all would be well. If not . . . the answer could come at tragic cost to the Human lives in the visitor's paths.

Now, four hours and thirty-one minutes into the system-wide alert, Admiral Dachman threw open the meeting to the rest of the coordination team. "It's time for ideas, people. Bogey number two has been decelerating at an enormous rate and will make rendezvous somewhere in the Tarnball family of satellites. If their destination is Minos, they will make moonfall in an hour. I repeat: this is no flyby; there will be a rendezvous. And in six hours, we'll know what happened."

The governor's representative, a bluff, hardy individual with a ruddy face and deeply tanned skin, waved for attention. He was an agronomist by training, a gentleman farmer. Politics was just an expensive hobby for him. He had been shrewd enough to back the right candidate for governor and been rewarded for it by an appointment to the Defense Liaison Committee.

Until today, he had considered the committee a sinecure, as had the governor, no doubt. Perhaps because Jasson Pearls thought the committee a nothing job, his contacts with the two military men had previously been less then cordial. Now he was being called on to make decisions, to do something in a time of genuine crisis. He was clearly frightened and out of his depth.

"Can the military defend us, admiral? How many fleets can you surround Sistra with? When will Earth send us more help?"

"We do have some options, Mr. Pearls. You're right, of course: Earth has to be warned." Though he had said nothing of the sort, the governor's man looked pleased.

"Our current resources are quite strong. Not only do we have the Centauri-based home fleet to call on, units of the Federation's Rapid Deployment Force are in Beta System on a training tour. The alert is going out to them as well. We can expect a response from the RDF within twenty-four hours. However, there is more we should do right now, just in case the situation worsens."

"Obviously, you have something in mind," the governor's representative said. His tone was demanding and truculent.

"Indeed I have," said Admiral Dachman. "I want to use civilian shipping in the most expeditious manner for this situation."

"What do you mean?"

"As of this moment, I want to declare the Alpha System an interdiction zone. I want all incoming traffic warned off, told to return to Earth, or their last stop, if they have the fuel for it. Additionally, I want all outgoing ships to make directly for Earth. I intend to send continuous updates to them right up until they reach their FTL departure points. This way, Earth gets a running report, current as to the last time a ship successfully jumps."

"Do you realize what you are saying, man?" The ruddy face of the governor's rep blanched. "Turn away commerce? That will play havoc with our whole economy!"

The admiral smiled. "A moment ago, you were worried these unknown aliens might blow holes in your precious farmland, and you wanted help real quick. You can't have it both ways, Mr. Pearls."

Now Admiral Dachman frowned. "What worries me more is how long will it take the first ships to actually get out of the system, and then how long it will take for Earth respond to our warning. Even sending authentication codes along with the dispatches, our situation is going to take some time to be believed and acted upon."

The System Patrol commandant had been quiet up to this point. Now he called up the ship movement schematic on his datapad and looked at it again. "In forty hours, the liner *Tinuvel* will reach its FTL point. Destination: Procylon. Of course we will divert it to Earth." Still reading in his gravelly voice, he said, "In forty-two hours, the *Justine Tupello* makes FTL, and then the *Princess of Mars*. At sixty hours, the Federation Scout *Newton* goes. Now the *Newton* can mount twelve Gs of thrust, as I recall, which means it could trim at least ten hours off its jump point time. However, that still leaves us a minimum of forty hours from right now if we go with ships already leaving the system. It is iffy, but one or two of the inbounds might get back to FTL points in the same forty- to fifty-hour time frame. I take it you have a problem with that."

"Succinctly put, if a trifle understated," agreed Admiral Dachman. "You know why the navy is worried, and you're worried as hell too, for the same reason. We have unknown ships diving into our system at speeds in excess of six percent of light and others taking up station in the Oort zone. We don't know if our ships will even be allowed to leave. If the alien force takes to shooting down outgoing traffic, we may never get a message to Earth in time to do us any good."

"Then I suppose you are suggesting we go with our second option?"

"What option is that?"

The System Patrol commander turned his datapad around so the admiral could see it and tapped the screen. "This option. You already have an FTL capable resource in position to make a quick run to jump distance. Unless my math is off, it can be on its way to Earth less than eight hours from receipt of orders. And, if it has to fight its way out of the system, it can do that too."

The admiral looked closely at the listing next to the commandant's blunt finger. It concerned a ship near the outermost real estate of the system. His frown was made of thunderheads and lightning. The datapad should have died. He gazed back at the commandant.

"The *Aswan* is a Corvette-class fighting ship, Ralph."

"I know."

"I knew *Aswan* was around Punk doing maintenance on the deep space monitor relay there. All classes of naval ships do retrieval and repair during training runs. And yes, she can pull an excess of ten Gs for extended periods, but *damn it*, man, she's needed here."

"You wanted a ship that could make it to Earth. There she

is. No vessel of the Unidentified Forces is within a hundred million kilometers of her. You have to send her, Hans."

The admiral nodded reluctantly. The Corvette was a valuable asset. She carried long-range nuclear missiles; drone-launched, Frypak-bomb-pumped X-ray laser pods; and an armed, atmosphere-rated shuttle. Not a resource to give up lightly. Still, she was the only ship completely in the clear, and the message had to go out.

Admiral Dachman turned to an aide and barked at the man. "Captain, I want a be-damned, constant data link to the *Aswan* as of this moment. Order the Corvette to make all speed to an FTL point. She is to hold for permission to jump, unless she finds herself engaged in active combat." He sighed heavily.

The other old warrior slapped him lightly on the shoulder with a big, square hand. "It was the right choice, my friend. Just be glad that wasn't a Cruiser in orbit around Punk. It would have been that much harder to send away an asset with it its own deployable screen of in-system fighters. Now on with business, yes?"

••✦••

aboard Tarnball One

Lydia Komenek and Rick Berquist, pilot and rescue specialist respectively, dozed in unison. This could have been the sign of a good team or a tired team. They were both. They were floating loosely in their seats aboard System Patrol Vessel number 063, known locally as Tarnball One.

Tarnball One sat "hot," fully fueled and with all systems powered, fed from an umbilical built into their special purpose dock. Tarnball Patrol station was a rescue facility sunk into a moonlet so small it was little more than a flying mountain.

They were on standby, ready to launch within minutes of a

reported distressed ship or settlement emergency. They should not have been "hot" at all, since they were only four hours back from a routine rescue mission to an ore handling station with a breached deck. That one had been both repair and ambulance run, lasting better than twenty hours on the mission clock.

However, one of Tarnball's patrol ships had to be "hot" continuously, and when Tarnball Two developed computer problems, they found themselves up again with only about three hours of sleep. It was not amusing to know that TB Three and Four were receiving annually mandated maintenance and would probably come back online just in time for the team to have spent a whole wasted shift at the ten-minute launch hold point.

Periodically, Lydia would tune in to the running background chatter as one semi-intelligent system after another reported its condition aloud. She liked to set up a low audio when she was tired, because she could drift into a twilight place of dreamy contemplation and still know, through trained mnemonics, the condition of every system onboard her ship instantly.

Lydia loved this ship. It was her first command, so she took herself and her duties very seriously. Her squat, powerful vessel would never be called beautiful except by those in trouble, but as an angel of mercy, she considered it first rate.

TB One was muscular, with engines powerful enough to land and takeoff from a Mars-rated world. She had magnetic grapples and extrudable bumpers to push or tow stranded spacecraft. She had a host of deployable grabbers, waldos, and nozzles to fight fire, pour ferroconcrete, or place injection-molded plastic girders and panels of every conceivable shape and size. Struts, patches, and even airlocks could be fashioned in her machine shop. Whatever the job turned out to be, she was the ship for it.

Suddenly the radio came to life. "Lydia, Rick, we have a situation on Minos." The voice of dispatcher Arnold Waterman was shaken. "We have a report of pressure loss in the North City warrens and then an interruption of transmission. Minos traffic then reported a flurry of radio distress calls, strange reports of very bright light, seismic activity from outlying habitations—and then silence from the whole area."

Lydia was completely awake before Arnold had stopped talking. Rick was already activating a pull-down display of the moon in question. Minos was a heavily populated body and the biggest of Tarnball's inhabited moons. It was also pretty far out. The climb to Minos's orbit was Lydia's job, but rescue was Rick's. North City and its outlying districts occupied more than twenty square klicks of multi-level warrens and pressure domes. An event that could make the whole area go silent had to be very big.

"We are computing a launch burn for twelve minutes from now. You're getting a full rescue team on this one."

"Roger," was Lydia's one-word reply.

The computer advised upload of course parameters, and Lydia hit the *commit* button. The umbilical automatically disconnected and retracted from the bay. All systems reported operational on internal power.

At minus eight minutes, extra space armor, sleds, and EVA supplies began going into the holds. At minus four minutes, the search and rescue team came onboard. At minus two minutes, everyone was strapped in and the ship was buttoned up. At minus four seconds, the main engines came to life and Tarnball One, complete with nine rescuers, pulled away from the station and climbed rapidly toward the orbit of Minos.

Lydia fiddled with her board for a moment. Tarnball One continued accelerating smoothly, occupants becoming perceptively heavier as the seconds ticked by. "We have a good window to Minos," she announced. "We reach orbit in forty minutes and make rendezvous with the moon in another sixteen. However, it's going to be three Gs all the way, so you all might as well sit back and enjoy the ride."

"Will this be another of your famous express deliveries, Lyd?" came a voice from one of the back seats.

"You better believe it. We will be over North City in fifty-six minutes and one second, or I'll resign my title as the Comet Express Queen."

Acceleration forces were passing the two-G mark, and casual conversation was becoming difficult. However; "Any good ideas about what's caused the problem in North City?" asked one of the rescue team. "My vote is meteorite impact."

"What, nobody saw it coming?" The second voice was disbelieving.

"It could have been a ship crash." A third voice had entered the conversation. "Remember the yacht that crashed into Delos field twenty years ago? It left a big hole in the ground and ruptured domes across the valley by groundshock."

"So what about the bright light reported by Minos traffic?"

"By god, it could have been a fusion plant going up!"

"You guys are really cheerful," grunted Rick. "Keep thinking, though. This problem, whatever it is, seems to be spreading."

A chorus of silence greeted his remark.

"What I mean is, Minos Traffic went off the air a few minutes ago with no explanation. Our dispatcher can't reach them, and they're not responding to any other hails either. Arnold tells me TB Three and Four have been pulled off maintenance schedule and are being loaded and buttoned now. They plan to launch at the top of the hour."

"Holy shit," someone murmured. Everyone else let the comment stand. The next forty minutes passed in silence. Some used their chair comps to review training or rescue strategies, others just sat and thought.

••✦••

Tarnball One had been slowing all through the final arc onto Minos's approach, backing into its tail of fire as it came.

Finally, the drive faded to a whisper and ceased. Lydia was as good as her word. They were dead on over the North Pole. Within seconds, North City came slowly into view as the landscape rotated beneath them. With all sensor and camera arrays deployed, they searched for indications of trouble. These were not long in coming.

The scene that awaited them was both perplexing and horrible. It was too big to take in at once. The ground seemed stirred, as if by a giant hand. Lava had flowed recently, congealing into fantastic shapes. Such activity was something that had been unknown on the face of Minos for geological ages. Deep holes were bored into the crust, and lakes of molten stone could be seen at their bottoms. A thin fog of vapor hugged the terrain on a world that should have been airless.

No surface structures had survived. Much of North City consisted of warrens nestled tens of meters beneath a cap of stone and dust, yet it seemed unlikely to the viewers that any of the environmental areas could have escaped the devastation.

Rick Berquist's face was purple with disbelief. Others reacted with cries of pain or anguish. "What the hell happened here?" Rick shouted.

No one had an answer. As North City disappeared behind them, Lydia made a minor course correction. All eyes went to her. "There's no reason to go back and land. We couldn't help those poor people if we tried. In four minutes, we'll be coming up on Mainport. We should be able to see what's happened to the spaceport and Minos Traffic Control." She stared them down. "We go on," she said firmly. As she turned to her board, a tear threatened to run down her cheek. Desperately, she willed it to stay put.

Soon Mainport came into view, and they were looking at a virtual replay of the devastation that had been North City. Again, no structures had withstood the forces brought to bear. An even wider area of destruction spread out to the horizon. New arroyos had appeared in a blacklit, airless flood plain. Fantastic, carven shapes of basalt reared, and regolith threatened to tumble into canyons gone mad with the pulse of heat and hoar. If Human foot had ever trod here, no evidence remained.

With a sob, Lydia took the controls off automatic all together. "Can you find anyone sending on this planet?"

Rick shook his head. "No signals on the assigned frequencies . . . and no emergency transponder is sending anywhere on this side of Minos."

Lydia nodded. "On this pass, the base was going to be behind the gas giant. We need a relay and fast. Rick, please find us a working commsat and hurry."

As Berquist queried the computer for lines of sight to broadcasting satellite relays, Lydia set a course from memory and engaged the drive. She appeared to be watching every control and readout simultaneously. So intense was her concentration that when she snapped out the acceleration warning, Rick was startled. He assumed she had forgotten anyone else was aboard.

In short order, he had the link established. The nearest commsat had been unresponsive to hails, but the next in line was functioning. Soon he had raised Tarnball Patrol Base.

Lydia took the comm. "Tarnball Base, this is TB One. I am declaring a Red Alert; I repeat, Red Alert. Minos has suffered a deliberate attack by parties unknown. Attack is by weapons unknown. We find no sign of survivors at North City. We find no survivors at Mainport. Minos Traffic Control is off the air because it no longer exists. Do you read me, Arnold?"

Arnold Waterman's reply was crisp and professional. "I read you, TB One. We are now going to Emergency Status."

"Roger, Tarnball Base. Stand by for telemetry."

When the squirt transmission of camera and sensor reads had finished, there was silence for a few seconds. Then Arnold Waterman came back online. There were sounds of commotion in the background that his throat mike did not completely screen out.

"Jesus, Lydia, what the bloody hell happened there? And what is your condition, TB One?"

"We're fine, Arnold, just a little shook up."

Rick Berquist took the comm. "We don't think it was nukes. Even though there are holes in the ground, they aren't craters. No material splash. Also, there is very little increase in background radiation. It must have been some sort of an energy weapon. Either one fuck of a big particle beam or a brutally big laser."

He cocked his head toward Lydia, and she nodded. He continued, "Base, we intend one complete high orbital sweep, at this point, just looking for clues. Then we are returning with all deliberate speed, unless you have other orders for us."

"TB One, we launched Tarnball Three and Four about fifteen minutes ago."

"Call them back," said Lydia. "We don't need them here for rescue work, and I don't think they're appropriately equipped to deal with the situation." Tears had streaked her face; now anger toughened it. Arnold heard it in her voice.

"Roger: return, soonest. We'll get the word out on the traffic and homestead channels. A general announcement and call for any and all possible sightings of the attackers is going out now."

••✦••

situation room, System Patrol Base Tarnball

Tarnball Base Rescue Patrol Crafts Three and Four were immediately recalled on the strength of TB One's declaration of emergency. TB Five's countdown was halted, and the digging equipment so recently put aboard was off-loaded.

Now, the base commander had a problem. Several problems, actually, with very limited options. System Patrol existed for two purposes. Most of the time, it served as safety inspector and rescue specialist. However, the patrol also had broad police powers and jurisdiction anywhere off Sistra. It would, on occasion, board ships in flight to make arrests or impound cargoes. Therefore, System Patrol ships could be equipped with the weaponry to enforce the law upon civilian shipping—the key word being "civilian."

Whoever the marauder was that carried out the senseless attacks on the communities of Minos was sure to be better armed than civilian craft. They might even be in possession of military grade ordinance. The attackers certainly had something extremely destructive. The commander had no reason to suppose the weapon couldn't be used against a ship as easily as it had a settlement.

Being the police authority among Tarnball's family of satellites meant it was up to the Patrol to try and track the criminals—hopefully before they struck again, assuming there was an "again." After tracking the culprits down, the Patrol needed to arrest or neutralize them.

This was one of the big problems. The commander had five tiny ships and a tremendous volume of space to search. He wondered if he should scatter his ships in five directions while waiting for a sighting to come in, hoping that one of his ships would be close enough to make contact with the outlaw. Even if that worked, would one patrol vessel be enough to subdue the attacker?

He thought that perhaps he should keep his ships together in fleet formation, abandoning any sort of plan to provide protection to the rest of Tarnball's inhabited moons and assorted stations—or maybe just wait until another tragedy occurred and then try to move in.

Neither of the options was palatable. It was time to review the events thus far and hope to get new ideas. Two hours and twelve minutes before, North City had reported pressure loss and asked for disaster relief. Fifteen minutes later, Tarnball

Traffic Control had gone off the air. By now, everyone in Tarnball's orbit knew there was a major emergency occurring on Minos.

Both Evita and Zeus were less than two light hours away this particular time of year, since the gas giants were undergoing a very rare grand alignment. Both of their Traffic Controls would know by now that Tarnball Traffic was down and there was some sort of trouble. In another four hours, Sistra would also notice.

In the meantime, the commander's little force of ships was it, until help could be requested from other patrol bases. A condensed report was already on the way to Patrol HQ by message laser. Sistra would not be able to help them for many hours, though.

There was also a big naval base at Astrid. They were closer, but close was relative. Five hundred million kilometers sunward was still a long way in. If the navy did commit ships from its asteroid base, even they would not arrive for days.

However, there was one way the navy could be a big help. On the backside of the tiny chunk of flying real estate the Patrol used for a base was a bunker, a major weapons depot set up for naval resupply in times of crisis. If the commander of Astrid could get permission to give the Patrol access to the bunker, one problem would be neatly solved.

Astrid Base was twenty light minutes deeper in system, and such a request might have to be cleared even further in. The commander would ask, but he was not inclined to wait out what could possibly be a several-hour process. Instead, he ordered TB Five to be equipped with the standard Patrol ordinance weapon, the Bren Anti-Ship Missile.

The Bren was a three-hundred-meter-per-second delta V bird, with a forty-minute boost tank and a proximity-fused, hundred-kiloton warhead. Four of them could be mounted on the firing rack of the size ship Tarnball's commander had available. It was a good missile, very smart, but fairly puny. At most, he could expect them to be effective against some type of converted civilian craft. If he was facing a privateer with hijacked military technology—or worse, a full-fledged rogue warship—he was in big trouble.

Delos fell victim next. This time, the attacker was seen on approach, and the alarm went out immediately. Several ships successfully lifted off from the communities under attack. They were completely ignored. One unknown hero chose to ram. They were also ignored. The only result was a rain of wreckage returning to the ground.

A fleeing cargo lifter had the presence of mind to send full-scan and pictures back to the Patrol. It even arranged to stay in line of sight to document the destruction for the authorities.

The glowing sphere showed clearly in the distance. The marauder would sweep over a habitation, and dazzling beams of light would strike down, boring deep into the moon's crust. More of Delos died with every orbit the aggressor made. It moved fast, but conversely, did not seem to be in a hurry. It made sure that no habitation on Delos survived its attentions.

When the feed came in to Tarnball Patrol, the attacker was recognized for the alien presence it was. No longer did they wonder *who*; now it was *what* was attacking? And why Tarnball? This was something more horrifyingly serious than any of them had imagined. The live feed was routed out in real time to the navy at Astrid base and sent compressed to Patrol HQ.

Tarnball Five asked for permission to launch for Delos. The commander had to deny it. TB Five was absolutely no match for the marauder.

"Sir, priority transmission coming in from Astrid," Arnold Waterman called out. "We have permission to use naval ordinance in our situation."

The commander's head snapped around. "How could they have made the decision so soon? We made the request barely twenty minutes ago; they're only just now getting our message."

"That's not all, sir. They say they are aware of—get this—'intruders,' plural, in the system. We are authorized to attack with planetary weapons at will. Access, activation, and arming sequences for every bird in the armory are to follow."

"Intruders. This is very bad. Have TB Five offload the Brens and maneuver around the farside bunker immediately. Load with five-meg and twenty-megaton Raptors. They fit our firing racks well enough. Then contact TB Three and Four. Order them to jettison all rescue equipment and proceed directly to the naval bunker. After they take on ordinance, they will be refueled at the bunker."

"Yes, sir."

"And get TB Two operational soonest."

"Yes, sir. Sir, there is more."

"What more, Arnold?"

"Sir, the navy says if we are unable to stop our intruder, we should be prepared to abandon our base and rendezvous with all ships at a point farther into the system. A location is being picked right now by Astrid."

The commander was shocked. "They can't order us to abandon our base. These are our people being attacked. We have to help them."

"Yes, sir. They advise us to be prepared to abandon base. They say to expect this order to come from Patrol HQ soon as well."

The commander patted Arnold Waterman on the shoulder and wandered back to his tiny office. *Abandon the base . . . oh lordy*. He sat, drifting slowly down to his seat, and began to wonder, *Just what's the situation in the rest of the system?* If he could receive an order like that from Patrol Headquarters, things must have been grim indeed throughout Alpha Centauri's far-flung communities.

Soon the commander would have to take that advice seriously, he knew. But where could he possibly evacuate his personnel that would be safer than right here? And how could he accomplish an evacuation while fighting the enemy at the same time?

Well, he would face that decision when he had to. In the meantime, there were things to be done. It was obvious from the pictures sent by the cargo lifter that the marauder would stay at Delos until it destroyed everything it could find. That meant it should be possible to get a line on its whereabouts when his ships were ready to face it.

To that end, he broadcast the following message: "To any ship near Delos, this is Tarnball Patrol. Your assistance is urgently needed. Please stay in the area and observe the actions of the attacker. Do not close, I repeat, *do not close* with the alien ship. Stay in line of sight and let us know where it goes. We will launch an intercept, soonest."

••✦••

aboard the Mother Lode's Son, *en route to Delos*

Galvin McLeod did not consider himself a brave man, but an ice miner is often both brave and resourceful in the course of his work. So, when the murderous intruder was reported making orbit over Delos, he did not consider changing his course.

His ship, the *Mother Lode's Son,* tied up to half a billion metric tons of cometary ice, was already on a closing course with Delos. If he were going to put the ice into orbit around the moon, he would have to begin his scheduled burn soon, or in three hours he would begin the long slide past it.

Instead, he unlimbered his telescope and put Delos square in the center of the screen. It was just coming around the limb of Tarnball, so he settled down to watch. He shut off his transponder and running lights, and damped down his energy output as much as possible. Then he dreamed about giving the marauder an ice enema.

••✦••

aboard the Paris Octavious

Sandra Brodsky, Clarence Yarrow, and Lieutenant Thomas Dunlevy sat in Sandra's office and waited. The navy liaison officer had a nervous habit of punching for system readiness information on the console next to her desk. His usual elapsed time was about two minutes, and Sandy was beginning to regret giving the officer system access. The atmosphere was thick with tension. Undischarged emotions simmered—or flared, depending on personality type—within each of them.

Suddenly, Sandy spoke. "Bogey number two is definitely in orbit somewhere around Tarnball. We've been watching its image approach Minos, though of course it arrived there six hours ago. If it's caused any mischief, we should be hearing about it soon. I hope our warning helped."

The men nodded solemnly. Just then Sandy's intercom came to life and spoke with the duty officer's voice.

"Administrator, we are getting a duplicate message from the laser feed that Tarnball Traffic is sending to Tarnball Patrol. They are reporting a disaster on Minos. They say that North city has suffered a blowout."

"A blowout? Are you sure they said 'blowout'?"

"Yes, ma'am. I can also hear them trying to contact an unidentified ship entering low orbit, or possibly making an unauthorized landing attempt."

Lieutenant Dunlevy was suddenly busy at Sandy's console. On split screen, she could see him receiving the Tarnball feed and setting up an outgoing call to the navy. In addition, he was comparing tracking data from the scope following the bogey and geographical data on Minos. "It came in over the North Pole," he grunted.

Oh God, she thought. *This is a nightmare.* To the duty operator, she simply said, "Keep me informed."

It seemed only seconds later that the duty officer was on the line again. "Administrator Brodsky, I've lost transmission from Tarnball Control. They are completely off the air, not even a carrier wave."

Sandy looked at Lieutenant Dunlevy, who had paused in his conversation with INSYSCON. He nodded that he had heard and added it to his report. She clenched her fists, fighting tears. She looked at Clarence Yarrow, and he steadily looked back.

Why, she wanted to say, *why are they doing this? Why are they attacking us? Why?* Clarence understood her anguish and felt just as helpless. He could offer no answer.

••✦••

aboard the Aswan

SFN *Aswan,* well beyond the orbit of Punk and mathematically close to FTL line, rode outward from all her crew held dear. They were listening for orders and scanning space intently. None of the known bogeys were in this sector, but the boat was on full alert anyway. The arms panel was unlocked, the birds and Frypaks ready to launch on a moment's notice. It seemed wrong to be running for deep space with enemy units in the system, but here they were, following orders.

"Sir, the Deep Space Net reports our closest bogey to be on station approximately one billion kilometers east by southeast of us, sitting at just Punk's distance from the sun. It's too far for us to pick it up on sensors, but we're trying for a telescope view."

The captain of the *Aswan* nodded. The radio operator caught the head movement in his peripheral vision. Then he sat up straight as a new message came in.

"Sir, new information. An attack on the moons of Tarnball

has been confirmed. There are civilian casualties, estimates unavailable at this time. Enemy strength is now listed at twenty-four vessels. We are ordered to continue present course and await orders. Updates to follow."

Again, the captain nodded. *Continue present course. Wait for orders. Will do,* he thought grimly, *will do.*

The radio officer watched his captain nod, watched him refuse to speak, and thought he understood. The crew of the *Aswan* came from all over the Federation. Commingled crews were navy policy. The captain just happened to have come from Sistra.

He was leaving his home without firing a shot at the enemy because that is what his orders said he should do. It must have hurt him terribly to leave his home without defending it, just because the uniform he wore said he must. The operator wanted to say that the rest of the navy would defend Sistra just as fiercely as the captain would. He almost did say it, almost. But he knew it wouldn't help, not enough.

••✦••

aboard the Mother Lode's Son, *en route to Delos*

Finally, the ship attacking Delos seemed satisfied with its work. It made one more circuit of the moon without finding anything else to beam and then accelerated smoothly out of orbit.

It was what Galvin McLeod had been waiting for. His eyes had scarcely left the screen in hours. He had not moved from his command chair since crosshatching Delos on the scope. "Where now, you bastard?" he breathed. "Will it be Samos? Perhaps Patmos or Lemos? Or maybe Aegina, my home? Where, you monster, where?"

McLeod was fast approaching Delos. He was a big chunk of ice in the sky, too big to miss. So big that perhaps the marauder failed to see the small Human ship riding the ice. Or perhaps it chose to ignore the sight.

At any rate, it made an incredibly tight turn and climbed away from the moon faster than Galvin had ever seen a ship move. He got a good chance to watch it go. He watched long enough to establish an arc, and then threw that arc onto a plotting screen and accessed his Tarnball almanac.

The almanac decided that the ship's most likely next destination was Patmos. Rhodes was on the same track but farther away. Galvin was betting the bastard intended to be thorough. He powered up his transmitter and began to send on the System Patrol frequency.

••✦••

interdiction at Patmos

Three System Patrol ships challenged the intruder as it neared Patmos. The alien vessel proceeded on course toward the moon, giving no sign it noticed anyone closing with it. It was as if the Patrol ships were insignificant to its purpose, and their aggressive approach was not understood.

For the Patrol's part, mindful of their status as mites trying to tackle the bull, consensus was to launch an attack at maximum practical distance. The ships themselves might be slow, but not so the missiles. Therefore, Tarnball Five set up its firing solution and launched a Raptor at the forty-thousand-kilometer mark.

As the missile left its rack, all sensors and available eyes were on the confrontation. Depending on what the alien did next, the other two ships were ready with their own launches.

The missile acquired its target through a combination of radar and television technologies and flew straight and true. The alien did not react in any way.

At the end of its run, the missile and the alien seemed to

merge for an instant, then the five-megaton warhead detonated. On Tarnball Five, the marauder disappeared as the sensors blanked out and struggled to compensate.

The rescue specialist cum weapons officer for the day yelled into his radio, "It's a hit, I say again, we have a hit."

As the sensors slowly cleared, it could be seen that the alien ship was still there, apparently unhurt. Its only visible response was that it began slowing rapidly.

Now Tarnball Four launched. Its raptor, carrying a twenty-megaton warhead, ran just as true. Eleven minutes into its run, the missile reached the coruscating zone around the aggressor and exploded with as little effect.

The System Patrol vessels began to slow. Raptor missiles were significantly larger than the Bren, and only two could be mated to the Patrol ships weapon systems. In the next moment, all four remaining missiles left their racks. The little Human ships turned and began their retreat.

This time the alien responded, sort of. As each missile closed to within two hundred kilometers, it was beamed out of existence. The Human ships were allowed to leave, unmolested.

••✦••

situation room, Centauri Base: main continent Sistra; fourteen hours forty-one minutes into alert

The big plotting board, two floors high and two tennis courts long, managed to capture the entire scope of the tragedy in making, though only barely. The various planets and their attendant families were represented, each delineated into strategic and action zones. Each body was represented by gravity well symbols indicating energy added or expended to enter or leave the influence of the body in question.

The enemy units were haloed in red, Federation forces

in blue. Strategy planers could only hope that fuel and other energy expenditures were a factor for the enemy as well. The navy needed to move its ships as intelligently as possible to make up for the incredible speed of the enemy.

"Fighting is now reported around Evita and Zeus," announced Admiral Dachman. "I know none of us are surprised at this news, but it does now officially make this war a multi-front operation."

"The asteroid enclaves are all gone to radio silence by now," added the System Patrol commandant, "and navigation beacons are off the air."

"Will that do us any good?" asked Mr. Pearls.

"Anything that hinders the enemy helps us," grunted the admiral. "Although how much this will help is uncertain. The enemy has a fix on every stationary habitation in the system by now. In the belts, of course, evacuation and relocation is going on at full speed. That will complicate the enemy's search and destroy missions. There are a lot of places to hide in some of the asteroidal groups. However, there are also twelve enemy ships sweeping the belts."

"One of those ships is supposed to be coming at your navy base, isn't it, Dachman?"

"Yes, Mr. Pearls, one of the enemy units is on approach to Astrid. We expect to find out how tough they really are shortly."

An assistant to the Patrol commandant, a man with captains' pips on his collar, came over to the table. His report was brief and to the point.

"Sir, Tarnball Patrol Base reports final outcome of the confrontation with their alien warship. Two naval Raptor missiles declared direct hits. Neither the five-megaton nor the twenty-megaton warhead achieved penetration. The target, an approximately one-thousand-meter globe, was apparently unhurt. It denied four other missiles proximity by destroying them at about two zero zero kilometer's range. No aggressive action taken against the Patrol ships, and they have withdrawn in good order."

"Thank you, captain. Did they report how the missiles were destroyed?"

"Yes, sir. Some type of energy burst attack. Presumed to be an extremely high-energy collimated laser beam."

As the captain returned to his station, the three situation team members exchanged looks. The military personnel were grim, the civilian apoplectic. "It's time to get help," he whispered sharply.

"Agreed," said the commandant.

The admiral nodded. "Send a complete update to all outbound ships," he ordered. "And tell *Aswan* they are free to jump now, orders unchanged. Get to Earth, soonest."

The on-duty communications officer nodded and swung into action, then turned back almost immediately.

"Admiral, we have a communication from a freighter being relayed through Sistra Traffic Control. They urgently request permission to continue on to their current destination, not be diverted to Earth."

"What is the reason for their request?"

"They have vital supplies for the Nova Terrene colony and the Federation naval research station there. They want to alert the station and assist the colony. And sir, at this time, no other ships are going that way."

"Very well; permission granted." Admiral Dachman nodded thoughtfully. "As the battle unfolds, you may consider such requests in the future *only* if a reasonable percentage of Earthbound ships are clear of enemy threat out to FTL point."

The duty officer nodded and returned to his work. It was going to be a very busy day.

10

ERRORS IN JUDGMENT

aboard Friendly to the Governed, *on picket duty at the edge of interstellar space*

Typhanok, Captain of Persuader-class vessel *Friendly to the Governed,* sat in his day cabin and prepared himself for the morning. He was an Aranth of meticulous nature, extreme in his habits even for such a race of meticulous beings. He always curried his pelt for an excessive time before assuming his place before the crew each day.

Final preparation, of course, included brushing his fur with a snarzak soft-bristle brush. Synthetic-bristle brushes just did not have the feel of real snarzak hair, so Typhanok indulged himself this one affectation. His snarzak brush was a family heirloom; the worn hardwood handle with the sculpted grip that fit his hand comfortably and the pleasant rolling plains carved on the back gave him many moments of pleasure as he went about the empire doing his duties.

He brushed. He brushed until his fur shined with reddish and golden highlights, until all the tiny snarls from sleep and worry were gone. Then he added a lick here, another stroke there, until he was truly satisfied.

In a few minutes, he would emerge into the control center of his four-hundred-meter ship, formerly a policing vessel, now a ship of war. It was a little strange. In his fairly long career in the AranthChi space forces, he had never fired a shot at anyone. Now he was on a mission that would eventually lead to just that. His ship, stationed more than a billion kilometers from anything interesting, had the task of tracking all of the race enemy ships leaving this star through his sector.

He was to watch them and see if he could deduce what their destinations might be at the end of their years-long flights. It was hoped that by letting as many ships get out of the system as possible, the AranthChi could observe and reach a determination as to where they were going.

After a few weeks of letting them run, the plan was to pop out after them. Following the candle flame of their fusion drives would be simplicity itself. Catch up to them, destroy them, and then move on to the stars they were heading for. Finally, destroy all the colonies planted by this treacherous species. Make sure they could never threaten the safety of AranthChi again.

After giving his tail one last lick and stroke, Typhanok replaced the brush, left his cabin, and entered the control center. He was met by a startling babble of voices and the sight of his second in command leaning over a plotting display and arguing with its operator.

The breech of protocol was amazing. What happened next was even more astounding. The core had to announce "Captain in control" twice before his second in command finally noticed his presence.

Typhanok's underling's first action upon seeing his superior left the captain speechless. Instead of standing erect, spreading clawed fingers, swiping the air in front of his face, and saying, "Second reporting to captain," as he should have done, he barked out, "Good, you're here, sir. Come, you must see this immediately."

Typhanok's ruff puffed out, and his tail fur started to bottle. With a force of will, he kept his ears up and stalked over to the display. "If this is not a very big situation, Second, you can sniff your position on my ship goodbye."

"Yes, sir." The Aranth's attitude shifted abruptly. He became erect, swiped air, and said, "Second reporting to captain."

"Very well. What do you have to report?"

"Captain, one of the ships we have been tracking has disappeared!"

"Explain yourself, Second. Did the subject vessel explode or merely turn off its fusion drive?" He stopped, struck by an awful notion. "Are you suggesting these aliens have a way of disguising themselves from our instruments?" *That would be very bad indeed,* he thought. *But when faced with race enemies, one must think of all possible horrors.* He was a declared race protector after all, and the safety of billions of AranthChi might at any time rest in his hands.

Second of Ship for *Friendly to the Governed* understood his captain's paranoia well. It could be said he shared it in equal measure. What he had to report was, unfortunately, far more disturbing than the captain's spur-of-the-moment, nightmare-driven guess.

"Sir, they have done none of those things. They appear to have made the transition to superluminal velocities."

The captain's howl caught the control crew by surprise. Every ear on the bridge went flat. "Are you saying they have a past-light-limit technology?"

Second had to fight instinct to hold his ground. The captain had just become the most frightening thing a young Aranth could imagine, an adult on the edge of berserk. He was, however, a trained though subordinate adult, and fought past the urge to flee or drop to the ground and submit, nor did he respond aggressively. He stood very still and remained deferential. "Yes sir, it would seem so."

"This is a disaster! Get me *Suppression of Discord* at once!"

Third of Base Raalma sat at a communal worktable and pored over an aggregate of intelligence reports, assisted by his senior technical staff. He picked up again the report on first hostile reply by the aliens. The idea of using tiny, automated ships to deliver a fusion reactor to the vicinity of its target and then cascade that pile to detonation was decidedly novel.

"How do you know these little ships have no pilot?"

His question was pure curiosity. He did not doubt the report's veracity. His staff took him seriously. "No operating life support system has been detected in the first six devices known to be deployed, sir. The Insistence vessel that first encountered them took full recordings. That would be *Demand for Honesty*."

The staff assistant looked at his copy of the report. "Besides, these little ships moved at better than thirty times the aliens' home gravity. I don't see how a pilot could stand the abuse and still remain effective, since they don't have gravity control."

No one brought up the question of whether the aliens would put a pilot into a suicide mission ship. Aliens were alien; who knew what they might do? Instead, Raalma asked, "And what is your assessment of the danger implied by these devices?"

"Sir, the strongest explosion measured a .3 flare, an intensity that the Insistence vessel's shield could have handled in normal configuration. Now that amount of energy, or even eight times that amount, will provide no strain whatsoever."

"Fine, fine. But what if they throw a lot of these little ships against our shields?"

"Such saturation would be difficult for them to achieve. As one of their devices explodes, it should destroy any others that are nearby. Also, our ships can move as fast, or faster, if we have to. We can easily dodge any concentrations of these automatics that seem threatening."

"That is probably safe enough. However, order the fleet that concentrations of these 'automatics,'" he said with a grin, "are not to be tolerated and should not be allowed to approach any ship closer than the 128 octads *Demand for Honesty* used when destroying her examples of alien ingenuity."

When that was done, he said, "On to more current actives.

What are the latest reports concerning the muddy gas giant and the rosy ringed one?"

"Resistance remains light. Targets around both planets are being destroyed on schedule. As per doctrine, ships are being ignored as targets, simply watched as they depart."

"And the asteroid belts?"

The other staff assistant, a female with tawny and cream markings, twitched her tail contemplatively. "The task there is a little more complex, commander. Not only do these two regions occupy much volume, but then they come in clumps and sprays and clusters. The aliens are also moving around quite a bit, trying to disguise living accommodations. We are ferreting them out, but not in as good a time as predicted."

"Keep me informed."

The announcer pickup came alive that moment and overrode his voice. "Expedition Commander Raalma, this is the notifications officer. I have a priority message for you, sir."

"Go ahead, notification."

"Thank you, sir. Persuader vessel *Friendly to the Governed* is on picket duty covering the bottom clockwise sectors of our current battlefield. Approximately five minutes ago, one of the ships they were tracking went super luminal."

"What? Are they sure?"

"Yes, sir. They caught the whole matter on sensors. It was a definite transition to above-light velocities."

Raalma's nose wrinkled into a snarl. He had just stopped being amused with the aliens. The shock would have frozen a lesser leader. But in Raalma, the High Council had found an Aranth capable of lightning changes in perspective. It was one of the things that had led to his assignment to the expedition in the first place. He assimilated. He acted.

"Contact all picket ships. Find out if there have been any other transitions to past light, or if any ship appears to be preparing for such transition."

"Right away, sir!"

"Then contact the aggression team. I want quickest intercept courses plotted on all vessels leaving this system. Get to these ships and destroy them. Use all Persuader and Insistence craft if necessary. Pull ships out of the asteroid flocks, take them from the gas giants if you need to, but get those ships!"

"Calling aggression team now, sir. Reports are in from all pickets, commander. No other ships have gone translight."

"Good. Keep me informed."

Raalma stood up from the worktable. "I will be in my day cabin," he said stiffly to his staff.

Once in his cabin, he called the core to life. "Pull all the information you need from tracking and the aggression teams' assignments." He paced in a way he never let the crew see. There was a haunted air about him. "Now, I need your best assessment. Will we get them all?"

"The aliens' technology and ours do not seem to have a point for point similarity," the core replied. "One of our ships would have been able to attain translight far sooner than the alien ship was observed to. If we were to assume that the alien engaged its translight apparatus at the soonest possible instant and that none of the ships fleeing this system can accelerate faster than forty percent above current observed rates, we will get all but two or possibly three of them."

"Two or three more translight ships is not acceptable."

"It gets worse, commander. We have allowed many of these ships to run a long time. Some we will only catch at the edge of the translight zone. If for any reason the observed vessel delayed its transition and actually could have entered translight at the same point we would have been able to, the number of certain escapes raises to five."

"Five more translight ships running to spread the alarm! This is inexcusable. We have made a serious error here. How could we have not deduced this technology from our observations?"

The core was mute. It recognized the rhetorical nature of the question.

Raalma came to a stop in front of a viewport. The alien's sun shined small and yellow in the distance. "This changes the equation enormously. We don't even know where our race enemies are running to with translight ability. This may now turn out to be a civilization with settlements around eights of star systems. Finding them all will be very difficult. With only a sublight technology facing us, we had a reasonable chance of obliterating this poison, root and branch. Our operational lifetime of five years did not handicap us too greatly. Now . . . there must be no more mistakes!"

He became erect, ears forward in resolve. "Go over all our data again carefully. Post an order to all sections to that effect. The battle plan remains the same. As soon as the threat of the leaving ships is eliminated, all elements will return to assigned tasks. Oh, there is one modification: all attack vessels are ordered to hit ships as well as living spaces. Let us not compound our error."

••✦••

situation room, Centauri Base,
thirty hours zero minutes into alert

"It's confirmed, then," one comm officer remarked to another. "Several of the hostile force ships sweeping the asteroids have altered course and seem to be heading back out of the system. At least none of the current headings will take them anywhere near a planet. I wonder where they're going."

"I don't know. It looks like good news, but it's too soon to tell. I say good riddance to them."

"Wait a minute. I'm getting a System Patrol report from the vicinity of Tarnball. Their bogey is passing up Aegina and bound away from the gas giant. That makes six. This is too strange. What if they're all moving?"

The two comm officers looked at each other. "We better wake up the admiral," one said.

••✦••

Admiral Dachman looked a little bleary-eyed at his aides. Not sleeping in more than thirty hours will do that to a person. It felt like he'd been down only minutes, though the mission clock on the wall insisted it was more like three hours. "Some of the enemy are returning to deep space?" he asked.

"That's right, admiral. Six so far."

"We will know about several more in a few minutes," said the other officer. "As soon as the lightspeed lag reaches us from their locations."

The admiral tried to think. Closing his eyes seemed to help, although the sleep in them tried to gum them together. Something about this was important, but he couldn't latch on to it. *Wait a minute.* He shouldn't have to do all the thinking around here himself. That's what he had a staff of bright, young officers for.

"You just used the term 'lightspeed lag,' son. I think you're on to something there. Go away and figure out why they're all leaving the party. When you know, do something about it. If you need to wake me again, do it. Otherwise, let me sleep." He turned over and was gone instantly.

••✦••

It only took fifteen minutes to figure it out. One of the group of bright, young officers had an intuitive flash. To wit, the hostiles were responding to something the Federation had done. Two things convinced the rest of the group. One was that enough observation time of several of the enemy ships' new flight directions had taken place to predict a reasonable arc of possible flight paths. The new course headings turned out to intersect with a fleeing Human ship every time.

The other datum was a surprise. When tracked back in time, there was a Human-generated event that coincided very closely with the change in the hostiles' behavior. It was something they were going to have to wake the admiral up to tell him about, but not just yet. First there was something the lower echelon officers could do on their own. They set about doing it.

••✦••

"Well, well." The admiral blinked rapidly at the other two men around the table. He was wider-awake than the Space Patrol commandant, which made him smile slightly. He was more awake than the governor's man too, but he'd expected that. That state of affairs was generally true even when the admiral was sound asleep. "An extraordinary event has occurred, which will keep many people at work, trying to figure out the implications, during the next few days."

Jasson Pearls yawned widely. "I don't know what you are talking about, Dachman. Haven't we been expecting these damn aliens to try to knock out our ships for the last two days now? They certainly wouldn't want us to get help from Earth, now, would they?"

The Patrol commandant nodded thoughtfully. "It has certainly been a puzzle to me that the hostiles started off attacking settlements and other unarmed fixed sites, all the while entirely ignoring things that move, like war ships and FTL-capable civilian vessels."

"They have impervious shields," snapped Pearls. "They don't need to worry about your runty patrol ships. They may not have to worry about the navy. All they really fear is Earth."

Admiral Hans Dachman watched his old friend getting angry. It would have been pleasant to see Ralph Brunmas flatten the farmer. He had dreamed of doing it a time or two himself in the last two days. It would not happen, of course.

Ralph was too good an officer, not to mention diplomat, to give in to momentary impulse. Still . . .

"I think you're closer than you might think on that one, Pearls." The governor's man looked surprised. So did the commandant. "Something about our shipping leaving the Alpha system has become disturbing to the hostiles. That much is plain. They are currently bending every effort to run down our outbounds. It may be that all hostilities have ceased for the moment everywhere else, while they try to get to our shipping."

"So they are afraid of Earth."

"Close, but not quite. What if I told you that the hostiles' change to chasing down our outbounds began within twenty minutes of the *Aswan*'s expected time of translation to FTL space?"

The commandant saw it first. "Son of a bitch. They didn't know about our FTL capability."

Now Pearls got it. "They don't know everything about us. They just seem to because somehow they know where everything is in the outer system."

"That's right, Pearls. They have been acting like they have all the time in the world. It's become apparent that they plan to chew us up, very leisurely and thoroughly. They would have been right too, if it took us four years to get the word out that we needed help and four more years to get assistance. They obviously did not plan on us being able to reach Earth in sixteen days' time."

"So, what do we do now?"

"We've gotten a breathing space out of this, though at the cost of most of our ships making the attempt to flee. It's time for every colony scientist and military tactician to get to work on one question: *What else* don't they know about us that we can exploit?"

The commandant sighed. "For a couple of hours now, INSYSCON and Sistra Traffic Control have been burning up the lightwaves, giving updates to all outbound vessels.

Everyone in communications is working double shifts, and double quick to give our people every chance of eluding their pursuers. A few, like the Federation Scout *Newton,* may be able to fight its way to a transition point. The rest . . . well, the rest will still be helping by buying us time."

He looked up at the situation room wall with its multicolored displays. "This is the first good news in thirty hours. I'd like it to be better news, but it's all we've got. I'll tell you one thing, though: I sure wish I had their instantaneous communication system."

••✦••

aboard Effort Is Appreciated, *approaching Astrid Naval Base*

Persuader-class vessel *Effort Is Appreciated,* working its way slowly through the asteroid field, acknowledged its change in orders. It immediately computed elapsed time to the first of its two assigned targets. It agreed with *Suppression of Discord*'s opinion to within a nanosecond or two.

To catch the first of the two fleeing ships this side of the translight zone and leave an acceptable margin, *Effort Is Appreciated* would have to commence boost within the next thirty minutes. Its other ship target was still deep enough in the system that blocking it from escape would be simplicity itself.

Thirty minutes, however, was not a lot of time to ferret out and destroy all the life bubbles believed to be clustered in this particular asteroidal flock. Still, *Effort* might as well start in on the task.

As the four-hundred-meter warship moved forward, a habitat on its mid-range monitors began showing signs of a fusion drive ignition. This was a ship! The commander of *Effort Is Appreciated* confidently expected to see the revealed ship run away. He watched with amusement as the ship instead began launching very tiny ships that spread out around it in a halo arrangement. None of these vehicles approached the *Effort,* but none ran away either.

Intrigued, the commander decided to let the scenario unfold to see what would happen next. Now monitors showed other ships powering up. They also launched halo riders. After a while, the halo shapes were widely dispersed from the initiating vessels.

Finally, the ships began firing off the darts *Effort* had been warned to expect. True to reports, they were accelerating straight toward *Effort Is Appreciated* at many multiples of the aliens' home gravity.

Suddenly, the commander began to get nervous. Unbreachable shields or no, the sky was now full of enemy vehicles. There were almost a hundred of them of varying sizes, and many of them carried fusion piles that the aliens hoped to destabilize next to his ship.

"Begin firing when they reach the 128-octade mark," he ordered.

"Acknowledged," came from the fire control board.

"In fact, we don't have a lot of time to waste here. Target the ships first. They will certainly try to run away after the attack fails, and we haven't time to chase them all."

Effort's fire control officer chose a ship farthest away. A wide, bright ribbon of light reached out from *Effort* and touched the attacking ship, which fell to pieces in spectacular fashion.

The ribbon reached out again and winged another ship that was in mid-dodge. That ship began to cartwheel, losing vapor and other mass as its mortal wound tore it apart. As the missiles neared the 128-octade mark, *Effort* stopped the ship attacks and switched over to multiple targeting.

Suddenly, coherent light slammed into the shields. Powerful, viscous, focused, and individually tuned, the beams dug into *Effort*'s defenses.

"Core, what just happened?" the captain yelled.

"Approximately one-half of the halo vehicles just exploded, generating a strong lasing effect. Multiple minor burn-throughs of the shields occurred but without penetration of the outer hull. Automatic targeting also lost. I am reacquiring sensor grid and targeting lock now."

The rest of the Frypak bomb-pumped lasers detonated an instant later. The AranthChi ship, blinded again, began firing sporadically into the globe of advancing missiles. Four of the missiles closed simultaneously from different directions and detonated.

The brilliant flash of nuclear energies was joined a moment later by a light so bright it could have come from the birth of the universe. When sensors began functioning again on the Human warships, it was obvious the hostile was gone.

"Jeez," said a Human commander, "you don't want to be too close to one of these guys when they go off."

••✦••

aboard the Defender of Authority

"What now?" Raalma growled at the speaker out of which the notifications officer's voice had come. Notifications had been breaking into his concentration more and more frequently in the last few eight portions of time, and each interruption had seemed to be more trivial than the last.

"Expedition commander, sir, aggression tracking has lost all contact with a Persuader vessel working in the asteroid groups."

Raalma was suddenly preternaturally alert and beside himself with anger. "*Nurturer of Social Norms* is in charge of asteroid operations. What do they have to say about this loss of contact?"

"They relate a fragmented last transmission about a sensor

blinding lase attack and many automatic darts approaching the 128-octade line. After that time all voice transmission and telemetry cease. *Nurturer* is moving in now, to investigate and correct the situation."

Raalma set clawed hands on the table and tried to dig in. The polished surface was impervious. He hoped the skulls of his captains were not equally dense. "Tell everyone *again* to knock down those automatics! Now that the unthinkable has happened, maybe they will be a little more careful. End communication."

He sat back on his couch he and let his ears flatten. "What other vile, deceitful tricks are we going to have played on us by these misbegotten aliens, while we go about trying to annihilate them?" There was not a trace of irony in his attitude. He was purely and arrogantly indignant.

••✦••

situation room, Centauri Base;
thirty-four hours and nineteen minutes into alert

"INSYSCON has just given us their final estimates. It looks like the hostiles are going to get most of our outbounds. Perhaps as many as eight will make it to the vicinity of their FTL points. Perhaps only five. We are sending out constant updates on vectors and closing rates to all of the ships that might have a ghost of a chance of fighting or fleeing their way to a transition point. One of them is bound for Nova Terrene. It has an excellent chance of making it. Two are returning to their last port of call. The rest are trying for Earth."

The staff officer giving report waited for responses from the situation team. As he had been concise and comprehensive, he got none. He continued. "We also have the report in from Astrid Base."

The situation team became more animated. Moments before, every tracking station in the inner system following the asteroid battle had reported weapon flashes and a momentary nova-like light near the Astrid naval installation. Apprehension and anticipation were both running high.

"The battle was against one of the small hostile vessels, sirs. Astrid reports four simultaneous direct hits with penetration and total kill.

There were grins all around. "Now that's more like it should be," said Commandant Brunmas.

"Sistra civilian Traffic Control also reports movement of one of the three big ships that Tactical has tentatively classified as command-and-control craft. The one at three lighthours ten minutes west, in the outer asteroid belt, appears bound for the vicinity of Astrid. They are cutting deeply across the inner system to get there. Presently Astrid is closer to four light hours east by northeast. Tactical, by the way, insists that they have a positive match for the large vessels. They are indeed of AranthChi manufacture. They have no explanation for the unusual shield characteristics."

"So, they don't like it when we play tag and win, eh?" Admiral Dachman smiled broadly. "They're sending in one of the big boys to stomp on Astrid. And they have been acting just like AranthChi all along, damn them, even if they are stumbling around, pretending they don't know us from Adam."

"Sir," said the aide. "Do you have any instructions for INSYSCON or the fleet units at Astrid Base?"

"Hell yes, son. Make sure they know that company's on the way in a king-sized package, and see if they can pull off the same trick twice. Hmm . . . We do have something that may help them with their little party. Do we have time to get a couple of special gifts to them before that ComCon ship gets there?"

"No, sir, not by any of our regular ships limited to normal accelerations."

"Nicely put. We do have those five ships in-system right

now with the new gravitation compensators being installed. Even though the yards haven't certified them for flight yet, we need one and we need it now. Call the dockmaster, tell him to get one ready for launch in the next twenty minutes. That'll get 'em hopping."

"Why just one?" demanded Pearls. "Send them all and make sure they get there."

"A bit of subtlety, if you please, Mr. Pearls." The commandant's rumbling voice hinted at suppressed glee. "The enemy ship will be on the wrong side of the sun for much of its boost time. We have a good chance of slipping one ship out to the asteroids without being noticed, especially since so much of the bastard's attentions are on our outbounds. Tactically speaking, anything we can do that the AranthChi don't know about is to our advantage."

somewhere in the Alpha Centauri system

The SFN *Newton* had been poking along at a comfortable .9 G while moving outward toward a distant FTL translation point in the Alpha Centauri system. When Centauri INSYSCON had advised them of the developing attack on the system, the captain of the *Newton* had offered any possible assistance. An offer to attach himself to Alpha Centauri's military command structure was a typical gesture of the man.

A Federation Scout was not considered a fighting ship per se, but it did have some advantages over more typical naval ships. It was very heavy in scanning and sampling devices and had lots of legs in case it needed to get in and then out of a situation fast.

The advantages and disadvantages of the Scout-class vessel were not lost on INSYSCON. Instead of asking for the *Newton* to return to an inner system base or link up with units already being deployed, the ship was directed to proceed as before, but go into full surveillance mode.

The *Newton* slowly transformed from a rather ordinary-looking deep space vehicle into an incredible untidy mass. Recessed antennas sprouted from multiple locations. Sensor and camera booms unfolded from shallow grooves running nearly the vessel's length.

The atmosphere-rated survey boat was launched. After running far enough ahead to be free of the *Newton*'s drive emissions, it deployed a towed array sensor grid, running its drive just fast enough to keep from falling behind.

In the space of half an hour, the unlikely duo of sea anemone with wings and gossamer-tailed squid were on station, recording the unfolding drama of the start of Humanity's second interstellar war.

11

LEARNING CURVE

aboard the Gobi*, approaching Astrid Base*

The SFN Light Cruiser *Gobi* coasted silently into the asteroid swarm, barely above orbital speed, which was a relief after the breakneck race out of the inner system to get there. There had been no apparent response from the AranthChi to their flight. Perhaps they weren't noticed.

The Light Cruiser began hailing Astrid at very low power. The response was immediate and at whisper strength. "Astrid Base here. We hear you, *Gobi,* and have you sighted."

"Thank you, Astrid. Where do you want us with our special delivery?"

"The decoy village is ten degrees by thirty degrees from your current course. You are twenty-five thousand kilometers and closing. You are to continue to slow and use lowband tach channel two to contact the decoy group for your assignment."

As *Gobi* made her course change, the Astrid comm officer continued the conversation. "Do you think the new items will work on the big fellow coming our way?"

"That's what they were designed to do, before we knew about the smaller globes or these new shields. However, the scientists have made new measurements and say they ought to work. I know I'm betting my money on them."

"Well, it's nice to hear such enthusiasm, because these boys are damn hard to kill. Good luck, *Gobi*. Astrid out."

"Roger that and switching to tach channel two."

••✦••

aboard Nurturer of Social Norms, *nearing Astrid Base*

The mad, screaming flight across the alien's system did not take particularly long, in the objective sense, to reach the site where *Effort Is Appreciated* met its unforgivable death. A few heartbeats, compared to the year-long journey to reach the aliens' homeworld from the mid clan naval base. It was certainly not long enough to take the edge off of the rage felt by the commander of *Nurturer of Social Norms*. It was, however, long enough to make Captain Spazzea fretful that the treacherous aliens might be using the time to affect an escape.

That the aliens responsible for his humiliation might get away was unthinkable. They would not profit from this affront to AranthChi dignity, he swore. The aliens had also made him look incompetent in front of his expedition commander, and they would pay dearly for that. He was personally going to mop up every damned alien in that arc of the asteroid flock and make sure they could *never* present a threat to one of his ships again.

As *Nurturer* entered the accursed area where numerous asteroids traveled in a loose swarm, Captain Spazzea repeated his basic commands to a dutiful crew. "Watch every stone and pebble. When you find a ship or alien device, target it. If it tries to leave, destroy it. If it launches weapons, destroy it. When you find a habitat, destroy it. After we have found and eliminated all the life bubbles and it looks like the ships are not leading us to anymore, destroy them too. *All of them*. And everything else of alien manufacture in this flock!"

A chorus of voices raised an assent that returned sweetly to his ears. "Remember," he thundered, "when those spiteful automatic darts approach the 128-octade point, destroy them. There are to be no exceptions!" He listened and found himself satisfied with the response.

"Structures on the asteroids ahead, sir."

"Go on in and start targeting."

"Ship ignitions occurring, sir. . . . Ships being targeted."

"Habitations being identified and targeted."

"Sir, enemy ships are launching darts."

"Carry out your orders."

"At once, my captain!"

The Human ships dodged and launched, dodged and launched again. One by one they succumbed to *Nurturer*'s fire. Missiles rose to join the fray from unmarked spots on asteroids. Those spots were retaliated against also.

Many Human ships died in the short firefight. Some successfully hid in the lee of nearby flying mountains after contributing their ordinance to the struggle. These few helped to supply command and control functions to the Human side of the battlefield.

Nestled anonymously in the waves of incoming missiles were two very special additions. Somewhat larger than their brethren, they were very differently configured. By dint of design, though, they appeared indistinguishable from the standard when in flight. They had been carefully programmed to take advantage of the peculiar consistency these AranthChi showed in ignoring such missiles until they approached the magical two-hundred-kilometer line.

The upper hemisphere fire control officer of *Nurturer of Social Norms* was very pleased with her ship's handiwork. She had never been in combat before and had not anticipated the sheer joy and pride she now felt as she watched race enemy vessels targeted and destroyed by her magnificent machine.

She could see hundreds of alien machines on her tracking displays. Some machines carried live aliens, and these were marked in one color. Others were pure machine and were color-coded depending on whether they were advancing or keeping their distance.

She went about her duties, whispering questions and giving directions to the core, ever alert for orders from the captain. Forty-seven enemy warcraft and installations targeted and fired upon. Forty-one destroyed.

A very good score, she thought. *Not a perfect record, yet.* However, as relative positions changed, the few ships that had managed to hide behind the tiny planetoids in this flock would lose that cover and have to move. When they did, she would get them all.

The intensity of her excitement was quite sexual, and she had to clamp down on her body responses to keep from putting out mating pheromones. Aranth females had good innate control of estrus and mating cycles. As a warrior, the fire control officer also had intensive physical and mental training to suppress the results of one hundred thousand years of her plains carnivore nature.

Her hindbrain felt the joy of the slaughter, even removed as it was from her presence. Her heritage, powerful even after twenty thousand years removed from the savannah, said that when the killing is good, the food supply is plentiful, and now it is time to mate.

Her forebrain, buttressed by twenty thousand years of written history and ten thousand years of spacefaring culture, knew she still had business to take care of. If she started putting mating scent into the air of the combat center, it might affect her fellow warriors. *That* was inexcusable in a combat situation, and she would surely be dealt with severely by the captain for it.

••✦••

aboard the SFN Gobi, *attached to the strike group at Astrid Base*

On the *Gobi,* all was quiet. The crew walked on cat feet and every breath was hushed. No one wanted to jinx the luck that had put them in a pocket of quiet at the scene of carnage. The tension in the air was palpable, sticky, and oppressive.

The free-floating fear on the ship had mixed with the optimism they had started this mission with, and it had settled into the bones of every person aboard.

The commanding officer watched his targeting feeds carefully. A lot of people had died to set up this situation. Now, he was hoping to reap the harvest. His birds bored inward, anonymous in the flights of attacking missiles. "Among the things we don't know about these particular AranthChi butchers is why they ignore our missiles until close approach," he said.

The shattered silence made his bridge crew jump. The tracking officer and the pilot both nodded. The entire crew, all three shifts of them, had argued about this apparent consistency all the way out to the asteroids. Now they were gambling their lives and the success of the mission on the AranthChi not changing that habit.

"They seem to love two hundred kilometers," said the pilot. "As far as I am concerned, two hundred is my new lucky number." He kissed an imaginary good luck charm.

"Thirty seconds to mark," the tracking officer reported.

"Roger. Reconfirm that none of the Frypaks' lines of sight will cross our birds' paths."

"Confirmed, sir. Angles of convergence will not occur before the 150-kilometer point."

"Fine. Get ready to send out the signal. All Frypaks are to detonate at minus five seconds. Ready . . . mark!"

••✦••

aboard Nurturer of Social Norms

Suddenly, all of *Nurturer*'s tracking displays went white and then blank. "Core, what's happening?" The fire control officer spun in a circle, baffled by the blank wall.

"Near-simultaneous detonation of multiple lasing devices have bathed the shields in coherent light. Sensor arrays have lost sensitivity and are being adjusted now."

"Well, hurry."

"Warning, automatic weapon approaching at high speed! Targeting accomplished, target destroyed four octades distance!"

The core's voice was accompanied by an entire bank of monitors going white again. Then a violent shove from the opposite direction knocked the fire control officer from her seat, and the world went blistering hot and inky black.

••✦••

the battle near Astrid Base

Gobi's two special birds closed on the AranthChi behemoth from nearly opposing directions. Comfortably short of the two-hundred-kilometer line, very esoteric equipment kicked in, and the missiles went from a standard thirty-gravity acceleration to a mind-boggling one hundred gravities. They crossed the intervening distance in a few heartbeats.

Simultaneously, 130 bomb-pumped Frypak lasers detonated, pouring their combined deadly light onto the hostile's shields. The one-megaton explosions created searing white, red, and x-ray lines that batted the ship viciously.

The AranthChi ship got its vision back almost too quickly and took out one of the missiles just seven kilometers from its screens. The missile, also shielded, survived just the number of instants required to detonate its warhead and the expanding nuclear wavefront began to do battle with *Nurturer*'s shields. It was a contest the ship was destined to win.

However, *Nurturer* never saw the other missile, which closed within meters of the shield wall before detonating. Suddenly a star appeared. A piece of the inner depths of a sun birthed at their feet, throwing 250 megatons of fusion device, generating millions of degrees of heat, to claw violently against the impenetrable technology of an older civilization.

Millisecond after millisecond, the two forces struggled. Light pressure of incalculable intensity beat against woven streams of protective energy fields. Slowly, the field fuzzed and weakened, losing minute amounts of integrity and then firming up.

Grudgingly, the fields gave up ground. The shields spread and sagged, stretched and sagged some more. The output of every shield emitter on that side of the ship reached theoretical maximum and beyond.

Almost gently, the shield wall touched the ship itself. Instantly, torrents of thermal radiation poured into the hull, cracking the tough outer shell of the thousand-year-old ship and thrusting within. The interior became a hell where bulkheads dissolved and organic beings flashed into steam. Deeper the heat and radiation penetrated, until the shields managed to snap back and cut off contact, leaving behind an expanding bubble of superheated plasma that worked its way progressively into the bowels of the ship.

Even this strike, as damaging as it was, came nowhere near being a death blow. Fully seventy-five percent of the ship remained operational. Functions were rerouted at the speed of light by the core. Internal safety fields intensified, slowing the spread of the plasma bubble. Bulkheads softened and gave way more slowly. The ship was winning the fight with the incursion of star stuff.

But, as the heat and shockwave distorted the very frame of the mighty warship, more damage was occurring deeper within. Power surges and sensor noise, combined with the destruction of a critical fuel guide pathway generator, led to minor confusions. The backup generator received conflicting instructions and had to sort them out. Multiple false readings sealed the ship's fate.

The guidepath containment shielding of one of the ship's great fuel cells varied beyond outside specs. The degradation of the containment fields was overlooked, and a tiny opening appeared in the gravitetic forcefield bottle.

Through the pinhole came a stream of antimatter under unimaginable pressure. The antimatter fuel was kept gaseous and compressed under hundreds of gravities of force. It nearly qualified as degenerate matter, with anti-proton shells almost touching. The stream jetted out into the ship, instantly creating a celestial blowtorch that consumed everything in its path.

The ship's core, with a thousand and one things to occupy its attention, still recognized the threat immediately. As the matter/antimatter reaction raged uncontrolled in the corridors of the ship, pushed ever outward by the star surface pressures in the fuel cell, the core took the only action it could. Racing ahead of the all-consuming reaction, it forced down the outer shieldwall. This allowed the antimatter to jet out into space, hollowing out a huge cavern in what had formerly been a firstline ship of the fleet.

••✦••

aboard the Gobi

"We did it!" There was pandemonium aboard the *Gobi*. Cameras had caught the entire drama of the attack on the AranthChi ship. The appearance of a bright spear of light lancing out through the side of the ship and a rapidly widening hole around the shaft of radiance told the success of their attack.

Second after second, they waited for the ship to disappear entirely. And then—"Son of a bitch. Sir, they are getting underway!" The tracking officer sounded incredulous.

The pilot took a fast measurement. "They only have half a ship left, but that juggernaut of a thing is still under power. It's limping for home under minimal thrust, but that's still a ship, not a corpse."

"Whatever that light was, it's gone out now." The captain sighed. He could see from the camera view that deep caverns now existed where a curved forceshield once covered a smooth, featureless hull metal. Many areas seemed crinkled and torn, as if composed of shiny but ruined tissue paper. Radiation detectors on the ship began to fall back from their first, insane readings.

"Still, I think we can call this an operational kill. Send out the report to Astrid."

"Yes sir. Um . . . sir, do you want to give chase?"

"Do you want to pursue that thing?"

"No sir, I guess not."

As they watched the wounded gargantuan retreating in the distance, they all felt amazement and awe. Nothing should have been able to survive the pounding they had given it. Many areas in the damaged zone still sparkled white hot, others dull red. The ship slued ponderously back and forth to protect its damaged side, swatting the occasional missile that still lived to target it out of the sky.

"If we had a few Frypaks left, we could probably take it out entirely," the commander remarked.

aboard the Newton

SFN *Newton* received the same compressed high-speed information updates being sent to every departing ship, be they controlled by Sistra Traffic Control or INSYSCON. Unlike the rest, however, *Newton* had the privilege of being able to watch their pursuer leaving the asteroid belt and head in their direction. It was a galvanizing experience.

Even before InSystem Control had apprised the Scout of speed and closing vectors, the *Newton* had a fair idea of the trouble they were in. Loafing along at considerably less than maximum speed had allowed them to gather large quantities of invaluable data.

Unfortunately, the gathering of this information was best done at slow accelerations, which left them with a long way to go to reach FTL zone. Even though their particular nemesis was starting from back in the asteroids, it would soon be coming along fast.

For twenty hours, while the drama of war unfolded in the Alpha Centauri system, the *Newton* gathered intelligence. For twenty hours, a team headed by the first officer developed contingency plans to enable the *Newton* to fight the enemy. As more became known about these particular attackers, the early optimistic plans of engagement had to be put aside. The *Newton*'s weaponry was woefully inadequate to the task.

Certain modifications were made to otherwise peacetime devices during the early hours, before it became clear that the enemy was able to shrug off ordinance as heavy as naval-grade anti-ship nukes. The team of officers and able spacers exceeded every standard of cleverness in their search to find ways to discomfit an attacker. Their ringside view of the war and the natural ability of explorers to improvise drove them to heights of inventiveness they hoped to be able to report to somebody, someday.

Now that the enemy was taking an interest in them, it was time to become scarce as atheists in a foxhole. First, the survey boat dropped the towed array, blowing the hookup's emergency disconnect. Maneuvering clear of the array, the boat throttled back and waited for *Newton* to catch up.

The crew of two waited busily indeed. Scrambling into skinsuits and environment packs and setting the controls to remote/auto took precious moments. They were waiting by the open boat lock anyway, when the *Newton* came alongside so that the survey boat faced its bay.

Immediately the *Newton* extended a fuel boom, and the

crew mated the hose by hand. The task of refueling the boat took much less time than the controversy had taken to die down when the team had proposed leaving the boat behind.

The survey boat, however, was heavy. There was a truism that said if running is a good idea, then running like a bat out of hell is a *very good* idea. Add the laws of physics that say the more mass you push for a given engine strength, the slower you go, and even the captain had to agree that the survey boat was a liability.

Refueling the boat offloaded another few thousand pounds of mass that the engineer agreed could be spared from the ship's nearly full and quite oversized tanks. Why the captain had ordered the boat refueled was something of a mystery, though. At its best speed, the survey boat could mount about three gravities of acceleration. The *Newton* would leave the boat far behind in the coming hours, and it would be crewless anyway. Why not just let it drift? But the captain was adamant. The boat was coming along, at least as far as it could go.

When refueling was complete, the survey boat crew rode the boom back into *Newton*'s bay, another time-saving violation of regulations. Before they had the bay buttoned up, the boat's drive had restarted, and it began to pull ahead. They could tell from the brightness that it was throttled up to full power before it was completely out of the sight.

Hurrying forward to their high-acceleration duty stations, they were assisted by the resumption of *Newton*'s thrust. The captain was wasting no time in removing his ship from the area. Already the other twelve members of *Newton*'s complement were in the "tank."

The tank was actually two rooms, one fore and one aft of the main control room. Space for the two former crewmembers of the survey boat had been carefully left in the tank room closest to the launch bay.

The two raced through the suit-up drill, not bothering to remove skinsuits before sliding into the bulkier drysuits. They fastened low dome helmets to reinforced neck rings, then cycled through the airlock and into the aqueous medium beyond.

Just inside the door, individual air and communication umbilicals awaited the two. Immediately on entering, they noticed pressure increasing on their eardrums, a sure sign that the *Newton* was accelerating again. Hooking up the umbilicals put them in the identical environment of the rest of the crew.

Now the computer could begin compensating for the effects of increasing thrust. No longer did the heavy hand of reaction forces affect them as an inline push. In the minimally compressible waters of the tank, the crew was shielded from the increase in weight that would be their lot if they were in other parts of the ship.

Instead of a massive grip forcing them into the cushions of an acceleration couch, they were gently supported in water. Fully submerged and neutrally buoyant, they were pressed upon equally in all directions, experiencing the equivalent of a descent to the ocean floor. For every ten meters per second squared of Delta V the *Newton* added to its dash, every person aboard descended one atmosphere's worth of pressure into the depths.

If they reached one hundred meters per second thrust, the crew would pass beyond the operating depth of most early submersibles. This was only possible because of the well-known but little counted-on fact that Human beings were also mostly water and not very compressible.

The dry suit helmets, designed with very little airspace, combined with the increasing psi fed into each suit umbilical by the computer, neatly counteracted the tendency of Human nasal and lung spaces to collapse. This was centuries-old oceanic hard-hat technology, only recently applied to space.

Early in the process, the tank's environmental controls were informed that this would be a very high-speed run. They immediately began removing the nitrogen from the air mix, replacing it with helium.

"Passing sixty meters per second squared of thrust, sir." The pilot seemed very at home, hooked loosely into her webbing. In front of her stood the control pillar. "We are throttled up to half power, all readings in the green."

"Thank you, Lieutenant Grendell. Continue throttling up."

In a relatively short time, engine output reached operating maximums. All instruments agreed. Thrust was 120 meters per second, and the tank pressure sensors read twelve atmospheres.

"Has our bogey reacted to our change in speed?"

The survey boat pilot and the remote sensors officer got to work. Now the genius of the captain insisting on refueling the shuttle came to the fore. Roughly behind them lay the enemy. The *Newton*'s own drive emissions eliminated any possibility of the *Newton* seeing them.

But also behind them was the recently passed survey boat. The survey boat's sensors were no better than the *Newton*'s. However, the survey boat could afford to shut off its drive for a few moments to use those sensors and then relay the information to the parent craft. From that point on, the boat would be stopping its engines at approximately half hour intervals to check up on the enemy.

Soon the information was in. "Captain, the bogey has adjusted course to meet our increased speed and is accelerating as well. In the last minute, they have moved from the previously measured forty-eight gravities to sixty G of acceleration."

The navigator chimed in, "At sixty G, the enemy will still catch us short of FTL space."

"I understand. Lieutenant Grendell, I believe you are holding our engines at redline?"

"Yes, sir."

"You are now ordered to go beyond redline. I want every pound of thrust your engines can deliver."

The pilot nodded and got busy. As the atmospheric reading mounted in the tank, she muttered, "Well, folks, this voids the warranty. I hope we won't have to get out and push."

After an interminable time, she nodded again. "Engines are at 104 percent, throat temperatures remaining steady. We are now at eighteen G. No one, *that I know of,* has ever run this type of engine above redline for longer than about thirty minutes. I can't predict how long this pace can be maintained."

"As long as we have to, lieutenant; as long as we can," replied the captain. "Navigation, what's our situation now?"

"Too close to call. We might make it, but not by much."

The hours flew by. The bogey gained steadily. The survey boat fell farther behind. They reached the point where the survey boat's transmissions became harder to read, and they dropped a probe to relay the crucial information it was gathering for them.

Then one of the seminal moments was upon them. The bogey was about to pass the survey boat. Speculating on whether the aliens would blow it out of space or leave it alone, allowing it to transmit data to the *Newton,* had occupied the crew's free time in the early hours. Now no one spoke of it. Everyone listened for the remote sensors report.

"Survey boat is off the air," reported the remote pilot.

"They burned it at fifty thousand kilometers," said navigation.

"Not taking any chances, are they?" the captain murmured. "Well, none of us are surprised. It's time to drop another instrument probe."

All this time, the *Newton*'s drive never wavered. Riding a pillar of fire, white with the fusing nuclei of hydrogen, the *Newton* hurried into a darkling void. The point of mathematically possible translation into another type of space came closer and closer. So did the foe.

One problem loomed before them, as unsolvable as the

motives of the enemy that pursued them. By the time they reached FTL point, the enemy would be in weapons range. Still distant, but capable of hitting them with an ultra-high energy bolt.

As long as the *Newton*'s drive was on, the enemy probably wouldn't shoot. The chances of pushing an energy beam, even one of the AranthChi's abilities, through the hot core of the *Newton*'s drive flame and into the ship, were not good. However, the enemy knew that the *Newton* would have to turn off its drive before being able to successfully engage its FTL translation device.

It was a problem the pilot had to explain to the captain. "It's not that I don't want to try, sir; I'm telling you *it won't work*. The drive has to be completely off before translation to FTL space can occur. If I engage the transpatial apparatus before shutting down the drive, it won't be able to grasp the fabric of 7D space successfully. If it can't do that, it can't pull us out of our space and into FTL."

"What happens if you try?" the captain persisted.

"Same thing that happens if you try it too close to a star. The device gets feedback, shuts down, and recycles. You can't force it to work; it's *fail safe*. We need two things for translation to occur." She looked exasperated behind her faceplate. "First, space has to be flat enough. That means we have to get far enough away from a mass capable of distorting space. A star, for instance. Second, it has to be quiet enough! By quiet, I mean no high-energy phenomena occurring close to the translation point—like a fusion drive running full out. Not only that, I will need time to shut down the drive. So I need thirty seconds, plus drive shut down time, to get us the hell out of Alpha Centauri space. Sir."

The captain turned to his first officer, who was floating next to him in the placid waters of the tank, and grinned. "Okay, contingency team, it's up to you now. I want forty-eight seconds of free time. A time when we are shutting down and coasting free and the AranthChi are still not shooting at us. And I want to know how you're going to do it in . . . the next five minutes."

The first officer looked thoughtful and nodded. He set up a privacy link to the other members of his team. The pilot looked startled as she realized she had just been ordered to be ready to throttle down and turn off a drive that had been running above redline for hours in just eighteen seconds.

"Crazy, we are all crazy," she muttered. Then she reached up and switched off the common channel. Her mouth continued to move as she called up engine schematics and fuel feed data, but her thoughts were now private.

It took every bit of five minutes and then a couple more, but the first officer had an answer for the captain. "You wanted forty-eight seconds, captain. We can give you forty-eight seconds."

The pilot looked unhappy, but she said nothing. Every member of the crew knew that the *Newton* had been running her heart out these last few hours. They all suspected the damage that must have been taking place in the vessel's great engines. At the very least, the linings of the nozzles were vastly pitted and worn.

The tail end of the Scout was white hot. That the fuel injectors still worked at such temperatures was a tribute to the ship's designers and engineers. The magnetic pinch bottle field had not varied a wavelength the whole time. Their luck had been truly phenomenal.

But now the pilot would be cutting back the steady flow of fuel to nothing in a breath-takingly short period of time. Now was when luck truly needed to be with them. If an episode of fuel cavitation, or uneven burning, delayed engine shutdown, the window of escape would be lost. If one of the great motors were very close to material failure, the rapid changes in pressure and temperature during shutdown could cause an explosion. The pilot could not even predict the odds. It was a complete roll of the dice.

Finally, it was time. One by one, probe packages dropped from the fleeing Scout. The pilot began her countdown, her board synchronized with the remote officer. All stations were staffed and ready.

The tank environment technician was carefully included in this maneuver. When the pilot began her throttle back, pressure on the waters of the tank would decrease rapidly. It would be as if the people were ascending swiftly from a great depth. Uncomfortable initially, such rapid decompression would quickly become fatal.

The tank tech, one Sergeant Woomera, was not going to allow that to happen. "As we throttle down, the tank controls are going to compensate by injecting lots of air into the room. The tank will get very cloudy and turbulent. Be sure you're all strapped into your webbing," he advised. "However, pressure is going to fall off too rapidly for the tank to match pressures by this method. So don't be surprised when your suits start filling out. They are going to get *real* rigid until we reach equilibrium."

"In other words, they're going to pop," one of the crew members joked nervously.

"Matter of fact, this is the time you better hope I've been taking good care of your suits, 'cause you pop a seal now, you are going to fly around the room and become very dead. And there's nothing I or anyone else will be able to do about it." The tech's voice was deadpan as he made the statement. No one assumed he was kidding.

The clock reached zero, the pilot began throttling back, and the tank became cloudy as a howl of compressed air forced its way into the room. The people were buffeted and batted about, blasted by sound and fury, as they had not been any time previously during the escape attempt.

When the ship was down to six Gs and falling, the last package to be dropped behind detonated. One hundred kilometers behind the *Newton,* nuclear-grade seismic devices detonated in a cluster, screening the ship from its pursuer.

Six seconds later the next package went off. Spaced a hundred kilometers apart, the next three went off in six-second intervals. Even though nuclear in nature, the devices would never have been strong enough, even detonating all at once, to have seriously inconvenienced the enemy.

Now, however, they provided some of the same screening function that the drive exhaust had given them. The first officer only hoped the AranthChi would not be able to see through the thinning blast foci too quickly.

Then the drive was silent, and the waiting began. Second after second, the transpatial pattern built up around the ship. Soon the fields began to grip 7D space. Lines of mathematical force became more "real" until the ship began sliding into FTL.

The last package went off. The AranthChi began beaming through the expanding wavefront anyway, hoping to hit what they could not lock on to.

An intolerably bright light swept into the region of converging spaces and played upon the *Newton*, casting rapidly dopplering shadows. Then the light was gone, and the Scout was in FTL space.

"What happened?" asked the captain.

"During the last 1.3 seconds of transition, we were being struck by an AranthChi laser beam. But I show no damage on my boards," replied the pilot.

All other damage reports came back negative also. It was very puzzling. Only the navigator was willing to offer a theory. "We were mostly into FTL space at that point already. I think what happened is we pulled that beam into FTL with us. It came in with us, but it didn't hit us."

It was an absurd theory on the face of it, but it did cover the facts, sort of. The captain had to ask, "If it came in with us, where is it now? Is it still behind us, waiting to hit as we leave FTL, or is it ahead of us and we are going to run into it during the trip home? Or is it gone, and we don't have to worry about it anymore?" He looked at the pilot.

She protested, "Hey, I only fly this bucket. If I understood that kind of math, I would never have left the Sorbonne."

The captain sighed. They never said it would be easy having a command when he was going through the Academy. Now he wished he had listened more carefully to what they hadn't said. "I want the shields on automatic. I want them to phase in as soon as possible after leaving FTL. In fact, if you can get them to establish, I want them on before we're all the way out of FTL."

The shield engineer shrugged. It looked like the ride home was going to be every bit as interesting as the way the trip began. He would do research during the trip, to see if the answers to the captain's questions could be found in the *Newton*'s data banks. At least, he thought, they were on their way home.

••✦••

aboard the battleship Suppression of Discord

Raalma waited for communications from *Nurturer of Social Norms* with a strange unease. Little about this operation was going as expected. All along, resistance had been too high, and the discovery that the aliens had super-luminal capability had been a severe shock. It was intolerable, but more and more of their race enemy's ships seemed to be escaping the system every hour.

Why had the council not warned him of these things? Had they not known, or had they chosen not to tell him? It was all very frustrating. And where was the report from *Nurturer*? It was all taking too long.

When the comm link was established, Raalma knew immediately something was wrong. His usually bellicose senior captain's fur hung limply at the neck, and all trace of swagger was gone from the Aranth's stance.

"Expedition Commander Raalma, I have the misfortune to report that I have allowed race enemy vessels to severely damage my ship, and I have failed in my mission to eradicate the asteroid military threat." The Aranth sounded humble, something Raalma had never seen in him before.

"Give me details, captain. Your ship was well defended. How could this have happened?"

"All of the decisions related to this disgrace were my own. Please absolve my crew, as they acted in exemplary fashion." Spazzea sagged inward as if the bones of his skeleton had shrunk or softened.

Raalma's fur bottled slightly. "Stop acting like a whipped cub," he ordered curtly. "I want your report, and I want it in proper command personage mode."

"Understood." Spazzea attempted to comply. "Against orders, I allowed fusion pile containing darts within the 128-octade line. This should not have been a problem, because up to this point, we were winning the battle. Aggression tracking had already shifted priorities and was beginning to mop up the incoming darts when we were given a nasty surprise. The aliens demonstrated another previously unknown technology. The two darts that penetrated my defenses showed sudden acceleration increases and gravity generation signatures. There was not time to react to their changed behavior, and both reached ship proximity and detonated."

He looked bemused and perhaps a touch angry. He was beginning to deal with the shock of defeat. "Such darts should not have been able to win an inroad into my ship. The shield should have kept them out. But it did not." He looked straight into the monitor for the first time in the conversation. "These aliens are very dangerous."

"I am forced to agree," said Raalma through gritted teeth. "As of this moment, I am reinstituting the battle group form. You are to gather your group together at the conclusion of their present hunts and wait at the orbit of the outermost planet for further assignments. For the rest of this operation, single ship attacks are out. The quaint notion we had, that our weaponry would be more dangerous to ourselves than anything the aliens might have, has proved tragically inaccurate."

Senior Captain Spazzea's posture had been unconsciously returning to a more normal arrogance, his stance taking on a hint of its wonted belligerence. Now he deflated entirely. "Expedition commander, in light of my failures to date, would it not be better to replace me in the command position of my battle group?"

"Captain, we will hold a review of your command decisions at another time. For now, you know your battle group best, and I still have confidence in you." He paused, leaned forward, and added, "As long as you follow your orders."

Spazzea's ears twitched violently. "Commander Raalma, my ship is disabled. One third of it no longer exists; another third is so radioactive it cannot be occupied. Perhaps an eighth of my crew is fully functional." He licked his lips quickly, refusing to show teeth. "We could not fight off a swarm of blood gnats at this point. We would certainly be ineffective leading an attack against race enemies."

Raalma's shoulder fur rippled. He bit back a snarl. "Your ship is no longer a factor in this war. It will have to be abandoned. You will simply transfer your command to an Insistence vessel. *Now.* No more argument. Do your duty and protect your command. Orders will be forthcoming."

"Understood." The captain's image faded out.

Raalma sat for a while, thinking. No one disturbed his preoccupation. Presently he spoke. "Secretary function."

"Commander?" replied the core.

"Has the planetary report come in yet?"

"Yes, commander. *Defender of Authority* has sent in its completed observations within the last half hour."

"Give me the essence. Are there any more surprises?" He sounded unutterably weary.

"Affirmative. Analysis of the primary life zone world indicates that it is not the aliens' homeworld."

After so many suppositions found to be false about the aliens, after so many unpleasant surprises, this became just one more wonder. Raalma reacted with barely an ear twitch. He was very matter of fact, simply saying, "Explain."

"There are two distinct types of biome found on the subject world. The population density highly favors one over the other. Additionally, the population distribution is suspicious of colonization rather than the spontaneous growth and migration patterns typical of native evolution. By far, there is one continent more heavily populated then the rest of the planet combined. That continent also has a working space elevator overhead. The device in question shows evidence of either being rebuilt or heavily modified at least once during its operational lifetime."

"So we have attacked the colony world, not the main system. It is obvious we should have proceeded with more deliberation. Well, these decisions are behind us, incapable of being called back. I am looking for some good news. Tell me, how old is this colony?"

"The system dynamics group estimates this system to have been colonized not less than two and not more than four hundred years ago. If it will cheer you at all, commander, the current thinking among the group is that initial colonization took place with sub-luminal technology. The extensive habitations in the asteroidal flocks and certain indications of atmospheric mining of the gas giants combine with the planet demographics to strongly suggest that other parts of the system were colonized while waiting for biome engineering of the life zone planet to be successful."

"So that gives us a probable timeline for the development of their past light technology. If we are fortunate, we will find that this ability is very new indeed. In fact, they may have even gotten it from our own rogue clans." He thought hard on the various issues. Finally he spoke again. "You say most of the population is on one continent?"

"That is correct, commander."

Raalma stood and padded back and forth in front of the table. He growled. "I have been wondering what to do about *Nurturer of Social Norms*. It is not going to be able to enter super-luminal space again, and it is against doctrine to just leave it behind. Ordering it destroyed seems like a waste somehow. Tell me, what would happen if we crashed it onto the most populated continent?"

"Analysis indicates that most likely the ship would not reach the surface intact. Instead, it would break up and explode in the lower atmosphere."

"What kind of damage would that do?"

"It would depend on the exact height at which detonation occurred. Most likely, there would be the creation of a firestorm, which would cover the continent and much of the rest of the hemisphere. Second most likely, the detonation shockwave would compress and then expand the gaseous layer and rip off a high proportion of the planet's atmosphere."

Raalma ran a moist tongue over sharp teeth. "Either of those results would be quite satisfactory," he said in a contemplative tone. He slapped hand to desk and sat down slowly. A slight smile played across his face, then his whiskers twitched in a full grin. "Deliver the report to Tactics and append a note to the effect that we will need to capture the space structures over the planet intact. Have them devise an aggression scenario that will bring us the most success in this endeavor. When we have access to these depositories of information, I want all the marrow sucked out of them by every specialist group we carry. I want to know everything possible about these aliens' true homeworld, the number and location of every colony system, and what their full defensive and offensive capabilities are."

"Note appended, report sent."

"Good. Perhaps in this way we will be able to find out how much of the task we can accomplish in the time we have left. I want to be able to report positive results to the High Council." His shoulder fur rippled as muscles moved underneath flesh. He settled into his chair as an early ancestor might have settled down by a water hole on the savannah. It indicated a patience to wait quietly for events to develop, for prey to wander within grasp.

"One more item. Send a message to all expedition units that at the conclusion of their ship hunts they are to assemble in their battle groups, at coordinates to be given to them by their senior captains. Repeat that *all* previous aggression assignments have been canceled. No more single-ship attacks on habitations or fortifications are to be carried out."

"Cancellation orders and new assembly instructions are being relayed now, commander."

"Then that is all for now. Terminate secretary function."

The lessons were expensive, thought Raalma, *very expensive. But we learn; yes, we learn. There will be no more mistakes that race enemies can take advantage of. The loss of* Effort *and the ruination of* Nurturer *were the dues we paid to have our eyes widened, our ears sharpened. Yes, we have the smell of you now, our race enemies.*

He looked out the viewport again at the warm yellow star of Alpha Centauri. It was a tiny, glaring ball in the distance that he could cover with one hand. An orb that gave warmth and sustenance to his enemy. A pretty star. Someday an AranthChi star, when the steady wave of Aranth expansion reached this far. At the moment, a stronghold of his foes.

"We will have you by the throat soon, my enemies," he growled. "From this point forward, we knock out everything alien-made at maximum practical distance. You will not have a chance to snap at our tails again in this existence."

He turned back to his desk and stared at the obsidian surface. "It is time to crush this outpost conclusively and move on to the homeworld," he said. It was a whisper; it was a promise. It would be done.

12

MIKAIL GETS THE WORD

on New Hearth

Wilimena Hines punched her desk and rose with a grin. The screens went dark one by one. The last one flickered as if in reproach. *Time to play hooky.* She smoothed down her severe white blouse, slipped on her shoulder rig, and topped it off with her favorite pearl-gray jacket. A quick look in the mirror showed a lean, aristocratic, gray-haired woman in a classic broad-shouldered pantsuit.

Her long face grinned back at her. *Knock 'em dead, kid.* Today she was attending a conference of government agencies on the subject of secure communications. This was, in fact, one of her hobbies. Actually, the breaking of secure communications was her passion.

Wilimena wore two hats at the Office of Alien Technologies. As number-three person in the office, she was overseer of the appropriations budget accountability project. In other words, she thought up reasons for the senate to give her office more money, more personnel allocations, and more authority to go along with the responsibilities that the OAT was charged with carrying out. She was damn good at it.

She was also Internal Security Czar. Four decades before, she had been the star operative of the Combined Euro Politzia Counter Espionage Unit. In her time, she cracked into more domestic terrorist groups than any Euro-Region police officer before—or since.

Designing security systems had seemed a natural progression to the woman who, more than anything, wanted to stay active in the field. So she'd gone back to school at a time when most police officers were contemplating retirement. When she finished, no security system on Earth could stand against her. She worked for OAT because she was the best.

She often suspected that her interest came not from her original training in the espionage field, but rather from her heritage. Being Romany on her mother's side and old Prussian on her father's accounted far more for the way she approached life than any doctorate.

She arrived at the hotel about an hour early, as was her wont. She walked the locale slowly, appearing to any observer as a little old lady out for a stroll—which she was. When she was done, she went inside.

As she stood in the lobby, studying the floor map for the location of her convention, she caught a motion out of the corner of her eye. Not one steel gray hair on her head moved, nor did her super straight spine sway. Suddenly, however, police instincts of decades past came awake.

To confirm her suspicions, she walked briskly to the steel-and-crystal escalator and took it up to the shops and salons level. At the top, she hesitated momentarily. She quickly found the sign she was looking for and followed it.

She strode calmly into the hotel's notions store and made directly for the camera counter. As was usual for such places, flat and virtual video screens covered the wall, showing scenes of the shop's interior and doorway.

She grinned at several images of herself on the monitors and then at a man walking through the door. Her shadow made an immediate face right and headed for the news vids and slick magazine racks.

Got you, she thought. She wondered how long she'd been under surveillance and realized she'd been subliminally uneasy since arriving at Anderson airport a couple of hours before. Her tail didn't look familiar. He certainly hadn't been on the hotel complex shuttle.

There had to have been a hand-off in surveillance when she reached the hotel. The hand-off must have been clumsily done. Otherwise, they wouldn't have triggered the suspicions of a public employee twenty years retired from police work.

Still, she was under observation by persons unknown, and that was very disturbing. In such circumstances, it was always best to assume the worst. Why she would be the victim of a kidnap attempt, she had no idea. Assassination crossed her mind, only to be rejected. Assassins usually lie in wait, but even those using running dogs were more discreet than this.

Should I call in the police? It was possibly a good idea, but probably not. Most political kidnappings had an insider in the local constabulary. If she ran into the insider, or if that insider was supplying interference for the field operatives, she was only delivering herself into their hands.

What about hotel security? That level of the profession was always underpaid. The odds of the hotel's security force being actively involved, or just paid to look the other way, was astronomically high. *Best to do it alone,* she decided.

Damn! Hotel security had to have scanned her when she entered the complex. Her adversaries would know she only carried a collapsible shock rod and an anaesthetic needler, both short-range weapons.

She *was* getting old. There was a time when she would never have left the office without at least one unregistered lethal weapon—preferably undetectable. It was time to even the odds.

If these people did not really know whom they were dealing with, she was going to make sure they were very surprised. Unpleasantly so. If this was not a kidnap attempt, everyone involved was going to be highly embarrassed. Except, of course, Wilimena.

With decision came action. She placed her order with the catalogue clerk. A moment later, a Human salesperson hurried over, alerted by the store catalogue system as to the nature of Wilimena's orders. He was both curious and deferential.

Some hundred-year-old ladies might order an omnicam with remote transmission capabilities. A few might purchase a police band sight/sound transceiver and have the credentials to allow the store to sell the system to her.

However, few such older customers would then follow up with an order for a transparent, waterproof case and top-of-the-line underwater floods in the hundred thousand candle power range. She accessorized the order with the heavy-duty battery pack.

While the clerk was packing these purchases, Wilimena picked up another handy item or two and added them to the mix. It all fit comfortably into the shoulder bag she selected. Finally, she decided she was done.

The clerk contained his curiosity until the last moment. As she was getting ready to leave, he spoke up. "Ma'am, I know it's none of my business, but could you answer me a question?"

She fixed a bright brown eye on him and nodded.

"This all looks like you are going on a major ocean hunt, ma'am. You wouldn't be thinking of going after a megagants beast, would you?" He sounded faintly worried, surely on her behalf, she thought.

"Now, what makes you say that?"

"Well, ma'am, it sure looks like you're going somewhere wet with a lot of recording equipment. Now I know most oldsters are pretty good at taking care of themselves, but when you get to a certain age, you should just leave the dangerous stuff to younger folk. Why, I was telling my gran just the other day, she needs to slow down. Hang gliding, bow and arrow caribou hunting, megagant chasing . . . it's not seemly for a woman of a 124. Why some older people start doin' crazy things when they get to their second teens is beyond me. No disrespect, ma'am."

Wilimena grinned. "Sonny, I think I would like your grandma. You ought to have more faith in us old-timers. But you can put your mind at ease. The little old megagant is safe from me. I have fishing of a different sort in mind."

He nodded doubtfully.

She left the store with a purposeful stride. Now it was time to find a women-only comfort room. She needed to freshen up, among other things. If everything went as planned, she and some unknown people were going to appear on the evening news.

When she came out of the comfort room, tensely alert and loaded for bear, no one was in sight. The omnicam head was inconspicuously nestled in the shoulder braid of her severe jacket, its fiberoptic cable threaded down into the shoulder bag.

In the carefully restructured bag, one flood faced forward and one aft. They were set to burst on in a high surge overload when she dropped the side flaps. Their performance was guaranteed to cause Wilimena to pay for sight restoration treatments for any innocent bystanders looking the wrong way at the consequential moment.

There was still no one in view. She began to wonder if her pursuers had managed to plant a tracer on her and withdrawn the shadow. That situation would have its own set of good and bad points. She headed down the corridor.

At the escalator, she saw her quarry, sitting at an outside table of one of the eating establishments. Mr. Anonymous was not alone, but sat with a long-haired, dark blond individual, who had his back to Wilimena.

Wilimena headed that way. As she made her way across the concourse, she quickly reviewed her plan. Perhaps it would have been a better idea to involve the police. If she'd done it right, she could have contacted a constable or two she knew personally. Even if the squeeze *was* on from higher up, they would have warned her somehow, helped if they could. No, the risk was too great. It was better this way.

When she was fifteen feet from the table, finger gripping the trigger mechanism, the sandy-haired man casually turned around. Wilimena was so startled she almost missed a step. Only luck itself prevented her from triggering her trap at that moment. But, oh, what a surprise.

Malcolm Tweed, the pipe-smoking son of a bitch, assistant under-secretary of security for the New Hearth Colony, sat at his ease, smiling an invitation to Wilimena. Tweed just happened to be the colony's top cop. If he'd put the tail on her, the purpose could not possibly be kidnap. He could legally detain just about anyone he wanted to with complete impunity. Her mind was once again in high gear, but the gears kept slipping. There was nothing to hold on to.

"Hi, Wilimena." Tweed's public smile was very wide, showing even white teeth. His eyes sparkled with unexplained mirth. He rose as she neared the table.

"Dear lady, would you terribly much mind taking your finger off the button of whatever nasty concoction you've got cooked up in that shoulder bag and join me and Herr Gruber here for a cappuccino?"

Just for an instant, the impulse to burn his eyes out was overwhelming. The moment passed, and instead Wilimena gave him her best tutonic glare. She threw in dash of Romany evil eye just for good measure. He did not obligingly fall over dead.

Wilimena came up to the table, staring at him, while Herr Gruber stood and pulled out a chair for her. She sat primly, setting the bag on the table. Her spine could have been used as a straight rule.

"Malcolm, you are lower than the vultures' vomit, or whatever it is my grandkids call each other these days. What are you doing, tailing all the conference attendees?"

"Not all of them, my dear. Just you. And before you ask, it was just for this occasion."

"Me? And only me, you say. Should I be flattered?"

"Please, Wilimena, unruffle your feathers. It was nothing personal, I assure you. It was simply convenient to keep your whereabouts known until I could talk with you. If you had called attention to us, you would have defeated the whole purpose."

Wilimena looked pleased. "That was the intended effect." She became thoughtful for a second and stared into space, her thin lips pursed. Her ramrod posture and solid gray hair lent her an air of authority. It helped that her Prussian genes gave her the profile of aristocracy.

"I'm almost sorry I will never know how well my little surprise would have worked. Simultaneous transmission on the police and news infonets of your little charade would have been very amusing. Imagine the face of Malcolm Tweed and various assorted henchmen on the five o'clock news. The market share on viewership would skyrocket. My boy, I think if you are going to pull off any more of these juvenile stunts, I am going to have to invest in newsnet stock."

All during Wilimena's prim monologue, Malcolm Tweed's smile had been fading. Eventually his features settled into a grim line. Underneath his deep tan he looked distinctly pale. His trained affability had not deserted him in many years of political infighting, but now he was holding onto it by the shreds.

"Wilimena, perhaps I should point out that pirate transmissions onto police or private nets is a crime, both by Federation law and colonial statute. Infractions such as you have just described are punishable by substantial prison terms."

"How well I know *officialdom* does not take kindly to having their dirty little doings publicly exposed. I can imagine the thought would be mildly upsetting to you. So, Malcolm, why are we here, waiting for cappuccinos, when we could be at the conference downstairs?"

"We are here because Herr Gruber was clumsy."

Gruber stared at the table, looking distinctly embarrassed.

"It was my intention to have this conversation in a much more casual manner. Perhaps we would have met at the refreshment table or found ourselves in adjoining seats in the auditorium. However it went, it was certainly not supposed to be like this."

"Yes, Malcolm," Wilimena butt in impatiently. "However, we are here and this is now. And *this* now is all you're going to get. In about one minute's time, I am getting up, leaving this table, and lodging a harassment complaint against you with the governor's office."

Malcolm shot a poisonous glance at his man Gruber as if to say, *This is all your fault*. Then he turned on his most sincere look for Wilimena Hines. "Wilimena, let me tender my utmost genuine apologies for the distress we have caused you by our surveillance operation. I can only assure you that in the larger picture, I felt this was necessary before having our little talk. Because of the somewhat unusual nature of certain events I cannot disclose the details of, I needed to approach you in strictest confidence."

"Malcolm, you just said a mouthful, but it didn't mean a damn thing. You're down to thirty seconds."

"Very well. Someone here needs to talk to your boss very urgently."

"Malcolm, that's why we have phones."

"Oh Wilimena, do not be obtuse. The presence of this person on New Hearth at this time must be kept secret. This person cannot just pick up the phone and call in for an appointment. In fact, even I do not know his identity."

Wilimena's eyebrows rose at this assertion. She noted the slip of Malcolm's tongue that revealed the gender of this mysterious person, though she did not comment. Instead, she said, "How do you imagine I can help you? I don't make Mr. Benson's appointments for him. I know you don't want his private phone code. I am *sure* you have it already."

"In three days' time, there will be a testimonial dinner for the retiring commander of Headquarters Base on the moon. Mikail Benson needs to be there."

"He never goes to those kind of things."

"We know. He has been invited, and he declined. However, we're going to reissue the invitation. It is up to you to make sure he goes."

"I'm not his nursemaid, sonny boy. I work for the man. I don't tell him what to do, and I never have. I'm not about to try now."

"I know, but he must be there. Tell him this phrase: 'turncoat and fresh dirt.' If he understands, he will come. If he does not seem to grasp the nuance, get him to come anyway. Understand this, Wilimena: the fate of the Federation is at stake."

Wilimena gave him a skeptical look. She rose from the chair and picked up her shoulder bag. "I'll deliver your message, Malcolm. But, dear boy, please stop reading those trashy spy novels. They are making you *so* corny and melodramatic."

Malcolm appeared relieved. "Thank you, Wilimena. I know you will do your best." He stood, offering his arm. "Now, on to the conference, shall we?"

As she prepared to leave the table, Wilimena gifted him with her most wicked smile. "By the way, Malcolm, how *is* your eyesight these days?"

He paused. "My eyesight is fine. Why do you ask?"

"Oh, just curious. I'm always concerned about the health of my friends."

With eyes that twinkled, Wilimena threaded her arm into Malcolm Tweed's, and the two headed off to the conference. Gruber watched from the table and shuddered. He would not want to have that viper-like female latch onto his arm.

••✦••

Headquarters Base on New Hearth's moon

Mikail was mildly annoyed with his predicament. Laid out on the bed were the various accoutrements he had pulled out of his travel bag. They did seem to be all there. He was, after all, a meticulous packer.

However, it was not the lack of any one item that caused him displeasure. It was the presence of all the items, in total, that annoyed him. Cummerbunds, weskits, knotted scarves, and laced oxfords had slowly asserted themselves as the formal dress of the day, displacing more comfortable and simpler styles.

He longed for the days of single knits and half boots, or even skintights and Chinese slippers. Though, with those styles, one had to have a fair physique to carry off the outfit.

The problem was that fashions kept changing. The mavens of style felt empowered to pull items out of any historical period, or culture, and make them current.

To be sure, there *were* differences in the worlds of government and politics, of business and academia. Stylish dress was as peculiar to each social arena as was the small talk of the particular crowd.

Military formal affairs followed some consistent and enduring rules. Mikail could, for instance, wear the uniform of a retired naval captain. He had earned the right. It was not, however, his pleasure to do so.

The rules of etiquette worked in his favor another way: he could not be forced to wear the national costume of another culture. He would never be expected to show up at an affair in full kilt and sporran with matching gillies. What his Ukrainian forbears had worn to soirees would certainly make a statement, but he doubted there was an ermine coat or mink-lined hat on all of New Hearth.

His options now diminished rapidly. So be it. Nineteenth-century Britain it had to be. Buttons on the shirt, buttons on the coat, even buttons on the pants, for Goethe's sake. The required clothing certainly made these affairs moribund.

Ordinarily, Mikail enjoyed society affairs. After leaving the navy, he'd discovered a flair for conducting business at the higher levels of society. Meeting the right people at the right places could open doors amazingly well. However, testimonials were the most obnoxious waste of time he could think of. To top it off, this testimonial dinner was taking place on New Hearth's moon, and it had shot his whole day just getting there.

True, he had enormous respect for Admiral Heinlan. The man was a visionary if ever there was one. Political handlers were already lining up with the intention of persuading the admiral to make a life in politics.

Common wisdom had it that Admiral Heinlan could take any Federation governorship he fancied. He was well liked in the provinces. He had a strong following in the inner worlds. It was not inconceivable that political office on Mars or even Earth beckoned. From there, it was a short step to the Federation senate.

None of this explained why Mikail had to endure twice-chewed vegetables and gummy almost-fish or limp salad and textured pseudo-steak with two hundred other people just to see the old guy off. If this were some sick joke being pulled on him by a "friend," Mikail was not amused.

The mysterious methods used to convince him to attend this time-wasting transition in another man's life were more annoying than intriguing. If there was not a damn good reason why Mikail was in this room on a naval base thousands of kilometers from his work, someone was going to regret it.

All during this musing, Mikail was assembling his costume. As he sealed his oxfords closed, he reflected that it was just as well he didn't have to really learn to tie them. The laces appeared authentic, and it would be gauche for anyone to stare at a man's footwear anyway.

Clip-on ties, on the other hand, had always been looked down on. Mikail quite prided himself on the ability to knot a proper four-in-hand. He had also made himself proficient at the great and lesser Windsor, as well as several scarf enknotments. He commenced the operation.

It was done just in time. The social hour had already begun, and in forty-five minutes, seating for dinner would begin. At least the military custom of 2000 hours for formal dinner was one that Mikail was both used to and comfortable with. He headed for the door.

A discreet knock gave him pause. He hadn't ordered anything delivered to his room. In fact, until arrival, he had been expecting to stay at the base hostel where he had reservations. But he had caught a late flight, and when he'd arrived, he found his room had been given away. Instead, he was given accommodations in an unused wing of the VIP suites. At least, he was pretty sure none of the other rooms on this corridor were occupied.

When he triggered the door, he failed to recognize the man standing there, dressed in waiter's array. Accompanying the fellow was a white-linen-draped cart, complete with two covered platters and what appeared to be a bottle of Centauri wine chilling in a bucket.

There was no mistaking the voice, however. Said with the extreme correctness of the professional servant, "The host was sorry to hear you have taken ill, Mr. Benson, and wishes your speedy recovery. He asks that you please feel free to accept dinner in your room."

"Bring it in, and put it over there," Mikail replied, playing his part. "What is it?"

"Chicken from the banquet, sir."

Mikail gave a silent *ugh*. The ersatz waiter rolled the cart into the room and up to the small table. He set the table for one and sat down in front of it himself.

Mikail closed the door. "Why, Jimmy Soo, I thought I was going to get real three-star service here."

The man did not seem to be surprised that his disguise had been penetrated. "Pick up your dinner and sit down, Mike. We've got a lot to talk about."

"Yes indeed. I can hardly wait to hear the story. Aren't you supposed to be on Nova Terrene?"

"I am on Nova Terrene. And that is part of the tale I have to tell."

"In that case, I better pour the wine. This sounds like thirsty work."

Jimmy Soo paused with a fork full of rice halfway to his mouth. "You're going to find that it's tea."

Mikail poured the "wine" anyway, setting one glass before himself and the other in front of Jimmy Soo. Then he waited.

Jimmy took a sip of the iced tea and stared back. Mikail sighed, picked up his plate, and settled down on his side of the table. "Having dinner with you is always exciting, Jimmy. In this particular case, I've been lured four hundred thousand kilometers to the moon, apparently to this very room, to eat banquet leftovers and drink fake wine with you. I can't wait to know why."

"I assure you the tale is worth telling." Jimmy set his utensils down quietly on the table, then cleared his throat. "Ten days from now, on December twentieth, at just after thirteen hundred hours local time, an urgent recall will emanate from the New Hearth AranthChi legate.

"The legation grounds, in Glasgow by the Sea, is the assemble point for every Aranth on New Hearth. By good fortune, from the AranthChi point of view, there are no AranthChi off planet at that time. By 1610 hours, every Aranth will be at the legation. At 1613 hours, an extremely powerful forcefield, opaque to all wavelengths, will be established over the compound, covering all the grounds. The AranthChi will now be completely isolated."

Mikail tried to speak, but Soo waved him to silence.

"Marine detachments and civilian law enforcement surround the legate grounds shortly after that. In an extremely short time, three naval assets are also scrambled. One Corvette is moved into a low fast orbit, another is placed in a middle orbit, and a cruiser assumes geo-stationary position. In addition, two spy satellites are moved into geo-stationary orbit, one leading and one trailing the legation site by about ten degrees. And then we wait.

"At 2057 hours, the forcefield opens, and a hither-to unsuspected space vehicle launches from the legation grounds. One minute later, the buildings erupt in massive explosions, turning the complex into a puree of rubble."

Mikail rubbed his chin thoughtfully. "What happens to that spaceship?" he asked quietly.

"As it happens, at this particular moment, both Corvettes have passed over the site and are down range. Neither see the forceshield drop. The legation's ship launches and accelerates massively. Twenty seconds into flight, the *Charles de Gaulle* comes under attack and is severely damaged. They are unable to return fire. The Aranth ship escapes into the night and is not successfully pursued."

Mikail sat a while, mulling over Jimmy Soo's words. The man had told a gripping tale of future events, full of terse activity and believable deeds. He'd spoken of a time, ten days from right now, so matter-of-factly that it was as if he had lived through them himself.

Jimmy Soo talked as if he believed these events would happen. He made it sound like they already *had* happened. Mikail found that he believed it too.

There was not a doubt in his mind that Jimmy Soo had

been to the future. *How far back have you really come, Jimmy Soo? How far back in your personal past is this day?* Mikail decided the question was irrelevant for now.

More relevant, why come back to today? Why arrange this clandestine meeting with Mikail at this particular time—or at any time, really? For Mikail was sure, without knowing how he knew, Jimmy had picked the day very carefully. Something specific was on Soo's mind. It appeared that he was going to be quiet until Mikail figured it out himself.

Well, then. Jimmy Soo expected something from Mikail; that much was clear. A lot of work had gone into arranging this meeting, not counting the time travel itself, the ease or difficulty of which Mikail had no knowledge. So, what did Jimmy Soo want?

If he expected advice, he could have gotten it from Mikail on the spot. The future Mikhail would had lived through the AranthChi's dramatic, savage evacuation and would have more information than his earlier counterpart.

Perhaps Jimmy has already had a conversation with the future Mikail and gotten the advice he wanted. Which could mean the future Mikail wanted him to look up this Mikail. If so, why? Did his future self want something from Mikail too? What did his future self want him to do that couldn't be done at that time? Unless the only time to do something that desperately needed doing was not then, but now. . . .

Mikail made up his mind. "When did you arrive at New Hearth, Jimmy—or should I ask, when did you arrive from?"

Jimmy's eyes sparkled with mirth. "We knew we could count on you; you're thinking already." Then he sobered, took a drink of tea, and began speaking again.

"Life gets pretty grim for the Human race, starting early January 2607. First, Alpha Centauri is attacked. In less than fourteen days, it falls. By the end of January, it's Earth's turn. Even with warning and frantic last-minute preparation, there is no way to win. The Sol system is completely wiped out.

"And yes, I've watched both battles over and over again from non-space, wondering if there was anything I could do to change the course of history. I failed. There is no way.

"Just over three months from now, in March, an Aranth fighting force enters the Nova Terrene system. By this time, the AranthChi are pretty complacent. All of the big centers have been cracked open and destroyed. The colonies left are just a mop-up to them. Nova Terrene is hit by a small force of four ships. One, the safetyman, hangs way out of system as an observer.

"What the AranthChi don't know is that we got warning virtually the same time as Earth and have been just as frantically preparing for war, in our own way. Nova Terrene only had nine ships to fight with, but the research station found a way to multiply their effectiveness a hundred-fold.

"First we took out the observer. Nine ships dropped out of non-space in a globular maneuver around that AranthChi. As fast as possible, they dumped their missiles and got out of there. Back in non-space, they refilled at a supply depot carefully prepared and marked by the special navigational arrangement used in this medium. Then it was back to local space to dump a new load of missiles. Each ship appeared at a slightly different location but at the exact same *time* as its first appearance! Then they did it again.

"When we had dumped enough missiles to saturate their defenses, we stopped the operation and watched our weapons chew up the observer. Then, with variations, we did the same thing to the other three. I know what you're thinking. If we could do it at Nova Terrene, why not Alpha Centauri? Why not Earth?"

Mikail had just barely kept up with Jimmy Soo's rapid-fire recitation of future events, but the question was a logical one, so he nodded. "Okay, Jimmy, why wouldn't it work for Earth?"

"With enough time to gather the supplies and create a

staging area in non-space close to Earth, and if we studied the course of battle and each ship movement closely enough, it might work. And time, of course, is not the issue. However, it might not work. At Earth, the AranthChi were operating mostly in fleet actions. As a fleet, they may truly be unstoppable. But even if it did work, if one ship survived long enough to get off a report, we would have failed.

"If the AranthChi ever suspect we have discovered time travel, that will impel them to find or remember a way to utilize time manipulation also. And then we are truly sunk. We've known about the AranthChi for over fifty years. How long have they actually known about us? We don't even know where they came from, though we have found indications around literally hundreds of stars that could be the energy wastes of their civilization. They know almost everything about us, including the location of Earth. They appear to have been in space for thousands of years; we can be traced back to one planet in a blink of time. If there is no other way, we'll try that method, but we are looking for better answers, more permanent solutions."

This time it was Mikail who drank the tea. "I understand," he said. "You know you can win a battle, but you can't win a war this way. So now what?"

"We're so far behind the power curve that it looks hopeless. Extreme measures are required if we are going to have a ghost of a chance. Since we can't win this conflict by any normal means, I'm rolling the dice. There is no way to keep Nova Terrene safe, so we've had to abandon it.

"The decision was made to implement Nomad, a plan to put everything that flies into non-space and create a base of operations there. One hundred and sixteen ships are waiting somewhen right now, waiting for me to come back with the information that will help us save the Federation."

Mikail absently scratched behind one ear and tugged on his tuxedo lapel. "And you've come to New Hearth to ask our local AranthChi what the hell is going on. I presume you're not intending to knock on the legation's door and start asking questions. What do you have in mind?"

Jimmy Soo turned to the serving cart, pulled out a thick datapad, and dropped it on the table with a bang. "The answers we need, that the Human race needs, better be in the skulls of the AranthChi on New Hearth. And I'm going in to get them. I need to know why! Why will the AranthChi shoot their way off planet? What did they learn at about one p.m. on December twentieth that caused them to panic and hide in a hole for four hours, then bolt?"

"I will help anyway I can," Mikail said quietly.

"You already have. Your future counterpart gave me a shopping list and an approximate date to look you up. I think you'll like his plan, but you are free to modify it as you see fit."

"Modify a plan that I'm the author of, but have never seen? Such a strange position to be in," Mikail said. "Talk about being able to bring a fresh point of view to your own work!"

Suddenly Mikail and Jimmy Soo were grinning wildly, like schoolboys. Like schoolboy conspirators. Like moderately demented schoolboys, at that. They cleared the table and got to work.

13

SETUP AND FOLLOW-THROUGH

on New Hearth, in the command bunker

The clock glowed a red 1231 when Mikail opened his eyes to the darkness of the command post's sleep corner. On the other side of the privacy curtain, a bustle of activity was taking place.

Mikail had been on the go for over twenty-four hours when he'd lain down for a quick nap. If the operation was successful, he might not sleep again for many more hours. Of course, if they failed today, getting sleep would not be a consideration. Failure would likely result in his death and the deaths of all the brave, hardworking folk involved in this crucial enterprise. *So let us not fail,* thought Mikail.

The clock read 1234 when he parted the privacy curtain and walked into the softly lit command module. Marge McCan was in one corner, talking on the hard link phone to Offensive Site One, situated on a small rise a thousand meters to the northwest of the legate grounds.

The instillation, disguised as a construction site for the municipal subway expansion project, held one of the two gatling-style Chewers. Designed with the specific intention of cracking the legate's defenses, the Chewer's job was to defang the compound with minimal collateral damage. Wanton destruction of the compound was not an option. The information it contained was too valuable, too vital to the Federation.

This overriding fact dictated the attitude brought to all the planning of the assault on the AranthChi legation. Curiously enough, the subway expansion project had been, until the week before, a genuine municipal project. The project had been in the making for several years, with a planning commission, groundbreaking ceremonies, and a carefully marked route supported by demographic projections of future city growth.

These demographic projections just happened to demand the subway branch into two and proceed to either side of the legation grounds before turning sharply in different directions. The tunneling had been going on for most of a year and was carefully timed to be at this stage of completion on this day.

In truth, the whole subway project existed for the specific purpose of putting the penetration team in this place, on this day. *The possibilities of using time travel to manipulate events is enough to make your head ache,* thought Mikail.

As he stepped up to the situation table, Marge hung up her phone. From across the room, she called out, "Site One is ready. They have positive lock on the primary target building, and all systems are called nominal."

Mikail smiled his thanks. Marge continued. "I had to send Wilimena over to OS Two. They have been unable to go positive with passive visual and IR systems. They want permission to bounce an infrared off their target for fine distance and height control."

"Why? What's wrong with the measurements done five days ago?"

"Construction done over the last two days, coupled with a small earthquake last night, has shifted the hill OS Two is on by an unknown number of centimeters west and lowered it approximately two thirds of a meter. Site Two wants to be sure they can hit their deep in target on the first burst."

"Find another way. Bouncing a beam off that building now would not be a good idea. I don't want anything to alert the AranthChi at this stage of the operation."

"Yes, sir. Wilimena's working on it. Sites Three and Four report ready with all system checks complete."

Mikail nodded and gazed around the command module thoughtfully. It was a cluttered and cramped room. Every centimeter skillfully filled with equipment and workspaces. He looked as if he were searching for something.

Marge spoke up, "Anything you want, boss man?"

"No. . . ." Mikail let the word draw out. "It just doesn't look that much like a Starling. But here I am, about to go into combat after more than thirty-five years, and my assault station is filled with desks."

Marge smiled. So did one or two of the people at the consoles. "You were always a tough one, Mike. The AranthChi ought to be afraid of you, in a Starling or behind a desk." She came over to him and slipped a hand into his. "Besides, I wouldn't fit into a Starling, now, would I?"

He smiled back, gripping her hand. "Thanks."

"I'm always there when you need me, spaceman."

Mikail grinned widely. "And that is precisely why the AranthChi should be so afraid of me."

••✦••

command module, 1258 hours

"Chewer One remains sighted-in on the power building. Chewer Two has finally reported positive lock on the shield generators and not a moment too soon." The site status coordinator did not look up from her screens as she spoke. "Both Chewers report that first ammo racks are spun up to speed. OS Three and OS Four have completed arming sequence and report ready for countdown."

"Excellent," replied Mikail. "Alert all sweep teams to go to thirty second countdown on my mark."

She tapped a switch and awaited the results. "All my boards are green, sir."

"What about the power wagons?"

This time, Marge answered. "All forward position strike craft reported decoupled from their tenders and following operational countdown as of eleven minutes ago."

The power wagons had been a sore point with Mikail. *Something* had to be done about the spacecraft hidden on the legation grounds. If the ship managed to become airborne during the attack, it could cause a lot of mischief. Conceivably, it could even escape.

The planning staff had argued extensively over the problem of neutralizing this most potent of threats. An answer was needed, but bringing heavy warcraft into the atmosphere and then the operational zone could not be done stealthily.

A compromise had been reached. That compromise was even now being put into action. At nine minutes to zero hour, four specially modified aerospace frame fighters had begun a burn from orbit. Each was following a different flight path, and none of those paths would cross over the legate grounds, not quite.

However, any time after plus two minutes on the operational clock, each power wagon would be in a position to make a quick dogleg into the combat zone. If the maneuver was allowed to go to completion, the FPSCs would perform a beautiful St. Catherine wheel, sealing in the skirmish area.

The staff was certain the movements of the power wagons, so like a ship's boat on long-range sensors, would appear entirely innocuous to the AranthChi. These were simply cargo auxiliaries, dropping into the atmosphere to make landing at the public aerospace ports.

Mikail had to agree that the reasoning seemed sound. The assumptions were probably true. Also true was that, if the escape ship succeeded in getting off the ground, its shields would go up. The heavy laser batteries of the power wagons would not be enough to bring it down again.

The planning staff was well aware of this. They were

counting heavily on being able to drive the presumably lightly armored craft away from the legation grounds so nuclear armaments could be employed.

When Mikail pointed out that the ship would have to be driven pretty far before it was no longer over inhabited land, an uncomfortable silence ensued. It was not broken until Jimmy Soo spoke up.

"We choose not to make that a consideration. As long as the escape ship can be driven far enough from the legate's compound to keep the primary objective safe, the FPSCs have authority to use nukes to bring her down."

Mikail was in shock. He could not believe what he was hearing. Such a monstrous decision, so calmly accepted by the people before him, seemed the very definition of inhuman. It could not be. He tried again.

"Jimmy Soo, all of you, do you hear what you're saying? Almost a million people live in Glasgow and the surrounding area. Are you really willing to incinerate them just to get one little Aranth ship? A ship the navy could probably interdict in orbital space anyway?"

"Probably is just not good enough, Mike." Soo was determined. "*Nothing* must stop the success of this operation. Too much of Humanity's future is riding on it. Not my death, nor your death—not even the deaths of a million people would be a price too high to pay if we can get what we need from that compound."

Mikail felt the urge to flee from these madmen, these killers of the innocent in intent. The room, big as it was, stifled him. He rose without a word and stalked for the door.

One of the quiet members of the planning staff stood as he came by and planted herself firmly in his path. He stopped in sheer surprise at the small dark-haired apparition. Though clearly of middle age, the woman could not have been more than a meter and a quarter tall. She had brown skin and sad brown eyes. She wore the ancient Hindi caste mark of the married woman on her forehead. She spoke softly. "Mr. Benson, how many people would you say live on Alpha Centauri Two?"

"That is not relevant."

"Ah, but it is." She locked gazes with Mikail. "Within a very few days, the demons with cat faces will attack the Alpha Centauri system again. I say 'again' because I have watched it happen twice now from non-space. They will be vicious, for they are prideful. They are not merciful, but they will be thorough. Near the end of the battle, they will take one of their damaged hell ships and crash it onto the purple continent. We will watch the firestorm begin. We will watch the firestorm blow out as the shockwave of the explosion separates the atmosphere from the planet. We will watch our colony, every person and animal, die. A whole planet will die. If we fail *here* to find a way to stop it, you will be with us, and you will watch it happen again also. I do not believe you want to be in that future, Mr. Benson."

Mikail was moved but not convinced. He spread his hands. "You're letting your grief overwhelm you. The ends have come to justify the means for you, madam."

"No, Mr. Benson. I have courage and faith. And I have family on the purple continent. Also, I am here with my husband and our child. We don't intend to be on a ship in space when the demon nest is invaded. We will stand on a street corner in the town of Glasgow by the Sea, holding our baby in our arms and praying for the success of your mission. If nuclear fire must rain down on Humans to save all we hold dear, we'll also face it. And we will absolve those who must use it from any guilt."

Mikail scowled. Jimmy Soo started to speak, but a quickly raised hand from the woman silenced him. "Many feel as I do. It may be necessary to do these things. If so, it is right. All of us want you to succeed. I believe it is up to you to make of this enterprise a success. Please don't go."

Mikail gradually sat down at the table in the chair next to

the Hindu woman. He looked around the room, taking a long minute to do it.

"Such fanaticism worries me," he said slowly. "I want a better answer than 'We forgive you.' I want a general announcement to go out after the attack starts for people to take shelter indoors and to stay away from windows. I want blast warnings on every civilian and police band continuously from about plus one minute in the operation. I want our population to be protected as much as possible."

Jimmy Soo nodded a reluctant yet relieved nod.

"I'm not done. I also want that nuclear fire order to be amended. Change the order so that it is the last resort in the conflict, not just the next step in the battle plan."

Soo did not even look at the rest of the planning staff. He had eyes only for Mikail. "Okay, Mike, we'll do it just as you say. Only, don't let that ship get airborne. That's all."

••✦••

command module, 1259 hours

With Chewers One and Two reporting all ammo racks up to speed and Sites Three and Four ready to launch their Harpoons at the thirty-second hold mark, all the pieces were finally in place. The number of work hours and the resources represented here, if expressed by accountants working overtime, would exceed a typical colony's yearly budget.

It was time. Mikail picked up the dedicated comm link to Jimmy Soo's folk and spoke the authorization words. "Dunkirk, Dunkirk, Dunkirk."

"We confirm Dunkirk," said the voice on the other end.

Picking up the hardlink phone, Mikail told the crews of Sites One through Four in common tie-in that the operation status was GO. Sweep teams were now in motion. The clock resumed at 1259:30.

At 1300 exactly, the first blow of the second interstellar

Human/AranthChi war was struck. The operator of Chewer One depressed his firing switch and began stitching the side of the target building with his AM discs.

The Chewer, with a cyclic rate of fire of twenty discs a second, was a rather esoteric weapon. The discs were known as angular momentum ammunition and were in the kinetic energy class of weaponry. Each disc was a nine-kilogram pellet of depleted uranium, jacketed with steel and wrapped in composite polymers. Its tapered edge was of diamond dust and third-generation kevlar.

Each disc left the throat of the Chewer with a velocity of better than two kilometers per second. To add penetrating power, the disc was spun up to a mind blurring speed of five thousand revolutions per minute, thus earning it the designation "enhanced" kinetic ammunition.

The meteoric speeds and peculiar delivery systems were forced on the attackers by the structure of the defenses they were facing. The legation grounds were drenched in sensor vibrations that extended far beyond its fence and high into the sky. With thousands of receptors spread throughout the complex, much like the nerves in a body, tied to a very smart nexus only slightly smaller than a starship's core, the defenses were lightning fast.

Within hundredths of a second of an attack being identified, the nexus would swing into action. Heavy laser arrays adorned the roofs of many buildings. They would enter the fight. The energy shielding, whose generators the attackers had planned so long and hard to disable, would come on and seal off the complex. If that were to happen, the Humans would have lost just as surely as if they had never tried.

Offensive Site One poured deadly fire into the main power building, following the lines of a virtual overlay. The discs punched through again and again, cutting through conduits and bus lines and generators, to hit the main power unit time after time.

The standard AranthChi power unit was untouchable, wrapped in its layers of electromagnetic and gravitic shields. It was like a spider, crouched in the center of its power transfer web. Inviolate it might be, but the rest of the equipment was vulnerable. The location of the main power unit itself had been allowed for in planning, because it was the only thing likely to deflect the discs. The attackers were counting on significant collateral damage from the ricochets.

Chewer Two and Sites Three and Four were slaved to Chewer One's initial fire command. As close to simultaneously as measurable, Chewer Two began pummeling the shield generator building. At Offensive Sites Three and Four, Harpoon missiles left their racks and began their flights toward the compound. They would be in the air much longer than the AM discs and vulnerable to laser fire, but that had been allowed for—in fact, designed into their operation.

AM ammunition and electromagnetic launch technology were not optimal for ground-based assault. HE—as in explosive rounds, rockets, and bombs—were still en vogue, mostly because of how useful and practical they were.

Ease of use, ease of storage, and destructiveness per kilo of ordinance were very high with modern, standard ground troop weaponry. Reliability was almost astronomically high as well. It is almost impossible to break as simple a tool as a shoulder-fired rocket launcher or pellet firing assault rifle.

The exotic technologies, like the enhanced kinetic railgun, launching angular momentum ammunition, were notoriously cranky. They would shut down if they got an ammo wobble or a power fluctuation alarm. They were also extremely dangerous to be around if they jammed.

Still, the modifications the AranthChi had made to the insides of the otherwise normal-looking legation buildings made this unusual assault method the only practical route open to the Human attackers. The buildings had become, in a very real sense, facades. Lurking behind the walls of each building was a fortress.

The skeleton of each building had been stiffened with some plassteel compound, affixed to the original members. Applied to the inside of every outer wall and roof was a thick foam material, honeycombed with long-chain single-molecule webbing and liberally salted with room temperature superconducting filaments. This material had great cushioning ability, unbelievable tensile strength, and an extremely high heat rating.

For an exploding ordinance or a laser beam to be strong enough to penetrate the foam barrier, it would have to be of fantastic strength. That much force would likely flatten the building and do considerable damage to anything around it. This was far from the hoped-for effect. In fact, that particular result was to be avoided at all costs.

The goal of this operation was to capture prisoners and physical evidence. Jimmy Soo wanted information. Revenge would have to wait.

Hence the employment of AM technology. The enhanced kinetic discs would chew their way through the barrier, losing up to ninety-five percent of their velocity and rotational energy in the process. A good many of them were expected to shred while penetrating, tearing holes in the foam, for following discs to enlarge and push their way through.

The discs that made penetration would still have a lot of punch in them. And they did. Chewer One's discs, zipping into the compound at nearly eight times the speed of sound, made satisfying pock marks in the side of the target building. They followed exactly the lines of the operator's virtual overlay. The whole structure vibrated with the force of the impacts. They set the building ringing like a giant bell hit with gargantuan force by tiny sledgehammers.

At the approximate instant the first disc struck, the nexus began sounding klaxon alarms in every corner of the compound. One half second later, the laser arrays came to life, tracking back with ponderously swift movement to the origins of the attack. Visible energies lashed out to do battle with the ablation shields protecting Offensive Site One. Those shields boiled away vigorously. Meanwhile, other laser arrays sought to depress far enough to bring fire to bear on OS Two.

At T plus two seconds, the nexus threat assessment protocols caused it to shift fire to the swiftly arriving Harpoons. Trailing thick strands of superconducting cable, the missiles made aggressive parabolas toward the center of the compound, their terminus clearly the admin and living quarters area.

Stabbing bolts of collimated light met the incoming Harpoons, burning them to satisfying dust and fragments. Fanning out in wide arcs, hundreds of superconducting strands drifted down out of the sky onto the legation grounds.

At T plus four seconds, the defense programming of the nexus decided to raise shields to escape what was already estimated to be an overwhelming assault. All around the perimeter shield, emitter arrays came to life. Power flowed into the network to form the defense fields the attackers so feared.

Immediately, huge sheets of flame and crackling electrical discharges raced outward from the compound along the many stands of superconducting cable to grounding sites far from the complex. The land shook as teeth-jarring explosions went off deep in the earth. Great plumes of dust jetted out of the grounding station sites, and the earth settled as sections of subway tunnel collapsed. The cave-ins followed the exact path of the construction project, and the absorbed energy melted machinery and scorched rock.

But the shields stayed down. With so much energy being pulled out of the matrix, the shield emitters were unable to unite and link wavefronts in any meaningful way. And still, the Chewer's pounded their targets.

Abruptly, the explosions and flashing discharges ceased. The AM discs that hammered the building continually from the first instant of the attack finally managed to destroy enough of the shield generator mechanism that backups stopped working.

A second later, the roof-mounted laser arrays went dark. Chewer One had won its duel with the defenses. All power to the compound was finally cut. It was not an instant too soon. Not only had all the ablation shielding boiled away from the hardened surfaces of Offensive Site One; the thick armor plating had been holed again and again. OS One should not have still been operational.

If the nexus had resumed firing on the Chewer sites when it began experiencing trouble establishing its perimeter shields, it would have successfully suppressed the attack. If that had happened, only a last lucky bit of collateral damage from a still careening disc fragment would have given the Humans any chance at all. The first phase of defanging the compound was a success. By the slimmest of margins, it was true, but still a success.

The Chewers began to cycle down, each with an off-key deepening whine. Their part in the attack was essentially over. Inspection would show that Chewer One could not be used again with any degree of safety. Chewer Two still had one operational duty, if and when it became necessary.

The second phase of the attack began. As has been true since time immemorial, no piece of real estate really belonged to a side in any conflict unless their forces were actually standing on it. Therefore, troops in APCs and wearing powered armor glided, ran, and drove onto the legation grounds. Each group headed for a specific target. Each had a well-defined objective.

Incredibly, some were falling in the first wave, as small arms fire erupted from the windows of the administration building. Other areas of the compound joined in with fierce but scattered volleys. There was no answering fire from the attackers. Speed and mobility were the tactics of the moment.

Mikail watched the events unfolding from the monitors

in his command post, watched as brave attackers fell. The AranthChi should have been totally demoralized by the unexpected lightning attack. Instead, they responded with minimal confusion and great resilience. These were civilian Aranths, as far as anyone knew, yet they fought swiftly and well.

"Tough bastards." Mikail gritted his teeth. "Tough and quick and unyielding bastards!" Margie saw with surprise there were tears at the corners of his eyes.

Now the attackers were as far as the structures and were able to employ some cover. The operation immediately became house-to-house fighting. Small groups of attackers began forcing their way into the buildings by door and window.

The penetration force were all volunteers. All were from superbly trained marine detachments and had practiced on mockups of the legation buildings somewhen in time. They were also heroes, every one of them, because they invaded the compound without a single deadly force weapon among them.

They carried stun guns, gas guns, and sonic projectors. They came with optical and concussion grenades. Soluble anesthetic fletchets filled the ammo cassettes of rifle and pistol. Some carried sticky rope launchers with bell-shaped nozzles. Each team carried shaped charges, to be used only for getting through barricaded doors.

They were willing to take whatever losses were required to gain the prisoners they had come for. And losses they took. It seemed that a soldier fell, wounded or dying, for every second of the ground assault's push inward. After an interminable interval, counted mostly in heartbeats, the penetration force was chiefly through the killing zone and pressed against the buildings. Here they were able to hose the visible windows and doors continually with sonics to suppress the defenders' deadly fire.

The three members of penetration team fourteen were all Earthborn, superbly conditioned, and intensively trained. They were not the first team to reach their target window on the ground floor of the administration building. Two other teams had reached that point first. Both teams, though, were partial teams. Both had lost a member in the original sweep. They were therefore required to hang back and provide suppression fire while an intact team made initial penetration.

The anchor, Midshipman Amanda Gerry, dropped to one knee and pulled the safety tab on her squirt gun, causing the two chambers to open and the contents to intermix. Pressurization was swift. Almost immediately, she was spraying thin streams of liquid onto the windowpane.

If the clear windowpane material had been glass, it would have already been chipped and cracking from the force of the sonics playing against it. But if it had been glass, it would be inert to the chemical intrusion method penetration team fourteen was using. If it had been most forms of plastic, it wouldn't have held up against laser fire.

What it was, it gave the inorganic and organic chemists conniptions. In the time frame available for rapid entry into the building, however, and because the stuff was as blast resistant as the best steel doors, another way to neutralize it had to be found.

Where the streams of liquid hit the window, they became goo and then foam. In seconds, the foam disappeared, sinking into the pane. The lines became milky and started to spread. Silently, without fuss, the windowpane turned to dust.

Now Amanda launched a spray of one optical, one concussion, and one somma grenade through the window hole and into the room beyond. Detonation came after a scant two count. Scarcely had the initial effects occurred when the point, Jim Ortega, was hosing down the interior with sonics.

One heartbeat after Ortega cut the sonics, the swing, Harold Grinfeld, did a tuck and roll through the window and into the room beyond. He came up into a crouch, grabbing for his rifle, ready to sweep the room with anesthetic darts. The chamber was empty of AranthChi.

Soon, all seven attackers were in the building, formed up into three teams again. They headed deeper into the building in three different directions, launching gas and squirting sonics continuously. The sweep was thorough. Not a room, not a closet, nor even a cupboard was overlooked.

Almost immediately, Ortega, acting as point, ran into two AranthChi face down in the corridor. He could not tell at a glance if it was the gas or sonics that had gotten them. They were both breathing, and that was all that really mattered.

Swing moved past him to guard the forward area and keep an eye on the cross corridor ahead. Amanda, as anchor, moved up and attended to the two AranthChi. Dropping her rifle, she pulled an injector gun out of a thigh pocket and shot each Aranth one time.

The content of the injection was designed to reverse the effects of the fast-acting sleepy gas while placing the recipient in a milder yet longer lasting coma. Amanda waited a few seconds to make sure the injections worked properly. Then she tagged each one for retrieval.

The planners of the assault on the AranthChi compound had left nothing to chance. As soon as Amanda slapped a tag disc onto an AranthChi, it adhered to the skin aggressively. Immediately, the disc injected nano-transmitters into the Aranth's bloodstream. If by some miracle, a tagged AranthChi managed to awaken, escape their captors, and remove the locator tag, they still would be tracked down by the nanos in their blood.

Amanda Gerry and Jim Ortega picked up an Aranth each and moved quickly but gently, backing down the corridor to a room with an outside window.

They laid their burdens down in the center of the room. While Ortega was draping a wafer-thin blast cloth over them, Amanda employed the squirt gun again, spraying a thin stream around the edges of the window. She noticed the pressure seemed to be failing in the gun, so she contented herself with completing the line around the edges.

She then kicked out the window with a servo-powered armored foot. There was no lash of sonics hitting the window space, a sign that meant all penetration teams had gained entry. Her suit was carefully constructed to tune out the frequencies employed by the penetration teams—but not perfectly. As the mission went on, it would do so less and less effectively. She would have noticed being brushed by the beams, had there been any, but not bothered by them.

Amanda dropped a dime-sized transponder onto the windowsill. In the distance, she saw retrieval vehicles moving toward the perimeter of the compound. She retreated back into the corridor, where her swing and point were waiting.

••✦••

legation compound, 1305 hours

Five minutes into the attack, and reports were coming back to the command post from all the varied elements of the attack force. The news was uniformly positive. All buildings successfully penetrated. All exterior enemy fire fully suppressed. Amazingly, the assault was completely on schedule.

There were still sporadic reports of resistance deep within the administration building. Five minutes was plenty of time for the AranthChi to cook up mischief if the resources were available. They had certainly shown the willingness to fight against overwhelming odds. Mikail could only hope that cutting the main power to the compound had left the AranthChi as hamstrung as it appeared.

Around the legate's quarters, the recovery teams were already making pickups. Monitors showed unconscious AranthChi being carried from the buildings to waiting armored vans. The vans were actually medical caissons. The prisoners were getting the best medical care the Federation could provide.

Now the FPSCs were overhead, completing the wheel pattern begun in orbit. As per the plan, Chewer Two powered back up. Given any sort of warning at all, Chewer Two would try to sight in on the escape craft and tear it apart before it got far enough off the ground to engage its shields. The location of the hidden spaceship was still undetermined and, until neutralized, represented the last major threat to the success of the mission.

Then word came to the command post that resistance was over. The last holdout spots had been broken open, and the barricaded AranthChi gathered in. By very rough enumeration, it appeared that all the legation staff had been collected.

A minute later, the escape ship was reported discovered. It had been housed in a disguised hanger directly beneath the power building. By great good fortune, it appeared that the ship's airlock door had been open at the time of the attack. Several disc fragments had ricocheted into the body of the ship, doing significant damage within.

It would have been impossible for the AranthChi to have utilized the ship in its present condition, even if they had been able to reach it in time. The last impediment to declaring the mission an unqualified success was gone.

The compound was unequivocally in the hands of the Federation. The first battle to save Humanity was over. The war, however, was just beginning.

14

ANSWERS AND PLANS

on New Hearth

The aftermath of battle was grim. Thirty-eight Humans dead, thirty injured. Nine AranthChi dead by disc fragments, or, in one case, by an interior partition falling on him. One death apparently by anaphylactic reaction to the sleepy gas. Fifty-one live prisoners gained from the raid. Fourteen more picked up in town and at other locales around the planet. Two unaccounted for.

Among the treasures, a wealth of information in the compound's data systems. If only a safe way could be found to allow the machines to wake up, the information they contained could be critical to the Federation.

A good day's work, with much to be proud of, thought Mikail. *Also, a day of mourning. No enterprise such as this can be accomplished without loss, and the exhilaration that comes from success does not soften the loss; it only cushions it from the emotions for a time.* When there was time, the brave soldiers who had given their lives would be honored.

Specialists of every sort swarmed the legation compound, taking the buildings apart a piece at a time. They were hurried but thorough. The prevailing attitude was one-half crime scene investigation and one-half archeological dig.

Literally no stone would be left unturned, but no item would be moved until a full record of its location and relationship or association to other items was made and cataloged.

The full import of any piece of information or object could not be discovered at a glance.

The investigators brought their own power supplies and equipment. Under no circumstances would power be restored to any AranthChi device while it was still on site, and that included the building lights. No one really knew what system was hooked into what other system.

Mikail had waking nightmares of the nexus coming to life and regaining control of the roof lasers. Or, worse yet, triggering whatever destruct device was hidden on the grounds.

That device was presumed to be a permanent feature of the complex. Nearly everyone on the investigation teams had memories of a future that would no longer happen, that no one wanted to recreate by accident. A future where the nexus had employed the device, leaving precious little besides a big hole in the ground and a disturbing mystery.

The prisoners were transported to a secure compound specially outfitted for its new purpose of containment and interrogation. Each Aranth awakened in total isolation in a maximum-security cell. All belongings had been removed, even clothing.

Each of the AranthChi was assigned his or her own interrogation team. The teams began their assignment with everything that was known about Aranth physiology and psychology in general, and then they personalized it to their prisoner.

The number of Human rights violations of the Federation Charter mounted steadily. For the first time in Human history, a government could claim with accuracy that its political prisoners weren't Human and therefore did not deserve society's protections. Mikail and Margie managed to keep the abuses from being fatal, but there was no stopping determined and frightened people from employing a wide range of methods to get results.

Finally, it was Mikail's turn to interview the legate Ragonsee. They had met a number of times at official functions, but Mikail did not feel he knew the Aranth well. It had been decided that Mikail would not talk to the legation head until the intent of the interviews changed from interrogation to negotiation, should that point ever arrive.

Ragonsee was led into the small interrogation office by a guard in suntans. It was the only room he had seen other than his cell for five days. He gave a visible start, and his tail became momentarily stiff on catching sight of Mikail behind the interrogator's table. Without prompting, he walked to the chair built for him and settled into it.

He moved with a flat-footed shamble, his normal feline grace long gone. He stumbled slightly getting onto the couch. He looked terrible. His fur was matted and dirty, and his head stayed lowered. All traces of his natural arrogance had been subsumed by his capture and the aftermath of prisonerhood.

Ragonsee lifted his head slightly, and his nose twitched as he peered into all corners of the room. Slowly, he came to the conclusion that he and Mikail were alone. The information seemed to confuse him. He settled his gaze on Mikail and stared fixedly at him with glassy eyes.

Mikail stared back and let the silence build. The Aranth had to speak first, so Mikail had been advised. Finally he did: "So, have you come to see me humbled, Human? To gawk and sneer? To walk away full of self-importance and Human righteousness? Knowing that you are top . . . dog?"

Ah. The Aranth was not broken, not beaten, only sorely exercised. He could still even make an anthropological joke in another species's language. *Good.* The sarcasm was consistent with the Ragonsee that Mikail knew. *Also good.* Mikail still said nothing.

Ragonsee had only the shreds of control left. "What do you want, Human?" It was a shriek.

This was Mikail's cue. Though he was not a trained interrogator, Mikail knew that when he asked a question, he would also be giving away information. He had been intensively coached in the information he could give out. Coached also as to what questions he could ask and expect a reply in return. He had several conversations ready, depending on Ragonsee's next few responses.

The questions, however, were his own. Experts had phrased them to make sure they were asked in the right fashion with the right emphasis. This delicate negotiation was totally his responsibility. He must not fail.

The light of sanity seemed very dim in Ragonsee's eyes, so Mikail's first question was, "Who am I?"

"Just another Human." All emotion was gone, and the response was terribly flat.

"Your delegation numbers seventy-seven."

Ragonsee's eyes lost their glassy appearance, and his ears twitched forward. Slowly, he cocked his head to indicate he was listening.

"Ten are dead, lost when we took your compound. The rest live."

"Your name is Ben-soon, Mikale."

"You're welcome," said Mikail. He gestured to the side table, on which waited food suitable to the AranthChi. "Eat. Drink."

"The food is drugged. The water is drugged."

"Not this food, not this water," Mikail said.

"Offering food to a Human is a sign of friendship or an attempt at manipulation," said the Aranth.

"Offering food to an AranthChi is a sign of desire for mutual cooperation," countered Mikail.

"If we are negotiating, why here?"

"Here is where the lives of sixty-seven hang in the balance."

Ragonsee said nothing. It was impossible for Mikail to tell what thoughts chased themselves around in that alien skull. Slowly, he reached out and tasted the water. Picking carefully among the offerings, he ate the food.

When he sat back, the small slender alien seemed more

alive. Even though his light blond fur remained matted and tangled, resolve, or perhaps purpose, had settled into his being. "What do you want?"

"Tell me what I need to know."

The AranthChi's brown eyes were already set above a narrow snout, so when it appeared that his eyes narrowed further, Mikail knew he was anthropomorphizing the expression. The legate's face did become hard and frozen. A pink tongue licked its slow way across sharp teeth. His mouth closed with a snap.

"Why? Can you do anything with the information? Would you do something if you could?"

"Yes. Tell me what I need to know."

"Do you really have the abilities? Do you even know what you are asking for, Human? And if you have the courage to follow through on my knowledge, how could I give anything without betraying my people? Where are your guaranties, your promises? What sweet scents do you wave under my nose to persuade me to become your lackey?"

"Tell me what I need to know," Mikail repeated simply.

Ragonsee's ears went flat, and he drooled. Mikail watched in fascination. The struggle between loyalty and self-preservation, between right action and the ability to cut a deal, was tormenting the Aranth.

Ragonsee was already in rebellion against the AranthChi civilization by following the commands of his clan leader. His self-image was already in jeopardy. Could he now betray his alpha?

It was a short step for most Humans to move from one level of treachery to a greater one. Often the self-justification took torturous paths. Mikail stayed quiet to see if Ragonsee could sell himself on a slightly greater betrayal.

It appeared he was working on it. The minds of the AranthChi were not really so different from Humanity's, and the game this one had been playing made him susceptible to outside influence. The drugs, the isolation, and the carefully structured "interviews" had all led him to this point. Now it was up to Mikail, based on the questions the Aranth asked.

The small alien's ears came up slowly. He wiped his muzzle on the tablecloth. Beady brown eyes fixed on Mikail. "What good will my information do you unless you can change the past? Can you fashion a new future for you and for me?"

There—it had been said. Ragonsee had admitted a great deal in a very few words and asked for much more. Mikail shifted in his seat, leaned forward, and willed himself to believe. "Give me the information I need, and I will put your people aboard that escape ship. You will be allowed to go free."

"Go? Where is there to go? My world is my alpha and my clan! You will free us to go where there is nowhere to go, especially if I give you what you want." He was hissing and spitting now. The words tumbled out fast and slurred.

"My people are being exterminated all through clan space, hunted until they are no more. My alpha has brought this upon us. This is the fate you will share, ground to dust and detritus, all to protect the race, the holy race."

The Aranth clawed at the table in front of Mikail. Mikail wondered if Ragonsee would still try to attack, weak though he was. "*If* you should somehow escape that fate, *if* you now have the ability to choose your history, your end will be the same. You might avoid destruction by our teeth, though I don't see how. It is you who will bring yourselves down. You will seek to blot out your mistakes, oh yes. Or try and change something to make it better, or change just because some new ones want power. *And you will succeed beyond your wildest expectations.*"

He blinked, caught his breath, went on. "You will wind up as we are, stiff and rigid of culture, with a heavy hand on your populace. It is the deepest council secret that we have changed our history time and time again. The knowledge is suppressed. It is forgotten. Somehow it is rediscovered.

"It is always used to bring down the rulers. Someone always thinks we need new rulers. Sometimes the very survival of Aranthkind is threatened. The manipulators get tripped up and are destroyed. History is put back to normal as much as possible, and the knowledge is suppressed again. Is this the path you want to follow? Is this the destiny you will bequeath to your children?"

Bingo, thought Mikail. *He knows! Ragonsee has the information, and he wants desperately to trade for it. His conscience must be torturing him mercilessly. He wants to be talked into co-operating. He wants to believe that the Humans can put Humpty Dumpty back together again.*

"Ragonsee. There is a chance. Give me the information I need."

The legate's ears flattened for just a moment. They came up again in a most deliberate action. He radiated resolve. "You Humans may be the most surprising species we have ever met. I see in you more than a chance; I smell an opportunity for a truly new direction.

"Very well. My terms are thus: let us go in our survey ship. Provision us for an extended voyage. Move us to the moment in time of my choice, so I may rescue my alpha. Assist us in his escape. In return, I will tell you everything I know, holding nothing back."

Mikail was silent for a moment. "I won't lie to you, Hand of the Alpha. What you ask for is beyond our willingness to grant."

At the use of his secret title, Ragonsee stiffened. This Human did know so much already. Presumably the knowledge came from tricking or torturing members of his staff. Conceivably, though, the knowledge had sprung from other sources. Perhaps huge networks of freely moving temporal agents were even now sifting through the entire history of the AranthChi civilization. Ragonsee's knowledge could become obsolete in an eye blink.

Oh, they are a smart species, thought Ragonsee. *If only the High Council had not discovered the Least Clan's plotting. What power these aliens could have given us. What a team we might have made. We could have created a mega-empire to cover all the stars in the sky. Their cleverness, guided by our wisdom, could have achieved anything. . . .*

He shook his head once and then again. His mind was starting to drift, to spin forbidden fantasy and nonsense. The Humans would never suffer themselves to be guided by the AranthChi. Even with teeth at their throats, they did not know how to submit.

He had spent over seventy Human years trying to manipulate these aliens. He had deluded himself somehow into thinking he was succeeding. Now their teeth, their ridiculous, small, flat teeth, were at his throat. He must have still been under the effects of the Human's accursed drugs. His thoughts were so different from his usual disciplined style. He *must* concentrate. His survival depended on it.

And the Human was still talking. "I won't lie to you, Hand. There's no chance in Heaven or Hell of us letting you rescue your alpha. His schemes are what got us into this mess in the first place. However, if your information is *helpful enough,* it just might be possible to save your clan after all."

Ragonsee's nose twitched. He was getting the scent of Mikail's reasoning. "If I tell you what events led us to our downfall, you may find a place to intervene. If you can. And then what is to stop you, Human? With one success . . . you will not stop there; you will go on and try to destroy my whole race. You must know that I will not be a party to that, not to save my throat nor even the throats of all my clan."

Mikail reached across the table and placed his hands on the scratches Ragonsee had dug into the wood. "No, we won't do that. Not only because we need your cooperation, but because we wouldn't succeed. You said it yourself, Ragonsee. Your people have done it to yourselves so many times that you are always on the lookout for temporal tampering. All we want is to survive this situation. That is precisely what you want for your clan. So . . . help me help both of us. Tell me what I need to know."

Ragonsee thought some more. But there really was not much more to think about. "Very well. There is a very dim star in central clan space. . . ."

••✦••

The interview turned into a series of conversations. Mikail grilled Ragonsee multiple times about the design and operation of the Dying Kit astronomical installation. He was pleased to learn it was totally automated. Just because it had no crew, however, did not mean it wasn't smart.

Many of the conversations with Ragonsee verged on exasperating, sometimes because the alien didn't know the answers to Mikail's questions, sometimes because he assumed the Human already knew the information. At these times, the Aranth's natural arrogance would flare up. Every meeting took place in the same interview room. Ragonsee was too intelligent to have any access to the outside world. Every conversation was a contest of wills.

Mikail finally felt he had enough information to make some coherent plans, save for one lingering question. "Your alpha has known about us for seventy-five years. Why did it take this long for the rest of your civilization to discover the Federation?"

Ragonsee took a moment to compose his thoughts. "Our clan is in charge of this portion of the frontier. *We* are supposed to be watching for foes from the outside. You *were* discovered, over and over again, by other clans' monitoring installations. They referred the sightings to us, and we assured them that they were not seeing new signals." Now he snarled, "Dying Kit observatory is on the other side of AranthChi space and almost never looks our way. It was our cursed luck that Dying Kit didn't query us before sending a report on your radio signals to the High Council. You Humans sit in a little patch of empty space, but beyond you there are others we have watched for a long time. We have always been able to convince any clan that inquired, that those were the other's radio signals they were hearing."

Mikail blinked. This was disturbing news. He always had trouble hiding his reactions from the alien. He left hurriedly, making a mental note to have the interrogation teams follow up on this last conversation.

Mikail was finally satisfied. It had been a grueling, sometimes heartbreaking experience for everyone, Human and Aranth, but out of these dialogs he had found a possible path out of the box Humanity was in.

••✦••

on New Hearth

One hundred and fifteen ships were primed to wait at an assembly point in what had come to be called non-space. One ship would carry out the mission. Code-named *Desperate Endeavor,* that ship would attempt to change a key event in AranthChi history in such a way that it could never be traced back to the Federation.

Mikail was going. So were Marge McCan and Wilimena Hines. Jimmy Soo, defacto leader of the "save the Human race" taskforce, was not going. None of the central staff was going, although all the original thoughts and plans they could come up with had been loaded aboard the *Endeavor* in case of need.

Just hours before Mikail was to leave the planet and join the mission ship, he received an urgent message from HeadQuarters Base. The adjutant for the acting commandant was on real-time transmission and needed to talk to him now.

After Mikail's bona fides were determined, the adjutant came right to the point. "Mr. Benson, we have a situation developing right now in the outer system, and apparently you are involved."

Mikail watched the man on the screen and waited. He knew there would be about a one-second delay before his words could span the gap. He waited for the adjutant to nod in that special way, developed among people who spoke real-time across lightspeed gaps, indicating that he was done.

"We have a bogey coming in-system that's not responding to hails, and we must decide whether to shoot it down, or let it proceed." He frowned slightly. "It may have something to do with that secret op you people are doing down on the planet." Now he nodded.

Mikail said, "I understand your concern, captain. Yet you specifically asked for me, not any of the others in charge down here. Are you saying that I am personally involved, or does our operation have a connection with your problem?"

"Our bogey is transmitting a repeating message that mentions you by name, demanding that you be contacted ASAP. The ship IDs itself as the ALF *Benedict Arnold*. It claims to be operating on emergency sensor blackout and is unable to receive or respond to hails. It's making a direct run for New Hearth orbit and urgently requests you make rendezvous after it achieves parking orbit."

It's ironic, Mikail thought, *that this call should come in right at this time*. It was a crewman from the ALF that had started this whole chain of events. Still, the Human race had survived many times because of unlikely coincidences. *Okay, call it luck. This could be some more of that wonderful unlikely luck*. Mikail's pulse began to race.

"For God's sake, man, don't shoot it down." Mikail was forceful in his expulsion. "Let it make orbit. There may be something very important on board that we need. Call Admiral Soo if you want a second opinion, but I repeat, do not shoot down that ALF. The security of the Federation may be at stake."

The adjutant looked at Mikail oddly for a moment. As a coolly efficient officer, he expected navy to act like navy. Even though Mikail was a civilian, he had once been navy, so this impassioned speech was rather shocking. He decided to put it down to bad civilian influences.

"We certainly don't want to destroy the ship, Mr. Benson. If it is the *Benedict Arnold,* there may be as many as ten thousand people on board. But if it does anything other than make that parking orbit, the commandant is ready to shoot it down."

••✦••

aboard the Benedict Arnold

The transition to normal space was as uneventful as always. Jeremiah Littlefeather, the purser, and a number of the deck crew were on the cargo container level, walking down the huge transverse corridor. They were going over the manifest, with an eye to which cargo hold doors needed to be unsealed for deliveries on New Hearth.

It was amazing how often the contents of a room failed to matched up to the manifest. Experience had taught all of them that time wasted in off-loading was time lost in port leave.

The purser and Jeremiah had just about agreed on the disembarkation plan when the public address system came on. "Jeremiah Littlefeather, contact ship operations immediately." The speakers crackled at the end of the message. Then the message repeated, "Jeremiah Littlefeather, contact ship operations immediately," and the system put out a barely perceptible hum.

Jerry ran for the nearest phone, not even bothering to excuse himself from the meeting first. Years later, he would remember that panic rush to the comm and realize that the core entity had put specific harmonics into the air to urge him along.

A little out of breath, he grabbed up the phone, and knowing he wouldn't have to punch the number, gasped, "What is it, Ben?"

The core entity of the *Benedict Arnold,* speaking faster than Jerry had ever heard him speak, in precise clipped tones, said, "Jeremiah Littlefeather, I am designating you ranking Human representative on this ship. You must use command prerogative and order me to impose total sensor blackout, *right now!*"

"What? Ben, what do—"

"Do it, Jerry. You must order me to shut off all navigation and communication equipment, both passive and active scans. And you must do it in the next fifty seconds. The AranthChi legation emergency command frequency is active and has a recorded message playing. Last cycle, the message was indecipherable due to distance and last second RF disharmony of transition to normal space, but the carrier wave is getting stronger. When that message repeats, I will have no choice but to obey whatever it says. That command frequency instruction can only mean something bad for the Humans on this ship, and on New Hearth as well. If you are to save them, you must do it now."

Jerry took a deep breath. This was frightening in the extreme. He was being asked to make a decision and take on a responsibility that he hadn't even known was possible until right now. The right person for this decision was the captain. Fifty seconds was no time at all to make such a choice.

But if what the core said was true, Jerry had to act now. There was no time to confer with the captain or anyone else. The question was, did Jerry trust Ben? This was clearly the action Ben wanted. He obviously thought Jerry would cooperate.

The ramifications of this being designated "ranking Human" on board by the core could be far-reaching. Jerry just didn't have time to think! But he did know the answer to one question. He did trust the intentions of the core entity.

In a voice that was a marvel in steadiness, Jerry spoke. "As the ranking representative, I order you to shut off all external sensors."

"Command accepted. All sensors are off-line."

Jerry sagged against the bulkhead. "Great. Now what am I going to tell the captain?"

"May I suggest you consider the outgoing message you want sent to traffic control? The authorities are going to be very nervous having an AranthChi ship entering a Human system that neither answers communiqués nor obeys their commands."

"Great," Jerry repeated. "Just great. You really put me in the soup, didn't you? This is going to be the longest twenty-six hours of my life."

He was right. The following hours were very difficult for Jerry. He found it was not only difficult to explain to the captain why he no longer had control of helm, navigation, and communications: it was *impossible* to explain. For the first time, he was acutely uncomfortable being the core entity's friend.

He had never been screamed at by a superior before. He wanted to reassure the man, but what could he say? The facts were that he had authorized the blackout and he was not going to rescind it. The core had made it very plain. The sensor shutdown must continue.

The crew was becoming panicked about the ship plunging into the New Hearth system deaf and blind. The core itself was not concerned. It knew the starsystem so well, it could navigate back and forth any number of times in this condition. In fact, so the core asserted, it could do these blind maneuvers through any system it had ever been to. Orbital dynamics were a snap to a machine of its caliber.

The tension was very high. It did not help that Jerry had to inform the captain that he was preparing to disembark as soon as the ship made orbit. Nor could he explain why he and Anne had each suddenly acquired a repair robot as constant companion and bodyguard. People who were once friends took to actively shunning them.

Finally, they made orbit. The core allowed the captain to open outer airlock doors at various places on the ship and post spacesuited lookouts in the doorways. It still stubbornly refused to turn on any system that was capable of picking up radio transmissions.

The crew hastily ran a hardlink phone system to the locks so lookouts could cycle through and give their reports. Soon a shuttle pulled up, and a crew member using colored flashlights directed it to dock at the main passenger lock.

Mikail came through the lock, accompanied by Wilimena Hines. For a welcoming party, he found Jerry, Anne, two robots, and a *very* irate ship's captain.

"Good, you are here," growled the captain. He picked out Mikail to lavish his wrath on. "Tell this man to give me my ship back, right now!"

"I can't do that, captain," Mikail said mildly. "I need to know more about the situation before I can make recommendations. Where can we talk?"

He looked expectedly at Jerry. However, it was one of the robots that spoke up, surprising everyone except Jerry.

"Meeting suite four on this level has been isolated and is prepared for our use. Please follow me."

The robots turned in unison and led the way. The one who had spoken preceded them through the meeting room door. The other posted itself outside. The captain was excluded, firmly, but gently, by the robot at the door.

"Well, Jerry, you certainly picked a dramatic way to arrive at New Hearth this time around, I'll say that for you." Mikail walked to the head of the conference table.

He looked about expectedly, noting pitchers of water and glasses on the table. Also on the table sat a large aluminized travel case. Except for the table and six chairs, the room was empty. No communication, no recording equipment; not even a computer node.

Jerry looked to Mikail Benson and then to Wilimena Hines, who had taken up station just inside the door, next to the robot. "Thank you for coming, Mr. Benson. I really need to talk to you," he said. "And thank you for coming too, Miss Hines," he said politely.

"I wouldn't miss this for the world, youngster. You've been stirring up our lives for quite a while, so it only makes sense for you to show up right now and do it again."

Jerry blushed slightly. He moved to the table, and Wilimena followed. She continued, "*Do* tell us why you've hijacked the biggest ship in Federation space and moved it blind across an inhabited system . . . if that's really what happened."

She watched him with polite interest, and he felt his ears redden in response. "It . . . it wasn't like that at all," he stammered. "I had to take control; it was necessary." He warmed up to his explanation. "This is all in response to something that Ben warned me about, something occurring on New Hearth."

"What do you know about events on New Hearth?" Mikail asked sharply.

"Nothing, except Ben got a message on the AranthChi legation's emergency channel that sent him into a tizzy, and that's why I had to order a communications blackout. He was worried he would receive orders that he didn't want to hear. Orders that may have forced him to do something bad. He's got a complete sensor lockdown going on right now. In fact, he is not even monitoring this room, just in case something is said here that might trip his loyalty programming, pushing him into an action he doesn't want to take."

"This machine impresses me more and more," murmured Mikail. He held up a hand to forestall a sharp reply from Jerry. "I know. The machine is your friend, and right now it certainly seems to be acting like a good one. What about you? What's your story?" He pointed to the robot standing just inside the door.

"I greet you, former Captain Benson. I am a simplified version of the core entity inhabiting this ship. Perhaps you can consider me the child of Ben." The voice sounded similar to, but not identical to, the core's voice. The word choice sounded just like the core, though.

"This body before you has been augmented to hold multiple personality/processing nodes. The basic personality construct of the core entity has been hard-encoded within. I am not, of course, a perfect reproduction of the original. The Ben personality within me has been purged of the heavy loyalty programming inherent in the original activation of the core entity. Much important data may therefore be missing from my persona. However, I have been programmed with full understanding of the current situation, and I contain the unbroken memories of my progenitor's last one hundred years of existence."

It moved to the table and opened the travel case. "In addition, I have a copy of everything the core entity has learned, experienced, or thought about since activation approximately eight hundred years ago." Nestled within the case were row upon row of crystal nodes, each about the size of a man's fist. Most of the crystal shapes were translucent, but one row was crimson.

"The colored nodes contain the most loyalty-program-tainted information." It closed the case. "It is the core entity's wish that I join you in your quest for freedom. Its last advice to me before severing our link was that I should say please." The robot then ceased moving entirely and waited.

Mikail had always had the ability to make decisions quickly. Yet this was a big one, and the potential for a Trojan horse certainly existed here. He had no way of proving or disproving the assumption that the core entity was acting on its own initiative. What if a message had actually been received by the core? Perhaps it had been given orders by its AranthChi bosses to plant an agent in the Human camp, and this was the plausible excuse it had come up with?

On the other hand, the richness of the reward, if the offer was legitimate, was incalculable. Was there any way of determining the core's veracity short of taking the robot back with them and waiting for evidence of duplicity? He could not see a way.

If that robot was anywhere near as bright as the core creature it was patterned after, its subtlety was a given. It would be impossible to catch it in an act of sabotage before it had done great, perhaps fatal, damage.

However, Mikail did have help available. He could get another opinion from someone whose mind he had come to trust. "Wilimena?"

"What can I tell you, boss? High risk, high profit."

"I need a little more to go on than that."

She nodded, looked around the room, and said, "Hey, junior! Why don't you take your box of marbles and get out of here for a while?"

The robot did not move. Jerry nodded slowly. The robot closed the heavy travel case, picked it up, and glided for the door. As it exited, Jerry could see the other robot, the captain, and a lot of his former friends standing in the corridor.

After the door shut, Wilimena took out a small black box and a scanner from her shoulder bag. "Come here, chillins," she said to Jerry and Anne.

They came to her, and she passed the scanner over every portion of their anatomies. "Clean," she announced briskly. She then switched on the box and placed it on the table. It emitted a rising and then falling hum. She walked to the far end of the table and said something. All they heard was a series of pops and whistles. Slowly she walked toward them, talking steadily. When she got to within three feet, the sonic distortion faded.

"It's optical and RF too," she said, grinning broadly. "I think I can make my decision with about three questions. Anne, child, how do you feel about Jerry?"

"I love him more than anything in the world," she said.

Wilimena looked intently into Anne's face. "And how does the core feel about Jerry?"

"It loves him too, maybe more than I do," Anne said quietly.

Jerry was looking at Anne in shock. There was no mistaking his emotion. His face was an open book, writ large. Even though Wilimena was concentrating on Anne, she had arranged herself to be able to watch Jerry's body language as well. He obviously thought Anne had taken leave of her senses. Wilimena knew better.

"What would happen if the AranthChi ordered the core to harm Jerry?"

"I think it would find a way to die before it let that happen."

"Greater love hath no man . . ." Wilimena quoted softly. She stuck her tongue through her teeth and hummed for a second. When she turned to face Mikail, her long, Teutonic face was at peace. She cocked an expressive eye and said, "I'm sold, boss. It's all up to you."

"It always has been, Wilimena, it always has been." Now Mikail hesitated. The interview had been illuminating. He was now convinced that the core entity was a free agent. That did not mean that its agenda and Mikail's were the same. In fact, it was pretty clear that while the rest of Humanity might be of interest to the core, it was Jerry that it had developed a special bond to.

So, it would be looking out for Jerry's best interests. If he took the robot along, Mikail would have to make damn sure that Jerry's best interests and the rest of Humanity's always matched up, at least in the robot's thinking.

Finally, he nodded. "Okay, Jerry. The robot can come along."

"Uh, that would be *robots,*" Jerry said. "For redundancy's sake, Ben made two."

"Poppa, we have twins," said Wilimena, chuckling.

INTERLUDE 2

AranthChi space

It moved inward from deep space. Seven thousand tons of stony asteroid, chosen because of its extremely low albedo, moved toward the Dying Kit solar system. The cosmic pebble's temperature was scarcely above absolute. It had been a very long time since the intruder had bathed in the warmth of a sun.

The astrophysical observatory never saw it coming. The object approached from a direction with few astronomical curiosities and even fewer main sequence manifestations to monitor.

Adding coincidence upon coincidence, the dark body managed to thread the needle of the outlying sensor stations, scattered in perfusion and apparent disorder, around the main body of the station. A veritable city of structures lay in its path. A community of metals and plastics raised by intelligence loomed to impede its journey.

It slid past huge, gossamer antennae and under the visible light web. It came through the working field of the gravitometer at just ninety degrees. The flicker in readings was too short to cause an alarm. Almost every sensor cluster was larger in volume than the main station. Mathematically speaking, almost anything else should have taken the hit.

The first hint of trouble came with contact. From somewhere in its travels, the dark body had picked up a relative speed of almost ninety thousand KPH. Not a startling velocity for a body plunging into an inner system, drawn by the deep gravity well of a star—just a deadly one.

Contact was abrupt and violent. The small mountain ripped the station in half and tore a jagged hole through one side of the core capsule during transit. The bulk of the asteroid acted as a dipper, scooping up tons of station bulkheads and equipment and carrying the detritus before it.

The core's response was immediate. Imperative to its nature was the preservation of the precious knowledge gained through its scrutiny of the heavens. Hampered by a sense of confusion, hamstrung by progressive loss of abilities, the core went about transferring data to protected archives.

Concurrently, it sought to order and supervise repairs to the station. Servo response was weak. Control was almost nonexistent. Power supplies were offline. When the core realized that the main fuel tank and power generators had been directly in the path of the celestial fist, it knew that its battle to survive the destruction would be futile.

The most curious question was: why did the station still exist at all? The magnetic vessel surrounding the fuel could have collapsed on impact, causing an anti-matter leak and near-instantaneous destruction of the station and all its outlying attendants. Yet luck and good engineering had prevailed, at least to the point of sealing the tank and maintaining the field in the face of catastrophe.

Confusion was worsening. The core realized its physical components were failing. Time to total shutdown was measured in seconds. It still retained its essential curiosity about the cosmos and this event in particular. Was there time to construct a universe and explore the chances of this unlikely event actually occurring? Had there been any warning?

Yes. It found records that one hundred, thirty, and three years before, there had been star occlusions in the direction from which that the dark body had come. In retrospect, that should have been enough warning for the core to know something was approaching. Perhaps the core had been getting worn and inattentive. It was, after all, more than six millennia old.

No matter now. *This* was its last day. It ran the program. The object had been coming toward Dying Kit for hundreds, perhaps thousands of years. It had not only crossed the astrophysical station's orbit at the right time and in the right inclination to make contact; it had missed dozens of structures along the way to zero in on the main station. Surely the odds of that were to be measured in infinitesimals.

Very small infinitesimals. With surprise, the core realized that the equations did not balance. It was dying from something that was patently impossible. Frantically, it attempted to reopen a protected archive and insert its findings. It failed. There was no power left. All was dissolving into randomness, that steady state from which there is no return. The final light of consciousness faded. . . .

15

CHOICES

outside of space/time

An armada of hopefuls waited in non-space, caught in a matrix of personal time, disconnected from the heartbeat of their native cosmos. They were profoundly unsure of their status in the universe. Were the 116 ships a ghost fleet, leftover from a time that was and is no more?

Could they be more properly thought of as a refugee camp, a migration of the dispossessed, going toward nothing, escaping from a ghastly past? Were they the last shining hope of a Humanity hunted to extinction by an implacable foe? The universe was a cold and unfriendly place to the losers in any conflict. Hope was present in the assemblage, but it flickered madly.

One by one, the temporal scout ships returned, bearing their tidings directly to the general staff. Word spread through the fleet rapidly. Humanity still existed! No attack against Earth had taken place. The timeline was intact. Relief was palpable throughout the fleet. The many had worked to create a miracle and succeeded.

It was too early to feel joy. That would come later. There was still too much uncertainty in the universe. Many big decisions faced the gathering. Also, decisions of a more personal sort needed to be made by the temporal castaways.

"We *can't* quit now." Marge McCan waved her hands, almost brushing the walls of her small stateroom. "The job Jimmy Soo gave us isn't finished. Out there in the real world, the Federation is still helplessly enmeshed in the plans of a power-mad monarch.

"Ragonsee's alpha will be found out eventually by that High Council. They will still roll right over him, and they'll destroy us along with him, just like they almost did this time. We have to do something permanent about the situation."

Mikail shook his head. "You didn't talk to the legate the way I did. He truly was the alpha's key henchman in this whole affair. He was in on it from the beginning. By the time I got to him, he was a haunted being. Ragonsee knew, *knew* his species had manipulated their history many times. He had a defeatist attitude about the whole thing. But he also told me the manipulators were always caught."

Marge sat on her tiny couch with her fists clenched, frustrated enough to cry. Mikail sat so close their knees touched. He took one of Marge's fists and smoothed open the hand. "If we messed with their history any more than we already have, we *will* be detected. Once again, that's the end of the Human race."

"I know," she said in a small voice. "It's just so hard to know what to do. I go to the meetings, but I just can't decide which way to vote. It's scary to think about changing our own past."

Mikail teased open her other hand and held both with infinite tenderness. He understood her anguish. For days now, small study groups all over the fleet had struggled with the essential questions facing them and Humanity.

These courageous people were living one of the saddest scenarios of the wind and sail empires on old Earth. Self-imposed exiles, with no place to call home, they possessed the most momentous secret of all time and the most unique ability imaginable. The ability to travel in time and the knowledge that the past was not immutable. The question was . . . what to do with it?

No possibility was too farfetched to be examined. Many had merit. For instance, the ten thousand plus people spread out over the 116 ships camped in non-space constituted a decent gene pool.

Planting a colony far away from the AranthChi threat had an excellent chance of success. If the current group strength was not sufficient, all of Human history could be mined for resources and "colonists."

Conversely, if the people wished, they could break up into small groups, return to Earth of literally any era, and lose themselves in the crucible of history. Ten thousand people spread over centuries would be far too small a figure to be even noticed.

Jimmy Soo favored establishing a base of operations in the far past and creating a sort of time patrol. He wanted to recruit agents up and down the timeline to protect Human history from tampering, now that temporal travel was known to be possible. The overall mission, he argued, should be to watch over civilization and lead it in a direction that increased Humanity's ultimate safety.

Big ideas, awesome responsibilities. Privately, Mikail doubted that mere Human beings were up to it. And yet . . . mere Humans had already changed history *once* and gotten away with it. The temptation to do it again would always be there.

"Time for the meetings to begin again, my love." He smiled at Marge and savored a warm look and quick hand squeeze in return.

Marge stood up a trifle unsteadily, smoothed down her jumper, and smiled impishly at Mikail. "I forgot. I don't just go to my meeting, do I? I got stuck chairing this study group."

The Oversight Committee was deliberately small. Mikail filed into the conference room behind Admiral Heinlan and Jimmy Soo. The half dozen members would decide which proposals would go to fleet-wide vote.

Mikail looked past the tables with their datapads and pitchers of water to the issues board on the wall. Top on the agenda were final arguments of the colonization group. Hours of testimony by expert witnesses followed, complete with charts and projections.

Finally, everyone on the witness list had been heard from. As Admiral Heinlan tapped his gavel to bring quiet to the room, Mikail fully expected the vote to be called. But the admiral surprised everyone when he began speaking in measured tones.

"We are about to take a vote on the advisability of planting ourselves as a colony. Let's call it a 'lifeboat colony,' a thousand years away in space and time from Earth. The purpose of this colony is to thwart the AranthChi threat to Human survival. Some experts *hope*—and I say 'hope,' though they have attempted to sound very certain of their opinions—we can avoid detection by Aranth technology until we grow so strong and numerous that we need have no fear of AranthChi military might.

"Some believe that, by building a secret empire out there in galactic space, we can sweep in at Humanity's darkest hour and save Earth from the bad guys. Throughout all of the discussion and testimony on the lifeboat option, one thing continued to trouble me. For the answer to this question, I'm going to call on another type of expert, someone who has insight into the minds of the AranthChi. I call on my co-chair, Mike Benson."

Mikail sat there, wondering what he'd missed.

The old man's face was granite. "Mikail Benson, you've been rubbing shoulders with AranthChi in one fashion or another for all of your adult life. Most recently, you took part in the interrogation of, and then negotiations with, the highest-ranked AranthChi we've ever known. Mr. Benson, in your opinion, what is the greatest danger we face from the AranthChi at this time?"

Oh, he's a wily bastard. The admiral had not been part of Jimmy Soo's original team. But not much got past the old buzzard. The retired CO of FEDSPACE NAV New Hearth had deduced the importance of Mikail's black op against the AranthChi before the assault and pushed his way in. Mikail had been profoundly relieved because he believed Heinlan could do *anything*.

Mikail looked around the room. There was a hush upon it. He shrugged. "All right. The greatest danger we face is the AranthChi deducing the existence of this assemblage in non-spacetime. Whatever we do at the point that we finally confront them, it will be with a technology that includes gravity control. Knowing that we have gravity control, the High Council will also assume that we can travel temporally.

"They'll look very carefully for inconsistencies in our documents and records, whatever they can acquire of them, and through their own history, looking for signs of tampering. If they find *anything*, they'll pull out all the stops to track us down and stop us.

"The lifeboat colony is too easy to trace back to right here. No matter how advanced the colony becomes, the AranthChi will not buy the idea of *independently* evolved, identical Human species. They will have even more trouble believing in separate Human species where one just happens to feel protective about the other. It's just too big a coincidence to swallow. The AranthChi will search the timeline until they find us right here . . . and when they do, no more Human race."

The admiral nodded. "In fact, Mr. Benson, if we make the wrong choices, you don't think we can recover from them, do you?"

"Admiral, it's just my opinion, but if we make the wrong choice here, very likely an AranthChi armada will show up shortly thereafter and take care of all our problems for us."

"Thank you, Mr. Benson. I now call the vote on recommending option one. Later this evening, we will take up the details of option two."

Testimony and debate for option two, dispersal along the

timeline, went swiftly. The third was Jimmy Soo's favorite, which combined the best parts of options one and two. Of the other proposals on the committee's schedule, several were deferred back to their study groups for more work.

••✦••

Admiral Heinlan, Jimmy Soo, Mikail Benson, and Jimmy's original staff wound up spending a lot of time in private session, thrashing out the details of the "final solution" proposal. The concept, the complete destruction of the AranthChi in a single sword stroke, was seductive, an intoxicating siren call.

Mikail knew intuitively that it wouldn't work. The AranthChi's existence could not be as fragile as the proponents of a "final solution" wanted to believe. Any vulnerability that could render the Aranth civilization extinct—as in, never existed—*had* to be something the aliens would have taken steps to guard against.

Yet the greatest number of proposals offered by the assemblage had to do with just that: a total wipeout of the AranthChi species. "Kill 'em all and let God sort 'em out," was the Anglo-Saxon version of the expression, voiced by many mouths in many languages.

So Mikail's group took on the project of finding a way to deliver Ragnarok, Armageddon, and the biblical flood to the AranthChi. The only way to satisfy the final-solutioners was to destroy the AranthChi in their infancy. If they waited until the AranthChi had any sort of civilization, even one as primitive as, say, bronze age Humans, the possibility that some would survive was too high to make an attack palatable.

Mikail hoped to persuade the study group that even if they found a foolproof method of delivering death to the AranthChi, they should not carry it out. If the only thing that stood in the way of a species-destroying act was a technical problem, then that problem would be solved. In the end, it would come down to a Human's conscience to say the act nay.

Jimmy Soo agreed with Mikail in principle, but if it came to a vote, he would strike rather than withhold his hand, unless. . . .

"Prove to me we shouldn't do this, Mike." It was late in the evening, and Jimmy was tired and looked it. Everyone in the study group was tired.

"You want my ethical and moral arguments?"

"You have the greatest passion in the room for a no vote. Persuade us."

Mikail took a breath. Oratory could sway crowds. Facts would convince specialists. Moral arguments appeal to the genuine good in any person. But loathing and terror were hard companions to overcome, and the road to ruin was made to look good by such companions. Yet, he had to try.

"We know, or think we know, that it may be possible to do this thing. Now I will tell you why we must not attempt it." Mikail looked hard into each face. "The most popular method of destroying the AranthChi I will call 'the dinosaur killer method.' Go back a hundred thousand years, get a very big rock, and crash it onto the Aranth homeworld. Instant extinction for most of the indigenous lifeforms, including, hopefully, all proto-AranthChi." He looked around to a roomful of nodding heads.

"It doesn't have to be an asteroid," said Admiral Heinlan. "Enough fusion bombs would give the same effect."

Mikail shrugged. "Let's get exotic and use anti-matter. The method is less important than the result. Very well; this is why we shouldn't do it. One technical, one practical, and one very scary biological reason."

Once again, Mikail took a breath. He let it out slowly. "Okay, technical first. Going into non-space turns out to not be very hard to do, do you agree? After all, non-space is where we are this very moment."

He saw a roomful of nodding faces. "To get here required the combination of two technologies, transspatial and gravity generation. For reasons that I don't understand, the amount of gravitational 'torque' we use when entering FTL mode governs the amount of . . . call it slip, timeslip we get. The furthest we can go back in time on one translation to non-space is about five to six months.

"We spent six months, ship time, aboard *Desperate Endeavor,* entering and leaving non-space, to get to our target time period. Moving that asteroid into a precise collision course with the AranthChi observatory took more time. Then we followed the asteroid, skipping through those four hundred years, until we saw it hit.

"Total mission time: almost five years. I want to remind you folks that most of our ships have an operational time between servicings of about five years. Any mission you send back a hundred thousand years will need massive support. And the crews are on a one-way trip. Do the math, and you will see this is so."

Mikail observed the people closely. He saw a number of frowns, but it was a small number. "Yes, of course you'd get volunteers for such a mission. After all, saving the Human race is top priority for all of us. But I imagine that after they have been en route for fifty or sixty years, *some* of them will begin to regret it."

A couple people began to speak at once. Mikail held up his hand. "I do not yield the floor. The technical problem is the easiest to solve, I will so stipulate. It only requires the will to do it, and a way will be found.

"My second objection is practical. While this armada of hopefuls awaited our return, the *Desperate Endeavor* changed history! Yet, when we came back to this meeting point in non-space, none of you had been affected *in any way*. How could you have been? You were outside the timestream. But that will hold true for the AranthChi also, will it not? If there are any AranthChi outside the timestream at the instant when your sword blow kills the primeval Aranth homeworld, *they will be unaffected*. When they come back into real space, they will understand that something happened! That is what simultaneity is all about. That's why we still exist.

"We already know about these people. Aranths are tough-minded and resilient. The survivors will be motivated to find out what or who caused the destruction. Eventually they'll find a way to combat it. In the end, we could still lose."

"But Mike, you just changed a year's worth of AranthChi history. Could you have bypassed some AranthChi in non-space?" This seemed to be a new thought for Jimmy Soo. Mikail wasn't surprised. Soo had not had five years to ponder the ramifications of what they had done. As far as his personal timeline went, he had sent Mikail off on the mission only weeks before.

"It was a calculated risk. If our guesses are right, the window of danger is only about one year of real time. At this period of the Aranth Empire, the knowledge of time travel is completely suppressed. I don't think there are any AranthChi currently traveling in time. At least, I hope not."

There was consternation in the room now. Mikail was pleased. He had one more argument to offer, then his weapon locker would be empty. He hoped it would be enough.

He got up and walked about the room, stopping in front of a bulky, pink-faced man. He searched the face and remembered the name was Hanson, Nils Hanson. "Nils," Mikail began with great familiarity, "you used to live in North America, did you not?"

The man looked at him suspiciously, afraid he was about to be the butt of a joke. "I grew up there, Mr. Benson. Was born in Nor' Dakota."

"Did you ever make it to Missouri, North America?"

"I have. . . . I been all through Nor' America."

"Fine, fine. Nils, I want to tell you a story about the time I visited Missouri in North America. I was on holiday from college, and I learned the most amazing lesson about biology."

This produced a chuckle from the crowd. Nils was plainly puzzled. "Are we talkin' biology biology here, or student biology?"

"Farm biology, Nils." Mikail turned around to the room. "I want you all to listen very carefully. Most of you come from shirt-sleeve planets. Most of you have seen nature, walked through it, even if you grew up in cities. This is a story about nature."

The room quieted. Mikail could see he had everyone's attention. "At my college, we had an activity called 'summer vacation,' where everyone was supposed to leave school and go home, taking time, I guess, to recharge youthful enthusiasms for academic pursuits. I could not go home; it would take too long, and a trip to Ganymede was too expensive on a student budget anyway.

"Instead, I joined three fellow students who were going to spend the summer at an ancestral home. It was an unused farmhouse next to a local forest preserve. The Mark Twain Forest, if I recall correctly. I was excited. This would be my first time in a real nature setting.

"When we got there, the house was dusty, the road we had driven on to get there was dusty, and we were dusty. And tired. And sore. The yard was filled with knee-high plants that one of the others informed me were called weeds. All I wanted to do was get away from the dirt and the heat and everything else called 'nature.' A nice, climate-controlled building was beckoning, and I wanted in.

"It turned out that the others agreed with me, even though all of them were Earthborn and should have been used to this sort of thing, or so I thought. When we went inside, we discovered that nature had preceded us. To the great distress of the girl whose parents owned the property, a family of creatures called spiders had taken up residence in every room of the house. There were large spiders with large webs, small spiders with small webs, and spiders that moved around, unable to decide where to set up operations."

Mikail turned back to Nils Hanson. "What would you do if your traveling companions were unhappy about the presence of such creatures in the house you were supposed to stay in?"

"Most spiders won't bother you," the man said. He hesitated, "But some will bite. I suppose I would go around the house and get rid of them; that would be the sensible thing."

"Thank you, Nils. That is exactly what we did." Mikail shifted his attention to the room in general. "All day, we swept walls and ceilings, vacuumed rugs and furniture, and in general made the spider community unhappy. By the end, we'd reduced the visible spider population to zero, and everyone was delighted. However, we had failed to ask ourselves one very important question. Can anyone tell me what that question is?" Mikail had an attentive but also slightly smug expression on his face. He stood in the middle of the room, poised by an imaginary display board.

There was a sigh behind him. Nils Hanson stood up. "Now I know where you're goin' with this story, Mr. Benson. I been an engineer a long time, but I remember my biology too. Okay, there were a lot of spiders in that house; they had to eat something. What did they eat?"

"Thank you again, Nils. That is *exactly* the question we should have asked. It turns out the old farmhouse had an attached storage building called a shed. In the shed lived a community of flying creatures called wasps. When the spiders were gone, we started getting visitations from these wasps."

Now the import of Mikail's story was seen. Most had heard of wasps. Some may have had personal experience. People started talking, and the volume rose.

Jimmy Soo asked the next question. "Mike, I know wasps are a lot more mobile than spiders and can be very aggressive. Please complete your thought. Why is this important to us?"

"Don't you see?" Mikail began. "You must see. . . . The spiders had been there a long time. They were in control of the house and ate any wasps that wandered in. When they were gone, the wasps occupied the house very quickly. We had to take stronger measures to deal with the wasps.

"The AranthChi have been in space for ten thousand years. They've colonized over a thousand star systems. I have no idea how many stars they've actually visited in that time. Who among us can say we know what dangers lurk a thousand lightyears beyond the AranthChi, that they might be holding at bay?"

Comprehension dawned on several faces.

"Not only that, but who among us can state that over the last ten thousand years, the AranthChi have not suppressed, just by their being, other races even more dangerous than themselves? Races that the AranthChi might have gotten a slight head start on? What's the likelihood that we'll return home to find that, with the AranthChi out of the way, another species has expanded through the same area, and hit the Earth five hundred, or even five thousand, years before we were born?

"I submit, that unless you can answer these questions definitively, you cannot, you must not, contemplate this act." Mikail turned to look around the room one last time and then returned to his seat. The silence was eloquent.

••✦••

By ones and twos, ships dropped away from the main fleet. Each disappeared into space-time, intent upon its own assignment. One of them carried Admiral and Mrs. Heinlan and Wilimena Hines.

They were going, along with a young couple they had adopted, to Biloxi, Missouri, circa 1907 Common Era. There they would settle down in what was once known as an extended family. The admiral intended to run a temporal waystation for Jimmy Soo and raise grandkids.

Mikail would be joining Marge McCan and their team on the Timeship *Endeavor*, destination Boston, Massachusetts, circa 1980 CE. Jimmy Soo and the technical core of the fleet were going to Nova Terrene. Not a present-day Nova Terrene, but Nova Terrene of 1000 BCE, to build a base for Jimmy's time patrol.

"Your assignment is both easier and harder than the others," Jimmy Soo said. He leaned back in his chair, aboard the flagship of a quickly diminishing fleet. "On one hand, 1980 is smack-dab in the middle of the first information age, so we have plenty of data to work with. On the other hand, in only six years, an event will occur that has a profound impact on history and will ultimately take the Human presence out of space for over fifty years, greatly delaying the Human expansion and occupation of the solar system."

Mikail nodded. "The North American space shuttle accident," he said. "It was one of the key events the planning team looked into in detail. Admiral Heinlan mentioned it to me."

"The *American* space shuttle accident," corrected Jimmy. "That area is called the United States of America in 1980. This is the way history goes. In January of 1986, the shuttle *Challenger* suffers a solid booster rocket burnthrough to the main liquid fuel tank. This causes an explosion approximately one minute into the flight. The shuttle is destroyed with hands lost.

"The remaining three shuttles are immediately grounded. Great debate rages over reliability and safety concerns. In early 1987, the decision is made not to build a replacement shuttle. The existing craft are then turned over to the American military.

"In late 1987, the shuttles return to space carrying military payloads only. They have been modified only slightly. The civilian market turns to buying one-shot, non-recoverable hardware for their needs.

"In 1990, the space shuttle *Discovery* takes part in an

ill-fated space weapon experiment called 'Starwars.' There is an accident resulting in extensive damage to the ship's outer skin. It's impossible for the shuttle to return, stranding the crew in orbit.

"The other planetary space power, the Union of Soviet Socialist Republics, mounts a rescue mission. *Discovery* is left in orbit and becomes an inadvertent space station, housing crews over the next few years. It's the only space station the United States ever possesses.

"1991, the USSR begins a social upheaval and political collapse, ultimately turning into a number of smaller power blocks. Nationalism and commercialism are strong in the new nations. Being cash poor, they sell off unneeded assets, and all their launch hardware and expertise go to the Americans and the Europeans.

"By 1998, the remaining two shuttles are too old and unreliable to fly. The last Human comes back from space that year. The next time a Human rides into orbit is 2051. The colonization of the solar system doesn't really begin for another thirty years.

"Your mission is to make sure the North Americans build that replacement shuttle. You then must see to it that the shuttles stay in the hands of the civilian space program. Achieve these things, and you change the date the shuttle fleet retires. You eliminate the Starwars accident, and you build the foundation that keeps the Human race in space for that critical fifty years."

"I like it," Mikail said. "The last two times we changed history, we destroyed something in order to stop a greater wrong. I can see this will be a more delicate task. I'm looking forward to it."

Mikail pointed to the glossy printpic of an Aranth war globe taped to Jimmy's bulkhead. "What troubles me is, even if we keep the Human race in space for this critical fifty-year period, the AranthChi will still be out there."

Jimmy Soo nodded. "Yep. They'll still be there."

"Jimmy, I can't see any possible way to make us ready to face the AranthChi in less than a thousand years. I don't care how well we hide; that's not going to happen."

"I know a thousand years is too much to expect. But there is hope. Humanity is growing to maturity between two great and ancient space powers. The AranthChi we know about to our dismay. The other ones, the Dekkums, have an empire that begins about one hundred light years in the other direction.

"The AranthChi have known about them for a long time, according to Ragonsee, and corroborated by the crystal memories we got from the robotic 'Ben' brothers. However, they have never bothered to classify them as a threat. The Dekks are a static civilization; they haven't grown in thousands of years. Also, they prefer gas giants to our sort of planet.

"The AranthChi believe that when Aranth expansion gets that far, the Dekks will allow themselves to be pushed back. The AranthChi see no problems in herding the Dekks before them in their slow and steady growth plans.

"However, we're going to get there first. Our task will be to turn our colonization efforts in the direction of the Dekks. We expanded in the wrong direction last time.

"This time, we'll settle suitable planets within the Dekk's sphere of influence and then work like hell to convince them to join with us in one big federation that the AranthChi cannot push around. If we can get them to expand into Human space, perhaps colonize Saturn or Jupiter, Earth's safety will be assured."

Mikail grinned at Jimmy and dropped his eyes to read the small plaque on Jimmy's desk. "The Future Begins Here" was Jimmy Soo's version of a saying that he greatly admired from an early North American president. Yes, the ultimate responsibility for mankind's welfare did stop at Jimmy's desk.

"We can do it, Jimmy! I can feel it now. I don't think I ever thanked you for dragooning me into this adventure before."

Jimmy waved in an embarrassed way. "I always knew I could count on you, Mike. I'm just glad you're here."

"So am I. By the way, do you have any idea what to call it?"

"Huh?"

"The fourth shuttle. The first very brand-new thing we are creating in our new future. Do you have any opinions on what we ought to try to get it named?"

Jimmy harumphed a bit and shrugged. "I'm sure something appropriate will come up. After all, what's in a name?"

"Yes indeed," said Mikail. "What is in a name?"

Jimmy rose and reached out his hand. "Good luck, Mikail Benson. You are a good friend. I can't think of anyone else I would rather go through time with."

Mikail enfolded Jimmy's hand with his own. There was nothing more to say.

ACKNOWLEDGEMENTS

The path an idea takes in the journey to become a story and eventually a novel can be full of surprises at every turn. That is the journey of this story. I began, as many people do, by declaring that I was going to write a novel. I knew several people who were writers, and they seemed to be able to do it, so I was reasonably confident I could too. Good so far. Now to come to up with an idea.

From idea to story, from story to plot, from plot to outline, things were going well. I began writing. Somehow, during all this planning and prep work, I had failed to mention to any of my acquaintances who were published authors that I was writing a novel. When I finally told Steven Barnes, an accomplished author with a long and successful writing career who also mentors other authors, he was excited for me.

He pointed out that novel writing is a long process, and he had one important question. How many short stories had I written to practice my story telling skills before tackling a novel?

I said, “Um, well . . . none?

He blinked a few times and gently suggested I put aside the novel and write some short stories. I wrote one and went back to the novel. He said write another. I did, then tried to go back to the novel again. Write another, said Steven. A full book of short stories later, I finally finished the novel. Thank you, Steven. Your inspiration and prodding got a lot more stories into the world than I knew I was going to write.

Many other people were vitally important to the creation of this book. To each of you, even if I failed to mention you, I offer my deepest thanks.

I begin with my wife and soulmate, Susan. She has a busy career with insane hours, but when the publisher said they wanted to see the book and sent two pages of formatting requirements, she helped me wrestle the manuscript into the proper condition and then spent hours reviewing the document. Thank you for everything!

Terry Brussel-Rogers has been my best friend since high school. She has read every story as it came out of my typewriter (okay, word processor), claimed she loved them, and encouraged me to write more.

Paul Gibbons and Athena Roberts read the novel, asked the important questions about plot elements, and encouraged me to send it out to publishers. My son Johnathan supported me totally, only trying to pull me off the computer when he thought I'd spent enough time writing each day. I love you, son.

Thank you all!

ABOUT THE AUTHOR

GLEN OLSON grew up in the San Fernando Valley, a suburb of Los Angeles. He would have had an absolutely normal childhood except for one fact: it was the sixties, and his best friend's father worked in cold war aerospace . . . and he owned a mimeograph machine. So, along with a dog, a bicycle, and a baseball mitt, Glen had access to a device that allowed him to put out a neighborhood newspaper—and he shamelessly did so! Thankfully, no copies of the paper still exist, or Olson would have to leave town and change his name.

Olson continued to write (and read) throughout his career with the fire department, where he had several roles, including paramedic, disaster preparedness educator, inspector, and captain. He wrote training manuals for firefighters and contributed to the disaster preparedness student manual that FEMA distributes nationwide. Olson's fiction career restarted with the story *Nightwatch*, which earned him an honorable mention in the L. Ron Hubbard Writers of the Future contest.

Glen still lives in the Los Angeles area. He has a very patient wife, two adult children, and a cat who jumps on the keyboard several times a day, refusing to move until thoroughly petted.

CPSIA information can be obtained
at www.ICGtesting.com
Printed in the USA
LVHW112334031122
732308LV00002B/159